# Chains of Satin

No portion of this book may be reproduced in any form without written permission from the publisher or author, except as permitted by U.S. copyright law.

This is a work of fiction. Names, characters, places, and incidents either are the product of the author's imagination or are used fictitiously. Any resemblance to actual events, locales, or persons, living or dead, is coincidental.

Copyright © 2024 by Delilah St. Rivers | Case Number: 1-13619173081

Cover design by Corvus Designs

Edited by Taylor Johnson

All rights reserved, including the right to reproduce this book or portions thereof in any form whatsoever. Scanning, uploading, and distributing this book without permission is a theft of the author's intellectual property. If you would like permission to use material from the book (other than for the purposes of reviews), please contact info@spellbound-publishing.com.

Thank you for supporting this author's rights.
Spellbound Publishing House, LLC
Austin, TX | www.spellbound-publishing.com
First edition: March 2024

The publisher is not responsible for websites (or their content) that are not owned by the publisher.

Identifiers:
LCCN: 2024932869 | ISBN 979-8-89123-985-2(hardback)
ISBN 979-8-89123-986-9 (paperback) | ISBN 979-8-89123-987-6 (ebook)

# Editor's Note:

*Chains of Satin* contains content and materials that may make some readers feel uncomfortable. Please turn to the back of the book for a comprehensive list of triggers found within the story. If at any time during your reading, you find that you are struggling or feel unable to continue with the story, please feel free to DNF.

Your mental health matters; please take care of yourself.

Each chapter of *Chains of Satin* has a song that accompanies the vibe and writing of that section. On the following page, you will find a complete playlist to accompany your reading preceded by the character's name and the page number on which that chapter begins.

Scan the QR code below to save the *Chains of Satin* Official Spotify playlist now!

I hope you enjoy; happy listening!

—Delilah

# Chains of Satin Playlist

Ethan - "I Never Knew Lonely" by Vince Gill

Chapter One, Petunia - "Hanging by a Moment" by Lifehouse

Chapter Two, Petunia - "Let Me Blow Ya Mind" by Eve, Gwen Stefani, Stevie J
"For me…Formidable" by Charles Aznavour

Chapter Three, Petunia - "Unwritten" by Natasha Bedingfield

Chapter Four, Petunia - "Crazier Best Friend" by Andi

Chapter Five, Petunia - "Drunk (And I Don't Wanna Go Home)" by Elle King,
Miranda Lambert

Chapter Six, Petunia - "Hero" by Bryce Savage

Chapter Seven, Ethan - "No One Cares" by Michele Morrone

Chapter Eight, Petunia - "Almost Touch Me" by Maisy Kay

Chapter Nine, Petunia - "Kiss the Girl" by Brent Morgan

Chapter Ten, Petunia - "Remember" by Josh Groban

Chapter Eleven, Petunia - "When God Made You My Mother" by Riley Roth

Chapter Twelve, Petunia - "Bring Me To Life" by Evanescence

Chapter Thirteen, Petunia - "Under Your Scars" by Godsmack

Chapter Fourteen, Ethan - "You Put a Spell on Me" by Austin Giorgio

Chapter Fifteen, Petunia - "All I Need" by Within Temptation

Chapter Sixteen, Petunia - "Watch Me Burn" by Michele Morrone

Chapter Seventeen, Petunia - "Insatiable" by Darren Hayes

Chapter Eighteen, Petunia - "More Than Friends" by Jon Robert Hall

Chapter Nineteen, Petunia - "(Everything I Do) I Do it For You" by Bryan Adams

Chapter Twenty, Petunia - "Slayer" by Bryce Savage

Chapter Twenty-one, Petunia - "That Should Be Me" by Maddi Jane

Chapter Twenty-two, Petunia - "Could I Have This Kiss Forever" by Enrique
Iglesias, Whitney Houston

Chapter Twenty-three, Petunia - "One of the Girls" by The Weeknd (with
JENNIE, Lily-Rose Depp)

Chapter Twenty-four, Petunia - "Inferno" Sub Urban, Bella Poarch

Chapter Twenty-five, Petunia - "Looking at Me" by Sabrina Carpenter

Chapter Twenty-six, Ethan - "Houndin" by Layto

Chapter Twenty-seven, Petunia - "Earned It" by The Weeknd

Chapter Twenty-eight, Petunia - "Touch" by Little Mix

Chapter Twenty-nine, Petunia - "Why Can't I Have Two? (2468)" by Caity Baser

Chapter Thirty, Petunia - "Super Freaky Girl" by Nicki Minaj

Chapter Thirty-one, Petunia - "Red Light Special" by TLC

Chapter Thirty-two, Petunia - "Bad Things" by Nation Haven

Chapter Thirty-three, Petunia - "Dirtier Thoughts" by Nation Haven

Chapter Thirty-four, Ethan - "Utopia" by Within Temptation

Chapter Thirty-five, Petunia - "Swan Song" by Within Temptation
"MIDDLE OF THE NIGHT" by Loveless

Chapter Thirty-six, Petunia - "Broken Pieces" by Apocalyptica, Lacey Sturm

Chapter Thirty-seven, Ethan - "Let Her Go" by Within Temptation

*To my fictional characters, for teaching me that I have no control over my stories and that they'll do whatever they please.*

*To Sphinx, my writing partner up until the day you tragically passed.*

*And, finally, the second half of my soul. Without you, I would have given up so many times.*

# Chains of Satin

DELILAH ST. RIVERS

PRESENT DAY
OFFICE OF DR. JOSEPH HALL

# Ethan

WHEN I WALKED INTO THE OFFICE OF Dr. Joseph Hall, I could feel the scrutiny as he took in my rumpled suit, greasy, disheveled hair, and the bags under my eyes. It wasn't normal policy for the psychologist to accept emergency appointments on his day off, but in the eight years he'd known me, it wasn't normal policy for me to need an emergency appointment at all, let alone on his day off.

"I'm desperate," I divulged over the phone twenty minutes prior. "My heart has never been so full as it has been these past six months or so, and now…" Unshed sobs choked out the rest of my sentence.

Now, in his office, I allowed the sorrow and panic to drown me, unleashing upon him before he'd even closed the office door.

"I can't sleep in my own room. I can't look at my kitchen. I can't even drive my car. Listening to music brings me more misery than joy. Her presence fills each aspect of my life; she's a specter moaning about, haunting the rooms of my soul. If she were air, she'd be no less needed for my existence. Please help me, my friend. My air is gone and I'm suffocating without her!"

Joseph looked down at the crumpled paper in my fist, no doubt curious. He gestured for me to be seated in the brown leather chair of his small office, and I dropped into it, not the least bit relaxed.

## DELILAH ST. RIVERS

"A broken heart is one of life's greatest struggles, something no one masters," Joseph offered. "No one is immune to it, but talking, like time, helps."

"I'm unsure talking will help anything."

"You wouldn't have called me if you truly believed that," Joseph said, sitting across from me. "Would you like to tell me what happened? Or, if you're unable, perhaps just tell me about her."

"How can one talk about the first sunrise of their memory, or the first time they tasted ice cream? How can I go about reciting a poem to you if you don't understand the language it was written in?"

"Maybe just start with how you met," Joseph suggested.

I ran a hand through my thick, wavy hair.

"I first saw her when Regal Cleaning Services introduced the workers that would be alternating shifts in my home. I'd just moved into the new house after years of renovation. She—Petunia—was in the lineup. While all the others were vying for my attention, she was polite and quiet; almost shy. I would have glanced right by her had she not looked me in the eye and blushed. I couldn't put her blush or her eyes out of my head for weeks afterwards.

"I was driven to distraction whenever she came around, finding relief when she wasn't working in my home. I could focus on work instead of mapping out in my head where she was or what she was doing."

I grew quiet as I thought about all the things I was too much of a gentleman to talk about: the way she smelled…the little dimple in her left cheek…the way her brunette hair shone in the light no matter how she styled it for the day…

Joseph brought me back to the present, clearing his throat.

"Did she know how you felt at this point in your relationship?"

I shook my head.

"It was clear she struggled with her attraction whenever we crossed paths, but I made sure to keep my own desires in check. It was a fun cat-and-mouse game for a while, but I remained strictly professional toward her."

"Until?"

I sighed, suddenly drained.

"This is shaping up to be a long story, my friend."

"It's my day off and you're paying," Joseph quipped. "I have all day."

"Very well." I sat back against the cushioned chair, crossing one leg over my knee. I toyed with the paper in my hand.

"It was a Thursday afternoon, clear skies with warm weather—"

# CHAINS OF SATIN

"The birds were singing?" Joseph smirked. "You're stalling, my friend. If you want to get through these messy emotions so you can think logically about your future, a purge is the best direction. Remember when I was going through my divorce? You suggested I do the same."

I looked out the window.

"I hadn't imagined it would be as painful as this when I suggested it. I applaud your courage," I admitted softly before turning to face Joseph once more. "To recite this, to relive this…they were the happiest moments of my life, truly. When I think about those times with her, I begin to ache for her."

Joseph nodded.

"She had such joy, this inner shine she couldn't keep to herself if she tried. Around her I became anyone I wanted to be, the very best man I never could hope to be on my own." I sat back further into the chair as I unfolded and refolded the paper in my hands. I despised the sting in my eyes as they grew misty before I drew a deep breath and spoke again.

"But I suppose your point is made," I conceded. "I'll start with our first real interaction, the moment that led to my discovery that she had the potential to be everything I had ever wanted."

*Six Months Earlier*

CHAPTER ONE

# Petunia

THE SPRAY OF COLOGNE IMMEDIATELY SATURATED MY sense of smell with notes of blood orange, leather, and a hint of charred amber. I inhaled deeply, closed my eyes, and savored the complex, sexy delight of his scent.

Careful not to linger too long, I ran the cleaning rag across the vanity top before replacing the elegant glass bottle. I inhaled again, imagining him standing close to me, before turning to fix the bed.

Tossing the comforter over fresh sheets, I made his bed presentable, imagining what his next nighttime adventure may hold. I blushed immediately, shook my head clear of any inappropriate thoughts, and smoothed the creases from his pillows. With one last look of longing toward the bottle of cologne, I set my thoughts to the next room on my agenda.

"Curious," a voice floated into the room from the doorway. "I do hope my fragrance is to your satisfaction?"

Ethan Richard Aldrich the Third's English accent rolled over me, and I realized he'd been watching me. Heat flooded my face and I spun to face him, arms full of his dirty sheets and my cleaning rags. I caught a glimpse of his stern expression before lowering my gaze, avoiding, as I so often did, the fury in a man's face.

"Forgive me, sir," I managed softly. "I'll pay back the value of what

# DELILAH ST. RIVERS

I wasted. I promise nothing like this will never happen again." I raised my eyes to meet his.

I could've sworn I saw something shift in his eyes and I looked back down.

"Never again?" He chuckled from his post. "Was that the promise you made to yourself the first time you did this? Or, how about the second time, when you thought no one was home though I was merely down the hall? Did you promise yourself it would never happen again those times, too?"

My face burned with guilt and embarrassment.

*He's been watching the whole time?*

I wanted to die right there on the spot.

"Or was it last week when you came in and cleaned my bedding? You'd sprayed it twice that day, then closed your eyes for a moment just as you did right now."

I looked up and Mr. Aldrich's eyes clashed with mine in a challenge, but I couldn't speak. Hell, I barely could breathe.

"I believe I'm still waiting for my answer regarding your… satisfaction." His voice was practically monotone, but that accent was deepening my blush by the syllable.

"The um…the cologne?" I stammered. *Get a grip, girl,* I chided myself. *Think of words, not his intense blue eyes studying my every move. Deep breath.* "I think no matter how expensive the bottle was, it was worth every penny, sir."

There it was again, that faint something behind his eyes. It was gone in an instant as he took a step toward me, slowly.

*Is he stalking prey or approaching a frightened deer?*

"Thievery is a poor choice of career change, especially when your spoils are literally in the wind." He stepped closer to me, demanding softly, "Tell me, what possessed you to do such a thing?" I caught the inticing scent of cologne mingled with his own bodily musk. This time I couldn't pull free from his gaze as he towered over me with his six-foot frame.

*Intimidation was always his weapon of choice* — I shook the thought from my mind. This man was not the monster from my past, haunting my dreams. He can't hurt me anymore. I swallowed hard before opening my mouth to answer.

"I'm sorry, sir. I don't know what I was thinking. It was spur of the moment, a stupid mistake." I took an earnest step forward, nervous words flowing in a barrage of information. "I honestly cannot lose my job. I won't let anything like this happen again. It was incredibly unprofessional and inexcusable, but I swear to you that if you forgive me, you won't regret it."

# CHAINS OF SATIN

I dropped the bundle of sheets that I'd been holding and fished through my pockets, finding a few scattered bills before thrusting the handful towards him.

"I don't want your money," he said, catching my wrist.

*Of course not*, I flushed deeply. *Mr. Aldrich has a fortune; why would he need a few of my measly dollars?*

"I don't find your offering trivial, either. I just don't want it." He released my hand gently and I forced myself to breathe.

"What do you want, then?" I asked, voice shaking with the fear of being fired. For a moment it seemed as though he'd turned into a wolf, hungry and ready to pounce, that odd flicker in his eyes once more. In an instant, it was gone again as he closed his eyes, swallowed and bent to collect the bundle I had dropped to the floor.

"Right now I want you to finish your duties," he began slowly as he handed me the dirty laundry. "Then I want you to come back tomorrow. And the next day. And the next, until I no longer require outside help for my home's maintenance. I'd also like you to try contain yourself from sampling my items in the future."

"Thank you, sir," I practically shouted in elation. "You won't regret it one bit."

I turned to walk out the door when he cleared his throat. I tensed. *He's not the same.* I breathed.

"Just out of curiosity, when did your company grow lax on your uniforms?"

I looked down at my jeans and plaid shirt with rolled up sleeves.

"I could have mistaken you for an imposter; if not for the messy bun on your head, I wouldn't have recognized you at all." His eyes glittered with mirth as they grazed over my body.

"Your normal Thursday girl was released from the company yesterday. I was called in this morning at the last minute and changing would have made me late. I figured it wouldn't hurt anything..." I trailed off. I hated my stupid blushing face and my inability to keep cool under what I believed to be his mild flirtation.

"The red-haired girl has been released from employment?"

"Yes, sir." I made a mental note about his ability to remember the name of the girl in question.

"Hm." Mr. Aldrich rubbed his finger across his bottom lip in thought before his eyes found mine again. "I like this look, perhaps more so than the dreary uniforms they provide you. I should like to see you dressed more comfortably while here at my home."

"Yes, sir," I responded softly, meeting his eyes to catch that flicker flow through his gaze once more before he turned and left the room.

## CHAPTER TWO

# Petunia

FOR THREE WEEKS I HAD BEEN ASSIGNED to his home with two other workers and I made sure to wear my work uniform each time. No man would dictate how I would dress, no matter how much his praise made me glow for days after he'd spoken to me.

Mr. Aldrich was home two days a week, handling business in his office, wandering the halls on his phone, or directing his housing staff with tasks. Occasionally, just out of the corner of my eye I would catch him glancing at me with a half-amused smirk on his face. I'd pretend not to notice, but a time or two we locked eyes for a breath before I blushed and looked away.

The real estate mogul was muscular, but lean, and never seemed to come across as haughty, untouchable or inhuman towards anyone in his employ. I never saw him come off as rude or demeaning; he had expectations of his staff, but was willing to be flexible as necessary. He treated everyone with respect and he was easy on those who were of fragile dispositions. When my colleague Marie had been dealing with a difficult pregnancy, he paid her maternity leave two months early so she could rest without worry. Beneath that chiseled exterior was a man of compassion and empathy.

Still, it wasn't in me to understand why I was so skittish around him. Sure, I found Mr. Aldrich beyond attractive, but it didn't explain my almost fearful reaction whenever we locked eyes or if he spoke directly to me when we were alone. I had been around heart-achingly gorgeous men without feeling a surge of desperate adrenaline. I knew that reaction came from somewhere years of therapy couldn't reach.

One Wednesday a month, everyone employed by Regal Cleaning Services would choose a home or a business contract and spend the entire day devoted to a solo deep-clean. Three weeks after the cologne incident, "Solo Wednesday" came around and with good reason, I chose the Aldrich home.

Wednesdays were days Mr. Aldrich would be in-office and the rest of the house staff wasn't scheduled until the evening. That meant I would have the large, twelve-room estate all to myself and I could do my job without anyone getting underfoot. It was perfect.

I slept in that day and decided to go in my casual clothes. I chose my denim jeans with a sleeveless black and white plaid shirt with a zipped-open collar and faux pockets in the front. The shirt fit me nicely with room to move and was long enough that it didn't ride high when I bent over. My black and pink non-slip shoes completed the outfit and I raced out the door only to show up a half hour after the start of my 8:00 a.m. shift.

First, I set my sights on the living room, working in a circular pattern around the room as I dusted, fluffed pillows, wiped windows and TV screens. After an hour, I moved onto the kitchen. I took out my phone, set my playlist of 80's ballads and 90's pop to shuffle, slipped on my wireless headphones, and began to jam out while cleaning.

I scrubbed counters and wiped windows to Air Supply and Blondie. I belted out Bryan Adams as I cleaned the stove and inside the oven. I took a metal whisk out of the ceramic bowl and held it like a microphone as White Snake rocked in my ears, pointing in sweeping circles as I threw my head back and forth to the rhythm of the music.

When it came time to sweep the mahogany wood floors, Madonna's "Vogue" came on and I became a one-woman show. I shimmied up and down the broomstick, swiveling my hips back and forth to the sensual beat. I bent over, both hands on the broom and shook my ass to the audience of the toaster, Keurig machine, and a row of cabinets.

Lost in the moment and movement, I twirled around, faked Michael Jackson's moonwalk a few steps and then threw myself into a semi-back-bend as the final "Vogue" echoed through my headphones. I collected myself and giggled at my own ridiculousness, sweeping the floor with my former dancing partner as my playlist slowed and eased into Alanis Morrisette's "Uninvited."

I closed my eyes and swayed to the haunting combination of strings

# CHAINS OF SATIN

and Alanis Morrisette's voice. The beat dropped and I became a wannabe sex idol on stage, thrusting my hips, belting out lyrics to the dancing-partner-turned-microphone and feeling myself up with my free hand. I grabbed the broom with both hands when the beat dropped harder, and gave myself a good, hardy spin.

...Only to crash into the chest of Mr. Impossibly-Blue-Eyed-Aldrich himself.

"Oh shit!" I gasped as he caught my shoulders to steady me. I ripped the headphones from my ears, panicking as I shoved them into my back pocket. His eyes followed my movements before they settled on my own, studying me. Neither of us moved. Neither of us said a thing. I swallowed hard and took a small step back from him, afraid to give my voice a chance to betray the panicked fluttering in my chest. His eyes drifted down to my throat and lingered on my lips before he opened his own.

"Are you alright?"

*My God, I would never get tired of hearing that English accent of his.* His eyes grazed over me and I quickly stepped out of his reach.

"The kitchen is almost done," I explained, bending over to pick up the broom. "I just have to mop and it'll be done, so I'm not really — I didn't wake you did I? I didn't expect anyone to be home, I mean your home of course, not mine, and really" — deep inhale — "you are developing a terrible habit of finding me at the most unfortunate times." I took another deep breath, cursing myself for babbling on.

"Unfortunate for whom?" Mr. Aldrich asked, smirking at me. If his eyes twinkled any brighter, they'd be mistaken for stars.

"I was just...I mean, I was certain I was alone and then..."

He smiled wider. I cringed.

"What are you listening to that has you behaving so...vivaciously?"

"Random music," I answered quietly. He reached down and tugged the haphazardly dangling headphones from my pocket and placed one side against his ear. My hand shook and I forced a swallow, frantically trying to gauge his reaction. "Sweet Child O' Mine" by Guns N' Roses. His eyes never left mine as he handed my headphones back. At this point I was making a very futile attempt to steady my breathing that had picked up due to my movement and his surprising presence.

"Interesting," Mr. Aldrich remarked. "And the device containing this music?" He held his hand out to me and I groaned inwardly. Other homes have a no cell policy, and I might have ruined this house for everyone else. I handed my cell phone over and watched as he touched the screen, pulled the headphones from the phone jack and turned the volume up.

"Now." Mr. Aldrich began as he turned his gaze back to me.

# DELILAH ST. RIVERS

"Perhaps something else to get your blood flowing?"

I'm not familiar with classical music but even I could recognize the signature rhythm of a waltz.

"I don't know the steps, sir. I've never waltzed in my life."

Undeterred, Mr. Aldrich pulled himself up straight, positioned his arms, and beckoned me to come to him. I quickly took a step back.

"Sir, I'm on the clock." I stared at his hands, my voice high with embarrassment. "I really shouldn't!"

"And you owe me at least an hour of your time, unless it was some other housekeeper who thieved from me in the form of my signature scent?"

I shook my head, my gaze immediately falling to my feet. He was right. *Technically he'd let me off the hook and it was a solo clean, so nobody could rat me out to management…and how exciting would this be, really?* I leaned the broom against the nearby island and carefully placed myself in his waiting arms, flinching softly as he touched me until I realized he was just locking me in.

"Deep breath," he murmured. "I've seen you move, the command of your body and nearly perfect timing with the rhythm informs me you are capable. Move with me."

The music swelled as he stepped and turned, pulling me with him. I hurried my less-than cooperative feet to catch up. He swayed and shifted, and I moved and stepped until—

"Ow."

I stepped back, horrified and embarrassed as he shook his stockinged foot back to life.

"I'm so sorry," I began, but he straightened, took a step toward me and gently took me back into his arms.

"You've been dancing alone for far too long. When dancing with another, there is a lead and there is a follower. I can take you slow, fast, twirling or dipping, but you must surrender to my movement. Close your eyes, and let your body follow mine through instinct." I looked at him suspiciously. "Close them," he whispered. His voice froze my bones, and I had to fight the shiver as I did as he asked.

"Now, trust me to lead you across the floor. I promise it'll be a delightful experience for the both of us." His breath was warm in my ear, the scent of him thick as it enveloped me. I took a deep breath, gripped him tightly by the hand and shoulder and we began to move.

I was still clumsy. I had seen a few good examples of waltzing from movies and TV shows, but part of being in someone else's arms while they lead means you can't always anticipate their next move. Especially during a dance you don't know.

As another song began to play, my feet refused to cooperate. I

# CHAINS OF SATIN

stumbled, overstepped and understepped in his arms, yet his grip never wavered. Patiently, he held me, whispering in my ear to relax, to breathe and above all: "Close your eyes, dear. If you look at your feet, you'll never trust them."

I felt wisps of his hair brush along my hand where I held his strong shoulder. I tried to focus, but his arms were a distraction, those muscles that bunched and tensed as he held me to him. With me tripping over my own feet and, occasionally, his I'd expected him to call it quits. Instead, the second song ended and another picked up without him letting me go. On and on he took me back and forth, twirling me occasionally as music continued to fill the room we danced in.

By the time he stopped us, a third song had finished and we were both flushed and panting. I opened my eyes to see him staring down at me. I cleared my throat and stepped out of his embrace carefully. My heart did a little skip as I tried to break the tension by doing a deep curtsy, bowing my head.

"Thank you for the dance, good sir."

He stared at me, his shoulder-length hair tousled, his eyes glittering and his chest heaving. He took a step toward me before hesitating, as though caught in thought, and swept into the most graceful, formal English bow. As he rose from it, Mr. Aldrich grasped my hand in his.

"The pleasure," he answered, kissing my hand as he continued to stare at me, "was all mine."

As he released my hand, I silently wondered if all this blushing I was doing around him was good for my blood pressure. I looked around the room, only to see we had ended up in the dining hall, quite a distance from his kitchen. I glanced at him as we began the walk back to the kitchen, filling the awkward silence with chatter.

"Thank you for being so patient with me. Your poor toes must be battered and bruised. I guess my brain got in the way before, but I think I was doing a little better with my eyes closed. Maybe?"

"You'd be surprised at the things you could enjoy with your eyes closed."

I jumped at how close his voice was to me. He continued as I turned again to face him.

"Every distraction just goes away, every other sense is heightened. Your body would be on fire with a touch you would barely register if your eyes were open." Mr. Aldrich gently brushed away the stray hairs across my forehead, making me close my eyes. My body delivered an involuntary shiver.

"I must say," he continued, walking around the island to retrieve

27

a bottle of water from the refrigerator, "I had planned on lounging today. However, I found our activities together a far more pleasant way to pass the time."

I couldn't help but to look down in shame and guilt. If I hadn't been so loud perhaps he would still have been relaxing on one of his very few days out of office. Mr. Aldrich came around and handed me a bottle of water.

"What is your name, by the way?" he asked abruptly, leaning against the island while I drank from the bottle.

"Petunia," I answered.

Mr. Aldrich blinked in surprise.

"Of all the names in the universe I had not expected Petunia."

I grinned and shrugged.

"My mother was always a...let's just say she was a unique person. She'd always say she had two children, myself and her art, and she loved us both equally. And it didn't matter what art she was creating, as long as it was hers. She'd paint, crochet, collect wild flowers to create collages and sang almost everyday, no matter what she was doing." I chuckled a little to myself thinking about her.

"I remember one time she pulled me out of school in the middle of a lesson, drove over an hour to a wooded meadow and we stood there, rain falling on us. She opened her arms and spun around. We danced and danced till we were drenched and shivering.

"We came home, baked a pumpkin pie from scratch and took turns in a hot shower while it was in the oven. By the time we were dressed, the pie was done. Dad came home to find us on the couch with a half-eaten pie, huddled under one blanket and sobbing over *Steel Magnolias*." I looked at him and grinned. "It's one of my favorite memories of her." I'd been tracing my finger along the smooth surface of the red marble counter as I spoke. Mr. Aldrich reached over and took my hand into his, compassion and sympathy filling his eyes.

"When did she pass, Pet?" he asked me.

"Mr. Aldrich—"

"Ethan, please," he interrupted. "It is just the two of us. I don't feel we need to be so formal with each other, don't you agree?"

"Ethan." I blushed as his name rolled off my tongue. "With all due respect, I don't go by the shortened version of my name. It's the one rule I have about myself. As for my mother, I'm sorry if I gave the impression she was gone. She runs an art class in a retirement home...at least that's what she thinks she's doing on an almost daily basis."

"What does that mean?" Ethan asked, taking two steps to me, still

# CHAINS OF SATIN

holding my hand in his. I was beginning to feel very distracted. I cleared my throat and leaned against the countertop.

"She has dementia. She lives with me and when I work, I take her to an outpatient treatment center. Most of the time they let her paint and teach with others  like her." My chest tightened; the all too familiar hurt began to spread and my eyes pricked. I took a deep breath and turned to back away, reaching for the roll of paper towels hanging above the counter behind me.

"Sweet girl," he murmured behind me as I wiped my eyes. "It's no wonder you spend so much time dancing on your own."

*What an odd take away from my anxiety-induced word vomit*, I thought to myself. I turned to him, puzzled at his statement.

"You carry all of your burdens alone, don't you, Pet?" My back was pressed against the counter once more as he moved closer until his hands were resting on either side of me on the countertop. "God knows how long you've been doing so."

"I...I don't go by 'Pet,'" I stuttered. *Curse my fluttering heart.*

Ethan's hair, slightly curly and golden brown, settled like a curtain around his face as he looked down upon me. He smiled softly, that wicked twinkle back in his eyes.

"I've afforded you some rule-bending, darling. Perhaps you could grant me the same courtesy on this one"—he held up a finger—"small thing."

It wasn't a question.

"Okay," I sighed, deciding to make it appear as though I had some choice in the matter. I flashed my eyes back up to him. "But only when we're alone. Never in front of others."

Ethan bowed his head slightly, then gave me the same wicked smile.

"I do hope to find you alone more often, then, Pet."

As close as his face was to mine, my thoughts immediately went to how soft his lips would feel pressed on my own. As my eyes grazed over his lips, Ethan stood straight once more and turned to hand me my bottle of water. I took it, downing the rest quickly to cover my deceitful thoughts.

"Now, tell me about your father," Ethan requested, leaning against the island once more, leaving our knees no further apart than six inches. I shot him with my own cocky smirk.

"Are you always so interested in your housekeepers' family trees?" I asked. The look on his face turned dangerously dark before he broke out in a small grin and let out a throaty laugh.

"You know..." He leaned toward me once more, sticking a finger in my face. "You're lucky you and I aren't—"

My mother's assigned ringtone screeched loudly from my cell, stopping him mid-sentence. My body pressed against his as I reached for my phone on the island, and I felt him tense as I answered the call. I looked up at him apologetically and stepped away.

"Hello?"

"I'm calling for a Miss P. Barlowe," a woman's voice answered.

"Speaking."

"I'm calling in regard to your mother, Mrs. Cassidy Barlowe."

"Has there been an accident?" I tensed, ready to bolt out the door.

"No ma'am, nothing like that." I relaxed back against the counter, sighing with relief. Ethan watched me intently.

"Ms. Barlowe, the treatment center staff find your mother an absolute treasure. She is courteous, kind and, simply put, a welcome sight while she is here."

I smiled softly.

"Unfortunately," the woman continued, "due to budget cuts, our branch is closing its doors to those who are using the outpatient service."

"Wait," I gasped, pinching the bridge of my nose. "What exactly are you saying?"

"Mrs. Barlowe would be a welcome addition as a full-time resident. She would have to be on a waitlist until a bed is cleared for her, but she would be able to enjoy her own room, have the freedom to either dine with others or get catering to her room, and she would be able to continue her art classes in the community room."

"If I decide this isn't the option that's right for her at this time?"

"We would be unable to provide further services to her from today on."

I scoffed.

"I understand budget cuts, but this isn't making sense to me. With your full house of permanent residents, doesn't it mean extra money to keep your outpatient program?"

"It can be difficult to understand, I'm sure." The voice on the other end of the line sighed. "Put simply, outpatients require temp and on-call services including nursing staff, janitors, and food department workers that our budget no longer has the funds to provide."

I grabbed the empty water bottle and walked around the island to toss it into the garbage while she condescended to me on the phone. I picked up a scrub pad from the sink and began to clean nonexistent spots along the counter, aggravation and anxiety triggering my need to move. Ethan stood, his eyes following me.

"I have to think of what's best for my mother. I'm sorry but being

# CHAINS OF SATIN

a full-time resident isn't it," I replied as calmly as I could while I tossed the scrub pad into the sink.

"I'm sorry you feel this way, Ms. Barlowe," the woman said, not sounding sorry at all. "When you come to retrieve her today, there are discharge papers for you to complete."

I froze, aggravation turning quickly to anger.

"Oh, no ma'am. My mother's outpatient service is paid up for another eight days. Your funding from the government may have been cut but you already have the money in hand to take care of her up until then. If you're telling me she isn't able to stay the eight more days she's paid for, then you're prepared to cut a refund check tonight when I come to get her."

"A refund check will be mailed to you. It'll take anywhere between seven to ten days to get to you."

"So it can get 'lost in the mail?' No ma'am. If you're telling me she cannot be there one day longer, you'll be cutting me a valid check in my name tonight or you'll hear from my lawyer!" Adrenaline surged through me as I hung up, tossed the phone on the counter, and let out an exasperated sigh as I gripped the counter's edge, and hung my head.

"Bad news?" Ethan asked softly from behind me. I turned to look up into those diamond-blue eyes

"You asked about my father. The truth is, he isn't doing so well. High cholesterol,  a lot of alcohol, too many years working multiple jobs, and life in general is catching up to him. I don't know how long he has left. That's why Mom goes to the treatment center while I work. He can't help her and there are days where I'm gone up to sixteen hours.

"Dad's retirement pays bills and his meds; my job pays everything for Mom. And now…" I sighed and shook my head. "Now I need to figure something out. I can't work and watch her at the same time, but if I can work from home it may be enough to support everything else she needs." My flushed cheeks reflected my guilt as I looked back up at him. "I may have to quit. I don't want to; it's a nice break for me to get away from it all and focus on something a little mind-numbing for a while, but I don't see any other way out."

Ethan looked as though he was going to say something, but I lifted my hand quickly to interrupt him.

"Don't worry, there are plenty of people who will take my place here. You won't need to worry about any lapse in services. The company is usually pretty good about that."

Ethan seemed to contemplate my words for a moment. I hoped he understood; I wasn't sure why it mattered so much to me that he didn't feel put out.

Finally, he sighed and shook his head, looking at me with an awed expression.

"A dying father. A declining mother. It's incredible that you can even smile some days." He took my chin gently between his fingers, studying my face. My heart stopped and my whole being to froze at the contact. "The strength in you is subtle, flowing just under the surface. Barely noticeable to those who aren't paying attention." He paused. "Do you even have a lawyer?"

I laughed. I couldn't help it. I descended into a fit of giggles as I shook my head no.

Ethan released my chin and retrieved his cell from his pocket. He punched in a text, received an answer right away and replaced his cell.

"Dance with me again, Pet," Ethan commanded gently, his arms outstretched like before. "I find you a most agreeable partner."

"I'm sorry, Ethan," I said, "but I'm not exactly in a dancing mood right now." It was faint, but I could swear I heard him growl under his breath. Then he sighed.

"I wouldn't stress yourself too much over this, Pet. With your returned money I'm certain there are other services that would be willing to help." He brushed a lock of hair behind my ear.

"I don't know. That place had so much to offer." I shrugged. "I'll figure it out. Maybe spending the time with her that she has left isn't such a bad idea either."

Ethan took a step back and walked to the refrigerator.

"If you will not dance, will you share lunch with me?"

I looked at my watch. *How was it lunch time already?* I nodded and his eyes lit up as he smiled at me. My lunch bag rested in its spot on the counter, and I retrieved my usual: a bottle of Diet Coke and a ham sandwich. Ethan lifted the bottle and turned it over in his hand, glancing from it to the sandwich.

"This is lunch for you?" he asked, looking back at me. I shrugged.

"It's quick and easy."

"Quick," Ethan mumbled before walking around to come behind me, taking both halves of the sandwich and the bottle of merciful caffeine into his hands. Before I could utter a sound, he tossed everything into the garbage.

"HEY!"

"That is not self-care." Ethan turned to grasp me by the shoulders. "Calories are spent so they may be replaced responsibly." He leaned in to whisper in my ear, "So they can be spent again." He stood upright and led me to the dining room table and pulled out a chair. I hesitated. His eyes

# CHAINS OF SATIN

flashed with that something that made my heart flutter in my chest.

"Sit, darling."

Still, I hesitated. I crossed my arms and glared at him.

*Wealthy people never get it,* I thought to myself. *He threw away a MEAL. Wasted it. Money I spent, just... gone.*

To my surprise, Ethan chuckled.

"Allow me to make it up to you."

I rolled my eyes. *Of course. Throw away my money and then order from a fancy place to flaunt his own. If that's his plan, he'd be nothing more than every other typical egotistical bullsh —*

"Pet." I looked up at him to catch a fire burning behind his eyes. "Pretend for a moment that you aren't angry, that you have an open and trusting mind. And pretend for a moment that you knew if you were to roll those sweet, blue eyes at me again there would be dire consequences."

I swallowed down nerves as he gestured once more to the offered chair. As I sank into it, he whispered, "Good girl," and my heart did flips as he walked back into the kitchen.

After a few more moments I heard him grunt loudly and curse just slightly. I rose from my chair and walked to the kitchen where I came upon him clutching a towel-wrapped hand. A chef's knife resting on the cutting board beside a haphazardly decapitated cucumber was all I needed to see.

"How bad is it?" I asked. He chuckled wryly and lifted his injured hand.

"Not exactly what I had in mind when I began this endeavor." Ethan shook his head and shrugged. I came around the island and reached for the towel. He pulled the whole bundle away. "I wouldn't want to put you off, Pet."

"Let me see," I commanded.

Ethan's eyes shot up at mine, and after a split second it was his own turn to roll his eyes as he held out his injured hand. I carefully opened the towel, ready to reapply pressure if it proved to be a gusher.

"It's not so serious, really. I—ow!" Ethan jumped and threw his uninjured fist into his mouth. An angry red gash ran across the base of his thumb. I pulled him to the sink and ran warm water over the wound to get the blood flowing and make sure there were no towel fibers in the cut. I leaned over, grabbed the bottle of soap, and began to gently wash the injury.

Ethan had large hands—thin but strong. As the water washed the soap and blood away, I could see just how deep the cut was. Had he been a man with soft hands or been more careless with the knife, he could have easily cut to the bone.

"First aid kit?" I asked, looking up to see him studying me.

"Master bathroom," he answered. "Allow me a moment, then it's all yours." He turned and walked out, while I used the towel to wipe up blood and water from the counter and the inside of the sink.

"So am I going to live?" Ethan asked with a chuckle as he returned, handing me the little first aid kit.

I grinned and shook my head. "I hope you have all your affairs in order, sir, this could be the end of you."

"Almost," he answered softly.

I chuckled as I painted iodine over the wound drawing a hiss as Ethan sucked in a breath. I patted it dry with sterile gauze and placed two butterfly stitches to close the gap. I finished by wrapping it with another thin strip of gauze and securing it with medical tape.

"You know, there are far less painful ways to get me to hold your hand," I remarked, my tone teasing. My laughter died away as I watched his demeanor change. His eyes grew dark as he drew closer and closer until we were just shy of touching.

"Are there?" Ethan's voice lowered to a predatory growl. "Pray, dear girl, tell me."

My heart hammered in my chest, and I was certain Ethan could hear it. The injured hand turned to caress my cheek with the back of his fingers while he leaned his weight on the counter with his other.

"We-well...um...there was...There...there was the, um... dancing?" I stammered, desperately searching my mind for coherent thought to form. Ethan inhaled deeply and released it with a dark chuckle.

"Maybe not entirely painless, my Pet," he whispered as he backed away. I stood still, frozen and practically quivering against the counter with my entire being flushed.

INSISTENT THAT I ALLOW HIM TO PREPARE me lunch after his injury, it wasn't long before I was presented with my first look at a genuine charcuterie board, complete with cheese, crackers, grapes, sliced strawberries, julienned carrots, chunks of turkey, and various dips and sauces. It was a veritable cornucopia, and my mouth watered at the awesome sight.

"It's beautiful," I said. "I don't know where to start!"

He chuckled as he set a pitcher of ice water and two glasses on the table, then built himself a plate from the board. I followed suit, and soon we were eating in relative silence.

# CHAINS OF SATIN

"Where did you learn to do all this?" I asked, breaking the comfortable bubble of peace.

"I minored in culinary skills while in college."

"It was time and money well spent," I complimented, placing a strawberry slice on a piece of cheese before eating it as one. He looked confused as he stared at me.

"It's sliced food on a wooden board. How is that impressive?"

"It's more effort in a lunch than I've experienced in a long while, and it only cost you one mishap." I shrugged and pointed at his bandaged thumb. "So, in my mind it's impressive. Besides, the way it's arranged, it's like art. Some of the simplest of things can be the most beautiful art, ya know?"

I watched a small smile creep over Ethan's face.

"How right you are," he said.

I smiled and blushed. Nothing more was said while we finished until I sat back into my chair, sighing with contentment.

"Feel better?" Ethan asked, refilling my glass with the water.

"So much," I said happily.

He smiled and rose from his chair, whisking away the plates to the kitchen. I stood and grabbed the board.

"Absolutely not." Ethan's stern voice rattled through me and I turned with board in hand. He took it and gave me a look that matched his voice.

"I'm still on the clock," I argued at his back. He walked to the kitchen with me following.

"Correction, darling"—he turned to me after setting the board on the counter—"you are on *my* clock."

I glanced at my watch and smiled up at his glittering eyes.

"Correction, darling," I mimicked him, loving the way his eyes widened a bit in surprise. "I am six minutes off your clock… sir." I held up my wrist, angled for him to see the numbers displayed on the screen, and I could almost swear I saw disappointment dance behind his eyes.

Straightening himself, he took a hold and gently kissed the offered hand, smiling softly before dipping into a half-bow.

"I hadn't expected to use all my time at once," Ethan confessed.

"Well, time flies when you're having fun." I smiled at him, my knuckles tingling from the touch of his lips. He didn't smile back; instead he took a step closer to me and reached out to tuck a lock of hair behind my ear.

"Oh," he whispered. "I fear you don't have the imagination to know just how true that is."

# DELILAH ST. RIVERS

My breath hitched in my throat. He smirked and walked around me, waving a hand over his head.

"Until next time," he called, leaving me alone to steady myself.

## CHAPTER THREE

# Petunia

WHEN MY SOLO CLEAN WAS FINISHED, I packed up my things and shut off all the lights downstairs. I stopped at the door before leaving and shouted "Good night" in the direction of Ethan's room upstairs without receiving a response.

It didn't take long to reach the nursing home, but the whole time my head swam with the memories of us dancing, me bandaging his wound, and him making lunch. That man, something about him…well, everything about him was so different from what I'd experienced before.

I was so lost in thought that it took me a moment to realize I had already parked at the nursing home. I turned off my car and sat against the seat, the ghost of his arm wrapped around me and the phantom of his breath in my ear.

I closed my eyes and shivered. I didn't understand all the events of the day, didn't know why he touched my face or kept stepping up close to me. Why did his body scream "I'm attracted to you" when the three months I'd been working in his home he acted positively indifferent?

I shook my head, straightened my shoulders and took a deep breath in an effort to shake loose the distractions that kept flooding my mind. I still had the issue of my mother's treatment center to contend with.

I walked into the main office where two nurses were seated beside

# DELILAH ST. RIVERS

my waiting mother.

"One minute, Mama," I said to her as I walked into the private office and closed the door. Melinda Davers looked up from her paperwork with a bright smile as she offered me a chair.

"I don't think that's necessary," I politely refused. "I'm just here for my mother and my check, as we previously discussed." I silently prayed I was convincing.

"Of course, Ms. Barlowe." She shuffled through the papers on her desk before handing me a check.

Surprised, I took the check from her hand.

"There's been a very recent change of hands regarding the building's ownership. All outpatients—including your mother—are to be allowed to stay with their current treatment in place."

I looked down at the check in my hand.

"Then why are you handing me this?"

"Oh," Melinda chuckled awkwardly. "The new owner has been in touch with your lawyers about our little misunderstanding. They insisted we pay back not only the eight days you've paid up to, but an additional three months for trauma our conversation may have caused your mother or yourself. We also offer our most sincere apology for being dismissive during our conversation. I am personally, truly sorry."

*My lawyers?*

"Thank you," I said softly. "I still have to have my mother here every other day or so." Melinda nodded at my statement. "So why don't I just hand this back and it will be enough to cover her treatment for the next few months?"

Melinda shook her head. "The new owner deemed the outpatient treatment unnecessary income, gave us a larger budget and is building a new wing exclusively for our center. Whoever your lawyers are, Ms. Barlowe, they are certainly effective."

Gratitude swelled in my heart. Free service, money back into my account, a new wing for patients…I was genuinely getting teary-eyed.

"Who was it that bought the building?" I asked after clearing my throat. "I would like to thank them personally, if possible." Melinda looked through her stack of papers again. She produced a plain paper with a company header across the top and handed it to me.

I gasped quietly.

"We were all a little surprised ourselves," Melinda answered. "It seems fortune favored us all today. Is there anything more you need from me, Ms. Barlowe?"

"No, thank you. I guess you'll be seeing us in a couple of days."

## CHAINS OF SATIN

I couldn't let this slide, not after all he had done. We'd only had one real interaction together to that point—what did he want from me? I decided that I needed to find out, and I drove with my mom back to my Regal Cleaning Services headquarters and brought her inside with me. In the office, I found Ethan's personal cell phone number in his file on the computer. I dialed before I lost the nerve, but was greeted by his voicemail. I sat in the office chair, feeling roadblocked. I looked over to my mother who had begun to drift off in the leather loveseat across the room. I glanced at the clock and saw it was after 10:00 pm—well past her bedtime. Promising myself that I would visit Ethan tomorrow on my day off, I rose from the desk chair, collected my mother, and headed home.

CHAPTER FOUR

# Petunia

*RING.*
*RING.*
*RING.*
*RING.*

"Ugh," I groaned, reaching for my phone from under the covers. My best friend Shay Williams's contact photo lit up my screen. "Hello?"

"Guess who has tonight and tomorrow off work?"

"That's awesome!" I exclaimed, happy for her but not enough to roll out of bed. "You totally deserve it."

"I totally do," she practically squealed over the phone. "I'm on my way to see my wifey with some cocktail dresses, a bottle of wine, and spa day reservations for two!" I couldn't help but be caught up in her excitement.

"Okay," I said, throwing the blankets off my body. "That's enough to get me out of bed on my day off."

"I mean, we could always ditch plans and I could crawl in bed with you. Gotta keep my wifey warm!"

"Only if you promise to be naked." I chuckled. *If your best friend doesn't make people question your sexuality, are they really your best friend?*

"What time will you be here?" I asked.

"Girl, traffic straight-up sucks right now so I'm guessing maybe

# CHAINS OF SATIN

another hour or so. Why? You busy? Got plans besides me or what?"

"Oh yeah, you know me, life of the party over here." I carried a towel to the bathroom as I answered her. "Nah, I'm just debating on a shower and shave deal. Besides, you know I always make time for you no matter what, shut up."

Shay laughed.

"Damn straight, bitch."

"I do have one stop to make at some point today. Other than that, I'm all yours."

"Alright, boo, I gotch —" Static filled my ear, and I winced away from the phone as I started my shower and adjusted it to the right temperature. "—there?" Shay came back on the phone.

"I can hear you now," I said, mimicking an old cell phone commercial. "All good."

"Oh, you know I am," she flirted.

"Better check on your head. If it gets any bigger you won't fit through the spa doors."

"Yeah, fuck you, too. Go, get ready so when I get there we can blow off steam like queens! I love you, boo!" Shay hung up and I shook my head, smiling. She was absolutely amazing.

After my shower, I called the Winding Creek Residences and Treatment Facility to see if they had an opening for mom in their outpatient schedule, then double-checked with our in-home nurse, Rico, to see if Dad needed anything. As usual, he waved me out the door when the horn blew from outside.

"I'm not going to let anything happen to Daddy while you're gone, *mija*. You just worry about getting out and enjoying life!" Rico ushered my mother and me out the door. "It's been too long since you've been out and about, and you know I live vicariously through you, honey."

Following his orders, I dropped Mom off at Winding Creek without a hitch and made it to the spa only a few minutes before Shay arrived. We signed in and were directed to a locker room where we could change into incredibly soft terry cloth robes. My fingers ran along the soft texture and I sighed with contentment.

"You about done feeling yourself up, girlie?" Shay stood with her hands on her hips. "'Cause I mean, it's not like we got hotties waiting for us to do that job for you or anything."

"Not quite…" I ran my fingers up my sleeves. "Almost," I mockingly moaned as I traced the belt around my waist and back up to my shoulders. "Okay, now I'm done. Let's go!"

We entered a big, quiet room with two tables for us to lay upon.

# DELILAH ST. RIVERS

Shay and I stripped and covered ourselves with the plush sheets. A man and woman entered the room together.

"Good morning. I'm Paige and this is Cory." The woman's soft voice was definitely suited for the calm ambiance of the room. "We are your massage therapists for today. We encourage you to relax. Feel free to talk to each other or just listen to the music, and you'll walk out of here refreshed and feeling like new women."

Of course my man-hungry bestie's eyes lit up when hunky Cory approached her table, and she blatantly grinned and gave me a thumbs up. I couldn't control the giggle-fit that overcame me at her reaction before we both settled in and let the calm wash over us.

CHAPTER FIVE

# Petunia

AFTER OUR SPA DAY, SHAY AND I got dressed up and decided on a night out at one of our favorite spots: Larry's. Much like the amazing afternoon at the spa, Larry's did not disappoint. Their mozzarella sticks never failed to bring on my happy-hum. Coupled with great music and a small-town atmosphere, it was a lovely place to go to kick off our evening.

"Ladies," Larry himself addressed us as we chatted at our table. "Always a pleasure when you come to town." He winked at Shay, who batted her eyelashes at him while sipping her daiquiri.

"So, I see two beautiful women enjoying my alcohol but no friend-zoned man or underaged driver. I assume you have someone coming for you after you're finished here?" Larry, being no less than sixty-five years old, was a flirt with a big heart. If you came for a good time, he was more than happy to help. If, however, you came unprepared to leave safely, he would charm you out of your car keys and call a cab or an Uber.

Shay pulled her keys from her purse and handed them to Larry. As with any small town, there was an honor system here, and the trust ran deep in Larry's parking lot.

"Don't worry, Larry," I said, getting up to grab yet another drink, teetering just a smidge. "I got extra money to play with so I'll pay for… the…oh shit." I felt my heart drop instantly.

# DELILAH ST. RIVERS

"What's wrong?"

"We never went to his house," I mumbled. "And here he did this incredible thing for me and I didn't even thank him." Typing as I talked, I quickly sent out an Uber request.

"We will be back for the car in the morning, old boy," I told Larry, kissing him on the cheek and thrusting forty dollars in his hand.

"Okay, girl, what's up?" Shay sounded intrigued. "Who's this 'he' and what was this 'incredible thing' he did for you?"

I handed the Uber driver a piece of paper with Ethan's address on it; luckily it wasn't too far from Larry's.

"His name is — ow! Jesus girl, what is in that bag of yours?" I yelled while rubbing my knee. Shay looked into her bag, laughed, and pulled out the wine bottle she'd promised to bring for the night. "I thought you left it at my house!" I laughed, watching her pull out a corkscrew as well. "Where's the sink so I can wash my hands first?" I teased, laughing while she took the first drink.

"Shut up and suck on this," Shay said, giggling as she thrust the bottle in my face. I wrapped my hand around the bottle neck and inhaled as I felt the first drops hit my tongue. I closed my eyes and drank until I couldn't hold my breath anymore. "How much are you going to leave for me, asshole?" Shay yelled and I giggled, feeling the heat of the wine and cocktails flood my body. I handed her the half-empty bottle with my eyes closed, savoring the light-headed sensation as we pulled up to Ethan's driveway.

"WHO IS IT?" a voice chirped through a speaker. The driver rolled down my window and I cleared my throat.

"Petunia Barlowe for Mr. Aldrich. And company. I forgot something, but if he isn't here I can come back on my next work day to deal with it." I silently applauded myself for the minimal verbal screw-ups in my stupor.

"He'll meet with you directly at the front door. Come on in." Shay looked at me in awe when she saw the house we were driving up to.

"Seriously, who is this guy?"

"I clean his home," I explained. "And he bought Mama's treatment center so she could keep going there."

My stomach tightened with anxiety as Ethan stepped out the front door. Clad only in a white t-shirt and gray sweatpants, his hands rested in his pockets as he watched the car approach with nonchalance. The car stopped, and I leaned forward to speak to the driver, slipping him a hundred dollar bill.

"Wait here, please. We'll go to Bonnie's on Third St. when we're

# CHAINS OF SATIN

done here. I won't be long."

My door opened, and Ethan offered me his hand to step out. I blinked, not having seen him move off his steps. I gingerly took his hand, placed my heeled foot onto the pavement and stood, leaning on him as I pulled my other foot out and placed it down carefully. I had been so careful making sure my footing was secure that I almost missed the savage hunger that filled his features before he cloaked it with a gentle smile. The hunger lingered in his eyes.

"I'm surprised you're here, Pet," he initiated. Shay let out a loud, howling laugh.

"Oh my God, did you just call her that? Seriously? Do you know who the last guy —"

"I told him he could." I bent down to speak to her before rising to meet his eyes and adding pointedly, "When we were alone." Our hands were still interlocked.

"I do apologize," Ethan answered. "I figured I may as well use it while I can, since I can't truly see how our paths would cross after today."

"Wait...are you firing me?" I swayed a bit, my stomach tightening up again. He steadied me by my elbow and cleared his throat, a trace of disappointment, anger and...hurt running through his eyes.

"You didn't show up for work today, darling. I had assumed you quit because of our interaction yesterday," Ethan explained softly.

"My best friend is in town and we are catching up. Today was a scheduled day off, sir. You've heard of days off, right? I do that too." I cocked my head to the side, and my heart flipped when I saw his eyes gleam. Something in his eyes made me remember why I was there, and I gasped, placing a hand on his chest. "Oh my God, I almost forgot again! Thank you so much!" Ethan took a step back to prevent a fall as I threw my arms around his neck, pressing my body flush against his in a hug. When he had us steadied, his arms circled around me, holding me, breathing quickly. "I don't know how or why you did it, but I'm so grateful to you for giving my mama a place to go so she can be treated and happy and...and..." The tears, an unwelcome but inevitable byproduct of the wine and cocktails, flooded my eyes. Ethan pulled back to hold me by my shoulders, reaching to grab the tissues offered from Shay within the car.

"You seem awfully certain I am the one who deserves this level of gratitude," he teased.

"The lady at the counter told me. She showed me the letterhead of your company. I tried calling you but the phone just kept ringing and —"

"What do you mean you tried calling? Forgive me, I don't remember giving you my number."

# DELILAH ST. RIVERS

I chuckled into the tissues. "I found it in our company's directory, sir. We aren't supposed to just go into it ourselves but I thought this warranted it."

Ethan looked at me for a moment, studying me as I dried my tears with the tissues. Then he burst out laughing.

"Quite the detective, aren't you?"

"Maybe."

Ethan looked me over again, seeming to take me in and contemplate my appearance.

"You look like you've never seen a girl in a dress," I laughed, trying to ease some of the awkward tension. His eyes found mine and he leaned forward ever so slightly.

"What I see before me could hardly be called a 'girl,'" Ethan growled softly. I wondered if it was dark enough outside to hide my blush from him.

"Wh-why did you do it, though? Buy the building?" I asked, hoping the question would distract my racing heart. "Why did you do that for my mother?"

"My sweet lady," Ethan said, taking me by my hand and leading me the few feet back to the car. "If your mother was in peril of losing her treatment center, others were too," he continued, opening my door to the Uber. "Not to mention, centers such as Winding Creek are hearty investments." He kissed my hand gently, releasing it and shutting my door. He crossed his arms over the window ledge and looked over between Shay and myself. "You ladies enjoy your night out. Be careful," he warned.

"I won't let anything happen to my wifey," Shay promised loudly.

"I'll see you on Monday," I breathed, tapping the back of the driver's seat.

"I'll hold you to it," Ethan said, staring into my eyes as he stood straight. He watched us drive away, his hands in his pockets before walking back inside.

"Did you see the outline of his—"

"Seriously?!" I interrupted my best friend's loud mouth. "That is a man I work for, ma'am!" I looked at her sternly as she lifted up both hands with a measured space between them. I blushed as we laughed together.

"I'm just sayin'...Wow!" She laughed.

"Give me that bottle," I told her, taking the wine from her and drinking the rest of it, the recent events playing back as I shook my head. "Ugh, I can't believe I hugged him."

"I can't believe you killed the bottle," Shay said dejectedly. I hugged her.

"I'll buy you a new one, all for you."

# CHAINS OF SATIN

BONNIE'S WAS A LARGER BAR THAN LARRY'S. The dance floor was always busy, which was perfect for dancing with Shay. With the music and the crowd, it was the perfect place to really let loose. After a couple of songs, we pushed through the crowd and down the stairs to find a table.

"Alright," Shay began as we sat. "Spill."

"What?" I protested. "I didn't do anything."

"Are you sleeping with him?"

"Oh."

"Yeah, 'oh.' That man is fucking gorgeous, but you can't be playin' like that with your job, boo."

I held up my hands and shook my head.

"It's nothing like that. We haven't been inappropriate at all. I've been cleaning his place for three months now. I actually kinda fucked up in my first month. You're gonna die when you hear this…I swear. I have never been near a man who smelled so good before, and I was cleaning his room and dusting and all that and…he caught me spraying and smelling his cologne." I cringed as I spoke the last words.

Shay, however, spit out her drink, laughing.

"Talk about some awkward shit!"

"Tell me about it. Instead of getting mad, he asked if I liked it."

"That's weird. Maybe he needed a woman's opinion. Or"—she leaned in conspiratorially over the table—"maybe he has the hots for you."

"Pfft, I wish," I answered impulsively. "But since then, I don't know. He gets so sweet until I pull a trigger word, which I swear I don't do on purpose, and he just looks so feral then."

"Trigger word? Really?" Shay stopped giggling and looked at me, her expression stern. "Goddammit, Petunia. What happened last time you were like that? Didn't you learn from that? You said it's not your scene anymore! You swore that sub/dom shit off! You promised me. Or did we forget that when he batted those pretty blues at you and told you that you were a good girl?"

"No, I didn't forget! And it wasn't even on purpose, not at first. But the addiction came back—that rush of control I felt over him when I could see how much he fought his own self-control." I sighed. "Nothing is going to come of this, I promise. He's a proper English gentleman who wouldn't overstep his bounds with the help. I promise."

"I worry about you, girl. You're the only person in the world I can turn to—the only one who gets me. I just don't want anything to happen to

# DELILAH ST. RIVERS

you again. Trust and believe: I'll kick your ass if you end up in the hospital again."

I smiled as Shay kissed my cheek and got up to get us drinks from the bar. I felt my phone vibrate in my purse and retrieved it to see an update from Rico:

> Mr. and Mrs. Barlowe are sleeping soundly. Hopefully you get back with juicy tea to share in the morning! 😊

I smiled and shook my head, shooting back:

> Good night, Rico. Don't wait up.

I looked up to see Shay returning with two drinks in her hands. Behind her, the men from the bar ogled her every move, and I couldn't help but laugh.

"What?" she asked, handing me a very potent Sex on the Beach.

"Those guys." I gestured behind her. "You just leave tongues hanging out wherever you go." Shay looked back and blew them a kiss before we giggled into our drinks. "You're an awful tease," I said, laughing. I missed this.

"You're one to talk! Teasing Mister Boss Man with your trigger words and then showing up at his house all done up just to say thank you." Shay rolled her eyes. "Not to mention, you didn't see his face when you threw yourself at him."

"Oh, God," I put my head in my hands. "He must've felt so embarrassed."

"Um, girlfriend, if that's what being embarrassed looks like, I don't want to know what he looks like when he's horny!"

"Oh shut the fuck up. He doesn't think like that. I'm a housekeeper, his employee. He's some wealthy English guy that probably has a different girlfriend every week. And I can guarantee they don't smell like cleaning solution." She laughed and I finished my drink. "Ugh." I made a face as I groaned. "I think I overdid the salt on that tequila shot. It's totally messing up my favorite drink."

"Come on," she said, grabbing my hand and leading me to the dance floor. Two of the guys from the bar found us and took turns dancing with the both of us, getting up close and pressing our backs to each other.

I turned around and grabbed Shay's shoulder during a break in the music.

# CHAINS OF SATIN

"My head feels funny. I'm gonna go sit down," I said in her ear, brushing off the wandering hands from the t-shirt-clad dancing partner.

"I'll help you back to your seat, sugar," Mr. Hands said. Shay took my hand and bruised off the would-be savior.

"I got you, girl!" Shay shouted as the loud music started back up and threatened to drown her out.

"Ugh," I groaned again. "I feel so stupid. I mean, look at me! I'm a hot mess. Why didn't I just wait till Monday to thank him? And I hugged him! What the hell?!" My head began to feel heavy, and I struggled to recall all the alcohol I had consumed that night.

*Cocktails at Larry's. Wine. Tequila shots, probably two? Sex on the Beach, I think?*

I felt like a lightweight; I'd handled so much more with more grace last time I went out with Shay.

"Baby girl, why are you trippin' so hard over it?" Shay asked, touching up her lipstick.

"'Cause just yesterday I wanted to kiss him. And...ugh, my head hurts."

"You didn't eat enough, you lush."

"I think I'll puke if I think about food."

"Hang on," she said, getting up from her seat and going to the bar. One of the guys, at this point it was hard to tell anyone from anyone, was suddenly beside me, handing me a cold glass. The blue-colored liquid and the thought of drinking any more alcohol made my stomach turn.

"No," I murmured. "I can't. No more right now."

"I bought this for you, sugar. Me and my pal. It was pretty expensive but I knew you'd be worth —"

"Hey, she said 'no,' my dude," Shay interrupted, thrusting a bottle of water in my hand. "Plus, we don't take drinks from strangers: 'Women's Party Rules 101.' Got it?"

"So I wasted my money? I thought you'd be more grateful. We're just trying to have a good time here, right?"

"It wouldn't be a waste if you drink it yourself," I slurred. The guy scoffed and walked away, mumbling insults as he sat beside his buddy back at the bar. I turned away from him and dug through my purse slowly, pulling out my phone.

"Uh-uh, we made a deal a long time ago that we wouldn't allow each other to drunk text!" Shay reached for my phone and I held up a finger as the call rang in my ear.

"Hello?"

"Ethan..." I barely breathed his name.

# DELILAH ST. RIVERS

"It's late, darling. Is something wrong?" Even in my stupor, Ethan's accent sent goosebumps down my spine.

"N-no. I'm…well, okay? I'm sorry I hugged you and it wasn't… was…um." I was really struggling to get the words out of my mouth.

"Petunia, listen to me. I insist you go home and rest," Ethan said patiently.

"No…no, sir." I giggled a bit, and glanced at Shay's horrified face as she mouthed "You're embarrassing yourself." "I need to say…. Something to you…" I carried on.

"And so you have. Quite elegantly. Is your friend with you?"

"Yeah. She…she's worried though. I can't end up in the hospital again. She'll kick my ass," I whispered the last bit into the phone. Shay wasn't a large girl, but she was strong, and in that moment I was truly convinced she would kick my ass.

"Hand her the phone, Petunia. Please."

My eyes locked on Shay's.

"See…He's not like You-know-Who. He has manners," I told Shay, smiling. I handed her the phone and everything went dark.

PAIN.

I felt it before I could even open my eyes. It was everywhere: my head, my stomach, my legs…

I groaned and tried to open my eyes, fighting to lift a hand to my head, but a larger one gently restrained it.

"Sh, Pet. I'm here."

"Don't…don't leave me," I could barely get the words out as the darkness took over once again.

CHAPTER SIX

# Petunia

LIGHT SHINED ON MY FACE. THE WARMTH felt so nice, I didn't want to move or even be awake. My right leg felt numb and heavy all at once. My mouth was dry, and there was pressure wrapped around my lower stomach. My headache from before was gone, replaced with light-headedness.

I sighed; this plush and amazingly comfortable bed and the pillow I was leaning against didn't feel the same as my own, or smell the same as my own. It almost smelled like…

*No.*

I chanced a peek through my heavy eyelids, flinching at the brightness. Across the room, Shay slept in a recliner. I called out her name, my voice scratchy and dry. Her eyes flew open and she sat up quickly.

"Hey baby girl," she whispered, kneeling at the side of the bed to take my hand. "How are you feeling?"

"Like shit."

"Don't wake up Prince Charming; he's been up almost a day and a half with you," she cautioned.

"What? Why?"

"'Cause you'd lose your shit every time he tried to leave. Even when I was changing your clothes, he had to hold your hand or you'd freak out

# CHAINS OF SATIN

and start crying, like ugly crying. That's why he's in bed with you."

"What?!" I had tried to keep quiet, but that last one surprised the hell out of me. I carefully turned my head, hoping he wasn't awake. My luck held, and he was sleeping soundly, his arm around me, breathing peacefully.

"I don't know what deity to thank for this, but, holy shit," I whispered back to Shay, who grinned and shook her head.

"Heal before you start thinking about the dirty stuff, you weirdo."

"What happened? I remember drinks at Larry's…Oh, God, being here with Ethan…and then…music? A bad headache, I remember that one. Not much else though." My heart pounded harder in my chest; I'd never not remembered a night out before.

"Fucking roofies," Shay scoffed. "I'm so sorry, sweetie. It's my fault; I was talking to those guys at the bar and one of them slipped it in your drink."

For a moment, I couldn't say anything, overwhelmed with the feeling of violation.

"Let me get you some water, boo. I'll be right back." She kissed my cheek and closed the door behind her.

After a moment, a tear fell. Then another. Before I could help it, my face was leaking onto the pillow beneath me. A hand reached up and wiped the side of my face.

"More bad dreams?" Ethan asked sleepily. I turned to him, shaking my head. He wiped the other side of my face free of tears.

"Shay just told me about the…" My breath caught in my throat, choking off the words.

"Allow me to get you a—"

"Here's your water, sweetie," Shay announced, holding a glass in her hand. Oh! You're awake." She acknowledged Ethan before demanding, "Help me sit her up."

After I was inclined and had a few sips of water, I sat back into the pillows, feeling a million times better.

"Roofies?" I asked Shay as I watched Ethan set my glass of water on the nightstand beside me. His cologne flooded my senses, and I shivered.

"Chilled?" Ethan asked softly. I nodded, though I was fine. He stood up and tucked me in before walking away.

"Wait, wait!" I called to him, unsure why the idea of him leaving sent a panic running through me.

"Restroom, darling. I'll return quickly, I swear to you," he vowed before leaving.

"Roofies," Shay answered my first question. "I'm so sorry."

"It's not your fault," I reassured her.

"Well, what if it was supposed to be for me?"

"Do you think that would have been any better?" I asked her. "With your past health shit, do you really think you would have needed that? Seriously, a little alcohol is fine, but God knows what rohypnol would have done to you. I would rather it was me than you anyday."

"Shut up," she said, wiping away tears before hugging me.

"Alright, so what happened? And how did I get into his bed, of all places?"

"You complaining?" she teased.

"Hell no," I giggled quietly.

"That's a much better sound coming from you," Ethan said, reentering the room. He sat on the edge of the bed and patted my hand. "Hungry?"

I shook my head. "I just want to know what happened."

"You handed me the phone, Ethan asked if you drank too much—"

"You called him?"

"You called, Pet. You were almost incoherent, so I asked to speak to your friend." Ethan's eyes studied me intensely.

"Oh," I said, a blush creeping over my face.

"And then you just passed out. I freaked out 'cause you wouldn't, like, respond at all. By then the phone went dead in my hand. I'm telling you I thought the worst—"

"I was already on my way," Ethan interjected.

"And then the two guys offered to help me bring you out of the bar. I was so grateful, and they were able to talk to you while you revived a bit, but you weren't in any shape to walk alone. They got you to the back entrance, which they said made sense to take you to 'cause it would be a shorter walk for you. They were getting between the two of us. Like, mad pushing me away, bro. And you know me: I'm getting really pissed off and start yelling at them, but they start telling me to back off so they could 'take care of you.' I pushed them hard, and they let you go or bumped into you or something, but you fell down the stairs…"

"Stairs did this?" I gestured to my leg.

"Baby, there were like two flights, and you fell over the railing onto the ground. I think there was a garbage bag someone tossed that saved your head from getting bashed in and it was so awful…" Tears leaked out of her eyes, and she squeezed my hand.

"You fell as I pulled into the parking lot. The men were spooked by the lights and tried to run. It is rather unfortunate for them that I have connections with the local police and first responders. They were as prompt

# CHAINS OF SATIN

as I needed them to be and were right behind me to apprehend them." Ethan reclined back onto his elbow as he finished his part.

"It was chaos with the cops and ambulance; money does make the world go 'round for sure," Shay continued. "The ambulance rushed you to the hospital and they tested your blood after they got you into x-ray."

"Broken in two separate places, but clean breaks as far as they could tell," Ethan reported.

"They wanted to keep you in the hospital, but you wouldn't stop giving them reasons you couldn't stay admitted. Fortunately for you, girl, Ethan has an on-call physician, so he was able to convince them to let you leave the hospital with the promise of in-home care. And since here is less chaotic than your house…"

I looked at him, meeting his gaze.

"This is such an inconvenience to you," I began, but Ethan held up a finger.

"Shouldn't I be the judge of what inconveniences me?"

"Well, yes, but—"

"Think nothing of it, Pet. You would have done the same if our situations were reversed." He sounded so matter-of-fact, and I couldn't deny it.

"I really do appreciate you," I said to him. I turned to Shay. "Can you help me to the bathroom?" As she stood, Ethan got up and helped pull me gently to a stand, supporting my weight while they led me to the door. He turned to go back onto the bed.

"You'll still…you'll be here?" I asked, trembling from the effort of my weakened body and hard-cast leg.

"Of course, darling."

I could swear as he sat on the bed that I saw a hint of his cocky smile.

When they were able to get me back onto the bed, Shay knelt beside me again.

"I hate to leave you, boo, but they need me back at work tonight. I was gonna tell them to piss off if you were still asleep, but you woke up. I'm really glad you're okay." She hugged me tight, while he went to the other side of the bed and reclined beside me. "Just don't say any more funny shit without me on the phone to hear it, got me?"

"Oh, God. What did I do?" I groaned. She laughed.

"Well, for one thing, you kept calling him 'Mr. Darcy.' Then you asked him if he wanted to kiss you. You told me you wanted five minutes alone in the room with him and you'd show him how to really be a dom—"

"OH MY GOD, STOP!" I put my head in my hands, mortified.

Shay hugged me again, laughing.

"Don't worry. He was such a good sport and a gentleman through this whole thing."

"Oh, God," I mumbled. Ethan's strong arms enveloped me from the side and I leaned into him reluctantly as he comforted me with soothing sounds.

"I love you, girl." Shay leaned over and kissed my head. "Take care of her. I'm trusting you."

"I love you too," I told her, lifting my head as Ethan held me tighter. The steady pounding of his heart had a calming effect on my body.

The door closed behind her and Ethan drew me in to his chest, bringing me to lay beside him on the bed.

"I'm so sorry," I repeated, embarrassment and fatigue washing over me.

"Shh," Ethan comforted me. "Rest now. We can talk later, but first you must rest."

My head shot up and he looked at me with surprise.

"My mom and dad! The nurse—"

"Come, darling," he said softly, guiding my head back onto his chest. "I've more than adequately compensated your nurse and paid another for your mother's care. It is all arranged."

Tears filled my eyes.

"No," I cried. "This is too much; how can I—"

"Don't you dare suggest repayment." The tenor in Ethan's voice rumbled in his chest as he interrupted me. "If it was an obligation, I'd be more reluctant to do it. Now, no more talking. No more crying. No worrying. You're safe. Just sleep."

"You'll stay?" I asked again.

"As long as you need me to, darling, I'll stay."

PRESENT DAY
OFFICE OF DR. JOSEPH HALL

# Ethan

THE OFFICE OF DR. JOSEPH HALL FELL quiet as I took a sip from my glass, needing some silence before I continued. Joseph made a few notes and reclined into his cushioned chair, removing his glasses and rubbing his eyes. Clearing his throat, he slipped his glasses back on and looked at me.

"Why do you think you felt so responsible for her?" Joseph asked. How could I answer such a question? Everything involving this woman was purely instinct on my part, purely primal. The need of her grabbed ahold and took root the moment I felt the connection. Admittedly, it was rather unhinged. I settled for a graceful shrug.

"I don't really remember the why of it. Perhaps it stemmed from a feeling of returning the favor from the incident in the kitchen. Her friend, Shay, wasn't wrong about the silly things Petunia muttered in her stupor. The one that stuck with me the most was a horrifying fear wrapped around the name 'David.' She'd apologize profusely and tremble whenever she'd utter the name. I'd asked Ms. Williams about this man who caused such distress, and she'd only share that it was Petunia's ex. He had put her in hospital with grievous injuries, and learning that was enough to make me see red."

"Do you suppose that was the start of you taking her in?"

"I would imagine it would make sense, wouldn't it?" I answered.

# DELILAH ST. RIVERS

"When she clung to me, begging me not to leave her alone, I stopped simply lusting after her. She cried out for me, a man who she hardly knew and shared little interaction in the time she'd worked for me. I could not resist such a siren call, not when it was coupled with her pleading eyes."

"The night she woke up and her system was cleared of all the insidious drugs, I was relieved at first. When she turned to me and asked if I would stay, I admit my thoughts became shameless. I couldn't stop thinking she was mine. She wanted me with her; she chose me. And I got to keep her by her choice without her brain being addled by drugs and trauma." I paused, shaking my head. "Then, on my first night with her as my responsibility in every way she'd allow, I let her down. She should have never felt pain such as that on my watch, and I berated myself for a while after she'd fallen asleep in my arms. Until she sighed. The sound of her being so content in my arms became an instant addiction, and I vowed that I would keep her safe from then on. Forever."

"You mean figuratively, of course?"

"Not then, I didn't. I meant it with every fiber of my being. Petunia, my Petunia would never know pain on any scale ever again." My fingers traced the rim of the now-empty glass. "Obviously, no one will ever be spared pain in any given time, but I was only thinking about the pain that I could prevent. She went through so much; truly I believe that while this last half-year has been the greatest for me, it could very well have been her worst."

I paused for a moment, the pain reaching into my heart and squeezing it tight.

"It went like that for another three days or so, her waking only to take her medicine or take care of bodily needs, until she gradually came about and could withstand some time between doses of pain medication…"

CHAPTER EIGHT

# Petunia

"AND HOW IS MY FAVORITE PATIENT TODAY?" An elderly man walked into the room where I sat on the edge of the bed, brushing my still-wet hair.

"Dr. Pakinowski, I bet you say that to all your patients." I smiled.

"Only the pretty ones," he quipped, setting his bag beside me and shooting me a wink. "Have you been staying off your leg, young lady?" The doctor knelt before me, lifting my leg by the heel. I winced, and he lowered it gently.

"Of course. Then again, I'm rarely left alone so I don't get the chance to use the hacksaw I have hidden under my bed and make my getaway."

"Remind me to check under the bed when this is all over and double-lock the toolshed," Ethan retorted, walking into the room on the back end of my sarcastic remark.

"Oh, I don't think you have to worry, son. This one isn't going to go anywhere." Dr. Pakinowski nudged Ethan and chuckled. Ethan looked at me and winked.

The check-up was quick, and Dr. Pakinowski declared me ready for mobility. At the end of the appointment, I was given a set of crutches.

"The beginnings of freedom, my dear," Dr. Pakinowski declared, winking back at Ethan. "Get yourself some fresh air and exercise. Before you know it, you'll be right as rain."

"Thank you," I said, extending my hand. The doctor shook it gently.

"I shall see you in a week or two, unless some emergency comes up."

"Thank you, Doctor. You may leave the bill in its usual place," Ethan said, shaking the doctor's hand as well. The doctor nodded and walked out, closing the door behind himself.

Ethan stood and grabbed the crutches in one hand, reaching the other toward me.

"Now?" I asked.

"What better time than now?"

I had a clumsy start. I tried to remember how I'd seen others walk with crutches and ended up almost collapsing to the floor. Ethan caught me around the waist as the crutches crashed onto the plush carpet.

"Oh boy," I said, looking up at him, blushing. "This is going to take practice."

"I could always carry you anywhere you'd like instead," he offered with a smirk. I rolled my eyes and shook my head.

"And take up more of your day by making you my personal piggyback ride? No, I don't think so."

Ethan's eyes bore into mine as he held me tight against him. After a brief moment, he let out a chuckle and shook his head.

"I could think of worse ways to spend my time," Ethan murmured.

"F-fair enough," I stuttered, a shiver coursing through me.

"Cold, my Pet?" he asked.

I shook my head and chanced a look into his eyes. He knew. I wasn't sure before; I hadn't been faced with the tangible evidence before, but I saw it then.

No.

He let me see it. He wanted me to see it, this incorruptible truth that he knew his effect on me. My blush deepened, and I had to close my eyes and take a deep breath to calm my racing heart.

"You know," he purred, "holding you like this brings back the memory of us dancing." He leaned back in to whisper in my ear. "I cannot wait to dance with you again."

I shuddered, and the leg supporting my weight gave at the knee, almost dragging us both to the floor. Ethan quickly regained his footing and swept me off my feet to lay me gently onto the bed, his eyes never leaving mine.

"It's practically charming," he began, kneeling on the side of the bed.

# CHAINS OF SATIN

"What is?" Damn my racing heart.

"The fact that you turn to quivering jelly at my whispered words. I haven't even touched you yet and you're already trembling."

Yet.

"You're an awful tease," I began, nervously laughing to break the intensity. "Awfully presumptuous of you to assume that—"

"Oh, darling," Ethan interrupted in a chiding tone. "I never assume. I also never tease. I may prolong a promised experience, but I always fulfill those promises." He dragged a finger softly across my lips and I couldn't breathe. He stood and kissed my forehead.

"Rest, Pet. Practice will have to wait for later, when you're more suitably dressed, and better balanced. And I have phone calls to attend to."

I looked down to find my bathrobe open and exposing the satin purple nightgown I'd dressed in. I looked back up at him and smiled sheepishly. Ethan smirked and placed the crutches their upright position against the wall and walked out the door, leaving me to relax into my pillows.

My trembling stopped none too soon after Ethan left, but his words lingered in my ears, echoing through my mind over and over, accompanied with his touch on my lips. I sighed and looked around, thinking about everything that had happened over the last month. My eyes strayed to the bottle of cologne he caught me spraying, and I couldn't help but smile through my blush at the conversation we held afterwards, how he looked when I threw out the phrases "sir" and "what do you want."

I smiled as I thought about the subsequent three weeks when I would go out of my way to catch his eye or get him to smile my way.

"God, I'm such a brat sometimes," I laughed to myself. *Well,* I thought, *might as well keep up the brat energy.* I wasn't tired as he thought and I was feeling pretty elated over the day's news. I pushed myself to a seated position and reached until I pulled the crutches to me. The thought crossed my mind to toss the pillows on the floor to cushion inevitable falling but decided they'd be more of an obstacle than a help. I situated the crutches under my arms and took a deep breath.

The first try set me back down again. I spread the feet of the crutches wider and tried again. *Success! I was standing on my own for the first time in a week!* The pride swelled in me, and I let out a loud breath. I decided to push my luck a little further and see if I could make the dozen or so steps to the bathroom.

I was sweating by the third step. The struggle of syncing my movements with the crutches and keeping my balance was all a bit too much. I turned, shaking and clumsy, and made it back to the bed, resting the crutches against the wall.

I smiled and was quite pleased. I lay back into the pillows, fluffing and rearranging them for better comfort before pulling the blanket up and settling in, smiling all the while at my little secret.

CHAPTER NINE

# Petunia

AFTER I WAS GRANTED A BIT OF FREEDOM in the form of crutches, Ethan reassured me that rest was my best friend. He said it would be at least a week before I would be in any shape to actually use the crutches, so I should take it easy until the time came. I let him believe that I was okay with waiting the week, but at night when I was alone, I practiced being mobile with the help of the crutches. It took two days of determination to even get a rhythm going and on the third, I sent the nurse away at lunchtime, claiming to be too tired for a bath.

As soon as the door closed, I gathered up my crutches and made it to the tub by myself, closing the door behind me. It was a bit tricky climbing into the tub without extra hands, but after a few minutes and extra care not to get my cast wet, I was able to sink into the tub with immense pleasure.

It truly was the greatest bath I'd ever taken by myself. The tub had room for four people to fit comfortably, and the steam from the water enveloped me like a pair of arms. I reveled in the solitude and peace of it all.

After about an hour or so, I'd managed to wash my hair without drowning myself entirely and decided I was ready to get out. I sat on the edge of the draining marbled tub to dry off, then threw on my bathrobe, having forgotten in my excitement to bring a set of clothes with me.

I reached out and opened the door to return to the bedroom, turned

## DELILAH ST. RIVERS

back carefully and, with the shoe of one crutch, pushed the towels in a pile. I was quite happy as I looked on at the scene with triumph. The maid, for sure, was going to find out about my independent escapades, but for now, this was all mine to bask in. I did this. I took care of myself. I smiled and turned back to the bed.

"I didn't want to startle you." Ethan quietly spoke from the opened bedroom door, holding a tray containing what I assumed to be lunch. My heart stopped for a moment, and I felt my face drain of all color. "I saw you weren't on the bed and panicked for the briefest of moments, until I saw, rather unbelievably, you. Doing this. How long, you marvelous creature? How long have you worked for this moment?" Ethan set the tray onto the stand beside the bed before returning to the doorway while I watched.

"A few days?" I felt guilty. I was sure his next words would be scolding me about the danger of the risks that I'd taken, but when I studied his face, his eyes glistened with emotion.

"Turn," he said, kneeling down on one knee, one fist against the carpet, the other held up by his face beckoning me. "Turn and come to me."

I did as he requested, slowly making my way toward him. I was only in my robe, and if I were to move too fast, there would have been no secrets between us any longer. As I moved, I found myself hypnotized by the movement of his fingers rubbing across his mouth while he watched me.

When I stood before him, Ethan wrapped his arms gently around my waist, holding me against him as he stood.

"You wonderful, glorious woman," he whispered in my ear. "How you impress me when I least expect it."

I blushed as he set me gently on the bed.

Ethan grew silent as his eyes drifted over me. He stepped forward and sat beside me, slowly taking the edge of my robe and straightening it, making sure I was fully covered. I held my breath, silently, if not foolishly, begging for just a touch. He gave me none. Only the terry cloth brushed against my naked flesh, and I almost whimpered.

"I forgot to take clothes with me," I quietly explained. Ethan smirked, his hands lingering on my robe.

"How in the world did you forget about clothes?"

His fingers were so close to my thigh that the ache for his touch hit me like a sledgehammer. I was tired and sore and still had a long way to heal, but I craved that which we never shared. He looked down at his fingers as he fiddled with the robe. For a split second my imagination was vivid and it caused me to shudder.

"I'm incredibly proud of your progress, darling, regardless of it being made in secret." He spoke quietly, and I smiled.

# CHAINS OF SATIN

"I hoped you would be," I said, matching his tone. Ethan's eyes raised and found mine. He opened his mouth.

"Pet—"

"I'm so sorry, Mr. Aldrich." The head of housing staff burst into the bedroom in a flurry. Ethan sighed and stood, shooting me an apologetic look.

"It's the nurse, Rico, for Ms. Barlowe," she said, handing him the phone. "He couldn't reach her on his own."

"Hello?" I took the phone and pressed it to my ear.

"Petunia, *mija*. Daddy needs you. It won't be long." There was no teasing in Ricos' voice.

"I'm on my way," I said, hanging up the phone and tossing it to the older woman. I looked at Ethan calmly.

"It's my father. I need to leave now."

# CHAPTER TEN

## *Petunia*

TIME MOVES DIFFERENTLY WHEN YOU'RE IN MOURNING. From the time I'd gotten that call to the time my father passed, it was a blur. But the days following felt as though weeks were drifting on by—listless and without direction. I couldn't tell you what I ate or wore, the words said at the funeral—any of it.

I *do* remember Ethan. I remember him placing me in the wheelchair to see my father laid to rest. I remember him being reluctant to leave my side at any given moment.

I remember the white rose I stared into as they lowered my father into the ground. It had an even number of petals and a spot of red like a blood drop on the innermost petal. I remember thinking it was quite fitting, something so perfect blemished by imperfection.

I also remember Shay. She'd driven to be by my side after Ethan called her and broke the news. She stayed through that first night after he'd been buried, she and Ethan sleeping on either side of me, the two of them trying to swaddle me in their comfort as I cried until dawn. After that, she was gone.

My house was filled with nurses and friends helping my mother through her own disorganized mourning process. After the reading of my father's will, my mom took a turn for the worse.

# CHAINS OF SATIN

She was full of rage, throwing things and smashing them, screaming in anger. I did what I could to help, but the nurses bore the brunt of her fury. Most days, at least one of the nursing staff suffered the brunt of her outbursts, some receiving bruises and scratches as they tried to subdue her. It was her lucid moments that brought about her true mourning as she suffered through the realization that her husband of almost forty years had passed, leaving her a widow.

The worst moments of all were periods of time where she'd regress. My mom would wander the house looking for my father. She once tried calling his old place of work. When it chimed as "disconnected" in her ear, she hung up and cried that he must have been being unfaithful. Those days I didn't know whether to lie or tell her the truth. Mostly I just prayed for her to be lucid again.

At one point, she'd mistaken Ethan for her husband. She went on about him forgetting to bring bread home, sharing with him how she burnt dinner, but begged him to understand that it was hard to be on her feet while carrying his elephant of a child. Ethan was gentle and kind with her, while I felt my heart breaking.

"Mom deserves so much better," I'd told Ethan one night, a few weeks after my father's funeral. My head was cradled in his lap as he leaned against my headboard, absentmindedly combing his fingers through my hair.

"You both do." His words were soft. I looked up at him.

"I wish there was something I could do for her—something from her bucket list or whatever. I asked her about it, but she just smiled and said she'd done everything she'd ever wanted. Except scrapbooking."

Ethan chuckled. I sat up to face him.

"Do you think she was serious?"

"Quite possibly." Ethan brushed his thumb across my lips. "I have news, Pet. Business is going to take me away for a week or two."

"Where to?"

"London, of all places. It's a good venture, and the potential for business expansion is huge. I'm rather excited about it." His eyes were glittering and hopeful as he smiled.

"It does sound exciting…When do you leave?" I was cautiously guarding my disappointment. Ethan owed me nothing at this point. He wasn't bound by relationship or duty—we were in a strange in-between place: not lovers, but much closer than friends.

It was rather curious, then, that Ethan's excitement looked somewhat tainted as he sighed.

"Early tomorrow morning."

## DELILAH ST. RIVERS

*So soon? It didn't feel like enough time.*

"Oh. Well, I'm sure you will have a great time with a ton of success. It's a pretty city, isn't it?"

Ethan reached for me, cupping my face with his hands as he shifted his body towards mine.

"Would that I could take you with me, darling," he whispered in a low, husky tone as he looked into my eyes.

"My mother," I reminded him. "And I would only slow you down with my leg. Besides, you know where to find me when you get back." I smiled, dragging my hand through his short-trimmed facial hair in a caress.

"Heaven help you if I have to come searching," Ethan growled. My heart skipped a beat.

"I wish I didn't have to take the pain medicine anymore. It would have been nice not to have taken it tonight."

"Why?" Ethan's chest moved fiercely as his breathing quickened.

"Because you'll be gone when I wake up," I whispered, wondering if I could say the rest without losing courage. He leaned in, closing what little distance was left between us.

"And?"

"And I...I don't want to..." *Breathe*, I told myself. *Let it out slowly.* "I don't want to miss out."

*So, so, so stupid*, I chided myself.

Ethan grinned like a wolf, the light in his eyes dancing. He leaned in so close, our noses nearly brushed.

"Tell me, what could you possibly miss out on?"

"I...well, I don't, it's silly..." My face heated with embarrassment. After a few seconds of silence that felt like an eternity, I felt his hand drift to embrace the back of my neck as he emitted a throaty chuckle.

"Ooh, my sweet Pet. I bet I know," Ethan growled, pulling me into a slow, soft kiss. I inhaled sharply through my nose, surprise and exhilaration drowning out all my senses. He pulled away slowly and our eyes met. After a breath, I couldn't take the tension. I threw my arms around his neck and met his lips with mine over and over until it slowed and deepened into something more primal. Intimate.

Ethan tilted his head and slid his tongue between my parted lips, groaning as I met him with the same fervor. He leaned into me, laying me back on my pillows, careful not to hurt my leg with the movement.

I grabbed at his hair, sifting through the silky, loose curls that I'd always longed to touch. He reached up, threaded his fingers through mine and pressed my hands down into the pillows beside my head. Ethan's breathing, along with his kisses, intensified as he ran a hand down my arm

CHAINS OF SATIN

before reaching and grasping at a breast, squeezing as I moaned into his mouth.

He broke our kiss, leaving me gasping as he trailed kisses down into the crook of my neck. He sunk his teeth into my flesh and I whimpered his name, the sensation toeing the line between pain and pleasure. My entire body lit up, almost electric as it begged for him to continue when he released his hold.

"Christ, my dear girl," Ethan buried his face into my neck. "How badly I just want to take you at this moment."

I panted, my head swimming from the combination of medication and heightened emotions.

"How badly I want to let you," I retorted, breathless. Ethan moved his hand from my breast to the pillow beside my head and rose to meet my gaze.

"I'm afraid I don't have the time to give you the proper attention you deserve," he said, tracing my jawline. He leaned in to kiss me softly once more. "I do believe you are most beautiful when you are looking at me with such desire." I reached up and wrapped my arms around his neck, pulling him against me.

"I really don't want you to go," I admitted softly, fighting the fatigue that heightened my emotions. Ethan laid on his back, pulling me down onto his chest.

"Shh. I'll be back before you get a chance to miss me."

"I miss you already," I whined, sleep pulling me under. He began stroking my hair again as he took a deep breath.

"I'm here, my darling. I'm still here."

CHAPTER ELEVEN

# Petunia

I SLEPT SO SOUNDLY THAT I DIDN'T feel Ethan move in the early hours of the morning. By the time I'd finally woken up, he was well on his way to London. I used my crutches to get to and from the bathroom before slowly creeping down the stairs—a fine art for someone with a cast and crutches.

Mom was at our small kitchen table, her head in her hands, as one of the new nurses comforted her by rubbing small circles on her back. All indicators pointed to this being a lucid moment for her. I took a deep breath and steeled myself for the interaction. "Mom?" She lifted her head, and her bloodshot eyes met mine. I walked over and sat beside her, leaning my crutches against the table.

"He's gone, right? Mary told me I'm not dreaming."

"He's gone. I'm so sorry, Mom. But I'm here." I took her hand in mine. "I'm here and Mary is here; Rico will be here soon, and Ethan will be back after his work trip."

"I like him for you. He seems like such a good boy. Much like…" Her breath hitched, and fresh tears poured out of her eyes.

"I know, Mama. I know. What if we gathered up all the shoeboxes full of pictures that you have and spent some time making a scrapbook? That may help both of us through this."

# CHAINS OF SATIN

"Oh, that's a fun idea." Mom smiled through her tears. "Honestly, I don't even remember what half of those boxes have in them."

"That's alright," I assured her, patting her hand gently. "It'll take me a bit to get the stuff around and carry it out of your room—"

"Don't you go touching my things!" Mom suddenly shouted.

"Mom…" I pulled my hand away from hers. "I promise I won't touch your stuff."

She shook her finger in my face.

"You people," she scolded, pulling away from Mary in a huff. "You come into my home and you're always moving and touching my things. Don't think I don't notice it, either. You're all thieves!"

It looked like scrapbooking was going to have to wait.

"I love you, Mom," I told her quietly as I got up from the table. I shot Mary an apologetic look as I walked away from the torrent of angry words coming from my mother.

I made my way back upstairs to my mom's room. The boxes under the bed held all the photos she'd ever taken, and I picked up the most recently filled box, opening it.

According to the dates on the lid, the photos were around two years old. The first picture was of her and me in front of the clinic where she was later diagnosed with Creutzfeldt-Jakob disease, a rare form of dementia that's cruel in its swiftness. By the time we caught it, she was already well into mid-stage dementia. Fits of violence, sudden bladder loss, and wandering around at night were becoming frequent. The good days were a more common occurrence than the bad ones at that point. I'd been in school, majoring in Ancient Mediterranean architecture, but when we got her diagnosis—then my father's aggressive cancer diagnosis shortly thereafter—I made the decision to take the time off and work to support my family.

The next few pictures were picnics, flowers, sunlight streaming through the trees, a time-lapse photo of the night sky, and me beside a baby deer at a petting zoo with my father in the background feeding a goat.

I sighed and closed the box, overcome by sadness. I tucked the box back in its place and rose from Mom's bed, straightening the blanket where my seated position caused a wrinkle.

Back in my room, I dialed Shay's number, but didn't get an answer. I shrugged and searched social media for a while, lying comfortably on my bed.

"Nia?" Mary knocked at my door.

"Yes?"

"You didn't eat downstairs, and your mother is refusing again." She walked into my room and handed me a lunch platter.

"I'm sure she will be hungry later," I reasoned, accepting the plated salad. "Thank you."

"She's resting for now. The scrapbook idea is a good one, don't give up on that." Mary gave me a kind smile and left me alone once more just as my phone chimed.

> Hey, baby girl. Emergency at work, looking at overtime. Call you tonight if you're awake. Love ya!

I smiled at Shay's text. My phone chimed again and I smiled wider.

> Landed safely. London would be more enjoyable if you were here by my side.

> Have an amazing time! I'm glad you're safe, thank you for letting me know...sir.

I giggled, imagining his eyes flash at me.

> Careful, Pet. Should you continue this devious teasing, I may not be held responsible for my actions when next I see you.

> If I do it enough will you forget about your business stuff and come back sooner? 😉

> Tempting. Terribly tempting.

I sighed, tingling from the tease. I took a selfie of me on the pillows, my hair splayed and a bright smile on my face.

> It's not the same as in person, but at least you can carry me through London on some level.

The picture sent, then the text.

# CHAINS OF SATIN

> You look incredible. I shall carry this and the lingering taste of your lips with me until I see you again. Get some rest, drink plenty of water, and I'll talk with you soon, my Pet.

> I'll keep my phone by my side.

———————

PROGRESS ON THE SCRAPBOOK WAS PAINFULLY SLOW over the next few days. Mom was rarely lucid, but I found comfort in the distraction when she regressed, answering her questions about the pictures to the best of my ability: who was who, when the events occurred, where we were. I'd also begun the physical therapy that I'd been pushing off, mostly at Ethan's insistence.

"It's only a couple of hours every day," Ethan said over the phone. "Your mother is in capable hands with her nurses, and it will help your leg mend better."

It was painful at first, doing straight-leg lifts and various other exercises, but by the third session, I was looking forward to the extra work.

"Yoga poses help too," my therapist told me, showing various poses on her computer screen. "These days, you can begin on your days off from here, so you're constantly working the muscles and bones." She gave me a printout of the poses to take home with me, and I looked forward to the at-home challenge.

"I'm home!" I shouted as I walked through the door, a feeling of accomplishment swelling in me after my therapy session. "Mom? Rico? Where a—" I stopped short, words failing me as I took in everything I saw before me. Papers and pictures were scattered in pieces all over the kitchen table and floor. The majority of the scrapbook I'd been working on lay open, its binding torn and the pages either hanging loose or ripped to pieces. Slowly, I moved through the kitchen, my anger and hurt building as I saw the zoo picture torn in half.

"What did you do?" I whispered to no one, tears streaming down my face. I scooped up what I could into a pile on the table and carefully knelt down, dropping my crutches as I cried, still picking up pictures and the colorful pieces of paper.

# DELILAH ST. RIVERS

I couldn't do it all. I couldn't handle another disappointment in my life. I rolled into a seated position, leaning my back against a table leg. I squeezed papers into my fists and brought them to my face, letting out a scream of frustration.

Arms wrapped around me as I let loose a torrent of ugly words to match my ugly crying. I cried out how unfair life was, giving so much to one person to try and carry on their own. It wasn't right; I couldn't deal with it anymore.

It took several minutes before I was calm enough to hear Rico's soothing murmurs through my own heartbreak. I pulled away from his embrace, and he handed me a box of tissues.

"I planned to clean the mess after your mama finally fell asleep, but you know how she is. She fought the sedative like a bull, *mija*." He stood and began separating the pictures that were still whole from the rest. "We can tape the ones that are torn—"

"That'll take forever."

"What else do we have but time, dove?"

He knew as well as I did that he was speaking the truth, so I nodded, wiping more tears from my face.

"That makes six sedatives this week alone. She's getting worse," I vocalized reluctantly, barely able to admit it to myself.

"Petunia, I'm not only here for Mama. I'm here for you, too. Speak your mind."

"I don't want to give her up, Rico. I don't want to fail her."

Rico hung his head, nodding slowly. "It may get more dangerous for her not to be sedated, especially at night. We need to do what's best for her, and for you, too."

"It can't get too much worse, right?"

"In my experience the more confusion and regression they have, the more it angers them. It's not unreasonable; the world they knew isn't the only one they experience anymore. Memories are stripped away, and sometimes they remember things long-forgotten for just a moment before they, too, are gone. Eventually we are going to have to think of more secure options. For her safety and yours."

I wiped a tear away from my cheek. Almost all the anger I felt melted away slowly.

"I feel like I'm a horrible daughter for even considering it. Our parents take care of us when we're vulnerable. Aren't we supposed to do the same for them?"

Rico rubbed my back.

"If only she was just old and frail, Petunia. But she isn't even sixty

# CHAINS OF SATIN

yet. She's strong, disoriented, sometimes viole — "

"Can we just stop? Please? God, I can't do this right now!" I picked up my crutches to leave to go to my room.

"It needs to be a voluntary decision before she does something that takes the control out of your hands, dove." Rico followed close behind as I climbed the steps. I stopped and looked at the floor, tilting my head to the side.

"Did you just threaten me? After all we've been through together, you seriously just threatened me?"

Rico's palms faced me in an attempt to calm me.

"No, no, that's not it. I love your family. I love working with all of you—even Prince Charming—but there are times when she's been a danger to both herself and those who work with her."

I made it to the top of the stairs where I fully turned to face him.

"She had scissors in her hand when she lashed out, Petunia. Had I been slower to react..."

"I can't deal with this, too, Rico. Please. Not right now. We just buried my father...It's just too much."

Once I was settled in my room, I pulled out my phone to text Shay.

> I wish my life wasn't such a damn mess.

> What's up?

> May have to put Mom into a home. She lashed out with scissors. How am I supposed to send my mother away?

> I'm so sorry baby girl. It's not easy, especially since you just buried your dad.

> Exactly. I can't stand thinking I'm abandoning her.

> You're not abandoning her if you're putting her in a place that could help her more, boo.

*Ugh.* I tossed my phone beside me without answering the text.

## DELILAH ST. RIVERS

Mom had so much help with her in-home care; what could they possibly do in a permanent residence that was different? All I could imagine was them locking her up and turning her into a medicated zombie. At least at home she could still be herself when she was lucid…I grabbed my phone.

> And when she's in her right mind and she sees what I've done, what then? She'll hate me.

> I don't know what to say to make this easier on you. I wish I was there to help.

Another chime announced a text from someone else. Ethan.

> Will you be awake in a few hours?

A wave of relief washed over me and I managed a small smile. I answered Shay's last text:

> Me too. It's okay, I just needed to vent. I love you and will talk later.

To Ethan, I sent:

> Yes, depending on how late you're talking.

His response was immediate.

> Wonderful. I have a surprise for you, Pet. I think you might like it, but you'll have to be downstairs in three hours. Can you manage?

> Three hours?

> Yes. It's a delivery. Can you be certain you'll be there?

I smiled; I loved surprises.

# CHAINS OF SATIN

> Absolutely. I've been taking less pain pills lately so I'll be awake. I promise.

> Perfect. I can't wait to know what you think of it. x

Shay sent another text:

> I have next weekend off, sweetie. Want me to come over and maybe I can help out a bit?

A surprise from Ethan for tonight, Shay coming to visit over the weekend, and a few days after that, Ethan would be home. It was almost enough to make the day better. Almost.

> If you don't have other plans you know I would love to see you!

> You sure you and Lover Boy won't be tangling the sheets?

> He's in London till later next week, you ass.

I laughed. I'd shared with her that we kissed, but I didn't think it would go any further than that. I couldn't even imagine it.

> He did say I'm getting a surprise in a few hours. Do you think it could be flowers? I've never gotten flowers delivered to me before, I'm so excited!

> Maybe he's coming home early to surprise you with a proposal!

I rolled my eyes.

## DELILAH ST. RIVERS

> Girl, we only kissed once. No declarations of love, nothing like that. Not even any kind of confirmation we're dating to be honest.

> You never know, you got them magic kisses!

> Not THAT magical...Besides, what if I don't want to marry him? What if he's not my type?

> LMAO!!! Who you kidding, girlfriend?

> Shut up, lol. I'm gonna let you go. Love you, girl.

> Love you too, brat. Send me a pic of those flowers or engagement ring so I can be jealous.

> Oh, I will. 😊

I set my alarm for ten minutes before 7 p.m., carefully turned on my side and tried to relax and put the day's events out of my mind.

## CHAPTER TWELVE

# Petunia

WHEN MY ALARM WENT OFF, I OPENED my eyes in momentary confusion. I would have turned it off and gone back to sleep had I not labeled it "Get the Door." With a few minutes left until Ethan's delivery was due to arrive, I changed into sweatpants and a black tank top before going downstairs.

I grabbed a glass vase from the top of my refrigerator and tossed a couple of ice cubes into the bottom before filling it most of the way with water. I wondered briefly if he could have possibly guessed that my favorites were tiger lilies. Either way, I'd love whatever flowers arrived. The house could use a bit of color.

When the doorbell rang a few minutes later, I glanced at the clock. 7 p.m. on the dot.

*Ethan should tip the delivery driver for being so punctual,* I thought to myself, pulling the door open.

To my surprise, Ethan was standing there, a small floral arrangement in one hand and a suitcase in the other.

"You!" I cried out, stunned by the simultaneous drop of the suitcase as Ethan's arms wrapped around my waist, lifting me in the air as we shared a tender kiss.

"I've been thinking about this moment all day," he whispered

DELILAH ST. RIVERS

between kisses. He carried me to the kitchen after kicking the main door shut and sat me on the countertop. His kisses began soft and quick but grew slow and intimate the longer we embraced. I kissed him fiercely back, grabbing fistfuls of his beautiful hair and wrapping my legs around his waist.

Ethan's hands tangled into my own hair, pulling my head back hard while he trailed kisses down my neck.

"Miss? Is everythi—oh!" Donna, an older nurse who occasionally worked with my mother overnight, stared speechless at us as we turned to stare back. "I'm so sorry. I heard the door slam and some noise and—you know what? I'll go check on your mother, dear." She hurried out of the kitchen and I stifled an embarrassed laugh. Ethan leaned his forehead against mine, chuckling.

"I'd intended to be more patient when I got here," he said, lifting his head and running his hands through his hair.

"I don't know, I thought it was part of the surprise. I'm not complaining." Ethan gripped the back of my neck and pulled me close to his face, a low rumble in his chest.

"Good thing. I'd have to stop you if you did." He kissed me deeply before pulling away.

"I'm glad you're here."

"Is everything alright?" He interlocked his hands with mine.

"You didn't come home early so I could dump my baggage on you," I scoffed, hoping this wouldn't kill the mood. I wanted him so badly, and his body between my thighs wasn't helping my frustration at all. His fierce blue eyes found mine and he took me by the chin, lifting my face to look at him.

"I'm here for the good and the bad, Pet. Tell me."

I hesitated.

"Tell me," he whispered against my lips, kissing me again.

*God, I can't think straight.*

"Tell me, Pet. Tell me." Ethan pulled away until his lips were just shy of touching mine. When I leaned in for another savory touch, he pulled out of my reach. His hand held my cheek. "Tell me."

I sighed.

"Mom may have to be put into a home," I shared reluctantly. "She almost hurt Rico with scissors today, and she destroyed the scrapbook we were making together. The pages we designed, the pictures..." My voice broke and I started to tear up, wiping them away angrily. "I bet you're getting sick of these stupid tears."

"What can I do to help?" Ethan asked. I shook my head.

# CHAINS OF SATIN

"It's something I have to choose and deal with, all on my own."

"Never alone," he began, but I cut him off.

"*All alone*. I alone get to carry the weight of the responsibility of my mother's future. I alone get to decide whether to risk her falling down the stairs and breaking her neck one night, or force her to live out the rest of her life surrounded by strangers, scared and alone."

"Come here, darling." He held his arms out to me for an embrace; instead, I took his hands into my own and looked up into his eyes. I needed to see them for this.

"You can't fix this. You can't take this from me or pay this off or decide this for me. But maybe..." I lowered my eyes and swallowed before meeting his once more. "Maybe tonight you can help me forget all of this? Just for a little while? I've missed you and I would like to focus on your return, if that's alright?" I placed his hands on my chest, ensuring he'd understand what I was asking.

The light in his eyes darkened as his pupils dilated almost immediately.

"You're certain this is what you want?"

"Yes."

Ethan pressed his pelvis into mine as he reached behind me, pulling me to the edge of the counter to feel his reaction to my request. I gasped as he leaned down, kissing me deeply and shifting his hips almost imperceptibly from side to side. It sent me reeling with need. I moaned softly in his mouth and he pulled my hair, tipping my head back to expose the length of my neck before breaking the kiss.

"Your words create an urgency in me, Pet. Do you feel how badly I want you?" He kissed my neck. "Are you as eager for me as I am for you?" Ethan nipped at my skin, causing me to whimper and clutch him tight against me.

"Why don't you find out?" I teased, panting. He growled and I felt his cock twitch through the fabric separating us. An arm snaked its way around my waist, holding me as I slid off the counter until my weight was supported by my good leg and his body. Ethan's other hand dipped below my waistline, teasing my lower belly.

"Look at me." he commanded.

I obeyed his command. The blue was almost completely devoured by the black of his pupils as he stared into mine. Slowly, his fingers sank lower into my sweatpants until he met my warmed flesh, already moist with need. I leaned back and closed my eyes.

"No," he grunted, pulling me upright. "Look at me. I need to see your eyes, darling." He caressed my labia before parting my lips and teasing my pulsating entrance. "So wet, sweetheart. So wet and needy," he observed, his lips pulled into a slight smirk.

I flushed. He stared at me as he teased me, rubbing his fingers against my skin but refusing to take the plunge into where I needed it most. Then, with a gentle kiss, he finally slid his whole finger deep inside me. He pulled his mouth from mine, freeing my moan into the air as he rumbled, "Oh, my sweet girl. I've only a finger in and already you're quivering."

"I was quivering before you did this, where have you been?" I joked, panting at his ministrations.

Ethan chuckled softly.

"Well, then…I wonder what would happen should I use two?" His lips found mine for a chaste kiss but pulled back to watch my face as he receded from me, then sunk back into my heated depths with the promised double fingers.

I was breathing hard as he plunged his fingers in and out, staring into my eyes, high on his power trip. I felt the coil in my lower belly begin to tighten, and I couldn't stop my fingernails from digging into his shoulder.

"No, my darling. Not yet, not here." Ethan's stroking slowed and he kissed me once again before pulling his hand away from me. I let out a small cry of dismay.

"I'm so close, Ethan," I practically begged.

"Not here," he repeated. "I'm going to take you home where we won't have to worry about waking anyone." He brought his fingers to his mouth and sucked my juices off them, groaning as he stared into my eyes. "Christ, you taste delicious," he whispered, sliding his tongue into my mouth to share the taste. My knees went weak and Ethan caught me, lifting me in one swift movement and, all else forgotten, he carried me out to his car, closing the door behind him.

FROM THE MOMENT I SAT IN THE passenger seat, Ethan saw fit to keep me on edge. Sitting beside me, he placed one hand on the steering wheel and the other on my thigh. My hand went over his instinctively as he looked at me again.

"Last chance, Petunia. We can get dinner then come back and get some rest, no questions asked."

I squeezed his hand as I lifted it off my thigh, slipping one of his fingers between my lips to bite it. His nostrils flared as he inhaled sharply, pulling his hand away to start the engine and shift it into drive. His hand found its place back on my thigh, skirting higher up and pressing against

# CHAINS OF SATIN

the heat of my groin. I sighed and reclined back into my seat, just enough to spread my legs for him.

"So eager," Ethan repeated as he smiled softly. His eyes never left the road as he inched his hand up until he was cupping my pussy in its entirety. Then he flexed his hand.

"Oh!" I couldn't stop myself from letting it out. He squeezed again, and released in a steady rhythm as my breathing quickened and the scent of my accelerating excitement filled his car.

We hit a red light and he pulled his hand away, grabbing my own as he looked at my flushed face and set my hand atop the firm bulge in his designer dress pants.

"Don't move, my sweet girl. I just want to feel your warmth."

I was surprised and couldn't help but run my fingers across his length. He growled and grabbed my hand, thrusting his hips upwards as my hand found its home once more.

The light turned green.

"Don't move," he commanded. He drove as I obediently held still, my heart pounding against my chest. Taking the final turn to his home, he whispered, "Bloody hell, that's good."

My heart skipped a beat at his words; my praise-kink was being nurtured, and we hadn't even made it to the bed yet. I couldn't help but keep my gaze on his face as he drove, almost angelic in his chiseled features with his high cheekbones, strong jaw and perfect lips. His hair, slightly disheveled, grew long, covering the back of his neck down to his collar, where it curled into itself.

Ethan was tall, of course, towering over me by almost a foot, but his frame complemented him without looking lanky. Having been in his arms, I knew he was muscular and strong, just enough to make a point without appearing intimidating.

Ethan's hand covered mine as he pulled up to his house. He brought my fingers to his lips and kissed them before leaning over and kissing my lips.

*He certainly seems to enjoy kissing me,* I thought.

"Dinner first, darling," he said, opening the door and exiting.

"I might be a little too distracted to have much of an appetite," I informed him as he opened my door. He leaned in, hanging onto the top of the car.

"What have you eaten today, Pet? Be honest."

*Oh my God, quit talking and just fuck me already.*

"A salad before physical therapy." I couldn't take my eyes off his hand as he moved it to rest on my leg.

83

"Hmm." He studied me for a moment before straightening. "Wait here, I'll be but a moment."

Ethan closed my door and walked into his home.

"Very funny," I growled in annoyance behind his back. "Like I'd get far."

He was only gone for two or three minutes before he came back out and announced, "It's settled. Amelia is preparing roasted chicken and various sides without a hint of peanuts," he winked as he told me.

"That's so considerate," I said in my best bedroom voice, "Sir."

He chuckled.

"I know what you're trying to do, you devious minx, but it won't work. We eat before we do anything...strenuous."

"Perhaps a compromise?" I offered.

"I'm listening."

"Dinner in the bedroom?"

"Oh, I never take food into my bedroom, Pet. Crumbs in the bed don't make for restful sleep."

I sighed.

"So eager, my sweet girl. Perhaps I could take you into the bathroom? Help you bathe and dress before dinner is ready?"

I couldn't help but smile.

"Alright then." He nodded. "Let's get to it."

He lifted me effortlessly in his arms and carried me up the spiral staircase to the master bathroom where a bath had already been drawn.

"But...I'm so confused!" I admitted as he sat me on the wooden bench beside the tub.

"I had a feeling you'd look forward to a warm bath. Would you like me to leave you to situate yourself?"

"I should make you wait as long as possible, like you are doing to me," I said with an impish smile. I reached for his hand, pulling him down for a kiss. He grinned against my lips.

"A game two can play, Pet?"

"A game I think no one wins, sir," I answered. Ethan inhaled sharply and kissed me again. I took my time as I unbuttoned my tank top, letting it hang open without removing it. His eyes lingered on my exposed flesh, warming me with his gaze. It felt like I had waited a lifetime to be looked at like this: with hunger, passion, and a little bit of something akin to adoration.

"I fear I should let you do this alone, lest I forget about dinner myself."

"I'm kinda hoping you do," I confessed, peeking at him from beneath

# CHAINS OF SATIN

my eyelashes. Ethan chuckled again and knelt in front of me. "Besides," I continued, placing my hands upon his shoulders, "it's hardly fair. You'll see all of me before I get to see all of you."

"Do you suggest we bathe together, then?"

"Unless you feel the temptation is too great to ignore," I teased.

"Shall we see if we have the fortitude to best it, darling?" He stripped off his buttoned shirt, his eyes gaging my reaction to his well-formed torso. He looked like a god.

"Remind me, if I ever get the chance to meet them, to thank your parents," I said, running my hands up his chest.

"My parents?" Ethan looked confused.

"For making such a beautiful man."

He grinned and looked down.

"My pants are still on. You've yet to see me in all my glory," he pointed out, smirking.

"Are they? I didn't even notice," I murmured, kissing his shoulder.

"This may be the most difficult thing I've ever had to endure," he muttered, wrapping an arm around me to steady himself.

CHAPTER THIRTEEN

# Petunia

"I SHOULD SEND A MESSAGE TO THE night nurse," I suggested to Ethan as he turned off the water. "We left in a kind of hurry and she might be concerned."

"I've already messaged Rico and he agreed to pass it on." He walked back around to face me, unbuckling his belt and slipping off his shoes.

"You've thought of everything, haven't you?" I asked, smiling up at him.

"I certainly try, though I do appreciate an element of surprise every now and again."

His eyes roamed my half-naked body, wearing a mischievous grin. I reached up and grasped both ends of his undone belt and pulled him close to me. I looked into his stunned expression before dipping my head and kissing the skin that lay just above the elastic of his underwear.

"Dear God," he gasped.

I kissed his flesh once more, and he wrapped my hair around his hand, yanking my head back.

"Surprise," I grinned up at him. His hardened expression softened and he chuckled before kissing me.

"My darling," he whispered, still holding my hair hostage, "what great fun we shall have." He released my hair, lowered his pants, then kicked

# CHAINS OF SATIN

them off. The underwear, black as night and hanging low on his hips, did very little to conceal his excitement. "Close your eyes, Pet." His command was followed with his thumb stroking my lips and I did as he requested. The water in the tub moved, and a breath later his hands wrapped around me from behind, soaking the back of my tank top as his hands found home on my bare breasts.

"Cheater," I scolded, my hands covering his. He kissed the back of my neck.

"How may I help you?" His words were gentle as he nibbled my earlobe.

"You may not." I pulled his hands away and turned to look down at him. "I've been doing this by myself for some time now and I'm pretty good at it. Now close your eyes, sir."

Ethan grinned and inclined his head in a short bow, backing away amidst the bubbles that filled the tub.

"No peeking. I understand it'll be an awfully tempting moment for you, but—" I wiggled my hips back and forth to inch the sweatpants down my legs "—fair is fair."

I turned to watch his eyes close, a smile stretched wide across his face that matched the one on my own. He was so exhilarating; I'd almost forgotten how much I'd enjoyed being around him while he was gone. Almost.

I peeled my tank top off my body after double-checking that he wasn't looking and situated myself into the tub, leaving my casted leg out and off to the side. I sighed deeply and relaxed into the corner of the large jacuzzi tub, the bubbles swallowing me to the collarbone.

"For someone who's a natural commander, you're incredible at submitting," I remarked. Ethan's form was still as his eyes remained shut. "It's safe to look now."

His eyes opened, and he took in the sight before him.

"My God," he breathed, staring. "I've seen you with less covering your body, but you've never been so enticing as you are at this moment. Knowing all I have to do is push the bubbles away to reveal all your secrets..." He closed his eyes and inhaled deeply. My heart pounded against my ribs at his reaction. His eyes opened, and he moved to sit beside me. "Would you like my help?" he asked, kissing my exposed shoulder. I smiled and dabbed a handful of suds onto his cheek before going under the water to soak my hair.

I came back up and wiped the suds from my own face to find him looking at me sternly as he wiped his cheek, causing me to laugh.

Ethan smirked as he plopped a dollop of bubbles on my nose.

## DELILAH ST. RIVERS

"Ugh, really?" I cried out. It was his turn to laugh as he reached over for the shampoo and began washing his hair. I followed suit, catching him watching me every now and then. It was only fair; I was watching him too. We bathed in silence, glancing at each other, and every now and then he'd lean in and kiss me, as though he couldn't go too long without feeling my lips pressed against his.

Ethan had stopped stealing glances and openly watched as I washed my body with the soft cloth he'd handed me. I caught his eye as I smirked and slid the cloth down my body to disappear beneath the bubbles. I exaggerated pleasure, parting my lips, tipping my head back and closing my eyes to let out a small groan. I'd been washing my upper thigh, but from what I saw when I opened my eyes, I'd successfully fooled him into thinking I was pleasing myself. Ethan reached down and grasped my wrist, his pupils dilated and focused on my everything.

"I think it's quite adorable, really," he murmured against my lips, "that you think your fingers could come close to bringing you the relief that you crave. You made yourself moan with yours, now I'm going to make you scream with mine."

Ethan slid his tongue into my mouth as he sunk a finger deep into my body, groaning an answer to the moan that passed from my throat. My hand trailed down his chest and dipped below the water's level before it was stopped suddenly by his hand, pulling it back up. He grinned, his lips stretched thin against mine as he drove his finger deeper inside me, rubbing his thumb against my hardening clit over and over in a gentle rhythm. He slid a second finger into me and I bucked against him, desperately trying to drive him deeper, my body begging him to rub me faster, harder as I felt my orgasm build.

I longed to touch him, to grasp tightly in my hand what I knew to be filled with the same passion he pounded into me. I longed to pump, to stroke and squeeze, to manipulate his cock the way he was manipulating my entire body, but he held my hand tight against his chest, forbidding me from touching him.

Ethan's thumb brushed against my clit again and I pulled my lips from his, begging with my eyes before my words could form.

"Please," I whimpered. "Please, I'm so close!"

"So close. Just a moment more, darling. Allow me to savor your magnificence gripping my fingers tightly, your warmth flooding my senses. Allow me just a moment more before I elicit those promised screams from you, my sweet girl."

His mouth had hovered over my neck as he spoke the words that threatened to take me over the edge as he stroked my flesh. I whimpered incoherently as I crept closer to the finish line; all I needed was one final push, a hard stroke of my clit, a deep plunge of his beautiful, skilled fingers to find the orgasm I was desperate for.

"Now, come for me, Pet," Ethan growled and sunk his teeth into the crook of my neck. He pressed so perfectly against my clit while stroking that sweet spot deep inside me that the orgasm ripped through my body with a vengeance. The explosion tore a scream of his name from my throat that ended in a wail as I rode wave after wave of undeniable pleasure.

Ethan held my hand tightly against his body as my climax lingered through his continued ministrations until I'd quieted and relaxed against the side of the pool. He withdrew his teeth, kissing the spot on my neck and finding my lips, consuming me savagely as though my mouth were to be his last meal forever. He pulled his fingers from my body and grabbed the back of my neck.

"Good girl," he whispered, pulling away from me so he could cup my face with his hands and examine my wildly ecstatic features. "I could take you now, hard and unrelenting. Your obedience in denying yourself until I gave my permission for your release has me burning for you."

He kissed my lips and then my forehead, lingering there for a moment while he caught his breath.

"My good, good, darling Pet," he gasped.

MY BODY SETTLED INTO A GENTLE HUM after several minutes of Ethan's soft touches, occasional kisses, and sweet words of praise. I was glowing under his adoration and didn't want the moment to end; the idea of this bubble we were in bursting was unbearable.

"What are you thinking about?" Ethan asked quietly.

"Nothing really," I sighed and opened my eyes, giving him a contented smile. "I'm just...floating right now."

"Hmmm." He leaned his forehead against mine, smiling to himself. "I'm thinking of all the ways we get to make this evening even more memorable."

"Already thinking about what's next?" I teased.

He pulled back to face me, his mouth curved into a devious smile.

"Always. With this, with you, always. Now, darling, I smell dinner. Close your eyes."

"Wait." I put a hand on his shoulder. I glanced downward before looking back up at him. "You didn't—"

"Trust me, my Pet, my time will come." Ethan took my hand from his shoulder and pressed a kiss to the back of it. "Now. Eyes closed. We mustn't spoil the surprise." I closed my eyes and heard him rising from the water. "Dinner smells delectable," he growled in my ear, his hands on my shoulders, "but I'm craving you for dessert." I shivered, my nipples instantly hardening. Ethan's throaty chuckle left the room as he retreated, closing the door behind him.

"Jesus, fuck," I whispered, gasping as though I hadn't breathed in hours. I pulled myself beneath the water once more to clear my mind. This man's energy was so intense and focused it was almost overwhelming.

When I emerged once more, the door was open and Amelia was carrying a bathrobe and a few sets of towels.

"Did you enjoy your bath, dear?"

"It ranks in the top ten of baths I've ever had." I grinned at her, which she reciprocated kindly.

"These are for you. Mr. Aldrich requests you call out to him when you're ready. He'll be waiting just beyond the door for any assistance you may need."

"Thank you."

She closed the door behind her just as I caught a glimpse of Ethan with black silk pants hung low on his hips. A matching silk robe draped around him, leaving his chest bare. My cheeks flushed and I leaned back against the tub, staring at the ceiling.

I'd never let myself go like that, especially with someone I barely knew. I hadn't known him for long, and I'd already given him so much of myself, my body, and my will. I had *begged* him. I wanted him in every way possible with a ferocity that frightened me. The longer I thought, the longer I dwelled on what just happened, and the more embarrassed I became.

*What if he really did find me too eager, like some kind of attention-craving slut that he could use and throw away after he was finished? What if I was asking too much from him? He took care of me, fed me, clothed me, kept me safe, hired a staff because of me, bought a building because of me...Would he think I just take and take without giving anything in return? Do I even have anything to offer him? Is he wanting a relationship, or is this just a fling for him? Does he think I owe him my body as repayment for everything he's done?* My thoughts continued to spiral as I dried off and slipped on the plush bathrobe.

*I wasn't that person anymore. I wasn't someone with sub energy who just gave and gave, leaving my self-care and self-love tank empty. What were his kisses, his touches, his kindness if not —*

A knock interrupted my thoughts, soft but insistent.

"Darling, is everything alright? If you need help I can come in."

"No, I'm fine!" The cheery tone in my voice sounded fake even to

## CHAINS OF SATIN

my own ears.

"You're certain?" Ethan sounded like he was pressed against the door, so close to me. "Are you out of the tub?"

I panicked.

"Yes, but I'm not ready to come out. I'm still…uh, I'm still naked!" I lied. I felt the urge to just go home and hide under the covers in shame.

The door opened slowly.

"I said I wasn't ready," I snapped, anger rising in my voice.

"Petunia…" Ethan approached me and knelt at my feet, looking up at me. "What's wrong?"

I pulled my hands away from his reach and felt heat rise in my cheeks.

"I just needed a minute alone. It's called having boundaries."

He reached up and caressed my face gently.

"After the heights of unaccustomed excitement, it's perfectly natural to experience a drop, Pet. Perhaps you're feeling uncomfortably vulnerable?" Ethan wiped a tear off my cheek. "We can take a moment and talk about it, sweet girl. Take all the time you need."

I shook my head, too stubborn and embarrassed to show him more insecurities than I already—stupidly—had.

"Allow me to rephrase," Ethan said, his voice dropping an octave. It was still kind, but more stern as he grabbed my chin and forced me to look him in the eyes. "We will be taking a moment to discuss this."

"I don't know what there is to talk about."

"Start with how you're feeling right this second, darling."

"I…I don't know." My admission was barely a whisper.

"Oh, my girl. I promise I can listen to whatever you need to share. This is my vow to you: as long as you trust me with the truth, I will always listen. Can you do that?" He leaned up and kissed my forehead softly. "Can you trust me?"

I took a deep breath and he knelt back down in front of me.

"It's embarrassing," I admitted.

"You have no reason to feel ashamed, I promise."

"But I feel that way," I sighed. "I feel ashamed at how easily I'm giving myself to you. I don't truly know your intentions. I don't know your kinks or how far you'd take them." I took a deep breath before letting the floodgates really open. "I don't know how to stop wanting you, how to stop needing you, how to be this…this…I don't know what to call it; exposed? Available? I don't want you to get what you want out of me, become bored when you realize I'm not actually up to your standards and take all of this away from me." My face heated as a blush crept higher and higher up my neck and to my cheeks. I was horrified at how much I was divulging, but I couldn't stop. "And I don't know how attached you are to me, so I don't want to become clingy and scare you off because you're only looking for a quick, momentary fling before moving on to the next."

"I never took you for a woman with such insecurities," Ethan said, and I looked down, away from his prying eyes.

"I hide them," I admitted. "To be honest, I'm afraid. I'm afraid of falling for you and you rejecting me after all is said and done. I'm afraid that you're going to take me through the motions of sex and possible dom control and then…"

Ethan rocked back on his heels to sit on the floor. He looked as though he was getting comfortable and settled in for a long while, much to my dismay. After a moment, his eyes soft with compassion, he asked through clenched teeth, "A dom has misused you in the past, my sweet darling?" I reluctantly shrugged.

"I've had a couple doms in my past." I shrugged, attempting to brush it off as I explained. "My first let me explore those words and find my place in it rather thoroughly, but when it came time to commit, he set me free. It was devastating. He said he only wanted to train subs, not keep them.

"The next—well the last, really—he was different. He pulled me in with words and the standard contract. He even collared me after a few weeks and I thought I hit the jackpot with this man. I thought he was truly going to love me and cherish me and be my own dom for life. After the collar slipped on, he got terrifyingly possessive and progressively disrespected our contract. It got to the point he was breaking this clause or that clause out of rage or spite if I did something he didn't like. By then he had me convinced I deserved everything he dished out—that it was what I signed up for and what I wanted. I've never had a slave kink or anything extreme like that, though. It took me years to recover from all the damage he did to me, both mentally…and physically." I whispered the last two words. They were the hardest. After a moment, I opened my eyes and looked down at Ethan. "I guess I'm still afraid."

My heart raced and I felt a chill, no doubt the effects of being highly stressed from my story. Ethan looked at me before slowly rising to his feet to pace the room.

*Christ*, I thought. *I just fucked this whole thing up.*

"I'm sorry," I said aloud to him. "I can go home. I should go home, you don't need this."

Ethan stopped pacing and turned to face me.

"You called me the night you were intoxicated, then drugged. You

# CHAINS OF SATIN

mentioned something about being sent to the hospital. Explain that to me."

I shook my head at his words. "I can't believe I mentioned that, it's not—"

"Explain it," he commanded me.

*What is his angle, here?* I wondered. *If he wants to know so badly...*

"The last night I saw him—my last dom—I was hanging from the ceiling of his basement by the ropes he'd tied me up in, doing a spread-eagle." I shuddered at the memory. "I remember wondering why he'd been bleeding from his hand as I looked down on him, not realizing it was blood from my body. He'd been whipping me so much that I barely could feel it at that point. And he—" I steadied my breath. "He added electroshocks and would zap me every few strokes of the whip. All of that, on top of..."

"Go on, sweetheart." Ethan sat beside me, his hand warm on my knee, as if to comfort me with slow, light caresses. I took a deep breath.

"He had me double-penetrated, just to help push my tolerance for pain. I was so good—at least I tried to be, but the pain...the fear...It was too much and he saw the tears. I was gagged and strung in such a way that I couldn't call attention to my need to stop. It was like that most of the time, at that point in our relationship. But I failed him that night, so he alternated between the whip and the shocks until he decided he preferred the whip. Then he didn't stop. That's all I remember, really. Next thing I knew, I woke up at the hospital. My back was striped from my ribs down, and I came away from the experience with nerve damage in both wrists and scarring everywhere he hit."

"Show me," Ethan commanded. The look on his face was unreadable. Slowly I opened my robe, exposing the rope scar under my right breast. He leaned over and traced it with his finger softly before tenderly kissing the mark. "Where else?"

I pulled the robe down past my shoulders and turned to face away from him. I lowered my robe until it pooled around my bottom, exposing all of the scarring on my torso and back.

Ethan spent several minutes kissing each and every scar with reverence. I didn't understand his reaction or why my tears fell faster with each kiss.

"Are there more?" he asked when he was done. I nodded.

"I can't...not yet. Maybe not ever," I tried to explain.

Ethan helped me turn to face him as I situated my robe. Before I could hide it, he caught sight of the scar that sliced through my lower belly.

"And that?" Ethan pointed.

"I'm sorry, I just can't." I shook my head.

Ethan took me into his arms and held me closer than he ever had before. It was only then that I noticed he was trembling.

"You're shaking."

"Rage, my Pet. Forcibly contained, rage."

I looked downward and began to pull away from him, intimidated and somewhat afraid that some of his anger was directed at me.

"I'm sorry."

"Stop apologizing," Ethan spoke slowly through gritted teeth as my eyes flicked up to meet his. "To think someone could have you and go out of their way to abuse you and...attempt to ruin you for their own twisted sense of sadistic pleasure brings me to thoughts of homicide. I've heard of cases of cruelty, but the sheer disregard for your life is maddening." He looked at me. "The damage he did to you, my God, Petunia. Not to mention the emotional trauma caused by his psychological warfare upon your psyche...How can you even consider trusting anyone, trusting even me after what that monster did to you?" Ethan took my hands into his own and searched my eyes as I sat frozen in my confusion. "Don't you think it could happen to you again? Do you *want* it to happen again?"

Quick as lightning, I reared back from him in anger and hurt to slap his face hard. The regret was instantly in his eyes, but it was too late.

"How dare you?" I growled. "My abuse doesn't determine my ability to be loved! I'm sorry if I don't conform to your idea of how a survivor acts, but I've never played the victim my entire life. I can't let what happened to me define my worthiness of love, even if it scares the shit out of me! Yes, I have tamped down my submissive side out of distrust and fear of fucking up in my life choices again, but I've been pretty successful in doing so until I ran into *your* ass. You made me feel safe and desired and wanted as a whole fucking person, not as a piece in your fantasy role-play bullshit."

Ethan's hand fell slowly from his offended cheek, his eyes studying me as I drew in a breath. His expression was unreadable as he knelt beside me, reaching to pull me in for a hug, but I rebuffed him, refusing to stop the tirade he'd unleashed.

"But if you don't want that or can't handle the depths of my past or how I've recovered years later, then I'll walk out that door and I won't even try to be anything to you. What happened to me is awful; it fundamentally fucked up my life. But it *made me who I am*. And if you're not the man who can love me the way I deserve, then I'll walk out of this damn house and find someone who can."

Ethan's eyes met mine for a moment before pulling his hand away. He took a few breaths and shook his head, his cheeks reddened, a look of shame and embarrassment on his face.

"I've acted no better than the monster you left," he said, sitting back

# CHAINS OF SATIN

onto his heels. "I'm...Pet, I'm sorry. For my words, my actions...I don't ever want to make you feel as though I don't respect you or the past that shaped who you've become."

My chest heaved from the emotion that settled heavily within and I studied him as he studied me.

"Everything you've said echoes with truth I cannot ignore. I've wounded you deeply, and it tears me apart to know I've caused you pain. Can you forgive this fool at your feet and let me do my very damnedest to erase every negative memory?" He waited, not touching me or moving closer.

"How can I trust you not to react like that again?" I finally asked, my voice filled with sadness, fear flooding me.

"I need only learn lessons once, my darling. One time. But I swear to you, should I forget my place with you again, you need only remind me, or make good on your threat. Your choice, Pet. Always. In all things, your choice."

I reached for his hand and pressed it to my cheek, his warm palm soothing as ever.

"I have a million plans tonight, love, but if you'd prefer, I can take you home and simply hold you the rest of the night," he said softly as he caressed my skin with the pad of his thumb. I felt the familiar prickle of tears in my eyes, and shook my head.

"I want to be here with you. You really hurt my feelings, but...you also apologize really pretty." A ghost of a smirk lifted the corner of my lips and I leaned forward to him, pressing his lips to mine gently. "I think you're worth one more shot."

"Yeah?"

I nod.

His tongue found mine and in our embrace, he told me of his pain for my pain, his anger, and his disappointment in a world that allowed such evil to reside in it. He held my face with both hands as his tongue caressed mine, his lips devouring my own with a soft moan. One hand slid behind my head to press me harder into his kiss while the other wrapped around my waist. My arms went up and around his neck, running my fingers through his curls that rested there, as my heart beat fiercely in my chest.

He lifted me and carried me to his bed, never breaking contact as he slowly opened my robe and found me wet and wanting with his fingers.

"The moment you tense up or tell me to stop, I will," he vowed before taking a nipple into his mouth.

"I'll kill you if you stop," I whispered.

PRESENT DAY
OFFICE OF DR. JOSEPH HALL

# Ethan

"SHE CRIED OUT SO BEAUTIFULLY WHILE MY fingers were buried inside her that it took everything in me to walk away from the bathtub. I was stronger than I knew at that moment—I've buckled for women who tempted me less—but I knew how quickly it would have been over had I given in right then."

Joseph cleared his throat and sat back into his chair.

"I want to focus a little more on her revelation to you. How do you feel you handled her confessions?"

My cheeks flushed as I shook my head, lowering it in shame.

"I confess I wasn't the most chivalrous in that moment. All I could picture was Petunia left hanging by ropes, sobbing and bleeding…I saw red. I didn't fully understand that phrase until that moment. When she talked about how he hurt her, broke her trust and destroyed her innocent outlook of the world, it was all I could do not to find him and tear him apart.

"I shouldn't have said what I said to her. I don't remember verbatim what I told her, but the look of utter hurt on her face—fresh hurt that I'd inflicted—stabbed me in the heart. It hurt me worse than the sting of her slap, which I know I deserved. She shouldn't have been made to feel the need to justify herself to me; I shouldn't have made her feel so when she'd been completely open with me."

# CHAINS OF SATIN

"It was a whirlwind of emotions throughout this night that you experienced; it's no wonder that you would flounder a bit at her pain," Joseph soothed. "You were in shock, I'm sure."

"She began talking about leaving because she didn't think she was worthy of what I could give her and I panicked. I didn't even have time to come to terms with her history, but the drive to keep her with me was too much to bear. I kissed her, pleading with my actions, begging her forgiveness because she alone deserves nothing short of support and kindness."

"Perhaps you did the best you could, given the circumstance. You, yourself, are only human; you're going to have reactions beyond your control at times. These are things you will have to forgive yourself for."

"It wouldn't be the first time I'd reacted badly to situations that I should have dealt with more carefully," I confessed, my voice thick with guilt. "I was filled with such passion every second I was with her, and whether that passion was lust or anger, it was at its height."

"She never had a reason to fear you, did she?" I immediately shook my head.

"I never hurt her, not on purpose at least."

"So, what happened next?" Joseph asked.

I couldn't stop the smile spreading on my face if I had tried.

"Nothing short of magic," I replied.

## CHAPTER FIFTEEN

# Petunia

MY HANDS TANGLED IN HIS HAIR AS he released my nipple and kissed his way up my chest, shoving his tongue into my waiting mouth as I groaned. His long fingers filled me and I spread my thighs wide for him, needing any and every part of him inside me. He pulled his fingers away from me and tugged his pants down past his hips and laid his body atop of mine once more.

I felt him press against me, firm and long as he moved his hips, teasing my soaking wet pussy with the tip of his cock.

"Please," I begged him, reaching between our bodies to grasp ahold and guide him into me. He grabbed my hand and pressed it by my head, shaking his own slowly, kissing my chin and circling his hips to smear my wetness all over my skin. Still he delayed.

I pulled my head away from him and looked up at him with equal parts confusion and urgency.

"Ethan," I whispered. "I need—"

"You need nothing and no one, my beautiful, strong girl." He kissed my neck softly over and over. "It is I who needs you. I crave you. I want you. Will you have me, Pet? Will you?" His hips dipped low and he dragged the head of his cock up over my clit to rest on my lower belly. I reached and grasped him with my hand, finally able to stroke his smooth, hot flesh, to

# CHAINS OF SATIN

love him with my own hand as he'd done for me.

Ethan groaned against my neck and my patience broke. I lifted my hips and pushed the head of his cock between my waiting lips. He pulled his face away from my neck and looked into my eyes as he slowly sunk his flesh into my body.

"Jesus," he cursed. I whimpered as my body stretched to accommodate his size. "I've never…you're so warm, so deliciously snug." He was all the way in, his body pressed so tightly against mine that we were truly as one. "Are you…" He swallowed and started again, holding so still inside me. "Are you alright? Is this alright?"

"More than," I gasped, pulling his head down to a kiss with one hand and grabbing his ass cheek with the other. My legs were up and around his waist and I moaned as he began to move.

He was slow at first, slow and deep as he withdrew wholly before easing himself back into me. The build of my next orgasm was almost immediate and I couldn't help but cry out as I soaked his bedsheets. He took the moment to bite down onto my neck with a growl as he picked up the pace, thrusting faster and harder into me.

"Oh, fuck," Ethan grunted as he arched his back to rise above me. "Fuck, you're so beautiful."

I stared up at his magnificent body, unable to withhold the series of increasingly loud moans as he kept up the pace. My body was his and he worked every inch of it as I was helplessly riding to a finish.

"Come all over me, my girl," Ethan gasped.

I released on command, my walls contracting around him, squeezing and soaking him at the same time.

"Good girl," Ethan smirked, sweat dripping down his forehead. "That's my good girl."

He leaned down and licked a hardened nipple and I took a moment to bury my face in his neck, biting down in the throes of orgasm. He temporarily slowed and grunted.

"Bloody hell," he groaned.

I held on for dear life, lost in the unending waves of pleasure as I marked his flesh with teeth and nails. He growled, lifted his body to sit back onto his legs, then brought my legs upward to rest against his torso. He wrapped an arm around them and thus I was pinned as he drove into me mercilessly. He leaned over and watched me massage my own breasts, stimulating myself for added intensity. I started moaning again, feeling that pressure low in my belly, the coiling spring about to snap any moment.

"That's it, Pet," Ethan said. "I'm almost there, my darling, so fucking close, but…*God*…I want you to come once more. Do it for me, you beautiful

99

creature. Come for me." He clasped a hand around my throat, giving it a squeeze. Adrenaline shot through me, sending me into yet another earth-quaking climax. I squealed and panted, feeling the world shatter around me, simultaneously killing me and breathing life into me with each crest and fall.

"Almost there." I heard his voice break through my cries as he grasped my thighs with his hands and drove himself into me. I felt him swell and I fluttered around his cock, spurring him on as I cried out his name. "Yes, darling. Oh, my God, yes!" He was panting, then letting go of my legs and pulling himself out of me, pumping his flesh quickly until streams of his seed shot out, coating my belly, groin and thighs.

Ethan fell forward with a sigh and caught his weight with both hands on either side of my head, sweating, breathless, and sexier than ever. He kissed my tender, swollen lips softly before pulling away and leaning on an elbow to look upon me. I swept the hair clinging to his sweaty skin off his forehead with the sleeve of my robe.

"Thank you," he breathed, smiling softly.

I grinned back and whispered, "You're welcome."

"That was...more—"

"Perfect than I ever imagined?" I finished, eliciting a chuckle from him.

"I was going to say more abrupt than I initially planned."

"Surprise!" I laughed.

"Surprise indeed. How are you feeling?"

I closed my eyes for a minute and reopened them to find him staring at me, patiently awaiting my response.

"Two things," I began. "One, I feel emotionally drained, to tell you the truth. I haven't told anyone outside of Shay, my parents, and the authorities about what happened to me, and the way you reacted wasn't what I anticipated. I'm sorry I slapped you, but I was expecting a more compassionate response, you know?"

"You're right," Ethan said, looking down at the mattress and nodding softly. "It was wrong, and I should never have asked you such a thing. It should never have even crossed my mind."

I appreciated his words and could feel that they rang true.

"What's the second thing you're feeling?"

I couldn't stop myself from grinning.

"Sticky," I answered, making him laugh. He rolled off the bed, pulling up his pants as he walked into the bathroom. I heard the water run for a moment before he returned with a washcloth and towel.

"Lay still," he commanded.

# CHAINS OF SATIN

The washcloth was warm on my skin and before long my body was clean and dry once more. As he tossed the dirty linen onto the floor beside him, he looked back at me, got onto his knees beside the bed and gently kissed the scar on my lower belly.

I smiled and felt him trace the four-inch scar with his fingertips.

"I hope someday you can reveal more of who you are to me," I said softly. "At least enough to make us even."

"I'm afraid there isn't much excitement in my story, but I am an open book for you. In the meantime, are you as hungry as I am right now?"

My stomach rumbled in answer, and I laughed. He closed my robe, tying the belt securely around my waist.

"Come, my dear." Ethan stood and stretched out a helping hand. "There's food to be gotten."

## CHAPTER SIXTEEN

# *Petunia*

THOUGH WE MADE IT WAIT, DINNER ENDED up still tasting like heaven. We sat across from each other and, aside from the occasional comments and looks toward one another, we ate in relative silence. After a while, Ethan rose to refill my glass with wine, and I couldn't help but smirk up at him.

"Are you trying to get me intoxicated, sir?" I winked.

"My dear, I have you in my home, all to myself. I have many stored-away ideas to explore with you during this rare opportunity. I'd hate for you to fall asleep before the night, and I, are through."

Ethan kissed the top of my head and I glanced up at him, puzzled.

"We just…I mean, we already…you know?"

"Are you tired or in discomfort, Pet? Would you rather rest for tonight?" His concern for me was genuine.

"Well, no, no not at all," I backpedaled. "I'm actually really okay right now. I've just never had an opportunity to, you know…go again."

Ethan sighed and shook his head, setting his glass down and lacing his fingers together. He leaned in closer across the table, resting on his elbows.

"You're going to have to forget all you learned and experienced from your past, Petunia. Those rules don't apply here. As for *my* rules…

# CHAINS OF SATIN

they vary from moment to moment, but the core of my morality stays the same: respect, communication, kindness. Those are essential for any partnership, whether it be business or personal. For instance, considering how long it's been since anything wonderful has been just about you, I feel that the focus of our evening should be on you. Out of respect for you and your experience." I took a sip of my wine to cover the blush in my cheeks.

"What is it, Pet?" Ethan's eyes didn't miss a thing.

"I'm not going to get away with answering with 'nothing,' am I?"

"Not a chance," Ethan answered, his eyes darkening slightly.

"I promise the answer isn't 'nothing.' It's more like, I'm feeling a little...out of secrets, at the moment. Like I poured my heart out to you and—"

"Regrets, darling?" he offered softly.

My eyes shot up to meet his. "No, oh, God no, nothing like that."

"What then?"

"Awkward embarrassment? I don't know," I admitted, draining my second cup of wine.

"Feeling vulnerable again, sweetheart?"

"I'm sort of used to feeling that way," I answered after a moment of silence. "I guess I just have to remember it's not always a bad thing. I have to learn to trust again, right?"

Ethan smiled and pushed his chair back.

"That you do. Perhaps we can start with you trusting me to fulfill my word?" He winked and slid himself under the table.

"What in the world?" I lifted the table cloth as Ethan pulled my robe open at my knees.

"Relax, sweet girl," he said, smiling devilishly as he pulled me closer to him by my hips. "I did mention something about dessert."

"Oh," I whispered softly as he guided my knees apart, grasping at my thighs before kissing and then biting one, then the other. He crept closer with his kisses and tender bites, and by the time he reached the apex of my thighs, I was already panting and aching for his touch.

My eyes closed and my head fell back against the chairback. I took ahold of his hair, releasing a quiet moan as he first kissed the very top of my groin, then dove into its moist center with the full length of his warm, wet tongue. His nose bumped up against my clit over and over, the double-sensation drawing a squeal from me. Ethan took his time stroking every part of my pussy with his hot breath, spongy nose and tender tongue. He nibbled and sucked, swirled and licked before he slid a finger inside me and sucked the flesh around it.

I was dying. I cried out, knowing there were others in the home,

103

but abandoning all societal restraints. He held me firmly to him, coaxing me until I felt my climax building, slow and patiently.

"Christ!"

"There's my girl," he whispered against my skin before pressing his tongue against my labia and sucking hard, his nose in constant contact with my aching, swollen clit. "Cry for me, Pet. *Come for me.*"

His voice barely met my ears, but it was enough for my orgasm to descend upon me, leaving me breathlessly calling out his name and tugging firmly on his hair. Ethan never stopped the movement of his fingers and tongue as I rode my ecstasy against his face. I'd broken out into a sweat from the torrent of pleasure, and still he kept on, steady and practiced as I began to quiet and still, my thighs trembling. Only then did he release me from his mouth, pushing my chair away from the table as he removed his fingers from my body. His kisses trailed up my slick skin as he removed his black silk pants.

"Never have I tasted honey so sweet," he mumbled, leaning forward to take one of my nipples into his mouth. "You are heaven." He stood and lifted me, taking a seat in my chair and settling me onto his lap.

"I need to feel you wrapped around my dick."

From my place straddling his body, his turgid flesh lay trapped between my thighs. He reached down and guided himself into the warmth that awaited him. I felt his hands grasp my hips from behind firmly, controlling my body as I moved back and forth on his lap. My hands cupped his face as I bent to slide my tongue in his mouth, tasting the intoxicating combination of my musk and his breath. He continued to guide me slowly but pulled his face away from mine.

"Tell me about the scar," Ethan whispered. I stopped moving in surprise but he gripped my ass and moved me back and forth.

"No, Ethan, not now," I begged.

"Now, my darling," Ethan groaned as he looked up at me, shifting his hips slightly which caused him to sink deeper into me.

"It'll…*God*…it'll shock you…dis-disgust you."

I didn't want to talk right then, my body was feeling way too good.

"No more than it'll shock you if I should stop." He thrust hard into me as he spoke. "Right. Now."

"That's extortion." I barely could form the words as I began to feel my impending orgasm. He slowed and kissed my collarbone.

"I'd like to think of it as positive reinforcement." He knew I was close, my hands tense against his shoulders, my nails finding home in his skin. He smiled softly and slowed my movement further.

"Wait!" I cried out, feeling my orgasm slipping away.

# CHAINS OF SATIN

"Tell me, Pet." His voice lowered as he jerked up into me twice more. "You may have your sweet release when you tell me."

"That's not f—oh, God, what if you ca-can't look at me the same afterwards?"

I was sweating, full of fear and need, desire and terror at his possible rejection. Ethan flicked a hardened nipple with his tongue, sending bolts of electricity through my body. I cried out and he smothered the sound with a deep, sensual kiss. This was agony. My mind was conflicted, my body was wracked with torturous desire, and he seemed to possess other-worldly patience when it came to tormenting me. Finally, I couldn't take it anymore.

"I was pregnant," I gasped, knowing full well my voice was barely audible.

Ethan stopped moving and slowly met my eyes.

"I can't." I took a deep breath, a shudder running through my body. "After what he did to me, I can't have children anymore." How odd it was to have Ethan inside me while I told him of my horrors. How odd it was that I still craved the orgasm I'd been denied even though I was crying.

"My poor Pet," Ethan moaned, resting his forehead on mine, pulling me tight against him. The movement shoved his cock hard and deep inside me and it just rested there, both of us panting and still.

"I'm sorry," I whispered into his hair.

"There's no need to apologize to me." His words were soft and after a moment, he brought my face down to meet his, kissing me softly. "If you'd rather stop and recover for tonight, you only have to say the word."

"You aren't put off?" I asked him. My heart was pounding in my chest. *Does my past truly not matter to him? And if not, why not?*

"What happened to you should never have happened to anyone, least of all you, my Pet. But it doesn't make you who you are. You are not your past, my darling. You came out of your endeavors stronger than anyone I've ever known."

"Ethan—"

"I find each moment you bare your soul to me a blessing, Petunia," Ethan said, sitting tall and grasping my thighs by my ass. "I could never truly know everything you've endured, but I'm happy to know the person you've turned out to be. I'm honored by your presence alone. It makes you all the more alluring, knowing how strong you are without being jaded by all of it."

I couldn't stop touching him, his cheeks, his neck, his hair, not a single patch of his skin within my reach was left untouched. I felt as though if I were to stop touching him, he would stop being real.

"If you're still alright, if you'd allow me, I made a vow," Ethan reminded me.

*Trust, right? I had to trust him.*

I nodded.

"Good girl," he whispered. "You held your end up beautifully. Now it's my turn to hold up my own."

He increased the speed with which he rocked my hips against his body. My clit stimulated itself against the rough patch of hair at the base of his cock, and in an instant I was right where I left off with my climax building. I didn't—couldn't—break eye contact as he met my hips with his, thrust for thrust. Without warning, my climax struck me dumb as it tore through me, punching the air out of my lungs and making my legs tremble as they tightened around his hips. Still he pressed on, pushing and pulling with fervor, sweat pouring down his temples as I cried out.

Without missing a stroke, he lifted me and swept his arm across the table. I was still crying out as he sent his expensive dinnerware flying to the floor. He laid me onto the table, and his lips found mine as the last waves of my orgasm swept through me.

"My sweet girl. Oh, my sweet, strong girl," he moaned against my lips, as he pumped and pumped until I felt him swell again inside me. "I'm going to come, my darling, for you and you alone."

"Please," I begged.

"You want it?" Ethan asked, looking into my eyes. I nodded and licked my lips.

"Fuck," he cursed as he pulled out of my body, moving quickly as he stroked himself until I grabbed him and pulled him deep into my waiting mouth. I wrapped an arm around his thigh and pushed him deeper. He came, his hot seed shooting past my tonsils. I looked up at him, gloating to myself at the bliss, which I created, displayed across his features. I swallowed over and over, forcing a groan from his lips as I sucked him dry.

"Oh, my darling," he cried as I eagerly drew the last drop from his flesh. "My marvelous darling."

I released him and sat up onto my elbows as he handed me his glass of wine. I downed it, wiped my lips, and reached up to kiss him.

"You truly are most magnificent," Ethan said, kissing me over and over.

THE CLOCK STRUCK ELEVEN WHEN HE SET me gently onto his bed, making me jump.

"What is it?" Ethan asked, fluffing the pillows on his bed.

# CHAINS OF SATIN

"It's awfully late," I answered. "Maybe I should head back home?"

"I'm sorry, I just assumed..." Ethan stopped with the pillows and looked over at me. "Is that what you want? To go back to your place?"

"I don't know." I tried, honestly. "I would really love to stay, but if I do and mom hurts herself, or worse..." I shrugged at him, conflicted.

"What if I compromised and stayed the night with you?" Ethan suggested.

"I can't keep quiet enough in my house, remember?"

"Admittedly, I could keep going with you tonight, Pet." Ethan chuckled. "There are so many naughty images that come to mind, but I promise, if you would bid me to do so, I would remain the perfect gentleman and only hold you as you sleep, nothing more."

"Ethan, you only just got back. Don't you, like, miss your home, or something?"

"My home will always be here. Right now, my focus is on what's best for you."

I shook my head as he took my hands into his.

"Why?"

"I'm sorry?" Ethan looked at me, puzzled.

"Why have you taken such an interest in me and my life? We're worlds apart, you know. It's like some kind of erotic romance novel cliché: the maid and the millionaire or whatever." I rolled my eyes as he grinned and licked my earlobe.

"Billionaire, actually. And, isn't it obvious?" He traced my jawline with his fingers, sending goosebumps over my body.

"Not really," I admitted.

Ethan smiled and kissed my neck twice before kissing my lips. I melted against him, coaxing him into a deeper kiss as he gripped my face and groaned.

"Of all the adventures I've been on in my life, you are the most exciting. Your heart is one filled with such kindness. You sacrifice daily without restraint, and you love with such wild abandon that I'm thoroughly intoxicated by you." His kisses burned my skin as he peppered my chest and neck with them between his words. "You've turned me into a man of lust and need, my Pet. More than that, knowing you has made me reach deeper into my self-reflection so that I may strive to be a better man...for you."

He laid me against the bed as he gently teased and maneuvered my hardened nipple through my robe. This was new. His touches were delicate, without so much as a hint of urgency in his kisses or his manipulations. It was almost as if he could stand doing only this all day long.

He probably could. But I was struggling. Ethan accused me of turning him into a lust demon, but he just *turned me on*. He made me want to lay in bed and ride orgasm after orgasm with him until I died. Every touch left me craving for more. Each kiss left me begging for another until it never stopped. If he was turning to Lust, I was Greed.

I moaned into his mouth and arched my back, pressing his hand harder onto my breast.

"Look at the wonder of you, my Pet," Ethan whispered as he pulled away from me and gazed down the length of my body. His eyes glittered with mischief. "Your legs are spread and welcoming even after the strenuous activities of the night. How deliciously should I reward such *eager* behavior? Tell me, my ardent lover, what would you have me do to you, do *for* you?"

"I want your tongue," I gasped, hardly believing my own words after he'd already pleased me so much. Ethan's chuckle came out like a growl as he mouthed my nipple again through the fabric of my robe.

"Where, my sweet girl?"

"Taste me," I begged. "Taste me to see how my body begs for you." Ethan stopped and looked up at me in surprise. He kept the look on his face as he lowered himself between my legs. He glanced down as his fingers caressed the bite marks he'd left on my thigh.

"Did you enjoy the way I've already marked you, sweet Pet?" Ethan purred.

I leaned up onto my elbows and looked down at him.

"Oh yes," I whined.

He reached up and palmed a breast, the warmth of his hand drawing out a moan. He smirked and, without pulling his hand away, dug into my right thigh, biting the supple flesh there. Releasing my leg, he trailed smaller, softer kisses upwards, moving closer and closer to my waiting, wanting pussy. He stopped and blew a gentle current of chilled air across my skin. I shivered.

"Please," I breathed, my words soft as a kitten's call.

"Please, what?" Ethan asked, blowing another gentle stream of cold air over me.

"Please, sir. Please, just eat me, fuck me with your mouth, I...I need..."

Ethan lay his mouth on as much of my flesh as he could and hummed. I squealed on contact and bucked as he tweaked and twisted my nipple softly. I reached down and grabbed his hair, panting and pushing him deeper between my legs. Just like before, he used his tongue, lips, and nose to make me belt out a symphony of cries and moans. Unlike before,

# CHAINS OF SATIN

Ethan took his time. There was no hurry in his movements, no urgency, no goal line to rush me to.

"God." I threw a hand into my own hair as I gasped. "I could happily pay you to do just this, day in and day out."

Ethan drew my clit between his teeth and delicately teased it. I called out his name as my thighs quivered around his head.

I was swollen and aching from all his attention, but he was so gentle, even as he brought me to a mind-blowing orgasm. I cried out again as the waves crested over me again and again, throwing both hands into his hair to hold his face against me. I twisted, and my body bucked and curved under the pleasure until it finally released its hold upon me, leaving me a shivering, moaning puddle on his bed.

Ethan pulled his mouth off of me and kissed my thighs, nibbling lightly as he crawled up my body. He leaned his forehead against mine, breathing deeply, as I slowed mine along with him until our breathing patterns matched. I reached between us to give him his own satisfaction but he stopped me, interlacing our fingers and holding our hands up by my head.

"No more tonight," he said, kissing my forehead. "As much as I want to bury myself inside you again, we can't distract ourselves from what's important. Answer me honestly, Pet. Would you like to go home?"

"I should," I sighed.

Ethan climbed off me, sliding a hand over my exposed breast, and walked over to his large, dark oak dresser. Opening the top drawer, he pulled out a pair of running shorts and a tank top.

*My* running shorts and tank top.

"How much of my clothing do you still have here?" I asked, puzzled. "I know Shay brought some things, but I thought we took all that stuff back to my mom's?"

"You have two drawers here, a couple dresses in the closet and three pairs of shoes," he explained, dressing himself.

"Okay, now I'm really confused."

"I really hope you don't mind, but I took the liberty of looking into your sizes." Ethan was watching me as I peeled the robe off my body and reached for the tank top. "I had a few things bought for you to replace some that were worn thin and give you a greater variety."

"I'm not sure how I feel about that," I confessed. He sat beside me and placed his hands over mine.

"It pleases me to do so. Should anything happen where you'd find yourself here for another extended stay, we're prepared."

He leaned over and licked my nipple just before I covered it with the tank top. I adjusted my shirt, then wrapped my arms around his neck. Ethan kissed me and pulled me tight against him, chest to chest. His hands tangled in my hair and pressed my lips tighter against his own. His tongue slid deep into my mouth until, at last, he groaned and slowed our kiss. He slowed it, but I never wanted it to stop.

"My vigorous, ardent lover," he muttered, shuddering as I kissed his neck. "Do you have any idea how delicious you are? How it pains me to not give into the temptation of you? Would that I could keep you like this, safe from all the troubles in the world." Ethan sighed and took my face into his hands. He looked into my eyes for a moment, then planted the tiniest kiss on the tip of my nose.

"Let's get you back to your home, sweet Pet. Duty awaits."

# CHAPTER SEVENTEEN

# *Petunia*

I WOKE UP ALONE IN BED. For just a brief moment, I wondered if the night before had been a dream until I saw flowers in a vase on my nightstand. I couldn't help but smile at the memory. My crutches and Ethan's suitcase rested against the wall beside my bed, moved there sometime after I'd fallen asleep during the night. As I grabbed my crutches and walked out of my room, laughter and music floated up the stairway from the kitchen.

Ethan's laughter.

Mother's music.

I made my way down the stairs after visiting the restroom and came upon my mother dancing gracefully in Ethan's arms. I leaned against the doorway marveling at my mom's face as she stared up with adoration at him, grinning softly.

*Me too, Mom,* I thought. *Me too.*

The music ended and Ethan pulled away, kissing her hand as he dipped into a low bow. Mom laughed.

"You always get tired of dancing before I do, Albert," she teased.

"You are, as always, so full of life, my dear," Ethan answered. He pulled out a chair and she sat, humming the rhythm that had been playing moments before.

"He's a good one, that man," Rico said as he came up behind me.

I blushed, turning my head to look at him.

"I'm sorry about yesterday," I told him. Had it really only been yesterday that I blew up at him? "You were right about the future. No matter how hard it's going to be, it's something that has to be dealt with. I just wish I didn't have to be the one to deal with it."

"When you get a second, I have a list already prepared of different facilities that specialize in her condi—"

"Good morning," Ethan interrupted, wrapping his arms around my waist and kissing my neck. "I trust you slept well?"

"I'll look at what you've prepared, Rico. Just set it in the living room and I'll find you with whatever questions come up. Thank you."

"You're forgiven, *mija*. It's a difficult time; I get it. Now, tend to your man while I tend to your mama." Rico winked at Ethan and went into the kitchen.

Ethan stepped in front of me, held my face in his hands and kissed me softly.

"I slept like a comatose child," I answered his earlier question. He smiled softly. "Thank you for giving Mom a moment to be happy. It was wonderful of you."

"I wish I knew her before her illness," he said, looking back at her with sadness for a moment.

"She would've kept you on your toes, that's for sure," I laughed.

"Can you make it back up the stairs?" Ethan smiled and took a step back from me. "There's something I'd like to discuss with you, in private, if I may?"

"Um, okay, yeah. Is something wrong?" I asked nervously.

"Not exactly. I'll meet you in your room." He kissed my cheek before turning and heading up the stairs. By the time I cleared my bedroom doorway, he'd opened his suitcase and placed two stacks of paper on my bed in front of him.

"Close the door, Pet," he said, rising from his seated position.

I did as he asked and sat on the other side of the bed while he leaned my crutches against the wall.

"What's this all about?" I asked.

Ethan knelt in front of me, taking my hands into his, kissing my knuckles. He leaned his forehead against them and took a deep breath, releasing it slowly.

*Now, I'm really confused.*

"Are you alright?"

Ethan chuckled and shook his head.

"I'm rarely nervous, my Pet. I find this situation has me quite…

# CHAINS OF SATIN

uncertain."

I reached down and lifted his chin so his eyes could see mine. It was an odd role-reversal.

"Whatever it is, it'll be okay," I assured him. "We can deal with it together, if you'd like."

His answering kiss was hard, almost desperate in its fervor.

"Alright, love," he whispered before sitting back onto his heels. "Ever since that day I found you in my room sampling my cologne, I've been drawn to you. Each moment we've shared is cemented in my memory, and I find that I cannot go a day without thinking of you, fantasizing about you, worrying about you. You drive me to distraction, my darling."

He closed his eyes and took another deep breath as I waited patiently, not knowing where he was going with all this sentiment. Finally, he looked back up at me.

"With your father regrettably gone and your mother needing to be placed in permanent care, I've had a thought."

"Okay?" I prompted after he was silent for longer than I was comfortable.

"What if you were to sell your home and come live with me?"

My jaw dropped but he held a finger against my lips before I could speak.

"Before you answer, I need to let you know my intentions are, mostly, selfish. I sleep better with you by my side. My days are happier when I spend them with you. And," he hesitated before leaning over and grabbing a stack of papers and setting them on my lap, "we could be... contracted."

I felt the color drain from my face as my eyes flew up to meet his cautiously eager ones.

"Only if you wish. I understand this is a big leap of faith for you, after what happened to you in the past. I understand if you refuse immediately, but I sincerely hope this is something you'd at least consider."

I sat quietly for a moment before looking at the contract in my hands, my heart pounding in my throat. It was a standard contract — complete with a list of options, information, do's and don'ts — it had everything except...

"There's no end date written," I pointed out, looking up at Ethan.

"I didn't...I didn't put one in," he answered softly. "I thought, if there's any time you'd like to...to cancel the contract, it's something that can happen at your discretion." His words were genuine, though his expression made it clear he didn't want such a thing to happen.

"And if you decide to? End it, I mean?" I asked.

"My sweet girl, there's not a force in the universe that could make me want to terminate this," Ethan confessed, kissing my bare knee.

"For the sake of full disclosure," I insisted. "Anything could happen, and before we even think about doing this, I'd like to cover all bases here. Nothing can be left out or one-sided."

"That is incredibly practical of you, my darling," Ethan said after a moment's thought. "Very well. For the contract's sake, if either of us wish to terminate, we must first discuss the reason before declaring a cease and desist. How does that sound?"

"I'm just so confused," I said softly, shaking my head.

"What confuses you?"

"I don't know where to start! All of this?"

"What did you imagine would happen here? Did you imagine that we would be stagnant, that I would do what I wanted with you and then abandon you? What did you think our next step would be?" Ethan's voice was patient, but there was an edge of something like panic in his voice.

"I imagined nothing! I couldn't! I'm not sure I still can...I mean, I'm having a hard time picturing this."

"Do you think so little of me?" he asked, loosening his grip on my hands.

"You? No, not you." I pulled his hands close to me, clutching them to my chest. "I mean, I certainly don't hold myself in the same regard as I hold you. In the grand scheme of things, I'm nobody. Practically nothing."

"I'm not sure I understand, my love. Have I not shown you that you are worth the attention of anyone, regardless of their status? I just don't —"

"You live in a world where your possibilities are limited by imagination, not the dollar. You can go anywhere, have the freedom to do anything you could possibly want, have anyone you could possibly love. It's a privilege to you. But me...I have a dead and buried father, a decaying mother, and no real assets to speak of. Not to mention I'm completely infertile, which means even my future is gone! To a man like you, I have nothing to offer!" I shook my head, drawing in a breath. "This whole fantasy has been incredible, don't get me wrong. The sex, the gifts, the tenderness... all of this has been a dream beyond anything I have ever experienced in my life. But I'm afraid of what will happen once you see that all I am is some common peasant."

Ethan scoffed.

"It's the truth! I can't offer you anything! I'm literally coming to you empty-handed! Meanwhile your future is filled with nothing but hope and vitality —"

"Ooh, I like that," he interrupted, sitting up on the bed beside me, and tucking a lock of hair behind my ear. I blushed hard. "Say it again for

# CHAINS OF SATIN

me."

"Vitality?" I asked.

He leaned in and kissed my neck, growling, "No, Pet. With *conviction*."

I was suddenly torn between being annoyed and turned on.

"*Vitality*," I drawled sarcastically before redirecting our conversation. "But, seriously, you heard me, right? I'm telling the truth here."

"Of course, my sweet girl." Ethan pulled away and searched my eyes. "It's all true. Except you're mistaken on an important part, Pet: I wouldn't be doing this with you if I wasn't certain you were the woman for me. I know your strengths, your limits, your pain, your joy." He kissed my neck again and whispered, "I know how you look when something makes you feel on top of the world and, oh, my dear girl, I crave that entirety of you insatiably." He kissed along my neck over and over, causing my focus to spiral.

"Insatiably?" I asked.

"Definitely. It means—"

"I know what it means." I struggled to keep my composure as he held my jaw gently in his hand. "It's just, no one's said that to me, even if they were infatuated with me."

"'Infatuated'?" Ethan pulled away from me, laughing. "A term for schoolboys who don't understand the full grasp of what it means to feel real passion and desire for a full-blooded woman."

"What would you call it, then? Why would you do all of this? You've never really answered that before."

"The truth?" he asked, caressing my face.

"No lies," I reminded him.

"No lies?" Ethan's eyes glittered dangerously as he smirked at me. He spoke slowly, his voice dragging over every syllable like a lover's caress. "My sweet Pet, everybody lies. Even you. You lie to your friends when you say you're fine. You lie to your mother, her nurses. You lie to yourself." With a strong hand, Ethan guided me to lie on my back as he loomed over me. "You even lie to me."

I shook my head.

"I've never," I said softly.

Ethan's smile grew, the dangerous look on his face one of a predator having successfully caught its prey.

"You're telling me you never lied? You weren't lying when you say you've never imagined anything happening between us? That before last night you've never had lustful fantasies of me holding you tight?" He wrapped an arm under my waist, pulling me tight against his body as I inhaled sharply. "Or touching your skin?" He caressed my cheek.

"Oh, God," I whimpered. My heart raced.

"Have you *never* imagined before all of this, looking in my eyes and finding nothing but the need for you filling them? The need to *fuck* you as I take your lips and press them against mine? The need to conquer and keep you as mine and mine alone?"

"No," I shuddered as he whispered the word 'fuck,' accentuating it to ripple through my body. I was losing this game, and I knew it. He knew it, too. He smiled as he planted a soft kiss on my throat.

"Liar," he growled. "Tell me about the first time you felt it, Pet."

"I don't know what y-you're talking about," I stuttered.

"You're lying again." Ethan's growl deepened as he nibbled my earlobe. I lost right then; I lost myself to him. Lost my resolve to win this battle of wills. I shivered.

"When I was introduced to you, the very first day I met you... shook your hand...smelled you..." I closed my eyes as I confessed, turning away from him in embarrassment. It was pathetic of me to hold a crush on a client from the first day.

"Did you go home and touch yourself..." Ethan growled as he reached down between my legs and cupped my heated pussy, "here?" He was breathing hotly against my neck as he spoke. "Thinking of me and what I could do to you?"

"Yes," I moaned.

He couldn't have known, but he was a damn good guesser. I made myself orgasm twice just that night.

"Did you cry out my name as you peaked in your pleasure?" My hands curled into his hair as he squeezed me, the heat of his hand seeping through the thin shorts I had on. "Did you picture my tongue inside you, or did your imagination dive straight to my cock pleasing you?" Ethan trailed his kisses down my body, my shirt the only barrier between his lips and my skin.

"All of it," I whispered. "All of this. More than this."

"I, too, found myself in dire need of release that day. I came as I pictured the way your eyes looked at me, your lips as you sighed your greeting. You teased me with your submission, even if you didn't realize it." Ethan grunted and took my hand from his hair and pressed it between our bodies to find his erection pulsating there. "I pleasured myself multiple times after I found you in my room, delighting in your secret adoration of my scent. I imagined rubbing my body all over yours so all you'd smell until your dying day was me. The day I found you dancing in the kitchen, I was dangerously close to bending you over the island and fucking you until you

# CHAINS OF SATIN

screamed my name."

I shivered and moaned, gasping for air as his palm picked up speed. "Oh, how you egged me on, darling. How you tortured me with your body as we danced together, with your breast as you reached for the soap to clean my wound. I felt that ample flesh brush against my fingertips, and it was all I could do to not tear open your shirt and pull it into my mouth."

My heart soared at his words, those blessed words that verified all the thoughts I'd had about his attraction to me. I gripped him tighter and he groaned, moving quickly as he slid his hand beneath my shorts and found me soaked with need. He shoved a finger deep and hard into me as I unbuttoned and unzipped his pants, crying out into his mouth as he kissed me. I found and sprung his hard, wanting dick free.

Ethan tugged down my shorts and, without further warning, he drove himself hard into my body, my hips matching his vigorous assault, thrust for thrust.

"That's my girl," he panted before conquering my mouth. On and on he pushed into me, filling me with his thick length until the inevitable build of my orgasm began to grow.

"I'm going to—" I gasped out.

"Hold it back, Pet, I want it to be together, *fuck*..."

"Come inside me," I begged. "I need to feel you fill me."

"Christ, baby," Ethan whispered, his cock flexing and thickening inside me. "Keep that up and I'll finish before I want to."

"Good," I teased. His hand went directly in my hair, gripping it tight while he sucked on my neck. "Come inside me, please...*please*...I need it. I need you, baby, please!" I couldn't hold back too much longer, I was on the precipice and with or without him, I was going to tumble over.

"Shit, Pet...Shit, I can't...Come, sweet girl, I'm going to—" He trailed off as his face twisted against my neck, groaning as he spilled his seed deep within me. His release sent mine into a flurry of explosions. Never in my life had I experienced an orgasm that felt so complete, pushing me to such heights while we came together.

We cried out, smothering each other's noises with passionate kisses, lost in the moment as if nothing else in the world existed.

When he was finished, he laid his head against my shoulder, one hand pushing my hair back as he tried to catch his breath. Meanwhile I continued to see stars. Finally, still inside me, he nuzzled his nose against my face.

"My beautiful, wondrous girl. How could you think you are not worthy of this when this brings us both so much joy? I don't care what you consider less than perfect about yourself. What matters is this: you and I are complete when we are together. I adore you, my Pet. I adore you beyond anything I've ever known."

CHAPTER EIGHTEEN

# Petunia

"DID YOU MEAN TO GO OVER THIS with me when you came to my house last night?" I asked as I flipped through the contract. He buttoned his pants as he stood before me, glancing over at the papers in my hands.

"It was my initial plan," Ethan admitted.

"Surprise," I laughed.

"Honestly, Pet. How do you feel about this? If it's too soon, or if you're trepidatious, we can approach this at a later time."

"Let's see what's all in here, shall we?" I still wasn't sure why Ethan had been so enamored by me, but I wasn't going to question the sincerity of his feelings for me. He'd done a damn good job explaining his feelings to me, and there was absolutely no doubt in my mind about my feelings for him. "You've checked your boxes already, but some of them should be explained."

"Of course," he said, sitting beside me and trying—but failing—to hide the joy in his voice.

"First, you've checked a hard 'no' for an open relationship, but then you've checked 'yes' for sharing. I'm not quite sure I understand."

"The bliss on your face when you're being pleased and the look in your eyes when you're full of lust and wanting are the most beautiful images I've ever seen. Once we're at a point where we're comfortable, I'd

# DELILAH ST. RIVERS

love to see someone drive you to those points before I take over, or help heighten the experience while we have sex." He looked away, tensing his jaw muscles. "But, I don't think I could bear the thought of someone else having your heart, my love."

"I wouldn't let anyone else close enough to try," I said quietly. "And..."

"What is it, Petunia?" Ethan looked back at me, taking me by the hand.

"I'm not so sure about setting up anything that involves another person, with or without you. It's not that I'm worried about temptation, or anything. It's just..." I shook my head.

"Honesty, darling. No one-sided clauses. If we're going to be as transparent as possible, there's no such thing as 'silly' when it comes to your needs. Do I have to pry it out of you?"

"It might be fun." I blushed, remembering how he pried all the other information out of me over the course of the previous night. When Ethan didn't crack a smile, I sighed. "It's dumb, but I can't get past a few things from before. Like sharing. He used to do that; share me with other people. There were frequent times where he'd actually sell me to different men or women and let them do what they wanted with me. Whatever they wanted. He told them..." I trailed off, the memory disgusting even to me.

"What?" Ethan prompted.

"He told them that I wouldn't enjoy it if I wasn't crying or screaming. It was like he set a goal for how far my limits could be pushed with each customer." It was a victory for me that only one tear fell from my eye this time.

"You have my word that such ugliness will never again come to pass. I'll never do as others have with this contract. I will not place hidden loopholes in the pages, nor will I dare to discard the contract under any circumstances. I swear I will take this one just as seriously as I do the ones I deal with in my line of business."

"I wouldn't be looking at these pages with you if I didn't think I could trust you, Ethan," I said seriously.

His eyes softened as he looked at me, then gestured to the contract.

"I knew you liked it when I called you 'sir,'" I giggled.

"When it comes from your lips, it sets fire to my loins." He reached up from behind me and kissed my neck. "What else did you find?"

"No pegging...Thank God. I mean, I'd do it if you requested it— there's very little I haven't done—but if it comes to strictly what I enjoy doing...that's like towards the bottom." I sighed and pulled away to look at him. "Buying me things?"

120

# CHAINS OF SATIN

"An important 'yes' from me, Pet. Not only would you be mine in contract, but mine in all other aspects as well. You'll need items for the occasional company dinner or social engagement, and," Ethan kissed below my ear, "it truly does please me to dote upon you."

"I'm just not used to it."

"I'll give you plenty of opportunities to become used to it. On that you have my word."

I sighed again, resigned, and left the box unaltered.

"The next page is about tools, toys, and the like. Remember, Pet, there's no shame in any answer you give. You will only disappoint me if you're being untruthful." Ethan kissed me and I nodded.

According to the list, he liked the standard stuff: satin whips, restraints, candles, ice, ropes, paddles, vibrators, the usual. I hesitated when I saw "ropes;" a flashback of the last time they were used on me caused me to shudder.

"Shh, my darling," he comforted me, rubbing my back in wide strokes. "Ropes aren't always necessary. We could use alternatives or forget them altogether until you feel more trusting and comfortable."

Ethan leaned closer to me to whisper in my ear. "I could always wrap you in chains of satin, instead."

I blushed and checked the box labeled "no," relieved that he continued to show how understanding he could be, and flustered as hell by his seductive suggestion. After that, we talked openly about the other things he'd marked "yes" to, and I found our likes were incredibly similar in regard to both what we'd like for me to use on him and for him to use on me. There wasn't much he left untouched.

"There's a blank for the aftercare section, darling. I assumed we could fill this out together, based on your likes."

I shrugged. "Cuddles for me, I guess?"

Ethan chuckled lightly. "Alright. Bubble baths, spa days...snacks perhaps?" he asked, looking at me. I nodded, smiling. "Gifts assuredly. Anything else?"

"Music?" I suggested.

"Oh, of course. If it helps, yes."

"And for you?"

"You allowing me to do these things for you is all I need."

"It's looking awfully one-sided," I warned, shaking my head.

"Alright, what do you suggest, my love?"

"Bringing you a drink? Inviting you to bathe with me? Tending any wounds you may have," I winked at him.

"Playing nurse, sweet girl?" He wrapped his arms around me.

# DELILAH ST. RIVERS

"That may be enough to make me hard for you again," he growled in my ear and I playfully squealed.

A knock on my bedroom door interrupted us. I sighed and pushed the contract papers into a bundle as Ethan stood and opened the door to reveal Rico standing in the hallway.

"Your mama is sleeping. Maybe we could talk about the options I told you about?"

*Less fun than my current paperwork,* I thought to myself. This was just as necessary, though, so I nodded.

"Would you rather I stepped out for this?" Ethan asked.

"If you don't mind, I'd really like you to stay," I answered. He sat beside me while Rico sat on the bed on the other side of me.

We went through the options, poring over various pamphlets. I looked closer at the more budget-friendly places, knowing Mom's insurance would only cover 30 percent of the costs. Two places looked good and affordable, but they were well over two hours away. Closer to home meant a higher expense. With my father's inheritance, my account could have supported her for months in a fancy residential living space, but it left little money for much else.

"Perhaps I could look into what's needed at Winding Creek and put her there full time." Ethan leaned in, placing his hands over the pamphlets. "At my disposal."

"She'd need access to specialists from the nearest metropolis. Last I spoke with them, they told me it was out of their budget," I informed him, turning my attention to the pamphlets once more.

"New management," Ethan reminded me. "New budget, new wing, and with me in cahoots with a few hospitals in multiple areas, I think we can make something happen. If you're happy with Winding Creek, that is."

"And the six-month wait? She—we can't wait that long."

"I'll see what I can come up with by the end of the week," Ethan said thoughtfully.

Rico nodded. "If it falls through, we can look at these options as Plan B," he said as Ethan and I looked at each other.

"Alright. We'll hold off until you're done figuring out what you can on your end," I said, taking a deep breath. "By Friday, we should have a firm plan."

"Thank you for doing this," Rico said, hugging me close. "I know it's not easy, but thank you for trusting me on this."

I smiled softly.

"Who else would I trust most concerning Mom's care?" I asked.

"I'm going to go start today's report before lunch." Rico looked

# CHAINS OF SATIN

between the two of us as he stood. "Will you be heading out sometime today or should I make enough for everyone?"

"Might as well make enough. If something comes up it can be set in the fridge for another time."

"Sensible as always, *mija*." Rico smiled and closed the door behind him.

I turned to Ethan, who was sitting silently beside me, looking off into the distance.

"What are you thinking about?"

There was no answer.

"Sir," I said in my most sultry voice, placing a hand high on his thigh. His attention focused on me instantly, and I smiled, victorious. "What were you just thinking about?"

"For *some* reason, I've forgotten," he growled, wrapping a hand around the back of my neck, pulling me close enough for him to nuzzle into it.

"Something had to bring you out of your thoughts; I wouldn't want you to get lost in them," I teased with my eyes closed. "Plus, we have unfinished business."

"The list of unfinished business is growing by the second," he murmured, leaning his forehead against mine and palming one of my breasts. I smiled, the heat of my blush filling my cheeks.

"We'll never get anything else done," I laughed as he went back into kissing my neck.

"Complaining, Pet?" Ethan whispered, his warm breath blowing across my skin caused me to shiver.

"Never," I exhaled.

"Hm." His throat rumbled. "That's my good girl."

He kissed my skin before sitting up and reaching behind me to retrieve the stack of papers that made up the contract between us.

# CHAPTER NINETEEN

## Petunia

THREE DAYS. THAT'S HOW LONG IT TOOK to get Mom a place in what was now Ethan's facility. She would have her own furniture from the house—as much as she could fit, anyways. We included her own mattress nestled in the secured bed frame. Her pictures were hung on the walls, and I was able to bring her easel and paints to set up a permanent art station in the corner of her suite.

Because she was going to be covered under Ethan, Mom was able to get the largest area for her comfort. She had an open-floor plan, almost as large as a studio apartment. The living room was large enough for her couch, rocking chair, and TV stand. The room also had a table facing a large window that looked out over the grounds. It held her paints beside her easel in her new, permanent studio spot. Her bedroom was huge, allowing us to comfortably arrange not only her bed and nightstands, but also a large vanity dresser with reinforced screws in the mirror to prevent it from falling.

On top of all that, Mom came with an entourage when the day came for her to settle in. Aside from myself, Ethan, and Rico, the specialist, Dr. Matthews, was there to greet her. He was a younger doctor, but his credentials were impressive, and he had experience strictly dealing with cases pertaining to Mom's condition. This was the best news of the day.

# CHAINS OF SATIN

Second best, actually. The best news was when we were talking around the living area when Ethan offered to hire Rico on at Winding Creek so he could remain Mom's caretaker. He was offered three times the amount he normally made, though I was sure Rico would have stayed for her without a raise; over time, he became the son my mother never had, and he loved her as much as I did.

When she was finally unpacked and settled, all that was left was to say goodbye to her and let her rest, which I found myself reluctant to do. I knew I was stalling. I knew that I didn't have to sort her paintbrushes or set up her toiletries just so…but I didn't want to leave. Finally, Rico had enough of my fussing and told me under no uncertain terms that Mom needed her rest, and I needed mine.

"I love you, Mom," I said, hugging her tightly.

"I love you too, chickadee." She smiled and patted my cheek. "I'll see you in a few hours."

*Chickadee.* She hadn't called me that since I was a teenager. She was humming the tune she and Ethan had danced to when he walked over and took my hand, leading me out of the door and closing it behind us.

I did fine. I did great, actually. We got as far as two complete city blocks away when the first tears started to form. Another traffic light came and went and I found myself sobbing uncontrollably. Ethan pulled over to the side of the road, got out of the car, then came around to my side. He opened my door and knelt beside me.

My heart was breaking. I had left my mother. I had abandoned her to a place that wasn't home with people that weren't me. Ethan held me tight as I emptied my misery onto his shirt, murmuring words to me that I couldn't hear over the afternoon traffic and my pain.

My guilt tore at me. If both of my legs were in working order, I would have taken the car right then and brought her back home. I begged Ethan, pleaded with him, to turn around. It would save him money and her heartache if he would just bring her home. All the while, he held me close, stroking my hair and waiting for the torrent to stop.

After what seemed like an eternity, Ethan held me at arm's length while I wiped my face with his offered embroidered kerchief.

"When we get to your house there's something I have to give you," he said, kissing my forehead as he stood to close my door.

"I've loved all your gifts and I'm not trying to be ungrateful, but I don't really want anything right now," I said quietly as he got back onto the road, clutching my hand in his.

"It's from your mother." His eyes never left the road as he spoke gently to me.

# DELILAH ST. RIVERS

"My mother?"

"She gave it to me yesterday morning while you bathed. She made me promise to give it to you after we drove back home from taking her. I hated keeping it from you," Ethan continued, pulling my hand up to his lips, "but when a man promises a lady, his honor demands he keep to it."

"Can we please just go back and get her? She can give it to me herself when she's lucid again…" My eyes were burning from all the crying, yet more tears came. "Please?"

Ethan sighed heavily. It wasn't fair to put all this pressure on him, but I knew one day, I would be grateful for his strength. He glanced at me, squeezing my hand as he shook his head.

"I detest that I cannot spare you from this pain. But we must understand this is for the best."

"It's not fair to her."

"I know, sweetheart."

When we arrived home, Ethan helped me in the house and guided me to the worn recliner that we hadn't taken to Mom's new home. He produced a folded piece of paper from the inside pocket of his jacket.

"May I bring you a drink while you read?"

"No," I answered as I took the paper.

"I'll be in the kitchen, should you need me."

I nodded, and with a gentle kiss, he left me alone with a letter from my mother.

*Dearest Chickadee,*

*I don't have the time to share everything I feel with you, so I'll make this as direct as I can. Your gentleman, Ethan, told me about the plan put in place for the future. He explained why and told me of your fight with your conscience over putting me in a home.*

*As your mother first and foremost, I need you to understand that I've never wanted to be a burden to you. The fact that I've been holding you back from living your life for so long leaves me feeling my own guilt. This man, this Ethan, is your future. You won't get anywhere in any aspect of your life, and definitely not with him, if you don't take the reins and start living your life for you. How can I be the mom I've always wanted to be if I get in the way of my own daughter's life?*

*I love you, Petunia. Don't think for a second you have done me any wrong. Don't dwell on your need for my forgiveness; there's nothing to forgive. I couldn't be more proud of how strong and beautiful you've become. You've done so well. Even in my worst moments, there's always a part of me that knows you love me, and I love you. Remember that.*

*I'll see you soon,*
*Mom*

I read and reread the letter until the words blurred and blended

# CHAINS OF SATIN

through my tears. It wasn't long before Ethan was behind me, rubbing my shoulders while I cried.

"I don't know what to do with this."

"With what?" Ethan asked.

"I can't help but feel guilty, but I don't know what to do with it or how I can make it go away. I know she said I shouldn't beat myself up but..."

"I know. I know. You've done so much for her and she acknowledges it. You need to live life, too, darling."

"Thank you for this. I needed to hear it from her. Maybe she knew I wouldn't believe it from anyone else but her."

"Your mother is a rare and spectacular woman, Pet."

I nodded and sat quietly for a moment, taking in the comfort his arms provided me.

"Maybe one day we'll be able to go through an entire week with no drama."

"It's not an idle drama, darling. Your pain is real to you. Tangible. It should be addressed head-on with all the support and patience it requires. Not many people understand, but as long as I breathe, I'll proudly be whatever it is you need to get you through whatever it is you struggle with." Ethan bent over me and planted a kiss on my lips.

"You've been here for a few months," I said, looking up at him after our kiss ended. "All this time you've been my rock. What about your own life? Your own dramas that are drowned out by dealing with mine?"

"One fire burns out another's burning. One pain is lessened by another's anguish. Turn giddy and be holp by backward turning. One desperate grief cures with another's languish." My heart thudded in my chest as he recited Shakespeare, eyes holding my own captive. His words flowed through me as he spoke low and with sincerity.

"Sit with me?" I asked.

Without hesitation, he lifted me to be seated upon his lap. I held my mother's letter against my chest and Ethan wrapped his arms tight around me. I leaned against him as he began to rock in the recliner, sending me drifting off to sleep.

IT WAS ALMOST DARK WHEN I WOKE to find myself alone and covered with a throw blanket in the chair. My mother's letter was pressed flat on the table in front of me, and I smelled something incredible being cooked in the kitchen.

# DELILAH ST. RIVERS

My phone was still buzzing, proving itself to be the culprit of my interrupted sleep.

"Hello?" I answered groggily.

"Hey sugar-tits. So about this weekend…"

"What happened?" I asked Shay, pushing myself to an upright position.

"My car didn't pass inspection so I've got to get it fixed. I don't have a choice, these are my only days off to get it done."

I sighed, rubbed my eyes and pinched the bridge of my nose.

"Hey, it's okay. These things happen, I totally get it."

"I know, but I really wanted to be there for you and catch up on how you're doin'. You never sent me a pic of your flowers either, you dick."

I laughed. "Yeah, they're in my room as we speak," I told her.

"Wait, so he actually sent you flowers? You were right! Were they tiger lilies?"

"No, pink zinnias with some red camellias. They're so pretty."

"Hm," Shay hummed in the phone before becoming quiet altogether.

"What?"

"So, I'm looking them up, red camellia means 'you're the flame of my heart' and the zinnia means 'thinking about an absent friend,' according to this poster you can get on Etsy. Sounds like he's hot for you, but he's keeping you in the friend zone." Shay was getting ready for a battle of words with Ethan, from the way her voice grew harder.

"Or," I laughed, "hear me out…He probably found some that he thought I would love. Not everyone knows flower symbolism."

"Yeah, okay," Shay answered bitterly. "I don't know, though."

"You're awake? How are—oh, I'll head back until you're done with your phone call, darling," Ethan interrupted before kissing me and leaving the room again.

"Hold on a damn second, girlfriend…who was that? Was that him? He's there right now?"

"Yes, he's here. You've missed a bit, but I can fill you in lat—"

"Oh hell no, you're not dropping a bomb on me like that then walking away. Nuh uh! I need the deets!"

"And I plan on telling you, but not right this—"

"Ugh! Okay fine, whatever. But at least tell me…" Shay's voice dropped to almost a whisper. "Did you guys do it? TELL me you guys had sex, at least one time when he got back!"

"Oh my God, seriously?"

"You totally did, didn't you? OH MY GOD you did!"

"I should go, good luck with your car—"

128

# CHAINS OF SATIN

"Come on, don't leave me hanging!"

I sighed and rolled my eyes.

"More like three times. Happy?"

I had to pull the phone away from my ear as Shay squealed.

"Okay, I'm going."

"No no, wait, come on…Tell me, TELL me he was good! Tell me that boy was packing what he was advertising!"

I blushed and looked behind me to make sure Ethan wasn't anywhere within hearing distance.

"I never had so many orgasms over an eighteen hour period in my life," I whispered. I had to pull the phone away again while Shay scream-laughed in joy. "Okay, now I'm really going to go. I love you. Do you need anything to help you?"

"Nah." Shay was still giggling. "You get back to Mr. Darcy—"

"Oh my God, I forgot I called him that," I muttered, my face getting hot.

"Uh huh, that shit was great," Shay laughed again. "But yeah, let me know when the wedding is 'cause I'm coming with bells on!"

"Oh hush," I scolded her.

"You watch, I'm gonna be right! Okay, love you, bye!"

"Ugh, you're exhausting," I laughed and hung up the phone.

I grabbed my crutches and met Ethan in the kitchen. He greeted me with a smile and hugged me gently so I didn't lose my balance.

"Dinner, darling," he said, gesturing widely.

"This is almost too pretty to eat," I laughed. I stared down at the two plates piled with lobster tails, shrimp alfredo with fettuccine, and broccoli. I looked back and found Ethan staring at me before I added, "Almost."

"My sentiments exactly," he growled, kissing me.

I blushed as he winked and pulled a chair out for me to sit. He sat across from me and we dug in, the quiet broken only by my happy sounds as each bite elicited almost wanton moans from my mouth. Paired with his expertly chosen white wine, it was an applause-worthy dinner.

"I would ask if this has been to your satisfaction, but I fear I'd find your answer to be a touch redundant," Ethan said as he sat back in his chair. The fork from his hand made a soft "tink" as he set it on his plate. I smiled.

"I'm in awe, really," I said, sitting back against my own chair.

"Then I shall declare it a success." Ethan grinned. "If you'll excuse me, I'll be but a moment."

He kissed me and headed up the stairs. My eyes followed him until he was out of sight, and then I started clearing the table. I'd no sooner

# DELILAH ST. RIVERS

set dishes into the sink when I felt his arms reach around my waist from behind, pressing his body against mine.

"Leave it to me, darling," he whispered against my exposed neck. He scooped me up, taking me upstairs to the bathtub and setting me on the closed toilet. "Can you manage here while I take care of the kitchen?"

"Yes, but I would have been happy to help you clean. You did cook."

Ethan shook his head.

"You've had a trying day, full of emotion. I have everything taken care of, including you."

"Thank you," I sighed and wrapped my arms around his waist, pressing the side of my head against him.

"Hush, Pet. It's only courtesy. I must admit, I'm still finding your excessive gratitude for the most simple things a bit off-putting." Ethan sighed and sunk into the embrace, wrapping his arms around me tighter. "In time you'll see what it is like when you are treated the way you truly deserve. But first, bathe. Call out if you need help."

He kissed my head and walked back down the stairs.

## CHAPTER TWENTY

# *Petunia*

THE NEXT MORNING I WOKE UP FIRST. I couldn't fight the uneasiness that settled into my stomach, as though something was terribly out of place in my mother's house. Unable to shake it by just lying there, I slipped out of bed and carefully made my way down the stairs, looking forward to easing my nerves with Rico's signature coffee.

The dark silence that greeted me in the kitchen momentarily confused me before a tidal wave of realization hit me at full force, practically knocking the wind right out of me.

Mom. Rico. They weren't there. It wasn't Mom's home anymore. I pulled a chair from the table and sat, the full weight of finality heavy on my thoughts. I hadn't taken into account what it meant to be in my parents' home without them there. I rested my elbows on the table and let my head fall to my hands. For the first time in my life I had no idea what to do.

*Coffee,* I decided. *When in doubt, coffee.* I got up and before long, my hands were wrapped tight around my favorite mug of steaming liquid, and I could smile for the first time since I'd woken up.

"I do love waking up to the smell of coffee," Ethan said, kissing my cheek before pouring himself a cup. He sat across from me, looking at me intently before chuckling and sipping from his cup.

"What?" I asked.

"I'm just trying to decide if you look sexier straight out of bed in the morning or just before you give into your lust."

I gave him a flirty grin.

"Have you decided?"

"Yes, actually," Ethan stated as he rose from his seat to refill my emptied cup.

"And what did you decide?"

"Why do you want to know?"

It took me a second to answer; several responses ran through my mind before I decided upon one.

"Perhaps," I said, dropping my voice to a seductive whisper to catch his full attention, "I'd like to better know the preference of my Lord and Master. Well, the man who *will* be my Lord and Master when the contract is officially signed." I put on my best demure smile while batting my eyelashes at Ethan.

"Hm," Ethan sighed deeply, the sound deepening into a low growl. "'Lord and Master.' You're going to have to be careful, Pet. That's borderline bratty behavior."

I couldn't stop the smirk as it spread across my face.

"That would be the case," I began, running my fingers around the rim of my coffee cup, "*if* I *fully* belonged to you."

He smirked and slowly made his way around the table. He knelt in front of me, slowly turning my chair until my knees were directly under his chin.

"*Fully* mine?" Ethan asked.

I smirked again, my eyes locked on his beautiful blues. He traced a finger around my naked kneecap so lightly that I could barely feel it.

"Do you think that you're safe from that claim because you haven't signed that silly contract yet? Do you deny the hold my touch has over you?" The malice in his eyes as he bent to kiss my knee sent a chill through my body. Ethan's smile grew wider. "Even as you tremble beneath my touch, you still question to whom you belong? Perhaps I need to be a bit more convincing."

*Oh shit.*

One hand trailed up my thigh while his other moved to guide my legs open. Further up he danced his fingertips until he was tracing the outside of my underwear, feeling the flesh beneath as my excitement dampened the cloth. All the while, I watched him with increased breathing, his eyes never leaving mine.

His lips curled into a sneer as he slowly, intimately began to stroke me through the fabric.

# CHAINS OF SATIN

"Tell me, lovely girl, have you always been so eager for a delicate touch? Do you always get so wet from the promise of penetration?" He fingered the elastic that held fast against my thigh, prying it away from my skin ever-so-slowly, teasing the warm, moist flesh underneath. I let out a little noise and closed my eyes, only to have them snap open as Ethan sunk in his teeth just above my knee.

"Eyes open, Pet," he cooed, placing a kiss on the offended spot.

I could do nothing but gasp in response as I obeyed. He smirked, that devilish glint in his eyes as he pushed his hand deeper beneath the fabric and stroked the bundle of sensitive nerves, nearly sending me over the edge.

"God!" I cried out, my body burning at the slight pressure he put onto me.

"No, *Princess*. Not even God himself can save you from me," Ethan snarled.

My insides ached for his touch as he continued to tease and tantalize in a steady rhythm, never with enough pressure to give me that ultimate peak. The burn began to intensify, and my pussy flexed and wept on his fingers. I whimpered as the need for release grew. And still Ethan stroked gently, steadily.

"Hold still, my Pet. No touching or moving, else you won't get your reward."

My whimpers grew with my need. He looked on, waiting with that infinite patience of his, and I began to pant loudly, sweating at the exertion of the moment. His other hand began to ghost-touch my thigh, matching the movement of his hand in my underwear.

Finally, I broke.

"Please," I whispered.

"Please, what?"

"Please...sir," I gasped. "God, I need to come..." I squeezed my eyes shut.

Immediately Ethan's teeth sunk into my thigh and my eyes flew back open to look down at him.

"You know what you must do to help with that, darling," Ethan whispered, sounding almost eager himself. I kept quiet, savoring his touch against my skin, not-so-secretly loving the burn of desire that flowed from the both of us.

"Tell me...tell me what other person could you possibly trust to give you satisfaction?"

"Please," I repeated softly, shaking my head. I needed release so bad, but I also wanted him to push me further.

"Whom else could you lay down arms with and place all your hopes and dreams upon? Tell me, dear girl, to whom do you *truly* belong?" His voice dipped into a growl at the end of the question and I sighed. He reached up with his free hand and palmed my breast, rolling the peaked nipple between his fingers.

"Tell me, *Princess*. Tell me and I'll grant you your sweet release. Deny me..." He bent and pressed his teeth around my nipple before replacing it once again with his fingers. "*Defy* me and I could keep this up. For *hours*. How long can you last, quivering, sweating, *wanting*, before you finally relent?"

Ethan kept his eyes locked on mine as he wrapped his lips around my clothed breast, the heat of his mouth enveloping my skin. My pussy pulsated hard with need and I snapped.

"You," I breathed.

"Elaborate. What about me?"

"You, I belong to you, I'm yours, fully yours. Plea—"

My words fell short as Ethan slipped two fingers inside me, using his thumb to pick up the pressure and pace of his attention to my sensitive clit.

Pumping his fingers deep inside me, he leaned up to whisper in my ear, "Good girl. Be sure to yell my name; I love hearing it from your lips." He replaced his teeth gently on my nipple, sending me soaring higher and higher until I finally cried out his name, grabbing onto his shoulders. I rode wave after wave of my pent-up orgasm while Ethan never broke the stride of his fingers.

It took an eternity to come down from the climax that left me spent and panting in my chair. Ethan studied my features. He pulled his fingers from me and placed them into his opened mouth, sucking the juices of his victory until they were practically dry. He grabbed me by my throat and shoved his tongue into my mouth, growling "*mine*" against my lips.

I trembled and shook in his arms, wrapping my own around him and meeting his lips with the same intensity, my heart pounding against my ribcage. His hair was locked in my hands as we kissed, the curls soft and thick in my fingers.

Deeper and deeper the kiss went. Moans and sighs passed between us until I felt a surge of adrenaline rush through me and I pulled his head back, exposing his thick neck, and mimicking the same movement he'd used on me countless times before. After a pregnant pause, I sunk my own teeth into his flesh.

He groaned but didn't move until I let him go.

"I'm yours," I whispered in his ear before I pressed my tongue

## CHAINS OF SATIN

against his neck and slid it upwards to suck his earlobe. His hands tightened around my waist. "I'm all yours, Ethan. But don't think for a second that you don't belong to me, too."

Ethan pulled away to look at me, his eyes piercing mine dangerously. We sat like that for an unknown length of time, gasping and staring at each other, the sexual tension so thick you could almost taste it. Finally, Ethan raised his hand and gently stroked my cheek, smiling softly.

"This," he said, kissing me tenderly. "This look right here, you raw with desire and possession? This is by far my favorite."

## CHAPTER TWENTY-ONE

# Petunia

IT TOOK A FEW DAYS FOR ETHAN and I to finish going over and finalizing our contract. We learned a lot about each other's likes and dislikes, how gently or rough either of us could take it, and what we liked outside of the bedroom. It was during this exchange that Ethan discovered my love of tiger lilies.

Ethan spent the morning we were to finalize the contract and have it reviewed by a lawyer making sure I had a wonderful breakfast and a back rub after a nice, hot bath. He even presented me with a beautiful set of sapphire earrings.

After signing, we agreed the contract would be valid two weeks later. Ethan also was going to use that time to help me with the whole housing situation, now that I had full power of attorney over my mother and her financial and medical rights. I did my best to include her in selling her home, but her responses to the subject varied from day to day. I realized it was better for all involved if we just moved ahead without her input.

"You're so patient, it's just…incredible how patient you are with me," I told Ethan once we came back to my house. "Normally it's hard with so many obstacles; most would walk away. And to wait for the contract to go into effect, rather than forcing the situation like I'm used to, is incredibly generous of you."

# CHAINS OF SATIN

"Would you rather have it in full effect right now?" Ethan cocked an eyebrow at me, his eyes full of laughter as they locked onto mine.

"No, I understand the importance of waiting; I'm not complaining at all, trust and believe. It's practical of you. I'm just reminded once again how very remarkable you are."

He brushed my hair back and bent to kiss me. I swear on my life I'd never been kissed so sweetly, so often, or so well.

"It is no more than what you deserve, Pet. What would you say to going out for dinner tonight?"

My stomach dropped, and I looked down at my feet.

"What is it?"

"I haven't gone out since I got hurt. I mean it's awkward with the crutches, but not even that..." I trailed off.

"Are you afraid, darling?"

"Not...not exactly? I'm kind of put off because of what happened."

"You don't speak very often about that night, Petunia." All teasing left Ethan's voice. "Would you like to?"

"Do I have a choice?" I asked, remembering the last time he asked that question. He cupped my cheek with his palm.

"In this you do, love."

*Ugh, why did that make me want to open up to him even more?* I sighed.

"I feel like the whole night was a disaster. We were so careful, we always were. Even though you hear the horror stories, you never think it's going to happen to you. You always think you're too smart or experienced for this to ever happen to you.

"And then it does. You pass out in one place and wake up in another—no memories of how you got there, what happened to you, or why. Even though I wasn't raped, I still feel so violated. Just the thought that it could have been so much worse makes me want to never go out again."

"To the very best of my ability, Pet, I understand. To be frank, it's enough to put me off seeing you go out alone ever again. My desire to be by your side at all times has increased a thousandfold since that night." Ethan looked down at our now-joined hands. "When I saw you fall, surrounded by those...barbarians, I felt murderous. I wanted to tear them apart for hurting you.

"You can't imagine the torment of guilt that followed when the doctor disclosed your diagnosis," Ethan stated quietly before kissing my knuckles.

"Guilt? Why would you of all people feel guilty? It's not like it was your fault any more than it was my friend's."

"You'd come to my home before going there. Had you stayed longer or—"

"Don't. Please don't do that to yourself. The only ones to blame are the assholes who did it. Not you, not her, not even me. Them."

Ethan sighed and squeezed my hands gently before looking up at me.

"Allow me this once to apologize, Petunia." He caressed my cheek, his eyes pleading. "I'm so sorry you went through such devastating events. Forgive me for being unable to protect you from the ugliness of humanity."

I wrapped my arms around his shoulders and pulled him close in an embrace, barely noticing the tears trailing down my cheeks.

"You're forgiven. Of course you're forgiven," I said, closing my eyes and kissing his neck.

Ethan pulled back and took my face into his hands.

"I'll have you know that nothing like that will ever happen to you again. You'll never have a need to feel unsafe, unprotected another day of your life. I swear to you."

"I know. I think I just need a bit more time before I go out. Even the thought of going out to eat makes me feel queasy."

Ethan sighed sadly.

"Damn them for causing you such trauma. Would that I could take it from you."

"We could always order in and watch a movie," I offered.

"Of course, my darling." He gave me a small smile. "What would you like to do beforehand?"

I thought for a moment.

"Visit my mom. I know she's okay, I just miss her."

"You don't have to justify it, my dear. Of course you should see her. I have a few things to tend to myself. Shall I pick you up at a designated time, or would you like to call me when you're ready to leave?"

"I'll call you," I said.

"Very well, Pet. Would you like help getting ready for the day?" He rose and handed me my crutches.

"No, thank you. It won't take me long." I stood and leaned into him for another kiss, which he readily obliged. "I could spend an entire day just kissing you."

Ethan chuckled.

"Perhaps at some point we may be able to make that happen, though I'd recommend chapstick to avoid abrasions."

Ethan's phone chimed, and he checked the text message and sighed.

"Duty calls, darling. I'll send a driver to collect you when you're

# CHAINS OF SATIN

ready, but, unfortunately, I must leave immediately." He kissed me once again before running upstairs to change. I took care of the coffee cups and rinsed out the pot. I was wiping off the counter when Ethan came back down and swept me up for another kiss.

"Can't get enough?" I teased as he headed out the door.

"Never," he admitted with a wink and a smile before closing the door behind him. Giggling and blushing, I took a deep breath and finished the countertop, then decided to call before I showed up to visit my mother.

"It's not a good time, *mija*," Rico said after answering.

"Is she having a bad day?"

"It's her usual lately. She's resting now; she got violent earlier. She may be out for the day, so I wouldn't want you to waste the trip."

"Alright, I understand. Thanks, Rico. I'm grateful you're there for her."

I sighed. I didn't have to deal with the whole mom situation first-hand anymore, but it was still hard knowing she was going through this and that it was never going to get better. I hung up with Rico after promising to visit another day and sat with my phone in my hands for a bit before deciding to call an Uber to head to Ethan's to surprise him.

Fifteen minutes later, I was walking carefully up the steps to his door. Amelia's friendly face greeted me and she took my coat.

"Mr. Aldrich is with a visitor in the study at the moment, love," she told me with a kind smile on her face.

"I'll just peek my head in to let him know I'm here," I whispered back, smiling. "I love surprising him."

I headed towards the door of Ethan's office and discovered, much to my piqued curiosity, that his door was slightly ajar. Ethan's voice drifted through the opening as I got closer to my target.

"...two years. What did you think would happen?"

"That you'd renew it, of course." The woman's voice was low, and her accent was the same as Ethan's. "It doesn't appear that you have another contract in place, so why not?"

I took a deep breath and decided not to linger in the doorway. I tapped lightly on the door before pushing it open and walking in. Ethan's look of annoyance quickly vanished when he recognized me as the intruder and he stood from his chair.

"Darling. Is everything alright?" He met me halfway and planted a kiss on my lips.

"I couldn't visit Mom today — sedatives were involved again. I may go visit tomorrow." I looked between him and the woman seated in front of his large oak desk. "I'm not trying to interrupt, I just wanted to let you

# DELILAH ST. RIVERS

know I was here. I can go—"

"Nonsense," Ethan interrupted, taking my hand. "You're always welcome here. Sit."

"What is this?" The woman's green eyes looked me over before looking back at Ethan.

"Forgive me," he said, returning to his chair after I'd been made comfortable. "You've come in with such a flurry I haven't had the chance to explain. Madeline, allow me to introduce you to Petunia. She and I are contracted in a similar fashion as you and I were."

I blinked in surprise, but recovered quickly. Of course he'd have a history of these arrangements; I just didn't expect to meet someone from his past contracts. I extended my hand to her which made her lip curl as though I was offering her a dead fish.

"It's nice to meet you, Madeline."

"Seriously, dearest, what is this? Are you putting me on? Not once did you mention you were with someone else."

"Technically we aren't going into effect for two weeks," I volunteered.

"Oh yes, our contract was pages long, it would take two weeks to go through." Madeline rolled her eyes.

"Actually," I stated, "we already signed it. It just won't take effect for two weeks."

"What ever are you delaying for? Are you getting a divorce, dear girl? An abortion perhaps?" She turned to Ethan before I could say a word. "Really, you ought to be careful taking in the lower class—"

Ethan slammed his closed fist against the desk, glaring at her.

"Enough. The details of my life, or hers, are not your concern." His voice never rose above speaking volume, but the deep rumble in his chest caused my heart to pick up speed.

"Whatever." Madeline settled in her chair. Her white dress suit shifted higher to show off more of her thighs, the movement appearing to be a calculated one. "You have a sub. It's not so unusual for a dom to have more than one."

"Yeah," I scoffed. "That's not happening."

Madeline's eyes shot in my direction.

"Since when do you speak for Ethan, little one?"

"I've properly introduced you both," Ethan growled. "So I invite you to use her name. As for your proposal, Petunia is correct. I will not take you on; even if she were not mine I would not. Our time is done, Madeline. Amelia can show you to the door once you leave the office."

Madeline looked me up and down again.

# CHAINS OF SATIN

"What happened here, dearie?" She pointed to my leg.

"I fell," I answered, looking back at Ethan, confused. *Why won't she just go?*

"You're broken before the contract is in place; you won't survive long." Madeline shook her head and leaned over to pat my hand. "And think of a less clichéd lie, sweet pea. I know how carried away he can get."

Ethan's face drained of all color, but it was me who spoke first.

"If you honestly believe he could do such a thing, then we are clearly talking about two different people. He helped me so much through a bad time, before we even started having sex —"

"Petunia —"

"And excuse me, but how dare you? So what if you knew Ethan in the past? You don't get to make assumptions about how he treats me or what he does for me, ever."

"Assumptions? And how dare I?" Madeline laughed incredulously. "Do you have any clue in that little American head of yours who I am? I'm nineteenth in line for the throne. I have money, means, and a pedigree going back hundreds of years."

"And yet no class," I said, my irritation finally showing. "Why are you here? There's no room for you in this relationship, so why haven't you left yet? Have we not made it clear to you where you stand?"

"Relationship?" She laughed harder. "Clearly you don't understand how he works. Ethan lusts after you, draws you up a six-month contract to sign, gets his use out of you, then sends you on your way. You don't really think he could form an actual *relationship* with you, do you? I mean, you don't think he actually could *love* you, do you?"

Visions of me bashing her face off the desk danced behind my eyes while the rest of my traitor face turned beet red.

"Oh my Lord, you poor thing," Madeline said, her voice gentle, almost concerned. "You actually think he has romantic inclinations." Her hands covered her mouth and she shot a glare at Ethan. "You've been known to be cruel on occasion, Ethan, but this is just inhumane. You took a poor, inexperienced girl and made her believe you were going to be her soulmate. How can you even —"

"I'm not inexperienced," I said coldly, having finally found my tongue. "I've been with the personification of inhumane, a man who did god-awful things that left permanent damage to me in every way. I know evil, Madeline. Ethan has been nothing but kind to me since I met him. You on the other hand..."

I left the sentence to finish itself. I rose from my seat and used my crutches to walk around the desk to sit upon Ethan's lap.

"Pet?" Ethan looked right into my eyes with nothing but confusion.

I shushed him gently before holding his face in my hands and bringing his mouth to mine. The kiss deepened and he inhaled sharply, his cock growing hard against my ass. I pulled away, kissing his nose and then forehead while he rubbed my arms. I turned to look at Madeline's horrified face.

"You have no place here. I hope there's no further misunderstanding," I growled while Ethan's lips found my neck.

"You've seduced him," Madeline whispered accusingly. "I thought he…but it's you. You're after him for what, money? You're whoring yourself out for a few dollars?"

Ethan ripped his mouth from my neck and glared at her with death in his eyes.

"You've come here unannounced. You've insulted me, my choices, and my companion IN MY OWN HOME!" I jumped as he shouted. "Get out, Madeline. Get out. And should you consider returning, I'll have you detained for trespassing." Ethan turned to focus back onto me.

"I'm sorry, my darling." His hand brushed my cheek and he nuzzled against me, our visitor no longer existing in our realm, even as she sat, glued by shock and disappointment, in her chair, speechless.

Our lips met, and all I knew was the smell of that incredible cologne, the taste of his mouth, and the feel of his hands as they roamed my back.

"I could take you right now. Your ferocity…your possessiveness… God, I adore you," he moaned, burying his face back into my neck.

I didn't know exactly when Madeline left. All I knew for the next hour or so was Ethan's mouth, his body, and then his name escaping my lips as we both reached our climaxes, right on his giant oak desk.

***

"YOU FIND MORE AND MORE WAYS TO impress me," Ethan said, helping me stand and fix my skirt, my leggings forgotten on the floor. "This is a side of you I certainly didn't expect."

"Did you think she'd scare me off?"

"I'd hoped not, but I sometimes forget the tigress that lies behind those pretty, submissive eyes of yours. Today, I find myself in awe and grateful for your tenacity, Pet." He kissed my hands tenderly and led me out of his office.

"I wonder though," I said, stopping at the living room and looking up at him, "if she'd succeeded and I left —"

"You could never have gotten far, my darling." Ethan pressed a

# CHAINS OF SATIN

finger to my lips to silence me, then ran his thumb across my jaw. "I would have truly let you go if you sincerely wanted to, but I would have at least sought you out to have that conversation first."

I kissed his thumb as he ran it back across my bottom lip and smiled.

"Was she your important business?" I asked.

"Heavens, no. That insulting intrusion interrupted my original reason for leaving in such haste."

"Which was what, if you don't mind me asking?"

"Not at all." Ethan kissed my head. "It was finding a buyer for your house, incidentally."

I looked at him in surprise. After a moment of stunned silence Ethan grew concerned.

"What is it, darling? I thought it would be good news."

"Can we sit?" I gestured to the plush couch. He nodded and led the way.

"Okay, look," I began as I set my crutches to the side once I had gotten comfortable beside Ethan. "I've lived in that house all my life. And I'm so grateful that you have all these connections at your fingertips that you can get the ball rolling, but you can't lock me out of the process. I'm not saying 'don't do it,' but I am asking that you let me be a part of selling the house."

"I seem to have been a touch overzealous in this project, Pet, and for that I apologize," Ethan said, looking down at his hands. "I shall make amends immediately. Please, wait here." Ethan went into his office and came out holding his smartphone. He quickly opened it to his company's website where my house was listed. "There are two people who are interested. Their agents are standing by to see who has the highest bid."

"Two!" I exclaimed. "Is that normal in such a short time?" My curiosity was getting the best of my apprehension as I looked at the listing.

"Would you like to sit in on the conversation?" Ethan asked, excited as a kid showing off a new toy. He really did love this part of his job.

"Please. I don't know much about it all, but I want to listen in anyways."

He dialed a number and switched to speakerphone. He received a number much higher than the asking price, told the agent he'd have an answer shortly, then repeated the process with someone on another line through a dual-number conference.

It turned into a bidding war, each line producing a higher amount than the previous one. At one point I was sure he'd forgotten I was there when he began pacing the living room, giving lavish descriptions of my home to each bidder. His passion was awe-inspiring.

# DELILAH ST. RIVERS

When the second bidder finally dropped out, we were left with an offer that was almost twice the original asking price. I was blown away. Ethan hung up the phone with the winning bidder, telling them they'll have their answer within the day. His hands were holding mine as he sat beside me to talk face-to-face.

"Do you accept the winning bid? Is this something you're truly ready for? I could end this now until you're ready and not give a damn, darling. It's entirely up to you."

It was a long while until I answered him. I was scared to take this leap with him, having never been to this stage with anyone in years, let alone completely without the safety net of my parents' house to return to. The thought of someone else owning my childhood home made me feel a little nauseated.

"My darling girl," he said softly. "I know we haven't known each other for very long. I know we've been rather unconventional with the pursuit of our companionship, but I have only your best interests at heart. If money is a concern, I took the liberty of acquiring your bank information so any and all money from this sale will go straight to you. Should the unexpected happen, you'll have security for your future."

Best intentions or not, I couldn't help but feel as though he overstepped. *How did he even get ahold of my bank information?* I took a deep breath and decided it wasn't worth a battle. Yet.

"Will you take a commission for being the seller?" I asked.

"No, Pet. Each and every penny will go directly to you, I swear."

"Then I refuse," I stated. He looked taken aback. "I won't go through with it unless you promise to take a commission. You put in the work, you should be paid."

"Darling, I don't need it," Ethan insisted softly.

I pulled my hands from his and sat back away from him.

"I don't care. It's the principle," I said, crossing my arms in front of my chest.

Ethan studied me, a small smile growing across his face.

"Are these your terms?"

I nodded. His smile threw me off, but I remained stern.

"Then I have no choice but to accept them." He held out his hand to me, and I took it, shaking firmly.

With a motion almost too fast to register, he pulled me to him as he fell back onto the couch, laying me squarely over his body.

"You're truly going to be alright, living here? Doing this?" Ethan asked, one arm around my waist while he pushed my hair from my face with his free hand.

144

# CHAINS OF SATIN

"I'm sure of it," I answered, pressing my forehead against his. "I might be a little sad for a bit, but I want this with you."

I rubbed my nose against his.

"That's an odd sensation," Ethan chuckled.

"What, you've never had an Eskimo kiss before?"

"Er, no," he laughed. "It was admittedly quite adorable, but I prefer the French way."

He guided my lips to meet his and spent quite a bit of time proving it.

## CHAPTER TWENTY-TWO

# *Petunia*

WHEN THE DAY CAME TO LEAVE MY childhood home behind, I handed the well-worn keys to the new owner and couldn't believe that all my time in those four walls was just…gone.

I stood outside the home and pictured all the things that happened during my lifetime while I lived in the home with my parents. The fights. The movie nights. The time Mom and I tried making a cake without a recipe and we ended up just making a mess. Snowball fights. Renovating the bathroom, just to have someone professional come in and redo everything because Dad wasn't as handy with installing a toilet as he thought. Dad's cancer diagnosis. Mom's condition. Nurses. Crying at night the first time my mother forgot who I was.

And just like that, it wasn't mine anymore.

Should I have waited till I knew Ethan more? Was I giving over too much too soon? Ethan had never done anything wrong to me; he'd never shown the slightest aggression, but I had never left everything to him, either. I'd never given complete control over every aspect of my life. Was I ready for this?

He did what he said he would with the money for the house, minus the commission he'd reluctantly taken.

*But if he had the ability to give money to my bank account, does that mean*

# CHAINS OF SATIN

*he has the ability to take it away too? Restrict it, much like...No.* I shook my head. *That's paranoia. Ethan can't change anything in my account without my signature.* We'd fine-tooth-combed over the contract together, and my copy stayed in a private lock box that Ethan didn't have access to at his insistence. There weren't any hidden clauses that allowed him to somehow gain power of attorney over me.

When we finally pulled into the driveway of my new home, I took a deep breath before unbuckling and opening my door. Ethan exited and came to my side to promptly shut my door. I frowned up at him through the window and was even more confused when he opened it again.

"We aren't going to begin this new stage in our lives without chivalry, are we?" Ethan asked as a small smile graced his lips.

I grinned in understanding, shaking my head as I lifted my arms behind me to reach for the crutches. Instead, Ethan wrapped his arms around my body and lifted me, carrying me through the opened door, and thanking Amelia for opening it as we passed through.

"Dinner smells good," I said through my giggles.

"Are you hungry, then?" Ethan asked, standing in the middle of the foyer.

I nodded, and he swung me around to carry me into the dining room, setting me gently onto the chair at the end of the table. He kissed the top of my head before sitting beside me.

Amelia brought out two steaming plates of lamb chops with an arugula pear salad and garden peas on the side. It was beautifully arranged, a message I relayed to Amelia herself. She blushed and thanked me for the compliment before bowing out of the room.

Ethan smiled at me.

"What?"

"It's going to be common, being served like this. If you get accustomed, would you lose your sense of propriety and manners, I wonder?" Ethan asked thoughtfully.

"It's doubtful," I said. "I mean, I'd try not to. I don't want to be one of those Miss Priss chicks who go Karen on everyone who tries to make their lives better, that's for sure."

Ethan chuckled as he ate. I took a bite of the meat and rolled my eyes.

"No, I don't think I could ever take food like this for granted."

"I imagine the events of the day were pretty overwhelming for you."

I sighed. "My imagination goes pretty dark sometimes and I have to remind myself constantly that you're a safe space for me. It's not easy to let my guard down, and it's equally scary to hand over the keys to a home

147

DELILAH ST. RIVERS

that I had full control over. 'Cause let's face it, even at the end there, I was the one who ran things."

Ethan nodded as he chewed. "One could understand that position. I'm certain if the roles had been reversed, I would feel the same." He looked back up at me. "For a moment, anyways."

We ate in relative silence until our plates were emptied. Ethan got up first.

"Shall we retire to the living room? I could put on a movie and we could relax on the sofa?" He held out his hand to me, helping me rise and adjust the crutches so I could move easily with them.

"That sounds heavenly," I answered, though I knew I wasn't going to make it through the entire movie. I hadn't mentioned it much to Ethan, but I'd started taking a pain pill through the last couple of days. I'd pushed myself far too hard and I'd go to bed with my leg aching from the excursions. He'd commented once or twice about how well I'd slept those nights, but I didn't tell him about it, for fear he'd think it was a setback and worry.

The movie played through, and as I predicted, I fell asleep at some point. I woke the next morning to find myself in Ethan's bed.

Our bed. God, that was weird.

Ethan was still asleep; it was one of the few times I caught myself waking before him, and I smiled. It was nice. Something about seeing him unguarded, without any expression on his face was like seeing him as a clean slate, untouched by the day's stressors or worries. He was beautiful to look at no matter what time of day I was looking, but he was angelic in his sleep.

I shifted slightly, my hip a little sore, when I realized I'd been changed into a nightgown. Ethan rolled over and wrapped his arm around me, pulling me close while tucking his other arm under my head to place his hand on my chest. He buried his face into my hair and took a deep breath. I closed my eyes and smiled.

"Good morning, my darling," Ethan murmured.

"Good morning," I answered quietly.

"Is it?"

"I think so?"

"Hmmm…" His rumbling purr vibrated his chest against my back. "Amelia found your prescription in your pocket after I'd taken the liberty of changing your clothing."

*Shit.*

"I don't think I'll need them much anymore," I explained. "I think I just overdid it."

"How you feel and manage the pain of your injury is nothing to be

148

# CHAINS OF SATIN

ashamed of, my sweet," Ethan said as he kissed the back of my neck. "It was a grievous thing, and you shouldn't feel as though you have any reason to hide things like this. I won't think less of you, darling. One day you'll be able to know this instinctively."

"I hope so," I admitted. I snuggled deeper into him, immediately learning that his mind wasn't the only part of him to have woken up just then.

"If you keep doing that, we're going to have to stay in bed the whole day," Ethan warned darkly.

"What's so bad about that?" I asked him, wiggling my ass against his morning wood.

"Temptress," he growled, his hand moving from my waist to my ass cheek, palming it before squeezing gently.

"Seriously, would that be so wrong? What if we stayed the whole day in bed, had our meals —"

"No food in bed, darling."

"Are you sure about that?" I asked, wiggling once more. His grip on me tightened and the rumble in his chest grew louder. "I'd get rest, you'd be able to spend our first entire day living together with me, and my poor little leg wouldn't hurt so badly."

Ethan's hand slid down behind me, and he lifted up the skirt of my gown, sliding his fingers into me slowly.

"You're so wet, you naughty thing. You've been thinking about this a while, haven't you?"

"I don't need to have dirty thoughts consciously around you, you're sex on legs," I moaned, loving the girth of his fingers penetrating me. He chuckled darkly before shifting his legs and mine to line himself up with me, sinking his teeth into my neck the same moment he sunk his cock into my body. The double sensation set me off almost immediately and I cried out, my hand flying up into his hair from behind while he thrust into me mercilessly.

"Fuck, baby," Ethan panted out. "God, you're so good."

"Ethan," I moaned, feeling the pressure build as he kept pace and began stroking my clit.

"Right there?"

"Yeah."

"You want it, baby?"

"God, yes."

"Unleash hell, *Princess*. Fucking come all over me," he grunted in my ear. The cord snapped inside me, and I felt the warm gush coat the both of us. "That's it, darling, that's it. Do it again for me, come on."

I felt as though I could do it for days on end, soaking our bed, drenching our skin in our lovemaking.

"You sing so pretty for me," Ethan moaned, moving his hand from between my legs to wrap around my breast. Gently he squeezed and slid his other hand up to my mouth. I sucked hard at his thumb while he gasped, thrusting erratically inside me. "I'm going to come, darling. Fuck, Pet, I'm going to come so hard."

And he did. Not seconds later he was groaning in my ear while his dick spasmed.

When he stilled, he kept himself inside while nuzzling my neck and kissing my skin wherever he could reach.

"How about that idea of staying in bed all day?" I whispered, barely able to catch my breath as I felt him soften within.

"Consider me thoroughly convinced," Ethan said, his own breath hard to catch by the sound of it.

"Breakfast or bath first?" I asked, beating Ethan to the punch.

"Is napping out of the question, darling?"

I laughed and turned to look back at him.

"No, sir. Calories spent must be replenished so they can be spent again," I recited as best as I could from memory.

"Using my own words against me, love?" Ethan raised his head, one eyebrow cocked.

"At least you know I listen," I laughed.

He kissed my shoulder and laid his head back down. After a moment, he turned to the phone on the nightstand and lifted the receiver to order us a breakfast that would sustain us for the entire day, in my opinion. I rose and went to the restroom, returning as he replaced the receiver.

"It's been in my room this entire time, yet I confess this was the first time I've ever ordered food for the bedroom."

"I suppose I should be flattered," I said as I climbed back into the bed and snuggled into his arms.

"Tremendously," Ethan growled in my ear.

I laughed and he kissed my cheek. After a moment of silence, I realized something.

"You know, it's a pity you don't have a television in your room."

"Why on earth would I consider such a thing?"

"We could watch romantic movies and make love whenever the mood strikes us, like teens in a movie theater," I suggested.

"Darling, I have a home theater," Ethan said. "We could just do that in there."

"That would defeat the purpose of declaring today a day of being in

# CHAINS OF SATIN

bed, wouldn't it?" I said.

"Damn," Ethan whispered in my ear.

"What?"

"Now that the idea is in my head, I'm finding it difficult to think of a good reason against it. If you could give me a moment, darling, we will have to pause our venture for this day and resume in, say, twenty minutes?"

"Alright. But you'll have to make up for it," I teased. I felt his hand sneak around me and squeeze my breast, first one, then the other.

"Have no fear, Pet, I have the perfect plan in mind."

At minute fourteen, our breakfast was delivered. Minute fifteen found Ethan back in bed with me, snuggling while picking at the fruit and french toast sticks. We started being silly, feeding each other and kissing between bites. He dragged a piece of pineapple up my neck and followed it with his tongue when there was a knock at the door, right at about eighteen minutes and thirty seconds. I groaned in Ethan's mouth, his tongue tasting like pineapple and my skin, a combination I didn't think I'd ever grow tired of.

"Come in," Ethan called, cupping my face and kissing me before turning to meet the intruders.

I'd expected a maid, or Amelia. I didn't expect to see two moving guys bring in a giant TV box and a wall mount kit.

"Ethan?" I looked at him questioningly. Realizing how naked I still was, I pulled the blanket up to my shoulders.

"Whatever my darling wants. How am I for time? Did they get here within the twenty minutes I promised?" He kissed my nose as I looked at the time on my cell.

"As far as I could tell," I said as I watched the men quickly assemble and program a new 75-inch TV on the wall facing the bed.

"All yours, sir," one of them said, tossing the remote onto the bed at Ethan's feet.

"I thank you, gentlemen. Your company's reputation is well-deserved. Amelia will see you out." Ethan gestured to the housekeeper who stood at the bedroom door. Both men bid their goodbyes and we were once again alone.

Alone to kiss each other senseless through the day while we flipped back and forth through the movies and binge-worthy series that peppered various streaming services. Alone to forgo watching anything as our attention was distracted by each other's bodies, crashing the breakfast platter onto the floor as we tangled up the sheets more than once; first urgent and wild, then slow and passionate.

"You are a wonder," Ethan gasped in my ear after a particularly

# DELILAH ST. RIVERS

passionate session. "That you could even think to keep up with me, that you urge me on beyond what I feel are my limits...You are a goddess."

"I think that makes us evenly matched, sir," I whispered back before his lips found mine. He grinned against my mouth and untangled his hand from my hair.

"Vixen," he purred. He pulled away and lay on his pillow facing me. I stared at him, catching my breath. "What?"

*I want to do this for the rest of my life.*

The thought came without preamble. I blinked in surprise, but smiled softly at him.

"I was just thinking about how great this is. How great you are," I said, wrapping my arms around his torso and cuddling against his sweaty chest. Ethan didn't say anything right away, just sighed and held me close to him.

"I think about it all the time," he answered back, kissing the top of my head.

"I think..."

"Yes?"

"I think we should have a bath," I laughed.

"I think that's a wonderful idea. In fact, I shall ring in the housekeepers and have them bring us fresh linen for the bed while we are otherwise occupied. As it is—" Ethan turned to check the time on his phone and his face fell in shock.

"Darling, it's past four! We truly have spent all day in bed, and missed lunch! Are you hungry at all?" Ethan sat up and went to start the bath before I could answer.

"I didn't realize it was so late. It's been worth it though," I assured him when he came back into the bedroom. Ethan grinned sheepishly as he crawled over the bed to hover over me.

"It certainly has. But I had forgotten, for some strange reason, about an appointment I've made across town. It should only take an hour or so, but it is imperative that I am not late. We have time left before I leave, so our bath is still part of the plan. Will you be alright here for a while until I return?"

"Of course," I said, my heart sinking. I really wanted to spend all day in bed. "I have the TV, and maybe I'll order food to be brought up here to continue our plans by myself." I winked.

"You're a devilish woman," Ethan scolded, his eyes darkening with desire. "I don't recommend doing *everything* by yourself. If I must wait, so must you."

"I don't remember that in the contract." I smiled wider as I wiggled

# CHAINS OF SATIN

away from him to go into the bath. He lowered his head until his grin looked malicious.

"You wouldn't dare."

"I guess we'll have to see how long your appointment lasts," I said, shrugging and entering the bathroom, my crutches slowing me down just a touch. I didn't even hear him move off the bed, his feet silent as he ran to me across the carpet. He lifted me into his arms and spun me to face him. I squealed with laughter.

"If my darling is feeling neglected to the point where she feels the need to satiate herself if left alone for only an hour, I shall be most ardent in my attentions in the bath. Perhaps, dear love, I should find ways to exhaust that part of you, to keep you satisfied until I return home."

His promise was first answered with giggles. We splashed into the tub and soon his fingers found me, leaving me moaning with pleasure, crying out in ecstasy, and, very shortly after, screaming his name until I could barely breathe.

## CHAPTER TWENTY-THREE

# Petunia

*"PETUNIA BETHANY, WHAT ARE YOU DOING, YOUNG LADY?"*

*"Mommy said I could make her a pie! I have apples, sprinkles, chocolate chips and potato chips. It's all of mommy's favorite things."*

I woke with the echo of my father's laughter in my head, the sun shining through the curtains momentarily blinding me until I rubbed the last remnants of sleep and a few tears away. I missed my father, my mother, my carefree childhood. I'd had dreams like that one and others that would spring out of nowhere, and each time I'd wake in the morning with wet cheeks. It never got easier.

I looked over to Ethan, who was still sleeping, and kissed his cheek lightly before rolling over and climbing out of the bed. As I walked down the stairs and into the kitchen, I was greeted by Hailey, one of the girls who worked with me at Regal Cleaning Services.

"Oh, Petunia! Hi, girl! How have you been?" Hailey wrapped her arms around my shoulders for a hug. We weren't close, but she was a hugger no matter who you were to her. She, along with everyone else in the company, knew my predicament and was no longer surprised to see Ethan and I together.

"I woke up starving and wondering what to make in the kitchen," I said, smiling. Hailey quickly opened up the fridge and rummaged through

# CHAINS OF SATIN

some things. "No, seriously, I can do it. You can get back to doing whatever so you don't get into trouble."

"Oh, it's no trouble, I'm due for a break anyways. I make a mean omelet, if you're interested?"

"That does sound really good, actually," I said.

"Well, you sit down and I'll get it whipped up in no time. Do you think Mr. Aldrich will want one too?"

"It wouldn't hurt to make him one if you don't mind. He's probably going to want something to eat when he wakes up."

"Girl, I'm loving your life right now. If I could, I'd break my leg so some rich guy will fall in love with me and take care of me forever," Hailey said, wistfully.

"Yeah, it didn't quite happen like that," I laughed. Regal Cleaning was family-owned, and they cared more than most places about their employees. After my accident, they offered to hold my spot should I choose to return after my leg healed and I was cleared to return to work. After everything that had happened, I wasn't sure if Ethan thought I would go back to work or not, and in truth, I still hadn't made up my mind.

"Did you hear Sophie got reinstated? Can you imagine?" Hailey began as she made her way around the kitchen.

"No, actually. I can't believe it. Once you're out for something like that, they don't normally take you back."

"I heard her grandmother has some kind of sway with the company people or whatever. Either way, hopefully she learned her lesson and won't try stealing again. She's lucky they didn't call the cops on her."

"Yeah, she lucked out. How have you been lately?" I asked her as she set a plate down in front of me.

"Nikki is going to be two in a few days. I can't believe how fast she's grown, it's crazy!" Nikki was Hailey's reason for working so many jobs. After her husband took off, Hailey was a single mom to a baby girl in a town miles away from any family. But true to her nature, Hailey never let her personal affairs affect her job or her personality. She'd always come in with smiles and baby pictures as her daughter grew.

As Hailey showed me some updated pictures, I looked back up at her.

"She's so pretty. How is she liking dance class?"

The proud mother began gloating about how much her toddler loved learning when I felt arms wrap around my shoulders and a kiss was planted on my head.

"Good morning," Ethan whispered in my ear. "How disquieting it was to wake and find you gone. Yet, to hear you laugh makes it all better

# DELILAH ST. RIVERS

again."

Hailey had turned to see Ethan, and she blushed.

"I made you a plate, too, Mr. Aldrich, at Petunia's insistence. It's nothing fancy, but I can promise it's tasty. I'm about done with my break so I'll get back to work and leave you two to your breakfast. I'll talk with you later, Petunia." Hailey smiled and walked away from the dining room as Ethan sat at the table beside me.

"How did you sleep?" Ethan asked after thanking Hailey.

"Really well, actually," I answered. I dug into the omelet and savored every bite. She was right; she knew how to make a mean omelet.

"I have to attend a meeting in a little while, but afterwards, I have such plans for you." Ethan's wicked smile lit his whole face up, and I couldn't help but smile back, my stomach fluttering in suspense.

"I can't wait to see what you cook up for today," I said, winking at him. He took my hand and kissed it as he rose from his seat.

"I'd begin right now if I didn't have work in the way," he muttered. He kissed me on the cheek, and I leaned into it, sighing in contentment. "I adore you, my sweet girl," he whispered before walking away to enter his office.

I smiled as I watched him disappear and then decided to go to the living room and call my mother from the couch as I relaxed.

"Good morning, honey," Rico answered from my mother's room.

"How is she today?"

"She's good. She's teaching her class right now." Rico's answer was slow and patient.

"This early?"

"It's the first of three she's decided to do nowadays," Rico explained.

"Does she not remember the classes after doing them?"

"No, sweetie. Not often. But she's in good spirits so we don't interfere."

"How has she been?"

"You know how it is, Petunia. She's good sometimes and other times...It's easier to deal with her bad moments while she's here rather than when she was at the house. We have more people on call and ready to move to help her when she gets out of hand. But...Oh, hey there mama! Guess who decided to call this morning and see how you're doing?" Rico's higher and more cheerful tone announced the appearance of my mother in her room.

"Can I speak with her?" I asked.

"Is that my chickadee? How is school going, sugar?" *College. Alright,* I thought to myself. *I can do this.*

156

# CHAINS OF SATIN

"It's going good, Mom. I miss you though! How is everything?"

"Oh, well…I miss you too, Petunia. Your daddy is out again, but you know how he works."

"I want to come see you today, is that okay with you?"

There was a moment on the line where all I heard was my mother's breathing.

"I'm suddenly very tired, sweetheart. But you get those grades up and start listening to your teachers. I'm not paying an arm and a leg for you to flunk out of school, hear me?"

"Yes, ma'am," I answered quietly. "I love you, Mama. I'll see you soon, I promise."

"She's set the phone down, Petunia. I'm sorry, but you can come visit her later today if you're up to it. I'll keep my eyes on her until then, of course."

"Thank you, Rico. You're the greatest."

I sat back into the cushions of the plush couch and sighed. These small, barely-there conversations happened more often than not with her anymore. I missed her, the *real* her. How odd it was to feel like she was already gone when she was still living.

Ethan's hands rubbed my shoulders, stirring me out of my thoughts.

"Penny for your thoughts?"

"I just got off the phone with Mom, is all."

"Is she having a bad moment again?"

"No. She was happy-ish. I was back in college to her this morning. And Dad was out on the road again." I sniffed a little as I shook my head. "You'd think this would get easier."

"Nonsense," Ethan chided. "This seems to be a long, tedious process that only gets worse as it progresses. You are allowed to feel your feelings, and you should embrace them. It's the only way to get through this without it swallowing you whole." He sat beside me and pulled me close to him, as he did more and more after each conversation or visit with my mother. I was grateful for him in moments like this. Grateful for his strength and his patience.

"Feeling a little better?" Ethan asked after a while.

I nodded and smiled up at him.

"Good. Come upstairs, Pet."

"I'm pretty comfortable here. We could go back to cuddling, it was nice," I pouted, giving him my big puppy-dog eyes.

"Pet," he warned. His voice dropped an octave and his eyes began to glitter.

"Ethan," I mocked before giggling.

157

## DELILAH ST. RIVERS

"*Princess*," Ethan growled, cutting my laughter off. "Don't tell me you forgot all about our contract."

My face fell with the realization that I'd indeed forgotten. He was right. As of this day he was my dom. He was my owner, and I belonged to him in every way imaginable.

"I'm deeply sorry, sir," I said softly. I pushed myself smoothly off the couch and knelt in front of him as gracefully as I could. My hands found their home on my knees and my eyes lowered to the ground. My body was still as a stone at his feet, in a pose that I'd practiced many times over the course of my life.

"My word." Ethan's voice sounded strangled, as though he couldn't pass air through his pipes enough to speak. "I've seen your feral side, buckled at your gentle side, rendered speechless at your protective side, but this...My darling, proper description fails me." He cupped my chin and easily guided my face upwards until I met his eyes. "Your submission is the most complete I've ever seen. It's truly a remarkable thing to behold."

"Sir is too kind," I responded automatically.

"Come with me, Pet," he commanded. I took his hand immediately and he guided me upwards while he took my crutches in his other hand. "You've had a trying time lately. I know this. I also know you have... certain expectations of what's going to happen between us from here on out, expectations that may need to be adjusted for our individual contracted relationship."

I looked up at him as he lifted me in his arms, not sure whether or not he invited my conversation, so I stayed silent while he carried me up the stairs.

"My focus is on you today, my darling."

Ethan set me gently on his bed. Our bed.

"Strip," he commanded softly.

I took everything off slower than I normally would, feeling his eyes feasting on my flesh as it became more and more exposed. He reached down and palmed my breast as he kissed me softly.

"You are so beautiful," he muttered as he pressed his forehead against mine. I closed my eyes and breathed in the scent of him, instantly calming my racing heart. The first tear slipped from my eyelashes and traced a wet trail down my cheeks only to be interrupted by the gentle sweeping of his thumb.

"I want you to lay on your belly and rest your head to the side."

Ethan removed his buttoned-down shirt and reached for a small black remote from the stand by his side of the bed as I did what he told me. The lights dimmed, and soft music began to play. Tchaikovsky filled the room. I didn't dare close my eyes, though the calming atmosphere he created made it tempting to do so. Ethan squatted in my line of sight and pushed a strand of hair out of my eyes.

"I have warm oil that I'm going to rub into your body. Do not move, even if you are tempted to touch me back, understood?"

"Yes, sir."

"As further temptation, I will be naked, and you'll be able to see for yourself how much I truly love touching you."

I gasped softly.

"Speak your mind, darling," he coaxed, stroking my cheek with his hand.

"That's unfair. I love touching you as much as you love touching me," I said.

"Do you?" Ethan smiled wickedly as he stood and unbuckled his leather belt.

"Yes, sir."

"Maybe I'll allow a small kiss from your sweet lips on my cock during my administration to you, if you can behave. Would you like that, my good girl?" he asked as his pants and underwear fell to the floor. My brain short-circuited as I stared at him.

*My God, he was magnificent.*

"Very much, sir," I breathed, eyeing his body hungrily.

He kissed the top of my head and very soon after I felt drops of warmth trail down my spine and then again from one shoulder to the other. His hands followed, firm but gentle, as they began working the tension out of my muscles.

"Darling, I want you to be the you of yesterday while obeying the one command I've given you. Talk to me, tell me your feelings about today. Don't fail to tell me about that overwhelmingly breathtaking display of your submission." His voice was low and soothing as he spoke, and I felt the practiced restriction of my submission loosen within me.

"I'm so happy to be with you here. It's just hard knowing that each time I pass my old place, it'll be owned by someone else. I can't walk through the door at any given moment. I know it's just…" I fumbled for the right word.

"Sentiment?" Ethan offered.

"Yeah, sentiment. But it's more than just four walls and a ceiling; it's so much more that I feel I'm lost. I've gained so much with you, and I don't want to seem ungrateful to you —"

"You are the most grateful person I know," Ethan interjected.

"—but it still hurts. The loss of everything. The fact that everything

DELILAH ST. RIVERS

has changed and the reality that one day I'll be without my parents for good...It sucks."

I let out a little moan as Ethan massaged a knot out of my back.

"All change takes time, sweet girl. I'm proud of you for sharing with me how you feel. You're such a strong woman. It takes real courage to confide in someone when you're used to not doing so. But if you think about it, you'll always have incredible memories from the house that the new owners will never be privy to."

He shifted his hands across my shoulders and I let out another moan, a little louder as he expertly manipulated the muscles there. I let out a series of soft whimpers as he found a knot cluster around my ribs and massaged those out as well. More pressure was applied soon after as he leaned over my body.

"You are sounding positively wanton, my Pet. Deliciously so," he whispered in my ear. "It's nice to know I can make you sound like that even when I'm not fucking you."

I stifled a giggle and blushed.

"I can't help it," I defended myself. "It feels amazing."

"Oh, I'm not complaining," he said as he sat back up and continued to rub his hands over my back. "In fact, the only downside is that my ability to maneuver around you has become a tad bit hindered by the physical effects of my excitement."

My blush intensified, and I had to fight the urge to reach around and take his cock in my hand, to caress and soothe it with my own massaging skills, but I remembered his command and sighed in frustration.

"In the meantime, how about we discuss your seamless transformation downstairs? It has been some time since you've had a dom — I know we've discussed that before — but that movement was as effortless as though you'd been doing it every day." He took me by my uninjured leg and gently moved it over, spreading my legs so his hands had room to work on the backs of my thighs. I shivered as his hands moved from my bare ass down into my thighs.

"I've been well-trained. I had gotten to the point that from the first signal I was an emotionless doll unless something extreme stimulated me. A few orgasms while bound or blood, maybe. Honestly, the sight of blood kinda makes me a little woozy, and I feel faint all over again...Why did you stop?"

"Get on your knees the best you can and face me, now," Ethan commanded.

I did so and began to assume the resting pose as before.

"Stop. Place your hands in mine and look into my eyes."

160

# CHAINS OF SATIN

Again I followed his order, startled to see his eyes watered.

"Well-trained? For..." Ethan took a deep breath and kissed my hands gently. I was lost; this was definitely not how I thought the start of my contracted commitment to him would go.

"You and I, we are under contract, yes?" he asked.

I nodded, my brow furrowed in confusion.

"Why did you agree? Honesty, Pet. Please."

I thought for a moment, then took a breath.

"I trust you. In all the time you and I have known each other, you've thrilled me, made me the most excited I've ever been, and I've never felt safer with anyone else. I don't want to be without you, and if there's anything I said that was wrong, I can fix it. I don't want to stop this." I was breathing hard, panic slowly building in my chest.

"Your answer..." Ethan began, before breaking out into a soft smile. "It makes me very happy. I want this with you, too, my darling, more than I think you can imagine. You've been trained to have the instinct of a fearful submissive, to do as you're told so you aren't punished. I don't want this from you."

My eyes snapped back up from my hands to his eyes.

"I want you willing, with feeling, having that touch of brat in you that first drew my attention to your charms." Ethan's fingers traced my jaw as he smiled upon me. "Sit here, my sweetheart. I was waiting to give this to you, and it may seem a bit sudden, but I think now is the right time. Close your eyes, Pet," he instructed.

I did as he asked.

"Open them."

A square box was held in front of me.

*It's too big to be a ring box, and not the right shape for a typical bracelet —*

"Would you like to open it?" Ethan asked, interrupting my thoughts.

I blinked rapidly and nodded my head, a smile passively forming on my lips. I lifted the box's hinged lid and gasped at the dazzling wonder that was held before me. I looked at him in confusion. This was a circlet, a type of crown one wore around their forehead. It was thin and diamond-encrusted the whole way around, set in silver. Under it lay a bracelet with the exact same details. Ethan lifted them out of the box and tossed the container aside.

"We've known each other, helped each other, and grown closer to each other over these last few months. I nearly leapt with joy in my heart when you signed the papers; you truly have no idea just how beloved you are to me." He kissed me before sitting back, holding the circlet delicately in one hand while the other held the bracelet. "I adore no one else above you. I want no one else in my life but you. And I know this is sudden, and probably too soon to be honest, and if it is, please tell me." Ethan set the circlet to the side and clasped both hands onto the bracelet. "I bought these, darling, this set for you. Would you wear this bracelet, wear it always and with pride as a collar?"

"Ethan..." I whispered. It took a few swallows to speak again. "It's...it's not a necklace?"

He looked down at it, turning it in his hands to make the light shimmer off the diamonds.

"No, it isn't. I can't stand the thought of anything around that pretty neck other than my hands. I knew this belonged to you as soon as I saw it." Ethan shifted closer to me. "The bracelet is a testament of my adoration of you. It is made of precious metal and stones to symbolize how precious you are to me. When you wave to others, the light will always be reflected off the diamonds, so you will always be reminded not only to whom you belong, but who belongs to you. This, I give to you to wear always. It will only be removed to be repaired or professionally cleaned.

"As for the circlet, you'll have to forgive the romantic in me. I saw it and I decided right then and there that should we partake in play, you'd wear it. If you would want to engage in a scene or whatnot, you'd be able to put it on and I would know instantly whether or not you'd want to play. A sort of nonverbal consent."

I was openly sobbing at this point, not daring to believe my eyes and ears, though my heart begged him to mean every word.

"Petunia," Ethan continued as my tears began to fall, "I want you to know that even when it's time to show your submission, you are not beneath me in any way. I desire for you to know that you are my priority in all things. When we have a moment to share that involves my dominion over you, I would very much like to have this item on your wondrous head as a signal that, during play, I am your 'Lord and Master,' without you ever forgetting that you are my Queen. As you are both in and out of the bedroom.

"Speak your mind, my darling, please," he said, setting the bracelet beside the circlet and pulling my tear-soaked hands from my face as I shook my head, unable to catch my breath. He looked at me in that dimmed light ,and his eyes were heavy and sad. "Sh, come to me. 'Twas too soon, I fear. I'm deeply remorseful, my Pet. Forgive me."

I couldn't bear to speak, the weight of the emotion threatened to choke me.

"My word," Ethan exclaimed after a few minutes. "You're shaking. Are you cold?"

# CHAINS OF SATIN

I shook my head as I tried to calm my crying.

"Would you like a drink?"

I nodded. When he came back to seat himself in front of me, he had a small towel and a glass of water, both of which I used gladly. He took the glass and set it on the table beside the bed.

"Would you like to wash up and go to bed?" There was panic in his voice. I looked up and found him looking as miserable and apologetic as he sounded. I put my hand on Ethan's and stared at him, both because I loved looking at him, and because I was steeling myself to put it all on the line.

"The —" I cleared my throat and tried again. "The gift."

"Put it out of your mind, Pet. We can approach this later —"

"No," I said loud and clear, stopping his words and his movement toward the glittering objects beside him.

*Courage*, I thought to myself. *He's safe. He's kind. He's good.*

"Did you mean everything you said? All of it?" I asked, my voice wavering but holding strong.

"Oh, Petunia." He hung his head before gathering me up in his arms once more. "I meant every word, and I'll spend as much time and effort as it takes to prove it to you."

"It's been so long, and the last time..."

"I know, and I understand —"

"But this isn't like that, and you aren't like *him*. I don't feel the same with you as I did with him..."

Ethan waited patiently as I took a moment to put thought into words.

"I don't think you're lying when you say I mean so much to you."

"I'm not," he swore.

"And I'm not so broken that I'm falling into the lap of the first person that's offered this to me."

"You are the strongest person I know, love."

I sat silently for a moment more. I wanted this. I wanted him in all his entirety and to keep this life with him as my own. I was terrified, hesitant. And still, Ethan waited.

"I want this," I said softly, tears falling down my cheeks again.

"Say it again," he said, the same disbelief in his voice as before. Ethan pulled away from me and searched my eyes. "Will you accept this, take this for what it is?"

I nodded.

"You will?" His voice rose in excitement.

"Yes," I said definitively, and Ethan grinned, kissing me over and over. He placed the bracelet on my right wrist, kissing my palm, my wrist, my hand, and finally my lips before pulling me close one more time in a tight embrace.

## CHAPTER TWENTY-FOUR

# Petunia

"SHALL I FINISH WHAT I STARTED?" Ethan asked after we had been entangled for a while. I smiled and nodded, lying back onto my belly, only to be stopped by him.

"I'll lay towels on the bed."

When I was situated, I watched him walk around the bed, his flaccid cock growing firm once more as he drank in the sight of my naked flesh.

I grew a little self-conscious and folded my arms over the scar on my belly. He took my wrists and set them back to my sides.

"I want to see you in all your glory," Ethan said softly. His fingers traced along my arms and down my side. "It's almost impossible to believe you're wholly mine," he chuckled softly as he touched the bracelet. "It's maddening, really."

"What is?" I asked. His eyes, which had been lingering on my chest, shot up and found mine.

"The lust you inspire, Pet. The need you pull from me, as though you are a succubus." He dragged his hand over a hardened nipple. The friction caused me to gasp lightly. "It was difficult for me to express how desperate my yearning for you has been as it engulfs and enflames me when I look upon your very being." He stood over my head and gently massaged my temples and down my jaw. "I've found myself, from the beginning, often lost in fantasies of you.

"Even now I fight back a primal urge to take you." He squeezed my neck gently as he leaned downward. "Taste you." He kissed me tenderly. "To make you scream my name and beg for more," he whispered in my ear, sending a shiver through me. "Christ, Pet. Being around you, even as I am able to lay claim to your entire body…" He sighed and crawled up onto the bed, aligning his body with mine until our noses touched. "It's as if my appetite is increased by what it feeds on."

"Stop fighting, then."

We were both breathing hard as our lips met, hastily consuming each other's noises as he tucked an arm up under my uninjured leg, opening my legs to him. He released my lips and sank his teeth into my neck as he plunged into me. I cried out his name as the sensations of pain and pleasure overtook me.

Over and over he drove into me, slow but hard, as his mouth met my flesh and his nails dug into my thigh for support. My eyes found his as he pulled his face back, watching me as he kept up the pace. He was an animal, desperate and primal as he picked up speed. My heart beat madly as I held onto his muscular hips, each connection with mine jolting me until orgasms ripped through me. I cried out as I clenched tight around him, every nerve of my body on fire while he kept driving on.

"That's it," Ethan gasped, sweat beginning to drip from his forehead. "Let it go, *Princess*."

My cries turned to moans as the climax subsided and he bent to kiss me again. "I want to watch you make yourself come," he growled as he unhooked my knee and wound his arm around my waist, pulling me up, still connected as one, to sit on top of him. He guided my hips to grind hard into him, shoving every wonderful inch of his firm cock into my body.

He took a nipple into his mouth and sucked hard until I couldn't stop from crying out in breathless wimpers, incoherent as they were. He laid back, reclining against the towered pillows as he released my breast.

"Ride it," he encouraged, pulling one of my hands onto my breast and the other between my legs to stroke my clit. "Good God, there's a vision." His voice dropped to a husky purr as he watched me move on him, making small circles around my clit and reaching up to pull at my nipple.

I was going too hard, too fast and I knew that I was going to explode too quickly. I could feel the familiar tingle start at my toes and build up my thighs, so I stopped manipulating my own body and reached behind me to glide my palm over his testicles as I kept riding him.

"Disobedie—good lord," he murmured, closing his eyes and tensing

# CHAINS OF SATIN

his thighs beneath me. "If you keep at it, I won't last."

I gave the flesh holding his balls one last light squeeze before letting him go and returning my attention to my own body.

"I'm close, too," I warned. "But for God's sake, don't move." The tingling within me intensified and swallowed my core as I circled my clit faster with my fingers. "I'm…I'm gonna come," I whimpered.

"Jesus." Ethan's eyes bored into mine as he stared up at me.

"I'm gonna — !" I cried out before my breath was strangled, and all I could do was squeal and buck on his cock, still stroking and stimulating him and myself as my squeals rose in a higher pitch and my insides squeezed and pulsated hard around him. On and on he pushed inward, thrusting as I came, crying out in descending pitches into his shoulder as I fell forward.

The orgasm began to release its hold on me, taking with it all my ability to move. No sooner did I catch my breathe than I turned my head, whispering "Fuck me" in his ear.

"Beg me," Ethan demanded, still moving within me from below.

"Please, I need you to finish me off," I whimpered into his neck.

Ethan shook his head with a smirk.

"Not good enough, Pet."

My eyes met his as I lifted my head off his shoulder.

"Please, *Master*? Pretty please, will you fuck me into oblivion? I need you." My whispered words sucked the air from his lungs ,and his eyes went dark as he savagely kissed me.

"Good girl."

Ethan pulled himself out of my body and moved out from under me. He crawled between my legs from behind and pulled my hips upward until I was right where he wanted me to be. He kissed the small of my back before entering me slowly, his dick still wet and warm from my orgasm.

He continued to move slowly, savoring this new position, but it wasn't long before he was thrusting hard and quick, forcing screams to emit from my mouth into the mattress. He reached down and grabbed onto a swinging breast, squeezing it almost to the point of pain before letting it go to give my ass a hardy slap.

"Fuck, Pet," he grunted as another shrill cry left my mouth, the sting on my backside heightening my pleasure. He looped a handful of my hair around his fist and pulled, bringing my face up from the mattress. "I want to hear that scream, *Princess*." He slapped my ass with his other hand, and my scream echoed around the room.

"Oh, my Pet. Oh, my good girl. Get ready. Get ready," Ethan panted out the words, releasing my hair and grabbing my hips mercilessly as he slammed against them. "Here, now," he ground out, shooting his seed into me as I came, triggered by the flex and release of his orgasm. He stroked in and out of me a few more times, grunting and cursing softly each time. Finally, he laid his chest against my back, wrapping his arms fully around my waist as we both fought to catch our breaths.

CHAPTER TWENTY-FIVE

# Petunia

A SOFT KNOCK ON THE BEDROOM DOOR woke me from the sleep of a lifetime. I pulled the sheet higher up on my naked chest as I turned and sat up carefully.

"Come in," I called out. I'd expected Amelia, but when the curly red-haired woman about my age walked in carrying a tray of various fruits with a few pancakes and a glass of orange juice, I was at a loss for words for a split second.

"Ta-da!"

"Sophie," I finally made out. "When did you start working here again?"

"Last week, actually. I'm surprised you didn't notice, but I mean, you're a little occupied." Sophie winked at me. "Mr. Aldrich met me at the kitchen and asked me to bring this up to his lady. I heard about you two through the grapevine, but I couldn't believe it! You don't seem that type." She laughed, and after a second I chuckled.

"To be honest, neither of us saw it coming. He was there for me one night, and we've grown closer ever since."

"Well, I'm happy for you," Sophie said, setting the tray down onto my lap.

"And I'm happy you're back." I took a sip of the juice and set the

# DELILAH ST. RIVERS

glass down. "Did they ever find those earrings at the Miller's place?"

Sophie shook her head. "I tried telling the son to tell the truth—I knew he had to have sold them or given them away—but he was a chickenshit and wouldn't fess up."

"What kind of boy does that to his mother and blames the help?"

"Only every privileged piece of shit out there," Sophie scoffed.

"That's just awful." I shook my head. "How did you convince the company to take you back? Jackson doesn't normally give second chances."

"They had no proof, and with all the people that quit from before, they need the workers. So I fought him about it. Obviously I can't work at the Millers' anymore, but I don't care. The wife is a drunk, and her husband is a huge pervert."

I raised my eyebrows as I took a bite of pancake.

"Oh, my God," I exclaimed. "Is it the normal cook downstairs?"

"It's Wednesday." Sophie rolled her eyes. "No cook, remember? Mr. Aldrich made this for you. Are they really that good?" She reached over to take a piece.

"Uh, not for you," I said, holding my fork in my fist.

"Jesus, Petunia, I was only kidding. I'm on a diet anyways; one bite will go straight to my ass."

The door opened and Ethan walked in.

"Ah, good timing, I suppose?" He leaned over and kissed me.

"Mmm, you smell the same as these delicious pancakes," I said softly.

"Alright, well I guess I have more to do downstairs," Sophie said, turning to leave.

"Hey, Sophie?" She turned as I called to her. "It's really great to see you again. I hope we see more of you."

Sophie looked at Ethan for a second longer than I liked and smiled back at me.

"I hope so too," she said and closed the door behind her.

"Perhaps you should release the fork in your hand before you snap it in half?" Ethan coaxed the utensil from my clenched fist. "What's the matter, my darling?"

"You'll probably laugh at me," I said, my stomach turning.

"Pet," Ethan murmured, turning my face to meet his gaze.

I sighed.

"You did this for me, something so nice, and she tried to take some and I was like 'What the fuck?' And then she stares at you—"

"You got jealous?" Ethan interrupted, a small smile growing on his face.

"I told you that you would laugh at me." I scoffed as I felt heat rise

170

to my face.

"Darling." He looked into my eyes. "To whom do you belong?"

"You."

His hand traced from my elbow to the bracelet on my wrist.

"Who's got you collared?"

"You." I couldn't stop the slow grin.

"Whose arms are these, that hold you close?"

"Yours."

"Whose lips, my Pet?"

"Yours," I said before his own met mine.

"And to whom do I belong, heart and soul?"

I paused and looked into his eyes.

"Say it," Ethan insisted.

"You are mine," I stated, wrapping my arms around him, returning his kiss.

"I could have a row of prostitutes and supermodels parade about me for an entire day, and still I'd only have eyes for you, my girl. Only you. I adore you."

I leaned my forehead against his, breathing him in with my eyes closed. He broke the silence with a chuckle.

"What?"

"This is the second display of jealousy from you, Pet. I'm finding it has a rather, mm"—Ethan paused, kissing my neck—"*licentious* effect upon me." He took my hand and guided it down to his lap to discover his hardened flesh beneath the fabric.

"Oh my," I breathed. "If only I didn't have to worry about my physical therapy today."

Ethan pulled his face away from mine and smirked.

"Greedy girl, worry less about this. It will always be here for you. I wouldn't have you delay your healing for something we can do at any time. And don't forget," he said, sliding off the bed, "I'm a very patient man, most of the time."

I smiled back at his admission.

"Finish your breakfast while I draw your bath. Maybe, if we time it right, I'll be able to stroke an orgasm out of you while you're in there."

AFTER PHYSICAL THERAPY, ETHAN AND I WENT to see Mom. She was sitting in the cafeteria area, eating applesauce, and doodling in a notebook with a pen.

## DELILAH ST. RIVERS

"There's my chickadee!" she exclaimed after seeing me walk in.

"How's it going today, Mom?" I asked with a smile.

"Oh, you know how students are, they don't listen like they used to," she complained. "But they're eager to learn, and passion is the biggest part of being an artist."

"Well said," Ethan complimented, squeezing my hand lightly.

"Oh." Mom glanced up at him, her expression softening. Her eyes teared up as she continued to look at him. Ethan and I glanced at each other before I reached out to take her hand.

"Don't," she said sternly, taking her hand away from me. "How long have I been here, Petunia?"

"About three weeks," I answered. "I come to see you almost every day without fail. Some days we have a great visit, others you either don't want to see anyone or you don't recognize me or Ethan."

"The physicians assure us you're responding well to the treatment," Ethan offered in an attempt to assuage her.

"Don't bullshit me, boy," Mom cursed. "I deserve to be home where I can die in peace—"

"Mom, you're not dying," I interrupted. "You have plenty of time left, and you're only here for your safety and those around you."

She scoffed. "That's worse!" she whispered aggressively. "Years of my mind falling to pieces, not knowing where I am most of the time or who I'm talking to...It's enough to make me want to end it all right now, while I still have some sense of control over myself and my life!"

"Mom..." I didn't have the words to comfort her, no way of knowing how to handle this level of desperation from the strongest woman I'd ever known. "I'm so sorry, Mom."

"What for, little bird?" Mom's voice was raised, and she placed her hand over mine. "What, the dryer? You were five, sweetheart, you didn't know dish soap didn't belong in there."

"*Hola*, Petunia. Prince Charming," Rico greeted us from behind.

"Young man, tell me you turned in your charcoal example," Mom demanded.

"I just handed it in, Mrs. Barlowe. I'm going to whisk these two away and let you get back to your business before we discuss my work. How does that sound?"

"Of course, dear," Mom answered absentmindedly. She picked up her pen and began doodling once more.

"How are you two this fine day?" Rico started as soon as we were out of earshot of my mother.

"Has she ever made threats of suicide or anything like that while

# CHAINS OF SATIN

she's been in here?" I asked him, ignoring his question.

"We hear these things all the time from our patients, especially ones that deal with mental issues, *mija*. We take all threats seriously and, yes, your mother has made a couple of statements that have put her on a watch list."

"I'm worried, Rico. She's never said anything like that before today. Is there anything she can actually hurt herself with?"

"Not without some creativity, dove. I promise."

"If I put some extra security detail into the building to watch her closely day and night, would that hinder the facility's ability to continue treatment?" Ethan asked.

"I'm sure if there was only a couple in plain clothes, it would be okay," Rico answered him after a moment's thought. "Uniforms tend to freak out some of the patients. You come up with the best solutions, Charming."

"He has a name," I teased Rico, who smiled and fluttered his eyelashes at Ethan.

"Oh, I know," he said.

I walked back over to Mom and hugged her around her shoulders from beside her, careful not to hit her with the crutches.

"I love you," I said, kissing her head. She looked up and patted my cheek.

"Sucking up won't get you a better grade than you deserve, but that was lovely of you to say anyways."

Ethan walked over and bowed low to kiss her hand.

"A pleasure, Mrs. Barlowe, as always," he said, smiling at her blushing face.

"You are most welcome to come see me whenever you want," she practically purred up at him. I stifled a chuckle. Mom was always a flirt.

As we walked out to the car, I hung my head.

I thought I'd dealt with some pretty disturbing things on this journey with my mother, but there was something completely unsettling about hearing my mother talk about suicide. In all my years, it was something I never thought I'd ever hear my own mother discuss with any degree of seriousness.

Ethan looked at me and sighed as he turned into the driveway at home and turned the car off. He reached over and caressed my cheek. I closed my eyes and leaned into his hand. God, I couldn't get enough of his touches.

"You're an admirable soul, Petunia. The world does not deserve you."

I turned my head and kissed his palm. "But you do," I whispered, looking at him.

Ethan's eyes flashed, and he smiled. "That's dangerously close to tantalizing, my precious wonder," he said softly.

"It could have been closer, *darling*. I could have done this." I slid one of his fingers deep into my mouth and sucked hard, moaning as I did so to watch his eyes widen and his chest inflate.

"Vixen," Ethan accused breathlessly as danger glittered in his eyes. I smiled sweetly as I pulled my mouth off his finger slowly, kissing it before fully releasing it. Faster than I could blink, Ethan grabbed me by the neck and brought his face close to mine without touching it.

"You act like you didn't enjoy that as much as I did," I purred at him.

"I've half a mind to prove here and now just how much I enjoyed that," he growled, and my smile widened.

"If it's my leg that stops you, you're not being creative enough." I cocked an eyebrow at him, taking note of how soaked I was becoming.

Ethan's hand tightened just a fraction. He stared at me for a second before breaking out into a devilish smile of his own. He loosened his grip and turned my head to the side before sliding his tongue from my shoulder and up my neck to latch onto my earlobe.

"You're right," Ethan snarled in my ear. "I haven't been creative enough. That changes now. "He sank his teeth into my neck, making me cry out, and soaking my panties further. "I'm going to take you upstairs, and you're going to see just how creative I can be, my sweet, bratty *Princess*. How do you feel about breaking in that circlet today?" He kissed my bite mark, and I shivered.

"Oh, yes, Master," I moaned.

Ethan pulled away to look at me, and I shot him another cocky smile, though I knew he saw the lust in my eyes.

"Brat," he growled. He pulled me into a deep, intimate kiss, moving his hand from my throat up into my hair and back down onto my breast. "Christ, you inflame my desire."

"I'm so wet for you," I whispered.

"Petunia, if you keep talking like that I'll take you right here in the car, regardless of who happens upon us."

"Then maybe we should go inside so you can show me your creative ways," I said, reaching down and stroking his cock through his pants.

"Capital idea," he murmured, kissing me a final time.

He pulled away, and soon I was whisked out of the car, into his arms, and carried into the house. Sophie and another housekeeper were

# CHAINS OF SATIN

laughing in the living room when we walked in, and they both grew silent as Ethan walked by. He turned before heading up the stairs.

"Sophie, Petunia's crutches are in my car. Have someone fetch them, and ensure they are upstairs outside of the master bedroom by dinner." He turned back to look at me. "She won't be needing them until then."

I kissed his neck, and he smiled.

"I adore you, my darling," Ethan said softly as I nuzzled his neck.

"And I, you," I answered.

"Don't forget," he ordered, looking back at the girls.

In the bedroom, Ethan placed me on the bed, then knelt in front of my seated form. He lifted the shimmering circlet out of the black velvet box and held it out toward me.

"Do you trust me?" he asked.

"With everything I am." I nodded, taking his face in my hands, kissing him softly.

"You remember everything we talked about? What the circlet means, how I feel about you? That even though I am your dominant, you are never beneath me? Your safety system, including safe words?"

I nodded.

"I mean it, Pet—"

"And so do I," I interrupted him. "I trust you." Ethan hesitated for a moment, and I leaned over to stroke his cheek. "If you aren't comfortable right now with this, we don't have to. We can wait." I never thought I'd ever utter those words to a dom. "But if you're alright with this, I promise I won't hold back from using the safe words if I need to, okay?"

"If you are certain," he said one last time, placing a kiss to my palm.

"I want this as much as you do," I assured him.

"Alright, my dear," Ethan said, lifting the circlet above me to settle it onto my head. "Let's begin."

PRESENT DAY
OFFICE OF DR. JOSEPH HALL

# Ethan

I REMEMBERED THAT MOMENT LIKE I WAS living it. It was all locked in me like a core memory. Every scent. Every movement. I took a breath and began to tell Joseph exactly what happened next:

I slowly exhaled as I released the silver circlet and took a step back. My sweet Petunia was exquisite in every way, poised and regal with the right amount of submission in her continence.

I'd feared her reaction would be similar to the first, until I met her eyes, and a ghost of a smirk curled her lips.

"You dare look upon me?" I snarled at her.

Her eyes dropped to her hands after the briefest of hesitations. Ooh, the brat wants to play today.

"Strip. Be careful, but be hasty," I commanded and watched as she peeled off her clothing at a speed slower than I knew her capable.

"You enjoy being impudent, don't you?" I asked, hooking a finger under her chin. I couldn't resist making contact with her skin at every possible moment. I made her lift her head to look at me from her seated position. Her eyes took my breath away. More grey than blue, I loved nothing more than staring into them while I buried myself deep inside her.

"Maybe a little, sir," she answered, winking at me.

"Whatever shall I do with you," I wondered out loud. I stood and took her

# CHAINS OF SATIN

*hands, placing them onto my belt. "Undress me, slowly," I said, holding up a cautionary finger. "Slowly, Pet. Or today may prove more intense than you anticipate."*

*She licked her lips and directed her attention to her task, and very quickly I found myself almost wishing I'd commanded speed. With deft fingers she pulled the belt, uncinching it before delicately grabbing the small metal prong and releasing it from its place. She glanced up as she slowly pulled the belt from the buckle. The sound of leather against metal made my fingers ache to rip it off and tie her up with it. I was not even undressed and already I was fighting to keep control.*

*Petunia slipped the belt from my pants and folded it in half, placing it in my open palm only after my flesh had been kissed. From there, my pants were gently tugged down my legs, and she made the unbuttoning of my shirt a slow, agonizing experience. I was breathing hard, and my chest was reddened by the time I stood naked before my darling.*

*"That's a good girl," I managed to whisper before I leaned down and kissed her lips in reward. Her disobedient eyes drifted over my form and landed between my thighs.*

*"May I suck it, sir?" Petunia asked so prettily.*

*My cock twitched in response, but I knew I'd revert to teenage quickness if she so much as touched me at this point.*

*"Selfish girl," I scolded her. "Your greedy mouth will have to wait." I knelt in front of her, holding her breast in my hand. "I'd like to use ankle restraints on you, but the minute you're uncomfortable, say your safe word and you'll be released."*

*Petunia nodded and I sighed inwardly. So far, so good, I told myself. I touched her cheek one more time, then took her by her waist and set her farther back onto the bed.*

*"The spreader bar will have to wait until your leg is healed," I explained as I used the velcro to secure her legs apart.*

*"My arms, sir?" Petunia offered, lying back and spreading them. The sight of her like that left me fairly intoxicated with lust. I shook my head slightly to refocus my attention.*

*"Not just yet, Pet. For the moment we test your self-control the way you consistently test mine." I kissed her ankle and reached under my bed to pull out a black trunk. Opening it, I selected a few toys and laid them in a row beside her as she watched.*

*A soft, leather flogger that made noise more than it stung.*

*An anal plug jeweled at the bottom of the base.*

*A riding crop.*

*A vibrator.*

*An external massager with a remote, providing seven different intensity settings.*

*Three satin ties.*

*Finally, I pulled out a folded emerald green weighted blanket.*

*I stood back and let Petunia look over the assortment of tools, gauging her reaction. She looked at me for a moment and smiled.*

*"Are they to be used on me or you, sir?" she boldly asked.*

*"Oh, my sweet girl," I began as I climbed onto the bed and kissed her tender neck. "I do believe that what you just did would be described as" —I nipped her earlobe— "a major fuck up." I finished by growling low in her ear and I grew harder as I felt her shudder beneath me. "Your color, my love?"*

*"Green," she moaned.*

*I slid my tongue into her mouth, sealing the kiss with my lips on hers, savoring the taste of her until I pulled away, holding one of the silken ties in my hand.*

*"Your arms," I commanded.*

*"Yes, I have two, just like you," she threw back at me.*

*"And what gorgeous specimens they are. Now put them above your head."*

*Petunia sighed and lifted them slowly above her head, exaggerating the lift of her diaphragm so her breasts pressed against my naked flesh. It was by sheer will that I was able to tie her delicate wrists together. When I was finished, I kissed each one.*

*"Color?"*

*"Green," she said softly, looking up at me.*

*"I've tied you into a position that I'd like you to stay in, no matter what. If you disobey, I shall cease touching you" —I rubbed my nose against hers— "playing with you" —my hands drifted down her arms— "pleasuring you." I ran my tongue up and over her hardened nipple. I moved back up her body to find her eyes glistening in the light, and I kissed her nose. "I'm also going to dim the lighting. It will increase the shadows and heighten anticipation. Still green?"*

*She nodded.*

*I lowered the lighting of the room with the dial on my wall. Her silhouette stood out against the sheet she laid on, her form of curves and mounds displayed ever so perfectly. I could have been content staring at her like this for the rest of my life.*

*Well, until my lust overcame that contentment, in any case.*

*"Now, my Pet," I said in a lowered tone as I approached her slowly. "You have been a rather naughty darling as of late. Your list of sins include: sucking on my finger, teasing me with dirty words, and defying me with bratty behavior. You moved slowly when I demanded speed, and you defied my demand of slow movement by moving quickly. You've tested my limits, sweet girl. And as I've previously stated, I'm going to test yours."*

*I watched her chest rise and fall rapidly. I picked up the leather flogger and made it glide over her legs and up to her hips, barely letting the ends touch her skin. I gently slapped the strands against her clit repeatedly before I bent and placed my lips against it. I stood and repeated the motion. The sound of leather against her flesh barely echoed in the room, overtaken only by the sound of her increased panting.*

# CHAINS OF SATIN

I kissed that magical place on her once more, slipping my tongue out to taste her sweetness for a brief second. I worked up her body, slapping the leather gently against her belly, her arms, and finally, those perfectly sculpted breasts. I struck one, then the other, watching in fascination as her nipples hardened on contact. She shivered, but never moved.

"You're doing remarkably well," I praised her, tweaking one of those precious peaks between my fingers as she moaned.

"This is nothing," Petunia said softly. "I can take so much more."

My gut curled at her words, but outwardly I smiled at her.

"This isn't about pain, my love. There's so much more that I can do for you that would still bring you to tears without doling out any negative sensations upon your person. To prove that," I continued, "I'm going to 'up the ante,' as they say. Now remember, no moving." I kissed her soft, parted lips as I cupped her entire womanhood, my hand pulling back soaked with her need. I still marveled at her constant eagerness for me. Never before had I encountered one like her. "I'm going to blindfold you, darling. Color?"

"Green," she gasped as I licked her glistening clit once again. I stood to grab the tie and straddled her chest. I began speaking softly to her while I went to work. "My cock has never been as hard as it is right now, Pet. It aches. While I tie this around you, you have my permission to make it feel better. Remember, darling, no hands. No other movement."

Her heated mouth engulfed my flesh before I had even stopped speaking, sucking the air out of my lungs as she did so. Had I been a less-controlled man, I would have fucked that sweet mouth into oblivion. Her tongue stroked and circled my dick as she sucked and moaned over it.

"Jesus, Pet," I said breathlessly as she sucked at my leaking cock. I pulled out of her warm mouth and finished situating the forgotten tie around her head, my hands shaking. "Now, my love, I'm going to give you five orgasms. Five. One for each act of insubordination on your part. Each time you peak, you will count it out loud. Should you forget what number you're on, you'll start back to one. Do you understand?" I sunk a finger inside her as I asked.

"Yes!" Petunia cried out. Her walls clenched tightly around my digit, shooting straight desire down through my cock.

"We may still have guests in our home, so the only sound you may make is the sound of your counting. Understood?"

"Yes," she whimpered.

"Color?"

"So green," she moaned.

Jesus, fuck, I thought to myself, absently placing a hand around my erection. I wasn't certain who would be more tortured at that point. I picked up the external massager and turned on the setting to three, placing it just under her clit,

# DELILAH ST. RIVERS

so she'd have the vibration against that and her labia. Petunia hissed as she inhaled sharply on contact and arched her back involuntarily.

I picked up the vibrating dildo and turned it on to the middle setting and rested it against one of her nipples. She inhaled sharply again before clamping her lips tightly shut. She was so good at not making a sound, yet even in the dimmed lighting, I could see her moving her hips ever-so-slightly.

"Now, now, we agreed not to move, my wanton creature," I warned playfully, placing both of my hands onto her hips and stilling them. I swore I heard her whimper in the slightest decibel, but I let it slide this once. "All these things going on, seeing you deliciously fight the urge to grind against my toys...I almost want to fuck you silly. That would be a true delight for us, wouldn't it, Pet?"

She nodded and I chuckled.

"Not yet, sweet girl. I get my five orgasms out of you, then we worry about the meeting of our bodies." I bent low over her so my lips rested just above her ear. "Is that creative enough for you?"

She trembled as she nodded, and I lifted the handle of the massager and moved it to the side, keeping the pressure on her body steady. I licked her swollen pussy, tasting her juices as I explored every nook and cranny of her, inhaling her unique scent. I could tell by the increase of her fluids and the irregularity of her breathing that she was coming close to her first climax. I pressed on, sucking and licking while the toys buzzed on her body, yet still she didn't come.

I glanced up and noticed her clenched face, obviously fighting off the waves of the orgasm I was working so hard to give her.

"Brat," I growled, climbing up her body, smashing the massager harder into her clit as my hips joined hers. The vibration of it almost ended me immediately, heightened by the sensation of her moist, hot pussy upon the tip of my steeled cock. "You're denying me my own victory and I won't allow it."

She shook her head, but I bent low and clamped my teeth around the unoccupied nipple, cutting her movement short. I couldn't resist pushing into her soaking cunt, feeling delirious with desire as my cock was swallowed whole, and I felt her begin to pulsate around me, proof positive that she was headed toward a climax despite her best efforts. I regrettably pulled out of her and removed the vibrator from her nipple.

"Now, you owe me your loss of control, Princess," I said through gritted teeth. I lined the silicone penis up, teasing it between her folds to get the head as slick as possible. "So give it up." At my command, I slid the cock between her legs. I knew the combination of vibrations would end her resolve.

Petunia panted harder and she began to moan.

"Shh, now, Pet," I warned her, delight building in me as I watched her approach the crest.

"I can't," she whispered between breaths.

I leaned over and purposefully groaned in her ear: "Come for me, Princess."

# CHAINS OF SATIN

*With those words, her body tensed, and she whimpered and panted as the vibrator moved between her legs, urged on by the contracting and pulsating within her. I grabbed hold of it by the base and eased it in and out of her, watching her arch her back from the sheer force of pleasure.*

*Petunia tossed her head to the side, and I could hear her hiss as she exhaled. Like such a good girl she was keeping quiet, though I could tell she longed to do otherwise. Finally, she settled into a gentle hum, and I watched her thighs relax as her orgasm played itself out.*

*It was probably the sexiest sound I had ever heard emitted from her lips when she panted out the word:*

*"One."*

CHAPTER TWENTY-SEVEN

# Petunia

"FIVE."

Tears streamed down my face, and my whole body ached as I forced out the word. My whole body trembled and I ached to my core. The sensation of pleasure after pleasure was something akin to torture without direct pain, something I was unaccustomed to in all my years of sexual play. "Yellow," I panted out, hoping Ethan would hear me, and that he wouldn't get upset. Immediately the vibrating tools were removed from my body and the restraints were taken away from my limbs. Ethan peeled the blindfold off my sweating face, and I laid still as he placed the weighted blanket across me.

"Here's water," Ethan said softly, putting the cold glass in my hand after helping me sit up. "I'm so proud of you, Pet," he whispered, caressing my arm and kissing my shoulder. "Take your time. You can decide if we continue or we call it a day."

It took such a long time for the fog to clear from my mind and for me to return to reality.

"What about you?" I asked.

"What about me?" Ethan's face turned quizzical. I reached between his legs and grasped his still hard erection. He shook his head. "That doesn't matter, sweetheart. It'll go away if left alone. All that matters is your care. I

# CHAINS OF SATIN

want you safe, in all ways. To me, that's much more important."

I rested against his chest, still stroking him softly. I loved the feel of him in my hand; the soft skin that coated the impossibly hard muscle was a fascination to me. It took a moment to realize he was breathing faster, though he hadn't moved at all. I smiled up at him.

"Are you close?"

"I've been close since the car," he admitted, his voice deep and broken.

I released him and kissed him softly. "Can you get my crutches?" I asked.

Ethan nodded and released my ankles from the cuffs, helping me to stand until I was steady enough to reach the bathroom.

"We aren't done," I said looking back down at his manhood and smiled as it twitched at my words.

I came back out feeling better, happy with the knowledge that I wasn't too tender for further play. Ethan was putting away most of the items, keeping out only the massager, the plug, the blanket, and the ties.

I sat on the bed in front of him and placed a hand on his thigh. He knelt down and kissed my forehead above the circlet, wrapping his arms around my shoulders and pulling me tight against him.

"Are you alright?" he asked.

I thought about being a smartass, or at the very least to tease him, but his concern touched me deeply.

"I promised you I would use my word the instant it became too much," I reassured him, kissing his lips. "I'm okay."

"Do you think you have at least one more in you?" Ethan smiled playfully, glancing over at the massager.

"Do your worst, sir." I cocked an eyebrow at him and smirked.

Ethan tilted his head to the side before looking up at the ceiling. An astonished smile spread across his face, and he chuckled. The look on his face a fraction of a second later as he lifted me and bounced me farther up the bed was purely primal.

"Daring me, *Princess*?" Ethan snarled as he grabbed my throat. "You shouldn't have." With his other hand he grabbed onto my breast, squeezing as he laid me down until I cried out. He bent down and bit my bottom lip. "No noises," he growled. He reached over and grabbed a tie in his fist. "Open that pretty mouth for me." I did as he asked, and he put the tie in it. "You'll pinch me once for yellow, twice for red, understand?"

I nodded, breathing heavily. He'd never gone completely feral on me before, and where the wild-eyed look terrified me with my ex, on Ethan it was just...hot. He grabbed the massager and put it on my relaxed clit,

183

bringing it back to life instantly. I cried out and clawed his shoulder as I could feel the buildup of orgasm number six rush upon me with supernatural speed.

"The anal plug is next. Blink once for green."

I blinked. Ethan popped the end in his mouth, rolled it around to get it warm and wet for easier insertion, his eyes on me the whole time. He lifted my legs and licked around and then inside my exposed hole, without even touching my aching pussy. He hadn't given me permission to come yet, but the double stimulation and the taboo of his tongue in my ass was almost enough to push me past the breaking point.

He pulled his face away and slowly inserted the toy, keeping steady but careful pressure until my body accepted the cone up to the jeweled end. My eyes widened as he smiled viciously, revealing with a firm push to the end that the jewel was a button, and the plug began to vibrate.

I unleashed an unholy howl into the bundled-up tie, throwing my head and squeezing my eyes shut.

Ethan grabbed my face and made me look at him.

"Still green?"

I blinked once through my tears, thinking if he didn't fuck me right then and there I was going to tear him apart. He grabbed my throat as he went to his knees between my legs, ripping the tie from my mouth with his own.

"Say my name." Ethan's voice was choked with animalistic hunger as he sank his cock into me.

"Ethan!" I gasped, staring into his eyes.

"Tell me I'm your master," he demanded, picking up speed.

"You're my master," I groaned louder, my head beginning to float with the euphoria of blood-deprivation and my body's overstimulation.

He began to slam into me, the wet slapping of his body meeting mine filling the room.

"I'm going to come. You're going to come with me, and when you do, I want the bloody world to hear you scream my name." Ethan grunted as he began to swell within me, prompting me to meet him thrust for thrust as I chased my climax with him.

When it hit, I felt like my body was filled with unleashed lightning as the merciless orgasm tore through my body. Echoes of his name bounced around the room, joined by his wordless grunts as he came deep and hard inside me.

"Ethan, Ethan, Ethan..." I repeated over and over as I rode tidal waves of agonizing pleasure for a full thirty seconds after his own climax was finished.

# CHAINS OF SATIN

"That's it, darling, ride it out," Ethan murmured, still stroking his cock in and out of me, even as it began to lose the steel within. His grip on my throat loosened, and he caressed the skin of my neck until the waves slowed and the orgasm subsided. He slowed as my voice quieted until all I could do was moan.

Carefully, he pulled himself out of me and turned off the vibrating toys. Tears spilled from my eyes as the rest of me began to relax; even more spilled over as he gently coaxed the anal plug out of me.

Ethan sat me up and removed the circlet from my head. When the barely-there weight of it left me, all tensions released, and a flood of tears flowed from me. Ethan's arms wrapped around me tightly as he rocked back and forth, humming tunelessly for comfort. Before too long my tears slowed, and I realized he'd wrapped the weighted blanket around my shoulders.

I didn't say anything for a long while and he respected my silence, giving me light kisses on my head and caressing my face and arms. I leaned in and cuddled against him, filled with tremendous gratefulness for this level of aftercare. I was so used to self-soothing after each session with my ex.

I sighed deeply, forcing myself to begin breathing regularly, matching his own. He handed me a tissue and I cleaned my face, leaning back against him when I was done.

"Water?" He offered me the glass again.

I nodded and drank what I could, handing the rest to him to finish off. He set the glass down and gently turned my hips so I was facing him more directly.

"How do you feel?"

"Incredible." I offered him a tired smile.

"Did I hurt you or take things too far?" Ethan asked, looking me over. Before he even finished his sentence, I was shaking my head.

"Nothing was done that I didn't want, or enjoy. I promise I'm okay. More than okay." I smiled wider, then kissed his lips softly at first, but I underestimated his need for reassurance.

He pulled me in as he slid his tongue into my mouth and inhaled deeply when I returned his passionate kisses. He broke off and held me close in his powerful arms.

"I adore you, my Pet, my Queen. I truly do."

I smiled through half-closed eyes, fighting the exhaustion valiantly but losing.

"Come, my darling. I know you're exhausted, but we must get you bathed, and your muscles need tending to."

# DELILAH ST. RIVERS

Ethan stood and took a few steps before stumbling just a bit.

"Whoa," he exclaimed, chuckling. "I suppose my own muscles are a bit overworked as well."

"It's no wonder," I said and was rewarded with a sheepish grin before finding his stride to the bathroom.

WE TOOK TURNS BATHING EACH OTHER, SCRUBBING hair, washing bodies, and snuggling while kissing and speaking sweet nothings in hushed tones. When finished, Ethan set me back onto the bed and helped me with gentle stretches so I wouldn't wake up sore and stiff from our strenuous activities.

"What can I do for you?" I asked him while we relaxed onto the bed.

"Letting me take care of you is all I need. Letting me touch your face, hold you close, bathe you and massage you after subjecting you to my more savage displays of affection is the most rewarding thing you could do."

"Well..."

"What is it, darling?"

"Thank you. Not for *you know*...That would be a weird thing to thank you for. I mean, thank you for everything these last few months, for taking care of me, my mom, and for being so wonderful. I've never felt so safe so consistently."

Ethan blinked in surprise before bending down to kiss me gently. "You've ruined me for anyone else in the universe, you know," he whispered against my lips.

"Should I apologize?" I asked, smiling.

"Never."

# CHAPTER TWENTY-EIGHT

# Petunia

"IT'S BEEN A FEW WEEKS SINCE WE'VE last discussed a dinner date," Ethan began one morning over breakfast. "I thought we might approach the subject once more, if you were feeling up to it?"

I looked up at him from my bowl of pineapple, my thoughts racing.

"We don't have to decide for tonight, love," Ethan reassured me. "But I was thinking sometime this—" His sentence was cut off by the sound of his cell phone ringing. With annoyance, he glanced at his phone and looked back at me. "Forgive me, Pet."

I nodded as he walked into his office. I finished my plate and took it into the kitchen, slowly but successfully.

"Darling?" Ethan called, backtracking when he found me in the kitchen. He smiled as he looked around. "Ah, the scene of our first dance," he said.

I couldn't stop the smile or the blush that crept up my face.

"And the origin story of your scar," I teased, taking his hand and kissing it. A soft growl emitted from Ethan's throat, and I winked at him. "Did your phone call go well?"

"Well," Ethan began thoughtfully as we slowly made our way into the living room. "I have an opportunity to take advantage of something that just came up, but it comes with a condition of travel."

# DELILAH ST. RIVERS

"London, again?" I asked him as we sat on the couch and he took my hand.

"Not quite so far, love. This time, it's in Charleston, in the lower Carolina state."

"Oh. Well, luckily you'll be in the same country this time."

"I'd like to ask you to come along, if you'd like to. It's beautiful this time of year and I'd love to take you around the city. What are your thoughts?"

"How long would we be gone?"

"Two days, plus travel. We'd leave tomorrow afternoon."

"Hm."

"Think about it," Ethan said quietly, pulling me closer to him. "The amazing things we could do in different places, the sights we'd see, the love we'd make…"

I couldn't stop the giggle that erupted from my mouth as he kissed my ear.

"It all sounds amazing and I'd love to go, but there's Mom. I don't want to miss out on making sure she's okay. Not to mention, I don't want to be tied down with the thought of something happening to her while we are supposed to be enjoying ourselves in between your meetings."

"What do you propose, Pet?" Ethan asked, pulling only his face from me to look into my eyes.

"I'm not proposing anything; just asking for some time to think about it."

"Of course, darling. I understand." Ethan tucked a strand of hair behind my ear. "But, at the risk of appearing overly optimistic, I shall hold off canceling plans until you give the final word."

"Thank you for understanding. You are so good to me." I leaned forward and pressed the side of my head against his chest.

"Might as well thank the sun for shining," he said, pressing a kiss to the top of my head. "Just as it was born to shine brightly, I was made to be yours."

"Silvertongue," I chuckled. "You know, you've already wooed me into being yours."

"Ah." Ethan's voice dropped an octave. "But to keep you, I must never stop wooing you. I've found that's the key to a happy relationship, no matter the commitment terms."

"Like you'd ever be rid of me," I joked.

"One couldn't be too careful."

"You're wonderful. I was thinking of heading out to see Mom in a bit. Would you like to come with me?"

## CHAINS OF SATIN

"As often as possible, but it may be a little uncomfortable with your mother around, don't you think?" Ethan asked, winking at me. I laughed and slapped his chest playfully. "In truth, Pet, I have much to prepare for this trip. Send her my best and as always, I will be right here when you return."

THE RIDE TO THE FACILITY WAS QUIET as I mulled over Ethan's offer to accompany him on his trip. This was a pretty big deal, something that took more trust on my part than any I'd shown him before, outside of the bedroom. I'd never been in a relationship where we'd traveled before. But with Mom's condition, the threat of her self-harming or even committing suicide hung over my head constantly. I was no closer to an answer when we pulled up to the entry doors.

"How is she doing?" I asked Rico, finding him eating a pudding at the service desk.

"She's sleeping," he answered. "But she'll be awake in a few minutes, and then we can go in to see her. In the meantime, how have you been?"

I smiled, appreciating his thoughtfulness as usual.

"I'd be worse off if it wasn't for Ethan."

"He's still being good to you, then? No crazy secrets popping up? No sex dungeons, or three foreign wives who mysteriously vanished? Dudes can get insane when they finally have their prize behind closed doors, *mija*."

"We won't discuss the sex dungeon—"

Rico belted out laughing, and there was no stopping the blush that overtook my cheeks.

"But he's been absolutely perfect, I promise."

"Mhm…then why the face when you came in?"

"He's taking a pretty big leap," I sighed. "I guess I'm just trying to figure out how I can turn it down without hurting our relationship."

"Now I'm doubly curious," Rico said, leaning into the counter.

"He wants to take me on a trip with him for a few days. I would be lying if I said I didn't think it would be a fun time, but I have a responsibility to my mom. I'm not the kind of kid that drops their parents off at a nursing home and then goes on with their lives and forgets about them. What if something happens to her while I'm gone?"

The look Rico gave back to me was full of compassion. His usual sass was nowhere to be seen.

"Your mama is in the best hands she could be in. You know all you've done for your parents while they were with you. You've put your

# DELILAH ST. RIVERS

life on hold, dove, and you can't do that. You know your mama wouldn't want that. She'd be telling you right now that if you don't do it, she'd pack your things, put you in the car, and make you go yourself. You gotta care for yourself, too, Petunia."

"She's awake." A nurse popped around the corner to tell Rico.

"Is she agitated?" Rico asked.

"She claims she's hungry. The rush order is in, just in case she goes and changes her mind before her normal lunch comes through. Other than that, she seems to be doing okay."

"Thanks, girl," Rico said, leading me to the room where Mom sat in her old high-backed chair, staring out the window.

"Hi, Mom," I said softly as I walked to her.

"Do you see the flowers out in the yard? Yellow." She pointed. "Your father bought me roses for our first date. Only, they were yellow. Yellow roses, can you imagine?" She laughed. "I cried as soon as I saw them, and your poor father was so confused until my father told him that yellow roses were a gift for friends."

"You never told me that story," I laughed. "He must've felt so embarrassed."

"He made sure the very next day that I had two red roses in my hand so I couldn't mistake his intentions." She smiled brightly as she looked back out the window.

"Your lunch is here, Mrs. Barlowe." One of the cafeteria staff rolled in a cart, catching my mother's attention.

"Oh, I'm not hungry, dear. Set it to the side and I'll see about it later."

"Now, little mama, if you don't start eating we will have to put in the feeding tube we talked about." Rico gave her a stern look as she rolled her eyes and looked back at me.

"They think I'm a child."

"They just worry, Mom. It's their job to make sure you do what you need to keep yourself healthy. We all just want you safe, is all. What if I share something exciting while you eat?" I offered.

"My own daughter joined the bullies." Mom shook her head but still gestured for the cart. As she began to slowly pick at the mac and cheese, I moved to sit on her bed.

"I've been invited to go to Charleston for a few days."

"With Shay?" Mom asked.

"With Ethan," I corrected. "It's a business trip, but he wants to show me the sights. I'm still up in the air about whether or not I will go; I wanted to talk with you about it."

# CHAINS OF SATIN

"Why wouldn't you go?"

"I'd miss you if I didn't come see you everyday. And I'd worry about you," I answered.

"If I could I would be packing your bags for you," she said calmly, while Rico did little to hide his laugh. Mom set her fork down onto her plate. "Ethan is a good man, you are a good girl. You're both young! You need to live a little without an old woman dragging you down."

"Mom, you're not—"

"Either go or don't. I can't make up your mind for you. But I tell you this: as of the end of this visit, you are not allowed to come back to see me until Saturday. Rico, you put this down. I'm serious, she's not allowed to come see me for the next four days."

"Yes, ma'am," Rico said.

"Wow, that's kinda bullshit, Mom. I'm just saying I don't think I'd be comfortable going so far away from you—"

"Well, you can be comfortable in that big house of his without him, too, but you won't be coming to see me." She reached over and patted my hand, her tone softening. "Go home. Pack your prettiest dresses and shoes. Enjoy the time you have with your love; Lord knows life is too short for regrets."

"It's still a shit move," I muttered, knowing she was right. Mom laughed.

"I love you, chickadee. And I can tell this guy of yours does, too." She winked as she picked up her fork and frowned as she looked closely at it.

"Why does the silver keep getting switched for the cheaper metal?" She glared at Rico. "Are you stealing again? Where's my silverware?" Mom yelled, throwing and hitting Rico with the fork. Her sudden mood change caught me off guard.

"Mom!"

"Don't you raise your voice at me, you nasty little beast. You're probably stealing too, aren't you? Where's my husband? Where's my home?"

"I love you," I said through my tears as I began to back out of the room. Rico pressed the red button on the wall and two orderlies came in, one holding a syringe. I barely made it out without getting hit by a flying plate of mac and cheese, dodging the food as it crashed against the wall beside me. I walked through the corridor and away from the commotion as I dialed Ethan's number on my cell. He answered in two rings.

"Petunia? Is everything alright?"

"Do you think you'd be able to come and get me from the

191

treatment center?" I asked. I heard shuffling and keys jingle together in the background.

"I'm on my way," he said. Through the phone, I heard the door shut amd a car start. "Would you like me to pick up anything on the way?"

"No," I cried, unable to stop the break in my voice. "Just you, Ethan."

"I'm coming, darling. Was it a bad moment for her?"

"It wasn't...but then it was. This sucks, it's just so hard." I took a shaky breath. "I'm sorry if I pulled you away from anything important."

"Think nothing of it, for nothing is more important to me than you. Are you inside?"

"No," I answered. "I'm sitting out front."

A few minutes went by and Ethan spoke again.

"There you are, pretty girl. I see you."

I hung up as he pulled up beside me and stepped out to open the door for me. He held me by my shoulders for a moment, then hugged me. I took a deep breath and turned out of his arms to get into the car, laying my crutches in the back.

"Where to?" Ethan asked as he got into his seat.

"Home." My tears began again and I cried silently until we pulled into the driveway. Ethan turned the car off and placed a hand on mine.

"I'm sorry you have to go through this." He brought my hand to his lips and kissed my fingers.

"When I got there, she was lucid and responsive, talking about my dad and flowers, telling me I need to live my life without regrets. Then she called me..." I turned to look out of the window, my emotions choking out my words.

"Your mother loves you and doesn't mean—"

"I know," I interrupted softly. "I know she does. My mother would slit the throat of anyone that talked to me like she just did. She would never stand for it. But to hear those awful, ugly words come out of the same mouth that had just said 'I love you'..." My head dropped and my hands covered my face as I fought against more tears. "She was so confused, asking for my dad and her home."

Ethan stepped out of the car and opened my door to scoop me from my seat. He sat me on top of the still-warm hood of his car and stepped between my knees. I leaned against his chest as he enveloped me in his arms.

"It's so hard," I cried into his shirt. "I just want my mom back. It's like I'm mourning her death while she's still alive, and I can't stand it! I just want her back."

"Oh, Pet," Ethan sighed into my hair. He gently placed a kiss on my head. "I'm sorry, my darling. I'm so sorry."

"I feel like a broken record," I said once I'd finally calmed and regained my composure.

"What do you mean?"

"I just have the same complaints over and over each time this happens."

"It's only that you feel the same hurt, my love. That doesn't mean you don't feel it as keenly the hundredth time as you did the first."

*God, that's exactly what I needed to hear, exactly when I needed to hear it.* A gust of wind blew and I shivered.

"Are you ready to go inside?"

I nodded and Ethan swooped me up into his arms and carried me in, leaving my crutches in the car.

"Rest, my sweetheart. You must be exhausted. I'll go out and get your things while you rest. Watch something on the television and try to relax until dinner. If you need anything, just call out." Ethan kissed my forehead, and I lied back on the soft couch, fast asleep before I could even decide what to watch on Netflix.

"I'VE DECIDED TO GO TO CHARLESTON WITH YOU."

"You're certain?" Ethan asked, studying me as I made my way into our room after my nap.

"I am. I know I made a huge deal out of it this morning, but after thinking about it and talking to Mom about it, she was right. I need to stop thinking that every action I do will somehow lead to her death."

"What did she have to say about it, when you talked to her? Was that the subject that set her off today?" Ethan asked.

"No, it wasn't. She said that if I stay or go, it doesn't matter to her. She was putting in an order to refuse visitors until Saturday."

"Well, then!" Ethan exclaimed, smiling. "She really is rather feisty, isn't she?"

"Where do you think I get it from?" I smirked. "I should change my name to apple."

"Good thing I love apples," he quipped. I cringed and he laughed. "Yeah, that was less suave than intended."

"I am serious, though. I want to come with you, to be with you and explore new places…Not to mention I'll get to see you out in the wild among the populace." I widened my eyes in mock shock.

# DELILAH ST. RIVERS

"Feisty indeed," Ethan said, kissing my cheek. He lifted me, carrying me into the bedroom and sat me in the lounge chair. The bed was covered in suits, dresses, casual slacks and pants, and all other items needed for our trip—all items needed for the *both* of us.

"Did I fail to mention my propensity for being an optimist?" Ethan slowly grinned.

"First that wonderful bath from our first night, now this...It's like you know just how irresistible you are or something."

"I certainly hope so. I put in an awful lot of work to achieve that goal."

"Humble, too," I teased with a wink.

"Humility is a pretense I care not to partake in, Pet." Ethan shook a finger at me and laughed.

"I'm glad you're not pretentious. You don't have to be."

"Would you like a drink?"

"No, I'm fine. I think I'll just sit and watch you do the work for me," I said, cocking my head and smiling innocently at him when his expression darkened a fraction.

"That's one, Pet. Keep it up and I'll leave packing until the morning."

"What?" My innocence was exaggerated in that one word as I batted my eyelashes at him.

"You know *what*. I'm busy, but never too busy to deal with my brat." Ethan's eyes shot daggers, though the corner of his mouth was upturned, egging me on.

"That actually sounds promising." I smiled up at him as he turned and made his way closer to me. "*But*, I'll behave so you can go on packing my things while I sit here and watch. It's kinda sexy anyways."

"Kinda?" Ethan asked quietly, still moving closer.

"Well it's a powerful sub-energy, with the whole act of service thing. It would be such a turn-on if it wasn't so...weak."

Ethan's eyes widened.

"Did that seriously come out of your mouth?" he asked, almost breathless in his surprise. "I'm tempted to jump straight to strike three for that one." He gripped both arms of the chair with his hands, his face barely inches from mine. I kissed his nose.

"No, you're right. We have to leave tomorrow and with so much for you to do, I'll behave," I answered, barely holding laughter back as I kissed his nose again.

Ethan seemed to debate with himself until he shook his head.

"Nope. I'm not convinced."

He stood and lifted me from my chair.

# CHAINS OF SATIN

"Bend over my lap," he commanded, as my heart began to race. He guided me gently onto my knees, helping me into position over him.

"I'd hoped you'd be bare for your first spanking, but this will have to suffice," Ethan mused softly as he ran his hand over my jean-clad ass. He grabbed a handful and I squealed.

"Sh, Pet. I need to hear you count to twenty, and I won't be able to hear you clearly if you make all that noise. I'd hate to get in the middle and have to start all over again." His hand went back to caressing me, and I could feel myself getting more and more turned on. I turned in time to see him plant a kiss on the spot he grabbed, locking eyes with me as he quickly raised his hand and let it fly.

The impact shoved my pelvis into his leg and I gasped.

"Count."

"One," I obeyed. He let loose a series of hits, never striking the same place twice. "Two. Three. Four. F-five," I counted out loud for him.

"Tell me why we are in this predicament, darling," Ethan cooed at me.

"Because I was being a brat while you were trying to work," I confessed. He struck me twice more, and twice more I counted aloud.

"I think it would be a good idea to not try testing me for my attention from here on out, don't you think, Pet?" He struck me three more times and my skin began to burn, though another part of me was reacting differently to the pressure that was being applied.

"Eight. N-nine. Ten!" I cried.

"I believe I asked a question," Ethan said, dipping his hand between my legs and finding considerable heat there. "Ooh, my sweet darling. Is the pleasure becoming greater than the pain?" The change in his voice and a newly growing stiffness in his lap almost broke me.

"Yes," I moaned.

"Perhaps I'll go back to my preparations and come back to this when I am finished."

"Please, sir," I began to beg. "I deserve being punished; you wanted to teach me a lesson. Please teach me the lesson! I haven't counted all the way to twenty yet."

Immediately he struck me three times more, harder and faster than those prior. I groaned; my orgasm was on the cusp of fruition when he stopped.

"Eleven. Twelve...thirteen." I shuddered in his lap as the first of my reflexive tears rolled down my face.

"Color," Ethan demanded of me, lust turning his voice husky as he spoke.

# DELILAH ST. RIVERS

"Green, sir." I was barely able to say the words. The completely hardened cock pressed against me twitched in response. He leaned over and bit my ass, his teeth digging into the denim. I gasped and grew wetter. His hand again rubbed over the bite as he chuckled.

"My hand is getting a bit tender. Let's call this one lesson learned," Ethan teased. "Shall we?"

I shook my head. I was in desperate need of him to finish it, if only to drive me to that peak of bliss that was just out of reach.

"I think you're searching for a reward for your behavior, darling. That defeats the purpose of this exercise, doesn't it? If I thought making you come would always correct your bratty behavior, you'd have had a dozen by now," Ethan cautioned, dipping his hand between my legs as if gauging my reaction by the heat that radiated from me.

"I'm going to have to get creative again," he continued thoughtfully. "What to do…"

The slow movement of his hand on my body without the direct attention to my hardened clit was beginning to drive me insane. My breathing grew even heavier the longer he kept up the contact.

"How many more are left?" Ethan spoke, finally.

"Seven," I whispered, feeling every inch of my body that was in contact with his.

"I dare say, I don't believe you can last seven more without coming. In fact, should you succeed, I will reward you. How does that sound?"

"Difficult," I admitted, my face turning red. He chuckled then struck me four times, hard but at a restrained pace. As I counted out loud, my body was chomping at the bit to have its release. I was so close, it physically hurt. I couldn't hold back the whimper.

"Shh, sweet girl. I know. I know," Ethan consoled me. "You want to come so hard, to feel that rush of adrenaline surge through your body, crashing into you and leaving you breathless as you float into bliss, don't you?" His whispered words were like porn in my ear, turning me on more than they helped to calm me down. I could do nothing but nod as I lay panting and sweating on him.

Without a word, Ethan gripped a handful of my hair, lifting the top half of my body off his lap, and further grinding my pelvis against his leg.

"And I wanted to finish packing for our trip before playing with you, *Princess*," he growled savagely, before raising his hand high in the air and finishing the last three strikes against my ass in quick succession.

On strike two, it happened. Encouraged by his hold in my hair, the denied orgasm ripped through me, the blinding heat rocking my body as he laid the final spank across my ass. I cried out wordlessly as pain and

# CHAINS OF SATIN

unbelievable pleasure fought simultaneously for my attention. I clutched his knee and clawed through the fabric of his pants as I rode it out, barely noticing his hand as he stroked my soaking pussy through my jeans.

"Eighteen," I gasped when my lungs found air once more. "Nineteen. Twenty."

"I'm surprised you could remember to count," Ethan chuckled darkly as he released my hair. My forehead leaned against his leg.

"I failed."

"I noticed. Now you won't get the satisfaction of your entire reward." Ethan sounded remorseful. "Instead, you shall thank me with that beautiful mouth of yours for making you come." He stood, lifting me in the air and kissing me. Our tongues found each other as he sat me onto the chair.

"How badly would you like to thank me, darling?" he asked, his voice thick and deep as he unbuckled his belt.

"I need to thank you with all my heart, sir." I glanced up at him. No bratting this time. "I hurt, but I feel so good. I'm grateful, let me show you how much." My sigh was full of lust as he released his weapon from the restraints of his slacks.

"You may," he said.

I wrapped my hand around the base of his erection and held it tightly as I slid my tongue around the heated head. I circled it lightly, listening to his grunts of growing anticipation until I took him in, fully, down to my hand and past my tonsils.

"Fuck," he whispered, tangling his hands into my hair, yet allowing complete control to stay with me. I held him in my throat for a moment before I began to move up and down his cock, coating it with my saliva and moaning for his pleasure.

I slid my hand up his shaft to follow my lips, maintaining a firm hold on him at all times, moving at a slow pace. Ethan moaned a guttural, animalistic sound that came from his throat, pushing my hand off his dick and gripping my hair tight. He rocked his hips to meet my mouth as he bottomed out against my throat again and again, increasing his speed.

Ethan looked down at me and our eyes met, my mouth and throat his to watch as he stuffed them over and over, eagerly fucking them. His thighs began to shake as I began to fondle his testicles, pulling and gently twisting the flesh between my fingers.

"My God," he gasped as he thrust himself deep, cutting off my air for a moment before backing away, only to do it again. Tears began to roll down my cheeks, but I never took my eyes off his chiseled form. I was being skull-fucked by a god and he was loving it as much as I did. The thought

# DELILAH ST. RIVERS

alone made me wet and wanting all over again.

Ethan's cock grew thicker in my mouth.

"I'm going to come down that throat," he groaned, his thighs tensing up for the launch. "Don't waste a drop."

I hummed in my approval, and that vibration was his undoing. He moaned as I felt the hot, salty liquid shoot against the back of my throat. I gripped his shaft again and pumped him as he purged his contents into me, watching me swallow it as I milked him.

The chest of his shirt was soaked and his hair was in his face, disheveled with sweat dripping from the ends. He trembled as he looked down upon me, watching me as I dragged my tongue under his cock. I opened my mouth and pooled the last of his semen from his head into my tongue, showing him the contents before swallowing. I kissed his deflating head for good measure before finally releasing my hold on him.

"That—" he started to say. I smiled at him as he gasped for air, no doubt trying to slow his racing heart.

"As I said." I interrupted, fluttering my lashes at him. "I'm ever so grateful, sir."

## CHAPTER TWENTY-NINE

# Petunia

I'D NEVER BEEN ON A PLANE BEFORE, but Ethan was my constant reassurance, and we arrived in South Carolina with barely any issues. Being in first class played a huge role in that, I'm sure. When we got off the plane, Ethan had arranged for someone to gather our bags and before I knew it, we were opening the door to our hotel suite.

Stepping in, my breath left me. The walls were covered in aged, delicate floral wallpaper that immediately flooded me with nostalgia. We entered the sitting room, and just behind the ornate oak furniture upholstered with eggshell fabric was a small table, seated for four. To my right, a step led from the sitting room into an area that was sectioned off by doors. One led to a large bathroom, with typical his and hers sinks, a standing shower, a soaking tub, and a toilet tucked away in a nook. The other door opened to reveal a king sized four-poster bed, the frame raised high off the ground. The wood of the frame was a walnut shade, and at first glance you could tell it was older than my grandparents. It was easily the nicest hotel room I'd ever been in.

"We could go out and sight-see, if you'd like," Ethan said, wrapping his arms around me from behind as I took in the view from the bay windows after we'd settled in. "Or we could stay in. It's your choice."

"Do you think it would be okay for us to stay in tonight and go

## DELILAH ST. RIVERS

wandering tomorrow? It's so close to dinner time."

Ethan's chin rested on my shoulder. "Not quite ready to share me with the world?" he asked, kissing my neck.

"Never," I teased, leaning into him. "Especially if you keep doing that."

"Greedy girl," Ethan purred in my ear. I smiled.

"Only because you're worth being greedy about."

"What will you have for dinner, darling?" He planted a kiss on my head. "Anything you want is at your fingertips. Or shall I surprise you?"

"Oh, I love surprises," I told him, turning to face him. Ethan grinned, the wicked expression spreading slowly across his face. "What?"

"Oh, I know of your love of surprises. I've arranged for a few during our stay here, and I have no issue adding dinner to that list."

"What are the others?" I cocked my head to the side, unable to stop my own excitement from showing on my face.

"Darling, *darling*, if I told you, it wouldn't be a surprise, now would it?" Ethan teased in his best imitation of Scar, his lips curling into a devious smile as his voice lowered to a rumble that ran through my chest and spiked my heart rate.

"Alright, I'll give you that one," I chuckled, asking instead, "When will I get them?"

"So eager!" he exclaimed, laughing. "But I'm not even giving you that."

"Any hints?"

"Not a single one," he answered, laughing again as I sulked. "You do look so precious when you pout. Just trust that when the time comes, it'll be no less than perfect." Ethan brushed a hair from my face and hooked my chin with his finger so I would look up at him.

"Trusting you is the easy part," I confessed. I leaned up and kissed his lips.

"Nothing makes me happier," he said softly. "Now, you sit tight, relax, and I'll order room service from the bedroom. No listening in or you'll ruin the surprise."

I took the time to go into the bathroom, and by the time I came back out, Ethan had finished ordering and was in the middle of laying out clothes to change into for dinner. I'd been wearing a plain blue t-shirt and jeans, but in front of Ethan lay two summer dresses, which he was looking at thoughtfully. He stroked his lower lip with one of his deliciously long fingers.

"Trying to decide which one would look better tossed onto the floor while you have your way with me?" I joked as I came up behind him. He

200

# CHAINS OF SATIN

smiled as he continued to look at the dresses.

"If that were the case, I would choose nothing and demand nudity."

"It would certainly save time," I laughed. He chuckled.

"How right you are." He gestured toward the bed. "Which one would you prefer, darling?"

"The blue," I answered, reaching for the sundress. Ethan pushed my hand away and sat me onto the bed. Tossing the crutches to the side, he grabbed the hem of my shirt and began undressing me, kissing my skin as it was exposed. He ended with a kiss on my lips as he tossed my shirt onto the floor.

Ethan's hands dipped down as he began to unbutton my pants and pulled downward, taking my underwear with them. He laid me bare before him on the bed, slowly crouching between my legs as I watched him kiss both of my bare knees lovingly. My desire for him descended upon me instantly, my scent permeating the air. He stood and lifted me, reaching for the dress and pulling it gently over my head, guiding the silken fabric down my body before kneeling in front of me once more.

"The color complements the beauty of your eyes," he commented. "You chose well."

Before I could utter any thanks, he grabbed my thighs and pulled me to him, his tongue darting out to taste me. I gasped, the sound soon swallowed by my moans as his lips and tongue made my knees quiver. I'd felt this man orally please me time and time again, yet it never failed to excite me, and never left me wanting.

A soft knock on the door interrupted us and I growled in frustration, flopping backwards against the mattress as he stood to answer the door with a wink. From the bedroom, I heard Ethan exchange pleasantries followed by the sound of a metal rolling cart entering the suite. I situated the skirt of my dress, cursed the timing, and followed Ethan's steps to the sitting room. He stood in front of the table as a member of the waitstaff unloaded and arranged the silver domes across the table. He showed Ethan a bottle of red wine and white wine to choose from, but before Ethan could decide, I interjected.

"Both."

Ethan chuckled. "Without knowing dinner, the challenge of choosing the wine is infinitely more difficult for you."

"Exactly. Choose both. We can have one with dinner and one" — I winked at him as he turned to face me — "with dessert."

"Madam has an excellent preference," the server stated, setting both bottles into a bucket of ice. It was exactly as they show in movies and I was stoked. Ethan saw him to the door, discreetly handing him a folded

DELILAH ST. RIVERS

bill before we were once again left alone.

"Come, darling. Tell me what you smell."

"Oh gosh, I don't know," I mused, thinking for a moment. "I can smell, steak? I think? Definitely some kind of meat. And fruit. Pineapple — I'm positive about that one. I don't know anything else for certain — it's all mixing and it all smells so good!"

Ethan grinned and pulled a chair from the table, beckoning me to sit. He gave me a sweet, lingering kiss as I did so, the effect of him warming my already blazing insides. He smiled against my lips and lifted the silver dome from my plate, revealing a gorgeously displayed lobster tail, a medium-well filet mignon garnished with parsley, and a little dish of melted butter.

He kept lifting the domes spread across the table, each one containing different side dishes, fruits, and an arrangement of two pieces of decadent chocolate cake topped with a single raspberry each.

"Wow. Is that caviar, too?"

I was stunned. It was all I could say as I stared at everything in front of me. This was extravagant, even by the standards set by living with Ethan.

"It is, actually." Ethan chuckled. "It's no Beluga sturgeon, but it is the finest the hotel has to offer."

"I wouldn't know the difference," I laughed. I pointed at the only untouched dome. It was placed in front of the seat between Ethan and I. "What's that one?"

"My curious girl," he marveled, chuckling. "Part of another surprise. Patience, Pet."

I smirked and reached for a piece of pineapple, signaling the beginning of our meal, as we did at every meal together. We ate in silence, glancing at each other every now and again, and taking our time. It didn't take long for me to feel satisfied. I tried everything, even the caviar, and found this dinner to be one of my top favorites of all time.

"Have you saved room for cake?"

"Maybe after a while," I answered, leaning back into my chair. He stood and helped me to one of the soft chairs in the sitting room, kissing me on the forehead.

"I've packed you a book to help you relax after such a meal. Wait here a moment," he said, retreating into the bedroom. When he returned, he offered me on of my all-time favorite books: *Maia* by Richard Adams. I smiled, taking the impossibly thick hardcover in my hands.

"I may forget you're here," I warned him with a wink, opening the book to the first page. "I tend to get lost in this one."

# CHAINS OF SATIN

"Well, we can't be having that," Ethan teased. He opened his phone and texted as he knelt between my knees. His eyes sparkled with mischief as his hands pushed my skirt up and he ran the pad of his finger over my clit. "Let's see how well you hold your composure and 'forget' while you read, darling."

"Not fair!" I gasped.

"I know, love. I know." He grinned wider and lowered his head to kiss the spot his finger had just caressed. "You're not reading."

"I'll be stuck on the same word the whole time," I whined.

"It sounds to me like you don't want to be reminded that I'm here," Ethan said, backing away from me.

"No! No, oh, God, no. I do! I *really* want to be reminded," I protested as he licked his finger.

"Then read to me. Help me understand why this book is a particular favorite of yours," he coaxed, sliding his tongue over my clit again.

I was quite proud of the fact that I was able to get through the first page and a half before the orgasm hit me, sending my focus from the book to Ethan between my legs, my trembling thighs, and the fact that my world was exploding.

My body was barely recovered when a soft knock once again interrupted our endeavors. Ethan pulled away, kissing my inner thigh tenderly as he rose to his feet and walked to answer the door. Some soft words were spoken and the door closed. I leaned my head back and closed my eyes, taking a few deep breaths as I closed my eyes. Hands grazed my arms from behind, pulling my own hands upward, *Maia* falling forgotten onto my lap.

"Meet your next surprise," Ethan whispered in my ear.

I opened my eyes and looked up, shifting to face him. Another pair of hands holding onto my knees caught my immediate attention.

A red-haired man around the age of thirty sat crouched between my open legs. He knelt in the common submission pose, his hands resting upon his lap as he sat still, looking up past me to Ethan with his deep brown eyes.

"This is Daniel, Pet. He is going to be our guest for the duration of our stay, should you choose to accept him as your gift. During the day while I am at these tedious meetings, he will entertain you by doing anything you please, whether it be by reading with you, watching a movie, or" — he nodded to Daniel, who began to lick and kiss my still-exposed pussy — "he may give you as many orgasms as you, or I, would like him to."

"Th-the contract? No sha-sharing?" I stuttered.

Daniel was slow and lazy with his attention, clearly one to savor

203

and enjoy his present duty. Ethan's eyes met mine.

"He's caged, darling. He cannot penetrate you, only give you the warm up while I'm gone. He is also barred from kissing, regardless of person or circumstance. It's grounds for immediate termination, as per his Master." Ethan's gaze flicked down to Daniel as he continued, "Daniel is into degradation and servitude. He wants nothing more than to do what he's told and nothing makes him happier than to be handled roughly, to be deprived of sexual pleasure, and to be ordered around. He's on loan from his own master and follows the same safety system we do if and when the time comes for him to use them. This contract between his master and myself concerns all things Daniel. What he does, his safety system, how he shall be rewarded, and how, if necessary, he should be punished."

Ethan handed me a small stack of stapled papers and I glanced over the words. Daniel was a slave, in all manners. He was to ask permission to do anything, even relieve himself. It was unusual for this small-town girl to come across someone like him, but with my ex, it wasn't a first-time encounter.

"He's yours, Pet. For tonight and the next two days, he's all yours. Do you agree with this?" Ethan's eyes could do nothing to hide the lust that burned behind them. His bright, blue eyes shone, boring into mine.

"Yes," I moaned as Daniel gently massaged my clit with his tongue.

Ethan handed me a pen and bid me to sign my name on the last empty line at the bottom of the final paper. As I did so, Ethan's hands slid down the front of my dress, and he rolled a peaked nipple with his fingers.

"I cannot wait to make all your desires come to fruition," Ethan whispered as he leaned over and took the papers from me. He set them onto the coffee table, then leaned to cover my mouth with his kisses, reaching to press the newcomer's head hard into my pelvis.

I squealed as Daniel sucked harder on my clit while Ethan's tongue dove into my open mouth. Breathing deeply, he pulled back and watched my face, twisting one nipple and palming my other breast as Daniel's firm tongue lapped at my soaking pussy. I twisted into Ethan's hand while grabbing Daniel's hair, grinding against his nose. I bucked as Daniel held fast to my flesh. Ethan's eyes widened and he bent low, pulling my breast out of the top of my dress and taking the nipple into his mouth. My unoccupied hand curled under and around Ethan's head as I moaned to the rhythm of Daniel's mouth.

With a groan, Ethan pulled away from my breast and stood, grabbing Daniel and pulling him to his feet by his hair. He threw him down onto the floor by my side, then pressed Daniel's face against my exposed nipple, still glistening from Ethan's saliva. He watched with darkened eyes

# CHAINS OF SATIN

as Daniel slowly licked and sucked on the offered peak.

"Are you ready for me?" Ethan asked, looking at my panting, sweating form through hooded eyes. I nodded. "Do you want me to fuck you while he sucks your breast and kisses you all over?" He took the turgid cock from his pants and stroked it with his hand.

"Yes," I cried out, desperate for him to fill me.

"I'm going to fuck you hard, *Princess*," he warned, his voice a low growl as he knelt before me, gripping his dick tight in his fist as he lined himself up with my entrance. "And I'm going to fuck you fast. Then, when I fill you with my seed, he's going to clean it up with his tongue and you are going to lay there and enjoy every second. Green?" My walls clenched at Ethan's filthy, sexy words. His fingers danced down my thigh and gripped my hip firmly as both Daniel and I nodded.

Ethan pulled me closer to him, wrapped my legs around his waist, and slammed his cock roughly into me. I cried out his name as he savagely beat against me, the simultaneous sensation of Daniel replacing his mouth on my nipple while Ethan moved between my legs brought me almost instantly to orgasm.

"Ooh, there's a good girl," Ethan cooed as he pounded me through the first orgasm and straight into another, my cries echoing off the walls of the suite. "Fuck...God, *yes*. I love this cunt. So wet. So tight—" His words were cut off by the snap of his hips against my body. He increased his pace just a touch, pulling my hips upward so he could dive deeper, sending me gushing all over his thighs.

"I'm not going to last," Ethan warned through gritted teeth. One of his hands snaked up my body and grabbed my throat as he continued to thrust into me. Daniel wrapped one of his own hands around my breast, squeezing and kneading it as he flicked my nipple with his tongue. I couldn't breathe as another orgasm ripped through me, punching the air from my lungs.

"Ethan," I gasped, riding hard through the pulsations that gripped his dick, causing him to groan.

"Sweetheart," he gasped back. "Oh, my sweet girl, are you ready?"

I nodded, licking my lips as Daniel's hand drifted to my other, clothed nipple. Ethan bent to kiss me roughly, trapping Daniel's hand against my chest, before pulling away and shuddering, his own orgasm making him twitch and grip my throat tighter. I cried out and pulled at Daniel's hair while he grunted and dragged his teeth across my nipple.

Ethan thrust into me, trembling with every stroke until he collapsed upon me, his sweating head trapping Daniel's stray hand between our bodies once again.

# DELILAH ST. RIVERS

"Ethan," I sighed as Daniel gave my swollen, red nipple a gentle kiss. I felt Ethan's head move as he lifted up to place his lips on my neck, then met my own. We lay like that in the chair, languidly making out, while Daniel sat still in his submissive pose, unwilling to disturb us.

Ethan's semi-soft cock slipped slowly from my body, spilling our intermixed fluids onto the carpet beneath Ethan's knees. He shifted his body over, motioning Daniel downward and grasped a breast as I inhaled deeply when Daniel's soft tongue tenderly went to work.

Ethan played with my breasts, making small circles around my nipples and palming the flesh while Daniel licked and sucked between my legs. The room was silent, broken only by the occasional sound of Daniel swallowing, my moaning, and Ethan's lips against mine.

"My girl, my own Pet," Ethan whispered in my ear, "does it feel as nice as it should? Is he meeting the high expectations I have for him, my love?"

"No one could ever feel as good as you," I whimpered back. "But, yes, it feels so incredible, sir. Thank you for my gift, Master."

Ethan groaned, and his head dropped into the curve of my neck.

"You keep it up and I'll have to ravage you again," he warned, his voice muffled against my skin. I grinned softly, then let out another small gasp when Daniel touched my clit with the tip of his nose. We shared another moment of silence, and I sighed as I ran my fingers through Daniel's hair.

"Ethan," I whimpered, the soft strokes of Daniel's tongue forcing another buildup within me. Ethan walked around me and wrapped his arms around me from behind, resting his hands gently back over my breasts. I reached my own arms up and folded him against me, allowing me to nuzzle his neck.

"Watch him, my darling. Watch him as he cleans you so thoroughly."

His fingertips dragged lazily across my nipples, making me further tense and clench my inner walls around Daniel's tongue. I gasped again as Daniel pushed softly against my clit with his nose again.

"Steady, my love," Ethan cooed as he kissed the top of my head. He pulled my arms from around him and held my wrists behind the top of the chair. "Stay just like this." His order, soft though it was, was command enough.

He took a few steps back and crouched on one knee, angling himself so he could see Daniel's movements and my expression. I locked eyes on Ethan, watching the knuckles of one of his hands press into the carpet while the other began to move along his bottom lip. The pose was familiar, reminding me of the first time I walked on crutches to him. I was aware I was being put on display for him. The thought brought warmth through my

# CHAINS OF SATIN

body, and the orgasm that was slowly building grew closer to peaking.

Daniel must've sensed a change in me. He rubbed his nose harder against that nerve bundle and took my soaked, swollen labia in his mouth and sucked. Ethan's eyes glittered as he watched me draw closer and closer to that finish I was chasing.

"There's my girl," he muttered. "You're so close, aren't you? Does it make you want it more knowing that I'm watching? Does it make you feel dirty?" His lips pulled up in a half-grin. "Slide a finger inside her, Daniel. Hold her tight to you, she's about to unravel."

Daniel did as directed, sending my body into a whirlwind of pleasure as he stroked my tightening walls. My whimpers grew to moans as the pressure built within me. I closed my eyes and threw my head back. Quicker than I could imagine, Ethan's hand was around my throat and I found his face inches from mine as my eyes flew open.

"No, you will not get lost in this. You will let me see your eyes as he makes you come. Though I am not the one giving it to you, we will share this orgasm together, do you understand? *You will not deny me this.*" He pressed his lips to mine in a punishing kiss before he pulled away to watch my reaction to Daniel's unhalted maneuvers. Ethan squeezed my throat tighter.

"Come hard. Now. Say my name," Ethan demanded. "Shout it, *Princess*. Shout my name as you come."

The orgasm coiled in my body before snapping loose, ripping his name from my lips as I squeezed Daniel's head between my clenched thighs. Daniel kept going, experience keeping him focused on just where to apply pressure to allow me to ride out the orgasm to completion. Meanwhile my eyes were locked onto Ethan's as wave after wave crested and crashed through me, my cries finally silenced by his ardent, insistent kisses.

When Ethan pulled away, he palmed my breasts as I found my breath, the climax finally retreating. I stared up at my most amazing dom and smiled softly. He unhanded my throat and pulled Daniel soundlessly from his position. Ethan lifted and placed me to straddle his lap on the chair I'd been occupying. He pulled me to him and began kissing my sweat-soaked face.

"That was the sexiest moment I'd ever lived through," Ethan said. "Feel me beneath you, hard and burning to bury myself inside you again. This is because of you, my sweet, good girl. Only because and only for you."

His tongue found mine and he grabbed my hips, grinding me against his clothed erection. I pulled my lips from his and flicked his earlobe with my tongue.

## DELILAH ST. RIVERS

"What was going through your mind as you watched another man please me?" I whispered in his ear.

"I wanted to kill him and hate-fuck you until you screamed for me," he growled as I kept grinding on him, creating a damp patch on his pants. "But God knows I couldn't take my eyes off the divine vision before me. The whole scene had me bewitched."

I cupped his face as he studied mine. His hands moved my hips slower, savoring the feeling of my hot, swollen sex stroking his own.

"You are so beautiful in any moment, but the look of lust and pleasure never fails to bring me to my knees, fully shaken," Ethan confessed. Keeping his attention on me, Ethan commanded Daniel to eat the dinner beneath the dome on the table. "Enjoy it," he told the man, "you've earned it. I'm going to make love to my darling girl one last time tonight." Daniel wordlessly obeyed, moving to the table to sit down and begin eating his room-temperature meal.

Ethan rose and carried me to the bedroom, his eyes boring into mine as he laid me gently on the bed, only pulling his body away from mine to strip off our clothes. He lay his body back upon me, his warm flesh warming mine as he began touching me everywhere, kissing me passionately.

Ethan shifted slightly and slowly entered me, never breaking the kiss, his thickness filling me almost to the point of pain. I whined in his mouth, and he started to lift off and pull out of me, but I wrapped my legs tight around him, pulling him deeper into me.

I craved the pain he was bringing and reveled in it with each thrust of his cock that strained my swollen muscles, his rhythm slow but hard. Ethan sucked then bit my lower lip before his tongue worked its way back into my mouth, cutting off my loud moan. His fingers twisted into my hair as my hands caressed down his muscled back to grope and fondle his ass before traveling back up to his sculpted shoulders.

"Christ, you feel like heaven," he whispered, trailing kisses down my neck.

"Pain," I whimpered. "Please make it hurt, I need it to hurt." I begged and pleaded with him as I succumbed to the edge of darkness that threatened to take over me. Ethan caressed my cheek as he looked into my eyes.

"Green?" he asked.

"Green. Please?" I begged again, dragging my nails down his shoulder. Ethan winced and groaned but still restrained himself.

"Call red if you need—"

"I swear, I promise I swear I will."

Those were the last words I was able to coherently speak as Ethan

# CHAINS OF SATIN

slammed his next series of thrusts into me, sinking his teeth into the soft flesh of my neck and refusing to let go. I let out a scream as he tore into me, ravishing my tender body, bruising my thighs with his fingertips as he gripped me tight. My head ached from his hands drifting into my hair, pulling it roughly to elongate my neck before finding my lips once more.

On and on he fucked me, hitting me deep and hard each time, sending me spiralling downward into that masochistic place within. Ethan bit my neck, my chest, my nipples, my ears. Everywhere his teeth met flesh, he dug into it as he pulled my hair tight and pounded against me.

"Say…words…" I panted. "Mean words…I'm…I'm almost there…"

"My whore," Ethan grunted in my ear. "My beautiful whore, taking this cock so easily…Do you like that? Do you like knowing you're filthy? That you're my fucking slut? I own you, your body, your cunt. I—"

"Ethan!" I cried out as the first surge of my climax rocked through me. He tensed up and his thrusts became erratic, his own climax building, seeming hell-bent on destroying me from the inside out. I clung to him for dear life; the sheer combined power of his strokes and his demeaning words in that sexy accent sent me to a higher plane of euphoria I had ever before experienced. My walls convulsed around him and I screamed into his opened mouth when his lips met mine. His cock twitched against the strain of my pulsating walls, and as he shifted me slightly upward, he drove himself deeper and released his semen against my cervix. I was drowning in pleasure; his release drove me further into my own orgasm, and I cried out for him again.

Ethan's orgasm subsided and he fell onto me, sweating, breathing hard, and speechless. His lips were still on mine, and his tongue searched and found mine. Meanwhile, my own climax wouldn't fade. With every microthrust of Ethan's hips I was still spewing electricity throughout my body. He released his hold on my lips and began petting my hair back from my forehead.

"Shh, Pet. My glorious darling, let it go. It's alright, let it go. I'm here," he murmured and soothed, until finally the waves passed and he was able to withdraw from me, still kissing my lips gently.

"Shall I clean her, sir?" Daniel had entered the room and was sitting beside the bed. I couldn't stop trembling, so Ethan turned us on our sides and cradled me against his chest.

"No. My darling cannot take anymore. Cover and move the cake pieces to the small refrigerator. Call for room service to clear dinner away. Then come to bed behind her." His hands were stroking my back. "Together we shall bring her back down from her incredible heights."

DELILAH ST. RIVERS

CHAPTER THIRTY

# Petunia

THIRTEEN HOURS. IT WAS THE LONGEST I'D ever slept in my life. When my eyes finally fluttered open, the first thing I noticed was Ethan missing. A different pair of arms circled my waist, and a body snuggled up against me.

"I didn't want to wake you, Mistress," Daniel said softly. "Before he left, your master said once you were awake I was to check you for any injuries, then ask if you would like to share a meal with me."

I smiled.

"Well, I guess you can start then."

Daniel's hesitation confused me; I turned to glance at him.

"Did you hear me? You may as well start with my back, since you're already there."

"I…"

"You have my permission to speak, Daniel," I said.

"I must ask for forgiveness, Mistress, but I have already checked on this side of you, from tip to toe."

"That was fast," I commented.

"You were still asleep while I did it. I know it went against his orders, but I was very careful not to wake you while I checked you over."

"That's still disobedient, and you know it. As your mistress I can't let this slide."

"I understand."

"Where did Ethan go?" I asked Daniel, looking over at the empty spot beside me.

"He has meetings all day, a luncheon with overseas clients, and another meeting with his company. He promises to be back for dinner," he responded without pause.

"Thank you," I answered. "As for your punishment..." I thought for a moment. "Ugh, I'm no good at this. I'm more of a bratty sub than I am any kind of domme."

"If it helps, my master would demand punishments from me. If I chose one I enjoyed, he'd pick something harsher, add to it, or even delay it," Daniel offered.

"You might as well finish looking me over," I said after a moment's thought. "Though you are technically mine, I am Ethan's and I suppose that would make you Ethan's as well, by default. So when he gives you an order, you are to obey it to the letter, understood?"

"Yes, Mistress."

"Then, afterwards, food. I'm starving already. Be quick, but make sure you miss nothing. Once we've eaten, I'll deal with your insubordination."

Daniel guided me onto my back gently, and I stopped him before he even began to touch me.

"If you find an abrasion, cut, bruise, discoloration or tenderness, you are to kiss it, understood? Gently. I feel like having lips on my body this morning." I gave my first real command ever, and I did it with a smile.

"Yes, Mistress."

He started at my fingertips and worked downward. He kissed a small bruise left on my wrist, a red mark under my arm and another on my shoulder. He gently turned my head to the side and kissed the bite mark on my neck, though it made me wince for him to do so. Afterward, he shifted my breasts carefully, heavy as they were on my chest, to see all the way around them before planting soft kisses on the tips of my still-swollen nipples.

"God, you're doing so good, Daniel," I said once I remembered to compliment him as little ripples of pleasure coursed through me.

"Your master said if he were to locate any injury I failed to report, he will be sure to keep me in a chair the rest of my visit, deprived of all attention and any stimulation."

"Wow," I exhaled. "That's impressively creative."

Daniel nodded and went back to work, kissing my hips where Ethan left reddened imprints. He lifted my legs, bending the knees gently

# CHAINS OF SATIN

before replacing them, slightly spread apart back onto the bed. His fingers gently brushed against my labia and I flinched.

"How tender is my mistress here?" Daniel asked before placing small kisses all across the irritated flesh.

"Not so bad, just a little sore," I answered softly. "I've dealt with worse."

"May I taste you, Mistress? I would love to make you feel better right now." The breath of his request fluttered against my clit. I inhaled deeply and almost gave in.

"Would it make you happy?" I asked him, running my fingers through his hair.

"Yes, Mistress," he answered, wrapping his hands around my thighs. I grabbed and jerked his head away from my body.

"Then your punishment shall be my denial. You looked at and touched my body while I slept, against orders. The fact that I allowed you to obey my own master's orders with your fingers and lips should be something to be grateful for, shouldn't it?"

"Yes, Mistress," Daniel answered, his soft hands never leaving my thighs.

"Are you finished with your inspection?"

"Yes, Mistress."

"And what will you tell Ethan?"

"Everything, Mistress."

I smiled. "Good."

"Would you like to join me for lunch, Mistress? I may call and place the order if you'd like," Daniel offered, still not moving a muscle. Once I released his hair, he slid back onto his knees with his hands on his own lap. His boxer shorts still showed signs of arousal.

"I'd love to," I answered, pulling the sheet back over my body and sitting upwards with some effort. "I'm not sure what I would want though. Something meaty that I can sink my teeth into...Burgers. Let's go super cheap to confuse the chefs here and get burgers with steak fries."

Daniel smiled, a dimple appearing on his right cheek, and went out of the room to place the order. I watched him move, his grace reminding me of a deer in the woods. Ethan's grace always reminded me of a panther on the prowl, even when he wasn't in feral mode. Even as he moved about his house on phone calls or whatnot. Both men were sure on their feet, but there was no mistaking who was predator and who was prey.

Daniel came back in and knelt at the side of the bed. "It will be ready in about thirty minutes, Mistress."

"That's enough time to get into a bath, I suppose," I said. "Thank you, Daniel."

"Would you like me to draw it for you and bathe you?" Daniel offered.

"No. I'm still punishing you for your disobedience. You can sit on the floor of the bathroom and watch me, knowing I probably would have wanted you to touch me the whole time if only you'd been a good boy."

"Thank you, Mistress."

"I can't wait to get out of this cast, though," I said more to myself than to Daniel as I rose and hobbled my way into the bathroom. "For an entire week after it's gone, I'll be under the shower, grateful to stand when I want to scrub away the dirt."

"How did it happen, Mistress?" Daniel asked as I started the bathwater and he took his position by the tub. I reached for his hand, and he eagerly raised it to help me climb in.

I began telling him about that night, how I fell and woke up in Ethan's bed afterwards. I told him about how I worked for Ethan and our first conversation, our dancing, and the cut on his hand all while bathing and washing my hair. By the time the tub was drained and I beckoned Daniel for my towel, he'd been caught up to speed with the shortcut version of my relationship with Ethan. A knock at the door took Daniel out of the bathroom while I began brushing my hair, and before long I smelled lunch. It smelled like it was going to hit the spot.

"Daniel," I called out as I left the bathroom. "Go and select one of Ethan's shirts for me. Put it on the bed."

"Yes, Mistress," Daniel answered, quick to obey. By the time I joined him he'd laid out a white, long-sleeved button-down. It was soft against my skin as I sat on the bed and put my arms through it, though the cuffs hung off my fingertips. Daniel knelt and buttoned me from the fourth button, his deft fingers working quickly to encase me in the silken fabric.

"It's see-through, Mistress," Daniel said as I stood.

I grinned, knowing that everything would be tantalizingly exposed through the shirt. I considered how Ethan might react should I still be naked under it when he came back tonight, and I sighed, wishing he were already here.

"You chose perfectly," I said to Daniel.

We ate, occasionally asking each other questions after I gave Daniel leave to speak his mind about things. I learned of his rough childhood, how coming out to his parents as bisexual led him to be kicked out and shunned by most of his family and friends. How drugs were a big part of his life until he met his Master at a night club. He had been stripping for cash, sometimes pimping himself out to survive, when he'd been discovered by

# CHAINS OF SATIN

the man who contracted him. Daniel shared that he was days away from killing himself before his Master found him.

"He taught me my place, taught me that I must love myself if I were to survive this life. He taught me how to turn my masochism into something constructive," Daniel said. "Being with him gives me the first sense of security I've had since I was a child in my mother's arms."

"Are you angry at your parents' reaction?" I asked him, wiping my face with the napkin on the table. "Did you end up hating them?"

"Oh, definitely, Mistress. I snuck into their house not long after they kicked me out with a knife — I wanted to kill them. But I got as far as the living room and saw all of our family's pictures. They'd taken down or modified every picture I was in. It was like I didn't even exist and it broke my heart worse than being kicked out. I ended up stealing a few things that I knew were valuable, but after that, I walked out and never looked back."

"Jesus, that's awful," I mourned. "Come and hug me."

Daniel rose, and I wrapped my arms around him when he sank to his knees beside my chair.

"Are you happy now, though?" I asked him as he laid his forehead against my neck. "I know you said everything about being secure and all that, but are you happy to be someone's slave that's loaned out every now and again?"

"Absolutely, Mistress. Without my parents being bigoted against everything that was different from them, I wouldn't have met my Master, found my place in life, and found a love that I never thought I would be deserving of. I also wouldn't be here, serving the kindest Mistress I've met."

"Flatterer," I accused, smiling. "I'm glad it all turned out the way it did for you. You seem like a great person and you do deserve happiness, no matter who is in your bed."

"Thank you, Mistress. I know it."

"Are you done eating?" I released him and pulled away to look at him.

"I couldn't eat another bite, Mistress."

"They make a great burger here, don't they?" I said, watching Daniel kneel back into position.

"Yes, Mistress. One of the best."

I folded my fingers together and placed my hands on my midsection, my thumb caressing the soft fabric of Ethan's shirt. A slow grin spread on my face as an idea popped into my head.

"Daniel, would you be willing to take a couple of pictures of me with my phone?"

"If this is what my Mistress wants, I will do it," he answered, following close behind me as I went back into the bedroom. I reached over to my nightstand to hand Daniel the cell. Sitting against the end of the bed, I laid my crutches beside me, on either side. My casted leg spread straight against the carpet while the other I bent upward, tugging the shirt up above my ass cheek and tucking the excess material between my legs. I leaned my shoulders against the mattress as I arched my back, looking at Daniel who had crouched four paces away in line with my bent knee. It was the perfect angle for a picture to tease Ethan without letting him see all of my feminine treasures.

I threw the opposite arm behind my head and slid a finger in my mouth with my other, pulling my bottom lip downward just slightly and held the pose while Daniel took a few snapshots.

"Your Master might find it hard to concentrate when he sees this," Daniel said, making me grin.

"That's the point."

I took the phone and opened my messages. I selected a picture and sent it followed by the message:

> I don't have your arms so your shirt will have to do.

Almost immediately, Ethan responded and the one word set my body on fire:

> More.

"He wants another one," I giggled. "Maybe I'll make him wait a bit." Daniel looked up at me with panic in his eyes and I laughed. "Alright, we'll send him one more."

I sat all the way against the bed and spread my legs. I unbuttoned the entire shirt, opening it just to my nipples. I grabbed the bottom ends of either side, pulling the shirt tighter to the floor to cover my exposed flesh between my legs.

Daniel faced me and lay prone against the carpet while I leaned forward, pressing my breasts closer together with my biceps. I closed my eyes and parted my lips just slightly, inhaling deeply before opening my eyes once more on the exhale.

> Exquisite, my Pet. One more.

"He's so demanding!" I cried out, not even bothering to hide my

# CHAINS OF SATIN

smile. It was such a thrill to picture him squirming in a meeting with clients, trying to hold it together. "Daniel, can you set the timer on the phone's camera? I want to make this one special for him, and it's going to involve you."

"I can hit record and you can select a single frame from it, if that would make it easier, Mistress," Daniel suggested. I nodded; I hadn't thought of that.

I stood carefully and pulled myself to the middle of the bed until my back was turned to the now-mounted camera. I lay back and moved until only my shoulders were off the bed, stretching my arms gently behind me. My breasts were pressed tight against the newly buttoned shirt. I bent the knee of my uninjured leg and beckoned for Daniel to crawl between my legs.

"That thing you wanted to do earlier, when you were inspecting me?"

Daniel nodded. "Yes, Mistress. To taste you."

"Do it, gently. Softly. Slowly. But do it."

I waited until his lips made contact with my skin, closed my eyes and imagined it was Ethan who was with me, Ethan who was licking and sucking me closer to an orgasm. Daniel slid a finger inside me and I moaned, edging closer to the finish. His tongue danced upward and his mouth latched onto my clit, matching the rhythm of his finger until I screeched when my orgasm crashed through my body.

"Daniel! Oh, God!" My voice was high and tight from lack of breath. "Daniel, don't stop!" My screams and yells turned into moans and whimpers as my body relaxed and Daniel slowed. He kissed my thighs and caressed my legs until my trembling stopped and my breathing returned to normal.

"Shall I retrieve the phone, Mistress?"

"Yes," I said, clearing my throat.

He got up as I rolled onto my stomach, and he showed me how to choose a picture from the video. It all looked pretty sultry, but in the best one, the look on my upside-down face was pure orgasm, and you could just catch the top of Daniel's head between my legs.

"The perfect angle," I complimented Daniel.

"Thank you, Mistress."

How I feel when I'm thinking of you.

No answer. For over fifteen minutes we held our breath and waited for a response that never came.

# DELILAH ST. RIVERS

"I'll call for room service to clean up from lunch, if that is what you'd like, Mistress?" Daniel eventually asked.

I nodded and rose from the bed, grabbing my crutches and heading to the sitting area. After flipping through a few channels on the television, I decided to call Mom and see how she was doing.

"*Hola, mija,*" Rico answered cheerfully. "Aren't you supposed to be looking at plantations and eating collard greens and grits while wearing big hoop dresses and clutching your pearls?"

I laughed at him.

"I'm in a hotel and just ate a juicy cheeseburger, thank you very much. One day in the South won't turn me into Scarlett O'Hara. How's Mom doing?"

"She's in the best mood I've seen her in, in a long time, honestly," Rico answered. "Maybe it did her heart, and head, good to know her daughter is taking a much-needed vacation and finding her own joy for once."

I smiled.

"May I speak with her?"

"She's sleeping right now; it's her naptime and all that. Would you like me to text you when she's awake?"

"No, I'll try again later. Thanks, Rico. I hope this good mood of hers holds out a while."

"Me too, little woman. Have fun, and then have some for me, okay?"

"Always. Later, Rico," I said with a chuckle and hung up.

I checked my messages. It had been almost an hour and still Ethan hadn't responded. After room service came and cleared away all evidence of my lunch with Daniel, the atmosphere suddenly got a little too quiet for me. I told Daniel to sit at my feet and rub them while I began to reread my book.

Before long I was swept away in the fantasy that lay in between the incredibly well-written pages. Between Daniel's expert foot massage, the hotel suite, the silence, and the comfortable couch, it was truly beginning to feel like an actual vacation. I was deep into the ninth chapter when the door blew open and Ethan stormed into the suite with murder blazing in his darkened blue eyes.

"Get out," he coldly demanded of Daniel. "Stand outside of this room and do not come back in until you hear your name called."

Daniel ducked out of the suite without so much as a glance behind him while Ethan turned his heated gaze onto me.

"Hey, I don't know what happe—"

# CHAINS OF SATIN

Ethan cut me off with the raise of a single finger. He took the book from my hands and set it on the table, then scooped me up and laid me down on the bed.

"Do it again," he commanded.

"What? Do what again? Ethan, you're scaring me," I said.

"The photo, *Princess*. Do. It. Again." Ethan crossed his arms over his chest.

*Oh, shit*, I thought. *He only calls me "Princess" when he's gone savage.* My thighs instinctively clenched together.

"All this over a picture I sent you?" I asked, confusion overtaking my good sense. Ethan's eyes flashed and he tapped two fingers on the bicep of the other arm. *Strike two*, the gesture meant. I hesitated a breath longer but decided not to test him further.

"Daniel had the phone over there," I pointed a shaking finger towards the wall behind me.

Ethan moved to roughly where I'd indicated. I positioned myself the way I'd been in the photo and waited. Ethan's eyes raked over my body and he licked his lips.

"Daniel!" Ethan shouted. I jumped at the sound while Daniel practically materialized beside him. "Where was the phone, exactly?"

Daniel took the phone and propped it as before.

"Now," growled Ethan at the both of us, "reenact this picture perfectly as before. I want her to climax now."

I didn't understand why he was so angry about it. *Why is he so aggressive about this one photo that he would leave his meetings just to see this done in real life? And didn't he give me Daniel to "give me as many orgasms as I please"? What the hell —*

My train of thought left me when Daniel's tongue found home against my clit as before and with embarrassing speed I was once again racing toward that finish line. I tossed my head back, closing my eyes as the first ripples of climax tore through my body.

"Open those eyes, *Princess*," Ethan demanded as the camera on the phone flashed. I locked eyes on Ethan as the phone recorded the whole event without him in the frame. I watched his chest heave and his face flush, a primal nature flashing in his eyes as speechlessness overcame him. I couldn't help but shudder as Daniel coaxed me through the main explosion of my orgasm, and I cried out Ethan's name.

Ethan stumbled backward into the wall behind him and slid down, the floor becoming his stabilizer as he watched me writhe in the final waves of ecstasy. I gasped for air, dripping in sweat as I rolled over onto my belly and away from Daniel's lips. I let my weary head fall over the side. The entire room was quiet but for the sounds of my whimpers and Ethan's heavy breathing.

Daniel waited a moment before coaxing me to sit on the edge of the bed, facing my dumbstruck dom as he fought to regain his composure.

"Leave us," Ethan spoke harshly, as though he'd been the one on the bed.

Daniel took his leave to the bathroom, and soon the sound of the shower running met my ears. After a few moments, Ethan rose to his feet, picking the phone up off the floor and scrolling slowly through as he took the few steps to reach me.

"The first thing I must do is apologize for frightening you, and if I've caused you harm, please tell me so I may rectify it," Ethan began.

I shook my head. "You didn't hurt me. And your apology is accepted, sir," I said softly, still coming down from my high.

"Secondly, I want to explain to you the nature of my outburst, which I'm certain you'd agree would best describe what happened here just now. Look, my darling." He offered me his phone that had my messages displayed on the screen. He held up my phone with my newest video, from which he selected a picture with the exact same moment captured. "Do you see it, love?" Ethan whispered.

*A bit dramatic,* I thought, but I looked between the two.

"I don't—" I began, but realized the difference almost as soon as I began to speak. My eyes were closed in the picture I'd sent him.

*"Look at me. I need to see your eyes…Eyes open, Pet…You will let me see your eyes as he makes you come."*

I didn't know. I didn't connect the dots until just then. Ethan knelt beside the bed as the whole thing dawned on me.

"I feel this completion when I see your pleasure. Jesus, it's the most beautiful thing I've ever had the privilege to witness, regardless of who is doing the pleasuring. On the other hand, darling, I feel positively cheated when I cannot gaze into the pools of your eyes, as though you are keeping me from sharing some of the most intimate bliss with you.

"I'm a tolerant man," Ethan continued, tucking hair behind my ear. "I'm also a patient one, and my temper is reined in the way a proper man's should be. However…" He looked to the ceiling and inhaled before taking my hands into his, dropping both phones onto the soft carpet below. He exhaled softly as he lowered his head to look back at me. "I'm so entirely wrapped up and consumed by everything you are that I cannot bear to have you deny me, even in a photo. Your eyes…" Ethan went silent for a moment as he studied me, our hands, my hair. "It never mattered so much before you."

# CHAINS OF SATIN

Ethan kissed me as he wrapped his arms tightly around my body and stood, breaking our contact. I reached for him as he adjusted his tie.

"I hope against hope that you'll forgive my outburst this afternoon."

"No, I mean, I get it now," I said timidly, reaching back up for him. "I just — I didn't understand, but now I do. Let me show you how much I understand,"

Ethan smiled softly and captured a hand, kissing it.

"I must return. I have one more meeting and then I'm all yours, darling."

"Ethan," I called to him as he turned to go, tucking his retrieved phone back into his jacket pocket. He paused and turned back to look at me. "Thank you for taking the time to explain it to me. I didn't know it meant so much to you. Now that I do, you can count on me working harder at not forgetting it, Master."

Ethan took a fraction of a second to look back towards me before shaking his head, eyeing me hungrily.

"Temptress," he hissed. "If this wasn't so important..." Ethan shook his head and turned to walk out the door but stopped before opening it. "By the way, Pet, I think I may add more of my dress shirts to your wardrobe. It's quickly becoming my favorite look on you."

## CHAPTER THIRTY-ONE

# Petunia

THE NEXT TIME ETHAN WALKED THROUGH THE door, he wa
pushing in a wheelchair. I'd been reading my book on the couch whil
Daniel was curled up and sleeping on the floor at my feet. When the doc
opened, Daniel sat up immediately, quick to defend me against anythin
that walked through, relaxing when he recognized Ethan.

"It's not too late to go out, if you're still interested," Etha
announced. "I'd thought we'd give those arms of yours a break while we d
it."

I smiled at him and lifted my arms towards him; he graciousl
accepted the offered hug.

"I missed you," I whispered in his ear.

"And I, you, my darling. It's almost 4:30, so if you'd like to go ou
and explore, perhaps we could also get dinner while we're out." Seeing th
panic rise in my face, he added, "We will be together—the three of us—an
we will get back to the hotel room before it gets too dark. You have m
word."

I relaxed a bit at his words and gave him a small nod.

"You're certain?"

"Yes," I assured him, nodding a little more enthusiastically thi
time. He broke out in a grin, then let his eyes fall down my body. In th

# CHAINS OF SATIN

time he'd been gone, I hadn't changed my clothes or put anything on under his borrowed shirt.

Daniel moved out of the way as Ethan moved to sit beside me and gather me into his arms. He leaned in and nuzzled my neck, inhaling my scent as he ran his hands down my arm.

"What I wouldn't give to take you dancing under the stars, my sweet girl. You can bet your life that I'll be adding that to the list of things to do when you're ready and able." He pressed his lips to my neck before standing in front of me and holding out a hand. "As devilishly tempting as it is to keep you in nothing but my shirt as we wander through the streets together in this heat, you must, regrettably, be made more suitable for the public eye."

I smirked and was tempted to tie the bottom of the shirt and throw on a pair of jeans, but he was right about that heat. The sun wasn't setting just yet, and even though it was after noon, the humidity would have me drenched before too long. I decided to go with the other sundress Ethan had packed for me, and paired it with white, strappy sandals. After both men sought to get me situated in the wheelchair, Ethan gave Daniel instructions to dress himself. Daniel was very quickly dressed in slacks and a gray dress shirt, the sleeves rolled up to his elbows. When all was said and done, we exited the hotel, Ethan pushing the wheelchair and Daniel walking beside me.

Our first stop was a plantation house called Drayton Hall. As we moved through the building, the tour guide shared the sordid history of the plantation and its inhabitants. The elegance of the grand wooden staircase, intricate plasterwork on the ceilings, and 1800s architecture were marred by the knowledge of the unspeakable acts of slavery and violence committed within the walls. The building had only been spared because the owner pretended the occupants of Drayton Hall were ravaged by yellow fever.

Afterwards, we took our time and walked through the City Market, looking through all the vendors' wares, watching in awe as a woman wove grass into a bowl and appreciating the fine pottery and handspun yarn. I'd never been to such a busy, diverse market in my life. All at once you could see baked goods next to metal sculptures, which lay beside jewelry that was displayed next to someone selling homemade soaps.

Ethan picked up a few things from the market that I'd admired. The woman weaving grass thanked us for our purchase of one of her larger vases. An older man winked at me as he handed Ethan a pretty bracelet with round onyx and hematite beads that fit my wrist beneath the bracelet from Ethan. Daniel himself bought a few souvenirs for his Master, including

# DELILAH ST. RIVERS

sandalwood-scented soaps and a dragon sculpture.

We'd reached the end of the market when Ethan leaned down and promised we'd return the next day.

"There's an enchanting restaurant we're going to, love, and I can't wait for you to see it," he said, smiling down at me.

*Just in time*, I thought as my belly began to loudly protest its emptiness.

We were driven to Halls Chophouse. The place was crowded and a line of people hoping to get in for a meal stretched down the sidewalk. I gaped at the sheer sight of it and looked up at Ethan from my wheelchair.

"I'm not sure this is going to be a good day to do this," I said to him.

Ethan grinned and patted me on the shoulder. He handed something to Daniel, said some words in his ear and watched as Daniel wove his way through the protesting crowd.

"Are you feeling chilled?" Ethan asked as he walked around the wheelchair and knelt in front of me, his hand resting above my knee. The sun had disappeared, but I was still comfortable.

"No," I answered, taking his face in my hands and kissing him.

He smiled sheepishly when we parted and cocked an eyebrow in question.

"I've gone quite a bit of time without doing that; you wouldn't want me to forget what it feels like, would you?" I teased him.

"Banish the thought!" Ethan exclaimed dramatically as he held my laughing face in return and kissed me back. He lingered, and the small kiss turned into something deeper, his tongue finding mine and consuming it. Each time I kissed him, it felt both familiar and just as new as the first time we'd kissed. We slowed before parting and leaning our foreheads together, coming back down to Earth. I grew conscious of the fact we were in public — the nearest person wasn't even five feet away from our embrace — and I blushed at the hushed whispers and wolf-whistles from onlookers in the crowd.

"Sir," Daniel's voice tore Ethan's attention from me. "Mrs. Hall is waiting at the door to seat us immediately."

"Jeanne is a wonderful woman," Ethan said, grinning. "She's southern charm and southern wit personified. You're going to love her as much as she's going to adore you." He gently maneuvered us through the crowd to the entrance where an elegant looking matron stood. She lit up as soon as she saw Ethan and leaned in for his kiss on her cheek. He immediately asked after her health as Daniel took Ethan's place behind my wheelchair, following the pair through the doors and into one of the fanciest buildings I'd ever dared to breathe in. Ethan introduced us as we found our

224

# CHAINS OF SATIN

table, and one waiter moved a chair to make room for my wheeled one.

"I'm assuming you'd like your usual course to start with?" Mrs. Hall asked. Ethan nodded. "Now, if you need anything at all, you just holler for your waiters and I'll make sure it's all taken care of for you."

Ethan took his place at my right and I laid my hand on his thigh.

"This place is incredible," I said to him softly. "All of this. I can't believe how great today's been."

"I'm glad you're pleased," he answered. "Do you have a personal favorite moment thus far?"

"This whole place is filled with history and amazing architecture; it's all incredible. I can't get over the ballroom of the plantation home, though. The academic in me can't help but admire it."

"One day," Ethan leaned over to whisper in my ear, "a room as elegant as that will be occupied by you and I alone. We will dance until our feet are sore, and then I'll fuck you in the very middle of the room until you forget your name, and the neighbors for miles around will know mine."

My mouth went dry as I began to imagine such a thing and I stared at Ethan as he winked at me, squeezed my knee gently with a smirk and turned his attention to the band on stage.

Classic jazz music began to play soon after we were seated, and after that, we had salads placed in front of us, along with tall glasses of iced water. I drank a quarter of my glass as we began to eat.

Ethan's hand rested on my knee and carelessly traced circles around it as he took small bites of his salad. Only slightly distracted, I ate my own food until the same waiter appeared and asked after our main dish choices. I chose the seafood special, something light to counter the heaviness of the burger I had for lunch and the heat outside. Ethan chose a wagyu filet and Daniel, being told to order what he'd like, ordered the dry-aged ribeye. Ethan then went on to order the lobster mac and cheese, broccolini, and pepper jack creamed corn for our sides.

As we ate, the music changed and new jazz began to play. I was so wrapped up in the ambiance of the place that I was unaware, at first, of Ethan's hand as his circling fingers slowly transitioned to caressing my thigh. I let out a soft moan as I took a bite of salmon, the moist meat flaky—a signature of a perfectly cooked filet—as it danced across my tastebuds. Ethan's hand gave a little squeeze of my thigh and I gasped, blushing red as I looked at him. He continued to eat his dinner as though nothing happened, ruining the illusion with a side-glance and a wink.

I smirked and rolled my eyes, digging into the last of the salmon and aiming for the helping of the lobster mac and cheese on my plate.

"*Oh my God!*" I cried out as the decadent flavor hit me at full force.

DELILAH ST. RIVERS

"Keep it up and I'll make sure the last thing you moan in this restaurant is my name," he threatened under his breath.

"Promise?" I asked, batting my eyes at him as I smiled. I took another bite and moaned as I closed my eyes. His hand pushed up under my skirt and I smiled wider until his fingers pinched my clit through my underwear.

"You're driving me to distraction," he growled as I took a moment to regain my composure. "Daniel, your mistress is being quite naughty at the moment. She is distracting me from my meal while she gets to enjoy hers. Terribly unfair, wouldn't you agree?"

"Yes, sir," Daniel answered.

"Move your chair closer to her and manipulate her without bringing about her release—discreetly of course—while I cut into the masterpiece that is on my plate."

"Cheater," I mumbled as Daniel's hand took Ethan's place and began to lightly drag between my parted thighs.

"And how is everything tonight?" Our waiter approached us and asked, inspecting our plates.

"Quite delightful," Ethan answered, the charm heavy in his voice.

"Would you be interested in dessert tonight, Mr. Aldrich?"

"I think the bread pudding would be sufficient for us," Ethan replied, turning to me. "Do you agree, love?"

I nodded and barely managed a smile as I tried to control my trembling.

"Bread pudding it is, then," Ethan declared, smiling broadly. He turned to me with wickedly glittering eyes and tucked hair behind my ear. "I do hope you never learn your lesson about being a brat in public. This is too entertaining." Ethan grinned at my blushed face and kissed me.

The evening wore on and my sensitivity grew with each stroke of Daniel's fingers. Visions of Ethan taking me into a restroom and thrusting into me danced through my mind with vivid clarity.

When dessert was placed before us, it smelled delightfully sweet and tasted even better. It was smooth and creamy against my tongue and I couldn't help—no thanks to Ethan taking control of my punishment once more—but to groan my appreciation. Ethan dug against my damp opening through the underwear and I almost came right in his hand.

"Ethan," I gasped in a whisper and he chuckled, continuing to play with me. "Please, can we go somewhere to finish this?" I put my hand on his thigh, sliding it up until I felt his firm, thick erection through his pants. "Please? I want you."

Ethan pressed against my panties once more before releasing me

# CHAINS OF SATIN

and pressing his fingers to his nose, inhaling as he looked right at me. I stared, breathing hard with my lips parted.

"Alas, they aren't saturated," he said, observing the digits. "Had you been naked beneath your clothes, I'd have you suck them dry this instant."

"Fuck." The word fell from Daniel's lips in absolute breathy admiration.

Ethan and I both turned to look at him — me, in surprise, and Ethan, in slight amusement.

"Do you approve?" Ethan asked. Daniel nodded. "Speak your mind, carefully."

"Your display of absolute domination is to be commended," Daniel said. "I'm sorry for speaking when I shouldn't, sir. I couldn't help myself."

"Only a fool would reprimand such a graceful compliment," Ethan stated, wiping his mouth with his napkin and setting it on the table beside his plate.

The waiter came by with the check and Ethan set a platinum card on the tray, pulling me against him to kiss me tenderly until the waiter came back with the card and receipt.

———

BACK IN OUR SUITE, ETHAN AND DANIEL both helped to dress me for bed. Under Ethan's instruction, the men took turns fondling my body with fingers and tongues. Ethan's kiss was dominating my lips while Daniel had one breast in his hand and his mouth clamped onto my clit. Ethan reached down and squeezed a handful of my other tit. I could do nothing as I sat on the end of the bed with Ethan behind me, kneeling on the mattress while Daniel was on his knees, on the floor before me.

"You were quite the temptress in that dining hall, weren't you?" Ethan asked softly after breaking off his kiss.

"You turn me into something wicked, sir," I said, smiling up at him.

"Did you enjoy feeling how hard I was for you?"

"I always do."

"If you enjoy it so much, my sweet girl, you should take it in your mouth and show me how much you liked it."

I nodded as Ethan kissed me again, freeing his large cock from his pants.

"Don't stop, Daniel," Ethan instructed. "Make her come often and I'll make sure your Master knows what an obedient slave you've been for us."

With that, Ethan guided himself into my opened mouth, entering slowly as he groaned, pulsating as he drove deeper down my throat. Backing out and easing in, he found a slow stride, filling and emptying my mouth with extreme pleasure. Daniel slid a finger into my soaking wet cunt and I couldn't stop the squeal that sent vibrations all around Ethan's cock.

"Your mouth is an oven, Pet," Ethan gasped, quickening his thrusts while holding my head in his hands. His palms covered my ears and his fingertips gripped my jawline as he moved with my head resting on his thighs. Of all the positions I've given someone oral sex in, this with Ethan was probably the most comfortable of them all.

My orgasm, delayed for over an hour and hurrying to hit home, built swiftly and unrelentingly. I whimpered and cried as Daniel's merciless movements held steady, gripping my thighs to hold me still.

Ethan grunted.

"Your throat tightens in such a pleasing way when you scream like that," he panted out, gritting his teeth as another squeal wrapped around him. "I love your mouth, my pretty girl."

Daniel sped up his fingers, thrusting faster and sending me over the edge. I bucked against Daniel's face and was set to screaming, the sound fragmented by the eager movements of Ethan's dick in and out of my mouth.

"Jesus, Pet," Ethan moaned. "You wild, unbridled woman; you beautifully unhinged creature, you're going to make me explode."

I began to quiet and still as my orgasm ran itself dry.

"Good girl," Ethan said, pulling himself out of my mouth to let me suck on his head. "You love this, don't you? You love his head between your legs while you're taking my cock down your throat, my sweet naughty girl, don't you?"

Slowly he eased himself back into the rhythm of fucking me down past my tonsils as I moaned low and loud, reacting to his words and Daniel's touches. I'd just come down from one climax, and the ball of fire was already growing in the core of my body once more. Ethan picked up greater speed, my saliva coating his thrusting dick with each movement as he threw his head back.

My thighs tightened around Daniel's ears, and he sucked harder at my clit in response.

"I want you to come for me...Come again, baby," Ethan coaxed. "Daniel, hurry, her sweet mouth is ending me."

Daniel eagerly quickened his pace, curving his fingers upward and stroking the knob of nerves within me that brought me to quaking heights. I jerked, but he kept a strong hold on my body so I wouldn't move.

"Yes, there's my girl. Right there," Ethan groaned as I felt him swell. I tasted the bead of precome that was pulled out of him. "Unleash

# CHAINS OF SATIN

hell, my love."

I arched my back hard and my arms flailed as my ordered release took hold and shook through my body. I cried out, my mouth muffled by his driving force.

"There, right there, oh there you go." Ethan shook, and I felt him surge forward as he emptied his load down my throat. I struggled to swallow, wrapped up in the internal thrashing of my body.

"*Christ*," Ethan cursed as his body jerked against me, the final drops of his climax draining into me. My thighs were still tight around Daniel's head when Ethan pulled his depleted member from my mouth and kissed my swollen lips. He murmured sweet words as I whimpered and moaned through the final twitchings of my own orgasm.

Fatigue took over me as the last tremors left. I honestly could have fallen asleep in the position I was in, yet Ethan instructed Daniel to help him situate me on the pillows, and as they were the night before, they wrapped themselves around me after Daniel turned off the lights.

"I should be a brat out in public more often," I whispered in the darkness, only to be answered by a slight chuckle from Ethan.

## CHAPTER THIRTY-TWO

# Petunia

I SAT BACK INTO THE PILLOWS THE next morning and felt Daniel's hand snake around my waist as he snuggled against my back, snoring softly. Ethan had another meeting calling his name, so he'd left Daniel and I once more for the day. I smiled and reached for my phone, careful not to wake him as I moved away, threw on the terrycloth robe, and made my way to the sitting room to call my mother.

"Well, well," Rico answered. "Look who it is. I'm glad you managed to pull away from Prince Charming long enough to call for your mama."

"Okay, Rico," I said, laughing.

"How's it going, girl?" he asked, apparently done with his guilt trip.

"We saw amazing things, took tours, and ate at a stupid-fancy restaurant. I went to sleep before my head hit the pillow," I summarized. "Is Mom awake?"

"Yes, and we are both happy you're having fun. Here she is."

"Hello?"

"Hi, Mom! How are you? I hear you've been doing well lately, so that's good news!"

"Oh, yes," she said. Her voice sounded like she could cry at any moment.

"Are you sure you're okay?"

# CHAINS OF SATIN

"Of course, chickadee. How are you?"

"Well, Ethan and I are having a wonderful time. I saw so many things and I've taken a lot of pictures to show you when I get back." I paused. "How are you doing, Mom? Really."

"I'm doing better, sweetie. I feel better now that my room is a little less cluttered and is organized the way I want it to be. One of my art pupils, Estelle, was devastated that no one came to her birthday yesterday, so last night I gave her my chair, a few afghans, and my ruby necklace as gifts. She lit up something fierce!" Mom chuckled weakly.

"The necklace Dad bought you? I'm glad you were able to brighten her day, but it's sort of sad that you don't have it anymore…What about your chair? Where are you going to sit now that it's gone?"

"Oh, hush," she chided me. "I don't need it all anyways. I think a good declutter was what I needed all along. Lucille and Georgiana both benefited from it. And Rico's niece is getting married; I was able to give him a pair of earrings he promised she would wear on her wedding day."

I couldn't pinpoint exactly why this made me as nervous as it did. She was giving things away left and right, but they were little things, and she said she felt better after doing so. Her room felt better. Maybe I was making a bigger deal out of it than I should have been.

"I guess without the chair there's room to put up another bookshelf. It'll give you an excuse to finish the series you've been working on reading," I said.

"Yesterday, Esther's son sold her stuff in his attic, and she lost hundreds of books—almost her entire collection! I let her go through mine and she ended up with a couple of bookshelves, too."

*Once upon a time she held onto books like they were my siblings,* I thought to myself.

"Do you think you'll marry this guy, chickadee?"

"Mom!"

"What?"

"Well, for starters, that's totally left-field for you. And secondly, we aren't even considering it right now, Mom. We're still trying to learn about each other and see if we even want to be together long-term. I don't even think he's thought about that yet," I said.

"Bah, you've got him hook, line, and sinker. Just wait and see." Mom sighed at the other end of the phone.

"You sure you're okay, Mom?"

"I'm fine, sweetie. I really didn't sleep well last night and I didn't nap today."

"Are you feeling stressed about anything?"

"You know, I've lived my entire life stressed about stuff; this is nothing new," she laughed. "I promise, I'm just tired."

"Would you like me to let you go so you can get some rest?"

"That's probably best, honey. I love you so much. Thank you for calling me."

"You don't have to thank me. I may be miles away, but I still think about you and still want to be sure you are doing alright. I love you, too, and I'll call again before I get on the plane back home tomorrow, okay?"

"That sounds nice." I heard the smile in her voice as she answered. "Goodbye, chickadee."

"Bye, Mom."

I hung up the phone and lay back against the couch. It was an odd conversation and something still didn't feel right about it. I mulled it over again and again, but each time Rico echoed in my mind with his reassurance that she was okay.

I stretched and groaned in slight discomfort just as Daniel was walking out of the bedroom.

"Are you in pain, Mistress?"

"Not really, just tense I guess," I answered.

"If it would help, I can give you a massage. My master claims I do them the best," Daniel offered.

"That sounds lovely."

"Is this a command, Mistress?"

I smiled at Daniel before turning my expression stern.

"Massage me until I am a bowl full of jelly!" I commanded, sticking my nose in the air dramatically.

"Yes, Mistress." Daniel's eyes twinkled with mirth.

Before long, I lay on my stomach on the bed and my robe was removed from my body. Daniel started at my shoulders and neck, careful not to press too hard on the bruise that still lingered from Ethan's passion. I sighed and moaned as his hands kneaded my muscles. It took only a few moments before the silence of the room was getting on my nerves.

"Daniel, play some music," I said.

Daniel obeyed without question and put on some music. I smiled as he happened to put on one of my favorites: Disturbed's cover of "The Sound of Silence." Happy and carefree, I sang along as Daniel continued to work away my tension.

"You should do that professionally, Mistress," Daniel commented. "With some lessons you'd be famous in no time." I blushed and buried my face in my arms. "I'm sorry if I embarrassed you."

His hands never stopped manipulating the muscles in my body,

CHAINS OF SATIN

focusing on my lower back to relieve tension I hadn't even noticed was there.

"You're forgiven," I said after a minute. "Compliments are one of those things I'm not sure how to handle well."

"If you'd like to talk —"

"Not really," I interrupted.

"Does it have to do with your scars?" Daniel continued silently.

I tensed back up and a cold shiver ran down my spine.

"You could say that. Let's not talk about it, okay? I'm just not alright with talking about things that happened in my past. I shared it with Ethan...mostly. He knows the worst of it." I blushed, remembering just how Ethan got me talking about it. "But as much as I told him about the physical abuse, I didn't delve into the verbal. I didn't tell him how I was constantly ignored. That the only time I was praised with so much as a 'good girl' was when I'd done something sexually. How I was trained to be the stoic, brainwashed, zombified sub who refused to say 'no' to anyone, no matter how horrible the request. How he'd laugh as I flinched as he faked a hit to my body, calling me names like 'bawlbaby' and 'dramatic.' How I can't even say my ex's name because it holds that much terror to me even after all this time. After all the good that's happened since."

Daniel's hands smoothed past my ass and down the back of one thigh, caressing and massaging my muscles as he spoke softly.

"And all this you didn't share with your master?"

"No. I mean, how does it compare to the physical stuff, you know? At some point it feels like it gets tiresome telling the whole story, so you focus on the worst stuff so everyone can understand what you went through and leave it at that. The more minor stuff just doesn't seem to matter as much."

"I know that if you were mine, I'd be pissed that you withheld that kind of trauma from me."

"What?" I turned to look at Daniel, whose eyes were blazing.

"If he doesn't know the whole story, he may trigger something in you that could set you catatonic with PTSD and not know what he did. As a dom, it is his job to protect you from everything, including himself. How can he do that if you keep things like this from him?"

"Well...I guess I didn't think about it."

"Him knowing would enhance the dynamic between you two because it would open creative doors to work *around* your full trauma until you're able to work through it."

"Ethan's been through some pretty shitty times with me. I don't think he should have to dive down that rabbit hole and live in the darkness with me, Daniel. He's too good for that."

233

# DELILAH ST. RIVERS

"How can he fully come to love everything that is you if he doesn't get to embrace every aspect of who you are?" Daniel sighed. "Your trauma and past experiences make up a huge part of that. He doesn't know you — he can't love you — if he doesn't know it all."

"Jesus, Daniel!" I cried out, moving away from him as I rolled to face him. He struck a chord in me, somehow found the deepest fear I had and said it out loud. "It's not that big of a deal. He can't miss what he doesn't know. Besides, *Dr. Phil*, who said he loves me anyways? We aren't at the point in our relationship to say anything like that. So it's not like I'm out of time or anything, God."

Daniel stilled and watched my face throughout my outburst. He sat back in his neutral pose, a careful eye on me until I stopped seething.

"I'm sorry if I upset you. Overstepping my boundaries is not something I do on the job. You have to understand that. But with a Bachelor's degree in Psychology, sometimes it's hard to keep quiet when I think someone may benefit from my studies."

"It's just not something I like to talk about," I said in apology as I rolled back into position. Daniel's hands resumed their work on my body. "You'd make a good shrink, though. All the others I tried for a while never got so much out of me."

"Our guest's talent for helping us feel better through bringing out our worst is uncanny, I'll have to agree, Pet."

"Oh no," I groaned in my arms.

*How long has Ethan been in hearing range? How much has he heard?* The questions circled my mind as Ethan walked closer to the bed.

"Daniel, draw your mistress a bath, would you? We must help her get ready for today's adventures." He kissed my head and helped me turn so he could lift me into his arms. The anxious knot in my stomach loosened with each passing second as I came to think maybe I hadn't been overheard.

"I missed you," I said, caressing his cheek. He smiled softly and pulled me closer to kiss my lips.

"And I, you, my darling."

He tapped the bathroom door twice with the toe of his dress shoe, prompting Daniel to open it. Gently, he lowered me into the quickly-filling jacuzzi. The heat began to seep into my body and I sighed.

"She is pleased." Ethan spoke over the sound of the running water to Daniel while never removing his gaze from mine. "Lay out something pretty for our lady; I will take over from here."

# CHAINS OF SATIN

"I HAVE QUITE THE DAY IN STORE for you, Pet, but I think we should have the hard conversation first."

My chest tightened, and I sat up in the bath as best as I could to turn away from Ethan. Anxiety crept up from my chest and wrapped around my throat tighter than his hands ever had, second only to the guilt I felt. I'd told a stranger things that my dom didn't even know.

"How much did you hear?" I asked softly.

"Petunia." My name was spoken slowly from Ethan's lips. "Look at me."

"Can't we just pretend I never said anything?" I asked.

"That's neither honest nor fair to either of us, my darling. Daniel isn't wrong. You should have told me, Pet. You should have told me all of it," Ethan chided.

"I couldn't." My eyes pricked and my vision began to blur. "What I said to Daniel stands: I've already shown you so much bad, and too much ruins relationships. What if you knew everything and decided I was too broken to deal with? There's so much I still haven't faced myself. I still get nightmares. Not as much as I used to, but still...I'm so used to carrying this ugliness alone that to willingly share it is almost impossible."

Ethan was quiet. His thumbs reached up and stroked my collarbone as he pulled me back into position leaning toward him against the side of the tub. I rested my head on his arm as his thumbs moved up and down in slow repetition.

"I'm sorry I'm so high-maintenance, Ethan," I said to him, closing my eyes. "It's the last thing I would ever want to be. And if this changes anything —"

Ethan scoffed loudly and pulled away, leaving my skin with only the ghostly reminder of his hands. I turned to look at him, fear that he was leaving me filling my entire being. To my surprise he was undressing with a quiet ferocity. He flung his clothes and shoes onto the floor as they were removed and stepped into the tub beside me, reaching for and holding my face between his hands.

"Do not misunderstand me, Petunia, I'm not happy that you consciously withheld this information from me. But I am not angry about the subject matter itself. You did nothing wrong, and even if you did, you never deserved the treatment you received in the hands of that brute.

"All of this that we share is about trust, Pet. *Trust*. I still envision a world in which you trust me with each and every aspect of your life willingly and openly. I need you to understand that I am here for you. Not just for sex or as a traveling companion; I'm here for *you*."

Tears fell from my eyes as I prepared him to guilt-trip me, but

# DELILAH ST. RIVERS

nothing more came from him as he wiped my tears from my cheeks.

"When I tell you that you are mine, do you understand what that means?" Ethan asked me, kissing me gently.

I nodded.

"Tell me, then."

"I live with you. I experience life with you. I sleep with you."

"And what do you get in return?"

"Happiness," I said, smiling.

"What else?" Ethan's expression didn't change as he prodded me for the answer he was looking for.

"Your companionship."

Ethan nodded impatiently.

"Of course, my love, but above all else, you're guaranteed security. Consistency. Safety most of all. That's what it means to me, darling. That when you are mine, you are untouchable to the rest of the world. When you are mine, your past, present, and future can do nothing to hurt you. I won't let it, Pet. I won't. And," he continued as he pulled my chin upward to meet his eyes, "it means that I trust you to do the same. I trust that I have your companionship, happiness, and security while I am with you. I trust you, my darling. I trust you. So you must trust me."

I sighed. Ethan was always right about things like this. He looked into my eyes as I nodded in understanding.

"But, in trusting you, I must trust that you'll tell me everything in your own time when you are comfortable. I won't force you to say anything you shouldn't, just as you shouldn't keep things from me that have any impact on our relationship. Are we agreed?" Ethan asked.

I nodded. "I agree." I answered him. "But I have a question."

"A question?"

"When is it your turn?" I asked.

He looked at me quizzically.

"My turn? I'm afraid I don't quite understand."

"I've bared so much to you—integrated so much of you in my life. I've told you about things I haven't told a soul and still you remain a mystery to me."

"How so?"

"All I know about your family is what anyone can google about them. I don't know if they know about me, or what they think. I don't know how you got to this country, or why. Or how you first came into this lifestyle you and I share." My racing heart never slowed as I talked. All the while Ethan looked on, an odd expression on his face, as though he was both studying me and looking inwardly. My bold confrontation would have

# CHAINS OF SATIN

been exhilarating and freeing if I hadn't been so anxious waiting for his response. His hands still clung to my face, but as I talked, his body stilled.

"Christ, baby," he exhaled finally, pulling his hands away from my face. He sat back on his knees and ran a hand through his hair as he looked away.

"I'm sorry," I cried out immediately, regretting it all that instant. "I can be so dumb. You'd tell me if or when you wanted me to know your personal life, and I should have respected that."

He chuckled darkly, and coupled with some slight head-shaking, I could tell it wasn't a happy laugh.

"I've done you a grave disservice," Ethan said, taking my hands into his. "Do you remember how Madeline mentioned my frequency in partners?" I nodded, a pit coiling in my stomach at the thought. "She wasn't wrong. The subordinates I've encountered have all had needs to fill and not much beyond that. I find myself falling into a rhythm from being expected to demand the soul of each contract without the demand of even a piece of mine in return."

"I wouldn't demand your soul, Ethan," I feebly tried to explain. "I just want to get to know the story of the man I care so much about."

I reached up and pressed my palm to his cheek, watching as he smiled and turned to kiss my palm. He pulled himself closer to me and held me in his arms.

"You aren't dumb. You have every right to ask anything of me that you want. And if you want to ask questions now, I'll take as much time as necessary to answer them to your satisfaction."

We ended up sitting side by side, his arm behind me and my head on his chest, tracing wet lines with my finger through his coarse chest hair. I began with his family, and he laughed as he immediately recalled being mischievous with his older cousin, Gerald, pulling pranks around his neighborhood where they grew up.

His mother was a hardworking physicians clerk who never missed a day of work. He described her as the personification of perfection. Ethan spoke softly of the nights she'd come home late and find tea in the pot waiting for her, courtesy of Ethan's father, which she'd sip to decompress from the day. His father would wait to hear the water running as she'd rinse her cup before approaching her for an embrace.

"Her name is Emily, after my great-grandmother. She's been retired for a few years but still likes the quiet and chooses solitude whenever she's able to."

Ethan's father, George, worked in the Department of Treasury for many years.

"He had a real knack for it and is said to have even taken advice all the way to the top."

"What does that even mean?" I asked.

"You know, I don't even know," he confessed with a chuckle. He went on, explaining how his father had one sister who died in a car accident when she was a small child. George never forgave his mother for driving drunk that night. Ethan only met his grandmother during formal occasions, but they were never close before her passing.

"Mum and Dad were quiet companions. The house was never filled with overly-loud laughing and racing around the furniture or whatnot. They slow-danced in the kitchen, had picnics in the park almost weekly and, if they ever fought, I never heard it."

"It sounds like something out of a fairy tale," I said with a wistful sigh.

"I remember looking at them and feeling so proud of how they loved each other, but to be truthful, I never saw myself in that situation. I always thought the companionship would be wonderful, but I never felt driven down the path with a wife and children."

"And now?" I asked.

"I think everyone's idea of a perfect future changes, based on how they grow...who they meet." Ethan smiled softly down at me and caressed the side of my arm.

I smiled as Ethan kissed my head and continued on. He talked about college and being away from his parents for extended periods of time.

"Then I met Claudine. I'd been with a couple of girls, but this was, well...she brought out quite a bit within me that I hadn't even known existed."

He explained how she initially took him under her wing as a sub, but he quickly found his true place. She'd introduced him to underground clubs and shows, expanding his understanding of both the thrill and the responsibility of being a true dominant in a world full of stigmas and fakes. Ethan's parents knew nothing, of course, aside from noticing the gradual shift in his confidence and overall demeanor. George had commented on the presence his son gained in college. They supported his choices in life and career change from finance, like his father, to company real estate.

"I'd brought Claudine home to meet my parents, and they loved her. Though we approached the family meeting as college sweethearts, in reality our passion for each other dwindled to a more platonic teaching relationship. Due to the discretion clause in our contract, no one suspected a thing."

We sat in silence for a minute with intertwined fingers as we soaked

# CHAINS OF SATIN

in the warm tub.

"Is there anything else your curious mind would like to know?" Ethan asked.

"Is my curiosity such a bad thing?" I teased.

"Not at all, my sweet girl," Ethan said, bringing my hand to his lips. "Your curiosity is one of the most fascinating things about you." He looked down at me with a small smile and brushed a wet tendril of hair from my face before kissing me.

"What's your favorite color?"

He smirked and leaned over to whisper in my ear an answer that sent chills through my entire body.

"*Green*, my Pet. It makes me absolutely feral when I see it around you in any capacity." His teeth grazed my neck and I shivered at the contact.

"Thank you for taking the time to share this with me," I said after clearing my throat a few times. "It's helped me get to know you better and the more I know, the more I'm able to please you, sir." I slipped my hand below the water to find him semi-hard until my fingers began to work him over.

"Christ, even your hands are heaven-sent," he moaned, leaning his head back against the tub.

I pulled on him gently, and he grunted before grabbing my wrist and pulling me from him. I looked up and found his darkened eyes searching for mine.

"We have plans today, little brat," he growled, leaning over and kissing me roughly. "Playtime comes later, and so will you. Countless times."

---

BY THE TIME WE REACHED THE END of the market, I'd accumulated a parasol, three more grass-woven items, a pretty leather hair clasp in the shape of a flying crow, and a beautifully hand-quilted hobo bag for my mother. Ethan bade Daniel to sit on an empty bench as he pulled my wheelchair up beside it, excusing himself for the briefest of moments. He returned with various trinkets to fill the hobo bag.

"You'll spoil her," I giggle-warned as he placed an ivory comb, a set of charcoal pencils, three sketchbooks of handmade paper, and a boxed necklace of an elephant family in 14 karat gold into the bag. He flashed a grin as he closed it and set it gently on my lap.

"It's bad luck to gift a lady an empty purse," he said.

"I didn't know that," I said thoughtfully.

"My mistress is looking a little pale," Daniel said to Ethan.

## DELILAH ST. RIVERS

"No, I'm fine, Daniel," I protested.

"Are you hungry, love?" Ethan asked. "We can find a place to eat, or"—he glanced up at Daniel—"we could go back to the hotel, have some room service, and get you your final surprise of the trip."

I looked at their patient expressions and when I realized it was my choice, I flushed. I didn't want to choose wrong.

"I mean, I'm okay with anything really," I began, but Ethan shook his head.

"It's your choice, darling. There's no wrong answer here."

"I am getting a little exhausted and overstimulated from being in a crowd for so long. Another area with a crowd might be a little too overwhelming for me. Maybe we could just go for room service?" I suggested, hoping against hope Ethan didn't want me to choose something else. He smiled instead.

"To the hotel, then. Daniel, give her a push to the car and I'll call ahead to order room service."

"Can I have a hint for the surprise? Just a little one?" I asked Daniel as I was lifted into the car. Daniel offered a small smile and shook his head. Ethan hung up with room service and climbed in beside me, while Daniel climbed in through the other side after loading my wheelchair into the trunk.

"If you keep asking, I may just change my mind," Ethan growled as he took my by my chin. I rolled my eyes and he kissed me, hard and impatient. "Brat," he whispered, gripping my bare breast tight in his hand under the top of my dress.

"You love it," I whispered back against his lips and reveled in feeling his mouth curl into a grin before his tongue found mine. "I want to feel you inside of me," I said when our lips parted.

"Shall I take you here and now? I'll roll down the windows and let the world watch me claim you as we ride by. I assure you no one would mistake your moans as cries for help." Ethan's lips trailed down my neck and his hand left my chest to run his fingers delicately up my thigh.

"Please," I whined, grabbing his hand and pressing it to my wanting, weeping flesh. He chuckled, the sound sending shivers down my spine as he first penetrated me, then pulled his hand away, sliding the glistening finger into his mouth.

"Not yet, *Princess*," Ethan whispered, biting down on my neck before releasing me completely. I stared at him in disbelief.

"God, you tease!" I cried, punching his arm. He laughed again and I pouted. "Fine, I'll just have Daniel help me till we get to the hotel."

The expression on Ethan's face immediately grew thunderous as

# CHAINS OF SATIN

he turned on me, his hand wrapping tight around my neck. I gasped and gushed at the same time.

"No," Ethan snarled. "You seem to forget that while he's your plaything for the duration of this endeavor, you are still mine even while in his presence. If I want you to crave me, beg for me, ache for me, and cry out for my touch, so shall it be until I say you can have your release. Understood?"

*Jesus fuck,* I thought, my heart hammering into my chest, and while my traitor cunt quivered with need deep inside me, a ripple of fear ran through me.

*Him.*

No...No, this was Ethan, not my ex. This was now, not my past. But I couldn't shake the thought of my past as I stared into Ethan's shadowed eyes. I swallowed hard and opened my mouth to respond.

"Yes, sir," I gasped.

His hands released me simultaneously, leaving me a heaving, wide-eyed mess against the seat.

"Good girl," he growled softly, his lips curling into a dazzling, victorious smirk that lasted him until we pulled up to the hotel.

An usher was waiting outside our hotel room when the elevator opened to our suite.

"As requested, your early supper is arranged on the table for your pleasure," the young man said, opening the door to welcome us in. Ethan thanked him while he pushed me through the doorway.

The silver domes were lifted by two others, presenting the three of us with an Italian dinner. Pastas, breads, soups, a beautifully executed eggplant Parmigiana, and a platter of braciole covered the entirety of the large table. I couldn't stop the gasp that left my lips, and I smiled tentatively up at Ethan, who did nothing but study my reaction as all was revealed. He tipped the men and closed the door behind them after they left.

Instead of steering me to the table, I found myself in the bedroom once more.

"Before we eat, I have something for you," Ethan said, walking into the closet and pulling out a dry-cleaner's bag and revealing a long red dress. It had one shoulder-strap, a scooped neck, and slits up both sides. He then handed me a sparkling, diamond-encrusted chandelier necklace to go with it.

"Ethan." I stared, barely able to breathe.

"You're stunning in everything, or nothing," he winked. "But seeing that it's our last night here, I figured I'd help us all celebrate with elegance."

"This is South Carolina...I can't even imagine what your idea of celebrating would be if we were in Paris or Madrid." I looked up from the dress to Ethan's uncertain expression. "Hey," I said softly. "It's the most beautiful thing I'd never even dare to wear. All of this, this whole experience has been so beautiful. Can you help me change?"

Ethan's smile broke wide and he shook his head.

"Daniel will have to. I have my own clothes to change. Daniel, when you are done with your mistress, your suit awaits you on the bed."

Ethan's suit was tailored to his tall, sleek body. It fell gracefully from his shoulders, outlining the dip of his waist and the curve of his ass down to his freshly polished black shoes.

Ethan bowed low upon seeing me.

"You are a goddess among men, Petunia. The beauty I see before me is simply undefinable." I dropped my chin to smile and blush at the floor, but he guided my gaze back up to him with a finger beneath my chin. "I've never said more sincere words in my life, darling. I'm more blessed than anyone can imagine that you are mine." With that, he kissed me.

"This is one of the best surprises I've ever had," I said, smiling at him.

"This isn't the surprise that awaits you, Pet," Ethan chuckled, his eyes twinkling with mischief. "This is simply dinner."

Daniel stepped out of the bedroom, and Ethan looked him over with a nod of approval. He wore a white dress shirt and tanned slacks that hugged tight enough to outline his cage. Daniel caught the direction of my gaze, and the ghost of a smile appeared on his face before he moved to pull out a chair.

***

"1992. A GOOD YEAR," ETHAN COMMENTED AS he sipped his glass of red wine. The vintage held a velvety hint of charred oak and paired perfectly with each dish of the meal.

"It is decadent," I agreed. "But you've barely eaten and we are pretty much finished...Are you alright?"

Ethan looked at me and smiled.

"Nerves, Pet. I'm rarely a nervous man, but I find myself uncertain and anxious about your gift, if I am to be honest."

Quick as a whip, my mind went straight to a proposal.

*He isn't so arrogant that he'd call marriage a gift. So what, then?*

"If you're so nervous, why wait? Better to rip off the bandaid, right?" I asked him, my voice eager. "Besides, anything...everything from you has been nothing short of perfect, so I wouldn't be so nervous if I were

# CHAINS OF SATIN

you. You have impeccable taste and I am a gracious receiver."

I beamed a smile at him. Ethan's finger grazed across his bottom lip, his expression that of a man lost in thought. Finally, he smiled softly and returned his gaze to meet mine.

"Why not, indeed." He rose and retrieved the business satchel he kept by the door, setting it onto the table. Flipping it open, he looked at me as he reached in, a sly gleam in his eye.

"What?" I asked as anticipation made me smile, though it quickly faded into shock as he lifted the black box that contained my circlet.

"I didn't know you had that with you all this time," I gasped.

"The definition of surprise dictates you shouldn't have, darling," Ethan grinned.

I stuck my tongue out at him, and he gently swooped down and took it between his teeth before kissing me. I giggled as he pulled away.

"I have a proposition for you, should you choose to agree. I put this"—he tapped the box with a finger—"on your head, you become the one in charge. We," he gestured between himself and Daniel, "become your submissives until you remove it by your own hands, with the intention that you are done with the role as our domme. What do you think?"

I started to smile like he was joking, but his unmoving expression froze my own.

"Wait, you're serious? You'd do this, like actually do this?"

"For you, I'd move mountains," Ethan swore.

"I mean, like seriously though? You're not talking about being a serious sub, like on your knees, doing my bidding, taking punishment, allowing me—no, *begging* me—to please you or allow you to please me? You're asking me to treat you as I treat Daniel?"

"You are among the most gracious of mistresses I've ever encountered," Daniel interjected. "It's not the worst thing imaginable."

"True role-reversal?" I asked Ethan.

He took a deep breath and on the exhale, he sank to the floor at my feet. My dom was on his knees, looking up into my eyes, and it left me breathless.

"This is intimidating," I said softly.

Ethan took my hand into his. "This is meant to be nothing more than fun. As you are a mistress to Daniel so easily, so too shall you easily be a mistress to me. Whatever you wish to happen, my love, that's what will be done. And should anyone, even you, need a moment or need to end this, we'll start by ensuring all parties know the safety system that is in place."

"Green, yellow, red," I recited, still dumbfounded. Ethan and Daniel both nodded. "Just for tonight?" I asked him, somehow needing the

## DELILAH ST. RIVERS

reassurance that he'll be in his rightful place when all was said and done.

"Say hello to your final surprise, darling. Assuming you accept." Ethan smirked in response. "I vow that no repercussions will come from tonight's exploits. I suspect that thought has crossed your mind as well."

I nodded.

"So, you...and Daniel. Both mine to command at the same time?"

"The very second this rests upon your head," Ethan answered patiently.

"Now I'm the nervous one," I admitted as I opened the box on my thighs. The circlet twinkled in my eyes as I placed my hands around it.

"I'm not demanding this, love," Ethan reassured me.

"I've never done it," I answered him, looking into the diamonds as they shimmered, flipping it carefully in my hands. I lowered my gaze to look at Ethan and I couldn't stop the devilish smile from spreading across my face. "But I'm willing to try."

Ethan's answering smile was filled with pride and joy in my decision to accept his gift. He rose up slightly to kiss me, his hand snaking its way around my head, pressing my lips hard against his as he removed the circlet from my hands with his free one.

"You magnificent wonder," he whispered. "I am indeed quite fortunate to call you mine."

With that, he lowered the circlet upon my waiting head.

## CHAPTER THIRTY-THREE

# Petunia

"YOUR WISH, MISTRESS, IS MY COMMAND," Ethan said softly, rocking his bottom back onto his feet.

Daniel got out of his chair and knelt onto the other side of me, his demeanor a much more fluid reflex of perfect submission than Ethan's.

"Say it again," I timidly told Ethan. His expression of devotion never waivered.

"Your wish is my command, Mistress."

"Ethan," I leaned forward and spoke softly, "I don't know what to do."

He took my hands into his and kissed them almost reverently.

"Whatever your heart desires, my lady; however you wish to direct your pets to please you."

"If my mistress pleases, embrace your deepest, darkest fantasies and let us play them out for you," Daniel offered.

"Anything?" I asked the both of them as I relaxed back into my chair, smiling softly as they both nodded. I had contemplated this scenario countless times in my head over the years, wondering what kind of domme I would be if my situation were reversed. Would I be benevolent? Soft? Hard? Would I have it in me to be a vengeful domme?

"Bring me to the end of the bed, Daniel," I commanded.

## DELILAH ST. RIVERS

Carefully, he lifted me and delivered me to the exact place I demanded. Ethan followed as I beckoned him.

"Undress each other," I commanded, leaning back on my hands. The twin pairs of eyes rested on me for a fraction of a second before Daniel's hands tugged off Ethan's coat.

"Slowly, boys," I demanded, taking in the sight of the two men taking my orders.

Ethan's hands busied themselves with the buttons of Daniel's shirt while Daniel did the same to Ethan's. I let out a giggle as Ethan's wrist got caught in his shirt sleeve and he struggled, shaking the garment while Daniel chased after it. The men began to smirk and very soon we were all laughing.

"I'm so bad at this," I cried out, wiping my tears with both hands to hide my embarrassment.

"No, my sweet mistress, not at all. A little lightheartedness is not an indication of a bad domme," Daniel assured me as he pulled the belt from Ethan's slacks.

"Besides," Ethan chimed in, unbuttoning Daniel's pants, "we don't have to be serious all the time. It can be fun all you want. There are no expectations here, love."

I closed my eyes and took a deep breath. Opening them once more to find Daniel pulling Ethan's underwear down to the floor from behind, careful to give me a slow peek as he removed them obediently. Even at half-mast, it was a glorious sight to behold.

"Ethan," I interrupted him as his hands rested on Daniel's hips, about to grasp the elastic of the underwear. "With your teeth." Ethan paused and stiffened slightly, shifting his eyes to me and finding no humor in them. "Go on, pet. Get on your knees and take them off with your teeth."

Ethan slowly did as he was told, taking the elastic gingerly between his teeth from behind and beginning to work the underwear off Daniel.

Meanwhile, Daniel—bless his heart—reached into the hips of his underwear and moved like he was going to facilitate Ethan's task.

"If you budge them even a fraction of an inch, Daniel," I warned, "I will not hesitate to flog you until you are crying for your mother." It was one of the more mild threats I'd heard directed at me, one that didn't taste foul coming out of my mouth in repetition. Daniel's hands didn't move, but he didn't remove them either. Ethan dutifully kept to task, the underwear slowly exposing Daniel inch by inch. I arched my brow.

With a barely-there smirk, Daniel looked me dead in the eye and pushed the band down to his knees where Ethan let them drop to the floor.

*Is Daniel seriously testing me?*

# CHAINS OF SATIN

Ethan rose and stepped back, looking between Daniel and me as if to gauge my reaction to Daniel's blatant defiance.

"Ethan, my darling," I said through clenched teeth, "did Daniel come with a bag of items to use in case he misbehaved?"

"Yes, Mistress." Ethan turned and retrieved a small black duffle bag from the bedroom closet, setting it on the bed beside me. Opening it, I found quite an assortment of floggers, cages, and one riding crop. I pulled the crop out and slapped it against my hand, breaking the silence that permeated the room.

"Why do I have this, Daniel?" I asked.

"I disobeyed, Mistress."

"Oh, dear. He doesn't even sound sorry, does he Ethan?" I asked.

"Not at all, Mistress."

"Why did you disobey me, Daniel? Have I been too kind to you? Too rewarding? Have you missed the sting and humiliation of the crop while you've been here with me?"

"Yes, Mistress." Daniel looked down to the floor as he answered.

"Down on all fours, Daniel. Face where Ethan is now. Good boy. Put your hands behind your back and your nose to the carpet. Do *not* rest your cheek on the floor or you'll be deprived of touch for the duration of your stay, do you hear me?"

"Yes, Mistress," came the strained reply.

"Ethan, come behind me on the bed and make sure my muscles don't get too sore."

Ethan chuckled under his breath as he climbed behind me. His knees were on either side of my hips. Gently he placed his hands on the small of my back and pressed inward and up, warming the muscles there.

I leaned back into Ethan and sighed, almost forgetting our little game with Daniel and the crop in my hand. I slowly circled Daniel's back with the leather tip, softly caressing his perfect skin before lashing out and whipping his skin, delighting in the hiss that escaped his lips with each sting.

"Daniel," I crooned, taking a small break to circle his back with the crop softly once more. "Oh, my poor Daniel. You forgot to count didn't you, little one?" I tapped on one of the dozen red lines that streaked across his back and buttocks. "Ethan, would you recite the rule we have about our punishments, darling?"

"No counting, you start over," Ethan quickly answered. His voice had dropped an octave and sounded thick with emotion.

"Your color?" I asked him, turning my head to the side to see him.

"Green, Mistress."

# DELILAH ST. RIVERS

"What are you thinking?" I asked him quietly as I smoothed the leather over Daniel's ass. "Tell me honestly."

"You've got my blood boiling with desire for you," he practically purred in my ear.

His words sent need straight through me, and on instinct my thighs pressed hard together. I turned and raised the crop to begin a slow but hard torrent of slaps, waiting until I heard each number cried out before moving onto the next. With each strike, Daniel moaned or panted his number and Ethan's hands dug into my skin. I was practically swimming with excitement.

"Thirty!" Daniel cried out as the final stripe blossomed over the back of his thighs. Ethan grunted softly as I slumped back against him, sweat coating my forehead, arms, and chest from my exertion. All three of us were breathing hard.

"You may now kiss my feet to beg my forgiveness, little one," I told Daniel after I caught my breath.

He crawled over and placed his lips onto the toes of my uninjured leg over and over, working up from my toes and around my foot to my ankle in a steady, slow pace, then sat back onto his feet in true submissive form.

"Ethan," I said. "I'm feeling unsatisfied with this apology. If he were your disobedient slave, would you accept a few measly kisses from his disobedient lips?"

"Hardly, my queen." Ethan's hands ran up and down my arms as he spoke in my ear.

"I don't recall ever telling you to stop with my back. Did I mention it or are you being disobedient as well?"

Ethan's hands immediately returned to my shoulders without missing a beat. He kissed the back of my neck, one of my most tender spots, and whispered, "Please forgive me, Mistress."

"Since it is not direct, malicious disobedience, I'm going to count that as a 'one.' Two more and you'll be the one with the red stripes."

A curious sound emitted from Ethan's throat before he forced out, "Yes, Mistress."

"I must agree with Ethan, Daniel. I don't think that suffices as an actual apology from you. You were so blatant in your defiance. It's a pity really. Not to mention you're hardly a credit to your master. We've been so good to you as our guest. We've fed you, clothed you, taken you out in public to enjoy the sunshine, and you can't even apologize sincerely."

I grabbed a handful of his hair and tugged him upward until he was face-to-face with me while he was still on his knees. A small gasp left

# CHAINS OF SATIN

Ethan's lips from behind while his hands never stopped moving.

"Are you ashamed to know that my dom makes a better sub than you?" I snarled in his face.

"Yes, Mistress."

"Tell me, Daniel, do you even want to continue playing? Am I not a good playmate?"

"The very best, Mistress!" Daniel cried out. His eyes began to tear and immediately I felt guilty.

"Your color," I demanded of him.

"Green, Mistress."

"Honest and true?"

"Yes, Mistress."

"Are you as ashamed of your behavior and your lackluster apology as you know your dom would be?" I asked him, back to the game.

"Yes, Mistress."

"Tell me about it, Daniel. Rub my feet and tell me about your shame."

Ethan growled quietly behind me as he continued rubbing and massaging my back and shoulders through the dress I was wearing. Daniel gently raised my good foot and began to twist his hands around it, kneading the shit out of it.

"I'm ashamed, my most benevolent mistress. You truly are a goddess among mortals in every fathomable way. The thought that I have let you down brings almost as much pain as it would if you were my master in life. I have failed you. I have failed my master, and for that it would truly be a mark of rare grace to be forgiven."

*That boy really knows how to apologize when driven*, I thought to myself.

"And yet you couldn't muster up the apology when given a chance. Perhaps I will make you leave if saying you're sorry is too difficult a task for you to complete…" I said thoughtfully.

"I *am* sor—"

"Show me, Daniel. I'm bored with words."

Ethan's hands were on the back of my neck, squeezing lightly until I shivered from his touch. Daniel's hands slid slowly up my legs to my knees, parting them, kissing each one as he did so.

"Love me, Ethan," I sighed. "With your hands, your lips; just love me."

With the words barely out of my mouth, Ethan's hands reached around and gently took hold of my breasts over my dress while kissing that sweet spot on the back of my neck. A moan escaped my mouth as both pairs of hands touched my body, while both pairs of lips covered my skin in kisses. Ethan rolled my nipples in his familiar way while Daniel's hands stroked my thighs, his kisses following his fingertips.

I began to feel impatient. I wanted to be stripped and fucked right then and there, but I also needed to savor this moment between the three of us. Ethan's hands untwisted my hair, and he breathed in as the cascade of dark brown hair tumbled down my back. He ran his hand through it repeatedly, kissing my shoulder and squeezing my breast at the same time.

"Undress me, my boys," I commanded softly. Ethan found the zipper and pulled it downward, kissing the flesh beneath it as it was exposed to him. Daniel reached up and pulled off the shoulder strap, and, using Ethan's technique, followed the strap with his kisses. From there, Ethan hooked his arms under mine and lifted me as Daniel slid the dress from my body in one slow, steady movement.

"My goodness," Daniel breathed.

"There are other uses far better suited for your lips than talking, Daniel. Your voice is lovely, but it's my second favorite thing your mouth does," I scolded gently as Ethan laid me back tight against him.

"May I kiss your lips, Mistress?" Ethan asked.

"Do you think you deserve it? Are you good enough for my kisses, Ethan?" I teased.

"Not even close," he answered as I wrapped my arms around him and pulled him into a deep kiss. Daniel pried my legs apart and continued to kiss the insides of my thighs, approaching the apex with such patience that I nearly screamed inside Ethan's mouth. Finally, Daniel's first tender kiss lay upon the dripping flesh of my pussy, followed by another and another. His warm breath upon my skin sent shivers through me as Ethan's tongue slid across my own. I took his kisses in earnest, claiming his mouth as my own while my thighs squeezed around Daniel's head. His tongue twisted and twirled around my clit before plunging into my hole, a rhythm I was quickly succumbing to.

"I'm going to—" I gasped as I reached my arms up and pulled Ethan's head to mine, forcing my lips harder against him. The surge of pleasure from Daniel's attention caught me hard and fast. Ethan sighed with me as he held my head cradled in one hand and tweaked and teased my nipple with the other. I bucked and twisted, caught up in the wrath of my orgasm.

I broke free from Ethan's lips and sunk my teeth into his neck, marking him as I'd only done once or twice beforehand. I released him and fell back into his arms, looking up into his eyes as I struggled to calm myself as my orgasm released its hold.

"My sweet mistress, I'm so sorry. Please forgive me," Daniel said,

# CHAINS OF SATIN

kissing my stimulated and sensitive clit over and over. "Please forgive me," he repeated as he slid a finger, then another into me, sending me dangerously close to the edge once again.

"Oh, there Daniel." I threw my head back to look into Ethan's eyes, feeling a second storm brewing within me as I reached down and grabbed Daniel's hair. His soft lips wrapped around my erect clit and he sucked, hooking his finger to stroke the inner spot until I was crying out and spiraling out of control once more. Ethan massaged my breast, twisting my nipple in his fingers again, strengthening the shockwaves that pulsated through me.

I rode Daniel's face, grinding him against me beyond the final throngs of my climax, greedily soaking up the pleasure it brought me until I could barely move my arm and hips, and I released him from my grasp.

"So beautiful," Ethan muttered as he stroked my cheek with his thumb.

"My mistress is kind as she is beautiful," Daniel said softly. "Please forgive me for my disobedience," he begged as he started kissing me again. His lips touched my clit and I gasped for the sensitivity that zapped through me. He didn't linger, instead crawling upwards from my throbbing flesh, continuing his mantra between each kiss.

Ethan and I watched as he placed contrite kisses up my body, past my navel, beyond my belly and onto a bare nipple. I gasped softly at the warm, wet contact. Ethan shifted slightly to the side when he'd first guided my head into his hands; I had only noticed when I felt his hardened cock swollen and pressed against my ribs. I reached down to grasp it tenderly, using only my sense of touch to explore that precious part of him that brought me such joy. I felt him twitch in my hand as I slowly stroked him, loving each inch with my fingertips.

Together Ethan and I watched Daniel work over my body with his kisses, taking the time needed to explore every inch of me that was made available to him. He reached between himself and I to plunge two fingers in me. I cried out, gripping Ethan's cock in my fist, which led to Ethan gasping and tightening his grip on my breast. Daniel kissed my neck over and over as he thoroughly fucked me with his fingers.

I began to feel a slight panic. This was not exactly out of my control, but it felt wrong. Daniel was owning me, using me, and it went against what we had agreed to.

"Dan—" My third tumultuous climax grabbed ahold of my air and choked the words I needed to say. Daniel ground harder, and he sucked at my neck as I twisted and squealed through the orgasm. Ethan petted my hair and played with my nipple once again as Daniel ripped his fingers from my body and pressed his caged dick against the soaked flesh, even as I still quivered, moaning with pleasure and frustration that he wasn't inside me.

I cried out from the contact, trapped between the two bodies and unable to move. He released my neck and pressed his nose against mine.

"Please forgive me, my dearest of mistresses," he whispered.

"Re—" I began, but before I could say the safe word, Daniel shoved his tongue into my mouth. Consumed by the heat of the moment shared between the two of us, Daniel seemed to forget the rules, his lips sealed against mine.

A roar erupted from behind me and in an instant, Ethan pushed me away and wrapped his hand around Daniel's neck, lifting him off my body. In the blink of an eye, Ethan had him pressed against the wall by the bed before I could even register the movement.

"MINE!" Ethan yelled in Daniel's reddening, panicking face.

I jumped off the bed, my circlet falling onto the sheets, and gripped Ethan's tensed forearm.

"Red!" I cried out. "Damn it, Ethan, stop! I called red!"

Ethan's hands loosened but didn't release their hold as he stepped back from Daniel's terrified face.

"Ethan." I softened my voice, seeking to calm him. He turned to me and I watched the anger dissipate as guilt and shame quickly filled its place. He turned to Daniel's trembling form and wrenched his hands away.

"Daniel, my God…I—"

"Go. Take a shower, wash, and find something warm—preferably alcoholic—to drink. Get something to dress in while I deal with this," I commanded, interrupting Ethan's stuttering. I waited until Daniel closed the door before turning to Ethan. I grabbed his hands and led him back to the edge of the bed.

"Breathe." I could feel Ethan shaking in my hands. "Ethan, baby, breathe."

I tried getting him to talk, but he sat in silence, staring down at our hands. I gave up and just sat beside him in silence, hoping my presence was enough to do the job.

"I ruined everything, Petunia," he finally lamented. "I tried to make this the perfect moment for you. It was all fine, truly. I don't know what happened. One moment I'm watching this display of epic proportions, and the next all I wanted to do was snap his neck with my bare hands. He kissed you and…and I…" Ethan shuddered and placed his head in his hands in despair.

"Ethan," I murmured and took him in my arms.

I saw the red flag. I did. I chalked it up to a good man who was

# CHAINS OF SATIN

pushed past a limit he either didn't know he had or chose to ignore in the name of love and a good time. So, I ignored the red flag as I stroked Ethan's hair, rocking us back and forth until he sniffled and pulled away from me.

"I'm sorry I frightened you, my darling," he said quietly. "I would understand if this violent display were enough to end things between us."

I shook my head.

"You didn't, it wasn't. Just before you lashed out, I was calling 'red.'"

"What?" I could feel Ethan get tense again.

"I think the moment and everything was a bit intense; I tried catching him before he pushed it too far...I felt it happening, but I wasn't quick enough."

It was my turn to feel at fault for the disaster in the air.

"What made you think it was going to go too far?" Ethan asked quietly while we heard Daniel begin to shower in the bathroom.

"He pressed...himself, against me. He was getting more and more vigorous and it just began to feel like..." I couldn't say it.

"Pet?" Ethan was struggling to maintain composure, I heard it in his voice.

"It was starting to feel like I was cheating on you." My eyes watered. "We'd done more intimate things in front of you, but it felt like you were getting pushed out of the scene and he forgot his place. But then you snapped. I didn't realize him kissing me could make you so..." I couldn't find the right word to describe what I saw on his face.

"Undone?" Ethan offered. I nodded. It was close enough. "I'd pictured this whole evening in my mind. You would be pleasured until you shook, we would service you in various ways and then we would go home, sated and wiser for this experience.

"But you exceeded my wildest expectations. You ordered, you positioned, and you punished. I was so in awe of you, of seeing that side of you so focally unleashed, that I almost lost control when you took the crop to him. You degraded him and I had to fight my restraint harder than even that first day we danced in the kitchen.

"Then he kissed you. I didn't see a domme accepting her slave's apology, but another man kissing the lips of the woman that was mine." Ethan kissed my hands and looked miserably into my eyes. "My behavior was abhorrent and there is no explanation for ruining this experience for you."

"You should have used the safety system, Ethan. It's what it's for, it's what we agreed to."

"I know."

253

DELILAH ST. RIVERS

I sat beside him, collecting my thoughts for a moment while Ethan's head hung with shame.

"I know I don't call all the shots here, but I think we should spend this last night with just each other. Any more with Daniel...I don't think it's a good idea," I finally said.

"You don't trust me." Ethan's voice was a mixture of hurt and acceptance.

"I'll talk with Daniel," I continued, reaching for the bed sheet to wrap around myself. The circlet fell to the floor and Ethan bent to retrieve it.

"I'm so sorry, my Pet," Ethan stated as he looked at the glittering object in his hands.

"I forgive you, Ethan. With all my heart, I forgive you."

I wrapped my arms around him and pulled him close, sighing in relief at the sense of familiarity of his arms as he leaned in and held me tighter than he normally did.

"I'll call Stanley and explain what happened," Ethan said while pulling away to dress in his discarded pants.

"Stanley?"

"Daniel's dominant. He has a right to know from me what happened and what you've decided to do about it." He stepped out of the bedroom, leaving the suite entirely to make the call.

"Daniel," I called out.

He came out of the bathroom with a towel around his waist and sat beside me on the bed.

"I'm afraid I took things too far," he began, and I flinched at the marks around Daniel's neck and his hoarse voice. "I, too, must ask forgiveness. I broke the rules. I was overwhelmed and consumed, complete rookie mistakes, and if I wasn't caged..."

I swallowed hard, not wanting to think about the what ifs.

"Are you alright?" I asked him.

"Not entirely," Daniel confessed. "He really scared the fuck out of me. I thought he was actually going to kill me. Of course it also excited me to the point I think I'll have cage-imprints for the rest of my life."

"Sounds conflicting," I joked softly.

"You have no idea," Daniel said. "I mean it with every fiber of my being, though, I really do. I am so sorry I got carried away. I know he's telling my master about it and God knows how that's going to go over. I let him down. I let your dom down, but I think none of that compares to how you must have felt in the moment —"

"Helpless," I interrupted softly, looking down at my hands. "Like

# CHAINS OF SATIN

all control went out the window. We played a game where I was in control, but in reality you are much stronger than I am, and you were easily overpowering me."

"Did I scare you?" Daniel asked, taking my hands into his.

"Not quite," I answered. "I think the worst of it was the speed that everything happened."

"I'm glad for it," Daniel said, kissing my hands one at a time. "It would be worse than what Ethan did if I knew I scared you. Not that I blame him at all—I understand why he reacted that way. He cares so much for you."

"I know," I said quietly. "I just wish he didn't erupt like that. I didn't think he was capable of such rage."

Daniel chuckled and held my face with one hand.

"Any man in love has it in him. If I were in his shoes, I would've probably killed me a hundred times over for the things I did to you."

"No, not Ethan. He permitted these things, he said he'd been planning this—"

"Imagining something like this is different than actually doing it," Daniel interjected, rising to stand as he spoke. "What about you? Are you alright?"

I nodded, hearing Ethan shut the door to the suite.

"It was a little scary, but with my adrenaline I wasn't focused on that. I didn't think of anything else other than to make things calm down as I stood there..." I trailed off, realization hitting me in the gut as I looked down at my casted leg.

Ethan walked over to me, kneeling in front of me to get my attention.

"What is it, darling? Are you hurt?"

"No," I said, looking at him, confused. "I stood and walked to you without my crutches. I stood on this leg, put all my weight on it without thinking..."

Ethan lifted it gently. "Do you feel pain now?"

"I don't feel anything remotely close to pain. I feel nothing; just a little stiffness," I said, my eyes wide.

"She mentioned an adrenaline rush," Daniel said to Ethan, who nodded.

"I think we will have to get you some pain killers for when the adrenaline wears off. I don't want you in pain, love." He gently set my leg down. "I have a bottle of pills in my day-bag, Daniel. Fetch them for her."

Daniel did as he was told, and I took the pills with a glass of water handed to me by Ethan, who then turned to Daniel.

"I cannot express the desolation I feel over my actions towards you," Ethan began. "You and your keeper entrusted me these past few days with your health and well-being and I abused that trust. I don't deserve your company and your dom agrees with Petunia. He has sent for you to return, where you will be punished for crossing the contracted bounds but also rewarded for the rest of the outstanding performance you've given us. You have my most sincere apology and my gratitude."

Daniel left with a generous kiss on my knuckles and a large envelope gifted from Ethan for his dom by way of recompense.

"I hope our paths cross again, someday," Daniel said to the both of us. "I meant it when I said I have no hard feelings." The door closed behind him and an unsettling quiet filled the room.

Ethan and I sat beside each other, adjusting blankets or fiddling with our own fingers for a moment as the silence grew awkward.

"Pet, I'm so—"

"I swear to God if you apologize to me one more time, I'm going to flog you myself," I warned.

"I don't like this silence between us, my love. How can I fix this?"

"What more do you need to fix? Daniel's forgiven you, his keeper is placated, and I'm fine. I think maybe you need to forgive yourself, Ethan."

"You're 'fine'?"

"Daniel made a good point while you were on the phone. You wouldn't have reacted that way if you didn't care so much for me."

"He's not wrong." Ethan kissed my forehead. "One last time, darling. Do you truly forgive me?"

"That's what I've been saying all along," I insisted. "What time do we need to be on the plane tomorrow?"

"Seven."

"Maybe we have time before bed to...you know?" I suggested, letting the sheet fall from my shoulders. Ethan went to look at his watch but found his wrist naked as I was. I laughed and reached for my phone on the stand while Ethan slipped his tongue across one of my nipples.

*Dead. Go figure*, I thought while I reached for the cord to charge it. Ethan palmed my breast before gripping it tight, causing me to lose my focus as I struggled to insert the charger into the phone jack. It needed a bit before it could turn on anyway, so I turned back to Ethan to find his pants unzipped and his erection exposed. I wrapped my hand around it as he sighed. I lowered my mouth onto him, my tongue sliding against his skin while tightening my lips around it to create a firm, wet grip.

"Oh, my sweet girl," Ethan crooned. "I'll never tire of that mouth."

I grinned slightly before opening my mouth to allow my tongue to swirl around his twitching flesh and turned back to look at my phone.

# CHAINS OF SATIN

Ethan shifted closer beside me to kiss my shoulder and upwards, onto my neck. He gently sank his teeth into the muscle as I held down the power button, and I shuddered.

"God," I gasped, closing my eyes and reaching my hand behind me and up into his hair once more.

"I want you, *Princess*." His husky voice sent ripples of goosebumps through my body as his hands roamed over me.

"You have me," I answered, dipping my head as his lips traced over the back of my neck.

"Bloody right, I do," he growled and suddenly I was lifted, turned, and straddling his lap, my phone falling to the floor as his cock pressed between us and our lips met. I leaned my hips back, coaxing him into my body. I moaned as he sank into me, filling me until our hips met. He held me there as he held my face, touched my hair, ran his fingers down my arms to grip my ass.

*Ding!*

*Ding!*

*Ding!*

*Ding!*

*Ding!*

"Damn," I cursed, breaking off the kiss to look for my phone as the notification chime repeatedly went off.

"Not yet," Ethan groaned as he guided me back to his lips. I rocked my hips, grinding hard into him, smiling at his need of me.

*Ding!*

We both groaned in irritation.

"I need to see," I said, holding his face with my hands. "It must be important, but if it's Shay, I might send her a pic so she can see what she's interrupting."

Ethan laughed as he leaned forward, holding me tight against him as I leaned to reach the fallen annoyance.

The screen lit up as I touched it and I read missed call after missed call from Rico, an unknown number, and the healthcare facility. I froze, unable to breathe.

*Mom.*

"Pet?"

Ethan's voice echoed in my head, distant and lost in the tumultuous din of panic that flooded my thoughts. I climbed off of him and held my phone with both hands, staring at the number of missed calls on my screen.

"Sweetheart?" Ethan was in front of me, trying to see the phone.

"I don't know," was all I could say as I tried calling Rico back.

No answer.

"Shit!"

"What is it, love?"

"Rico, the front desk, and someone else have been blowing up my phone and now I can't get Rico to answer. Did you get a call? They'd call you if it was a true emergency, if they couldn't get ahold of me, right?" I asked, desperate for hope to cling to.

Ethan's face blanched.

"No," I despaired.

"I turned the ringer off after my meeting this morning. I didn't want us to be interrupted," he explained as he retrieved his own from his business jacket.

Two missed calls from Rico.

Four from the facility.

"It's eleven-thirty, love. The front desk is closed and Rico is probably asleep. We will stop there as soon as our plane lands in the morning, before we even go home."

"Can we see if there's an earlier flight? I'm sorry, but it's Mom and I can't...I don't see how I'll be able to sleep tonight," I said, hoping he'd understand.

"Let me make some calls and see what I can do, Pet," Ethan said. "Just remember, darling, we don't know until we know, alright?"

I nodded and Ethan took his phone to the sitting room, dialing numbers and talking with various airlines for a good hour or so.

All to no avail.

"I'm sorry, sweet darling," Ethan said as he crawled back into the bed with me. "We cannot leave any sooner."

I leaned in his arms, setting my phone beside the bed with the ringer turned all the way up as it charged.

"I'm sorry the mood is killed." I half-heartedly smiled up at him. Ethan shook his head as he brushed hair from my eyes.

"I would rather enjoy you when you aren't burdened with worry, my darling. For now, lie with me. Allow me to kiss you to sleep and we will face whatever comes together. I will not leave your side come what may."

PRESENT DAY
OFFICE OF DR. JOSEPH HALL

JOSEPH SAT IN HIS CHAIR, QUIETLY SMOKING his cigarette while I sat across the room, my hands in my hair as I tried to blink away the unbidden tears. The sun was setting, though the lights had yet to turn on outside. I couldn't appreciate the brilliant, dusky sky painted in the bold colors of the sunset. How could I? What business did I have knowing beauty when all I knew to be beautiful was gone?

"She was too forgiving, I think," I mumbled miserably. "I know what I did had to have sent her back to the past abuses she faced, yet she was moaning in my lap not two hours after the event. When I read her goodbye letter, I thought immediately of that moment with Daniel and how I would have strangled him against the wall right there in front of her in my anger. Maybe it was so easy for her to walk away because she never truly forgave me, in her heart."

"Unfortunately it is not beyond the realm of possibility, my friend," Joseph said quietly. "Did you hear from Daniel afterward? Was there any permanent damage to him?"

"Stanley gave me an update a week after we returned. Daniel was given 30 percent of the money in the envelope and a bit of time off, both to heal and as repercussion for what he did."

"And did he heal?" Joseph asked.

# DELILAH ST. RIVERS

I nodded.

"I had lunch with the two of them after Petunia left, mostly to check in and offer any other recompense for the incident, though partly to see if maybe she had gone to see Daniel. I know they had no romantic feelings, but Daniel and Shay were the only two she ever really talked to outside of the house cleaners, so I took a chance. They hadn't seen or heard from her, of course."

"And you feel as though she lied when she said she forgave you?" Joseph asked.

"I'm not saying she lied. I'm just saying…maybe she didn't forgive me as wholly as she thought she did."

"And if she was just placating your feelings by sweeping it under the rug and genuinely lying to you about it?" Joseph asked.

"I don't know!" The irritation that bloomed within made my voice rise uncontrollably. "I don't know, alright? I don't know if she lied, I don't know if she was telling the truth. I could only trust what she said to me and move on with it. I allowed her to take the lead in everything, and if she was really lying, she didn't have to be with me. She could have demanded I go to counseling to prove I would do anything for her. But I don't know and it's killing me, Joe. It's killing me thinking about her holding in that fear for as long as she did. She and I slept together so many times—what if it was because she was afraid of me?"

"Easy, Ethan." Joseph sat up in his chair as I paced the room. "I don't even know the full story yet, right?"

"Right," I said after a minute, though the truth of my fear and pain had sent me into a panic.

"Let's not spiral here, buddy. Focus on that night, when she had the missed calls."

I took a deep breath before finding my seat again.

"No one texted her? Or you for that matter?"

"No. Just missed calls. Even I thought it was odd because Rico texts everyone."

"That would have saved her some panic, I think," Joseph said, thoughtfully.

"Not really," I said with a small smile. "Petunia would have panicked even with texts. She would still be trying to call through the wee hours trying to get as much information out of everyone as she could, forgoing sleep."

"Tenacious," Joseph chuckled.

"Quite. The promise of physical contact was all I could do to get her to lie back against me that night…I watched her fall asleep that

# CHAINS OF SATIN

night. I remember everything about it. I remember the way she smelled. I remember how warm her body was pressed up against mine. I remember kissing her until she sighed and closed her beautiful eyes to leave me for her own oblivion. I said it that night, Joe. I love you. I whispered it in the dark, so quietly that I knew she wouldn't hear me, but I had to say it.

"This woman took me at my worst, held me close and refused to give me up. I made up my mind that night that she would be my wife. Not some sub obligated by contract to me, but *my wife.*"

"Why did you wait until she was asleep to say it?" Joseph asked, clearly exasperated.

"Because I didn't say it for her. I said it out loud as an acknowledgement of my own feelings for her. I didn't want to say it to her, for her benefit. Also, I didn't want to hear it back in some monotone. I didn't want to not hear it in return, either. She would tell me in her own time."

"The fact she hadn't said it to you up to this point is proof that the words mean something to her," Joseph remarked.

"Precisely." I took a long drink from the glass in my hand and set it down. "I'm in the 'home stretch' of my tale, as they say."

"Really?" Joseph asked.

"I can imagine the hefty bill I'll be getting in the mail from you," I joked dryly.

"Double time and a half, for it being my day off," Joseph said, smiling.

"More than worth it, my friend." I sighed as I stretched my long legs out. "You've certainly earned your keep today."

Joseph chuckled. "Alright, so home stretch. You return home and find out what the commotion was all about?"

"We did, indeed."

CHAPTER THIRTY-FIVE

# Petunia

THE DRIVER PULLED UP AT THE HOSPITAL entrance soon after our arrival home, and Ethan stepped out, carrying the crutches to me from the trunk. Rico rushed to me, hugging me tight. His face was swollen from prolonged tears as he led us to a small conference room. His voice wavered as he tried to formulate the words, and my heart sank with each passing moment of silence.

"Where is she?" I finally asked him.

"The basement." Rico's tears spilled over and he took my hands. "I'm sorry, Petunia."

*The basement.* People, myself included, go their whole lives to the same hospital and don't know what every floor contains. But I knew the basement floor. My father had just been there a few weeks ago.

*The morgue.*

"But, how?" I could barely get the words out.

"We're waiting on tests. She was un-unresponsive when I fo-found..." Rico closed his eyes and rubbed his face with his hands.

"I want to see her," I demanded. Tears filled my own eyes, but I angrily brushed them away.

"The autopsy has alr-ready started."

I looked over at Ethan and found him already on the phone. He

# CHAINS OF SATIN

stood and walked out of the conference room, and I sat in the silence he left behind.

"What happened, Rico? She was fine. I called her while I was away and everything. She was fine! Where were you?" I pounded my fist on the table as I yelled. "Where were you, Rico?"

Ethan came back in, tucking away his phone. "It'll be a day or two before they know anything," he explained as he placed a hand on my shoulder. "I've hired my lawyer in your name so everything can be done with as little impact on you as possible." He turned to Rico, who was still staring at me, heaving and horrified. "I've used said lawyer to ensure you have a few weeks of bereavement time for yourself, Rico. For all you've done for her family, you deserve it with no financial repercussions."

Rico looked up at Ethan. "Thank you, Mr. Charming," he said before turning to me. "Petunia, *mija*, I am sorry about your mama. You know I loved her, too."

When I didn't respond, he got up and walked out the door. Realizing there was nothing else for me to do, Ethan and I soon got into an Uber and rode home in silence. I couldn't stop mulling over the last conversation she and I had.

*"Esther has my books...Lucille and Georgiana have gotten things too...I love you, chickadee...Do you think you'll marry this guy?"*

*Had she known it was coming? Had she known she was going to —*

"Darling?" Ethan broke through my thoughts, and I looked up to find him outside with my car door open. He lifted me, carried me inside, up the stairs, and laid me down on the familiar softness of our bed.

He removed my sneaker and sock from my good foot while I watched wordlessly.

"What can I do, sweetheart? What do you need?" His voice sounded distant, even though he was right beside me.

I couldn't answer. I couldn't feel. That weird numbness, the same numbness that washed over me when my father passed, returned. When no answer came from me, Ethan wrapped his arms around me and held me close to his chest. I snuggled deeper into him.

This whole thing reeked of *déja vu*; the only difference was my location. This time, I couldn't look at the room I was in and find traces of my life with my parents. I wasn't surrounded by memories and ghosts of laughter ringing through the walls that comforted me. There was nothing I could focus on, nothing for my mind to cling to while it prepared to mourn.

I was lost.

"Are you tired, my love?" Ethan asked.

I could barely make myself shake my head. I wasn't tired. I wasn't anything.

263

# DELILAH ST. RIVERS

"Do you need to be alone, Pet?"

*I need my mother to be alive,* I thought. *I need her to be alive and okay, to smile and sing. To dance in the rain with me one more time and to hold me. I need her to tell me she'd never leave me. I needed her arms around me.*

I didn't notice the tears on my cheeks until I felt Ethan wipe them away. That small act of kindness broke through a small part of my barrier and I wrapped my arms around him. I let go of the anger, the guilt; I let it all go into a torrent of tears.

ETHAN STAYED BY MY SIDE AND SUFFERED through the worst of the depression and guilt I was tortured with. My mother had died while I was away having fun. I was ashamed and I pushed Ethan away, sometimes even blaming him for her death. Still, he held firm beside me, no matter how ugly my mood got, or how stubborn I was about blaming myself, no matter how miserable I knew it made him.

Within a month, the timeline of my mother's last days came to light. She'd been clever about the whole ordeal for one suffering from dementia. With each gift she'd given to various ladies of the facility, she told stories of how she suffered from this malady or that pain but was offered no help from the doctors. Naturally, the women she'd spin these tales to had suffered genuinely from such pain, and they were more than willing to spare a few doses of medicine to help their poor art teacher.

The day my mother died, she had a light breakfast, a light lunch, written her will and plans for her body and possessions, and by the time Rico had come to her room to wake her from her evening nap and check her vitals, she'd taken all of the pills she was given and was unresponsive.

The women responsible for giving her the medicines were removed from the facility and relocated until the law could determine what to do about this whole situation. Ethan's lawyer had confided in me that I could sue him directly for his clinic's negligence, but I refused. Shay, who had come and spent the week of the funeral with me, none of which I could even recall, had pushed for it.

But I refused. For all my ranting, none of this was anyone's fault. Not the women who'd been sympathetic, not Rico's, not Ethan's. None of this was anyone's fault but my mother's.

The last bit of official news came from the life insurance company. Mom had taken out several insurance policies over the years totaling three-quarters of a million dollars. I was to receive all of it.

"I thought because of what happened, I wouldn't get anything."

# CHAINS OF SATIN

Ethan looked to his lawyer for that answer.

"Though most people think this, it's a Hollywood misnomer. Typically, most insurance policies have a 'suicide clause.' In most of them, the person taking out the policy has a period of twenty-four months where the beneficiary will only be returned the paid premiums of the policy. Your mother took her last life insurance policy out on herself over forty months ago. Ergo, you get the entire thing, minus taxes and such, of course."

I'd fully expected to receive nothing. Now this man was telling me, with the sale of my house, the money I'd saved and received from work and the facility, and now the insurance, that I was officially a millionaire.

"I don't deserve this," I cried softly into the pillow when all was said and done. "I want to just give it all away. I don't deserve any of it."

"Shh, sweetheart." Ethan tentatively ran his hand up and down my back. The last few weeks had strained our physical relationship as well. "Let the mourning period pass before you decide to do something that could affect you for the rest of your life, darling."

"I don't deserve it," I repeated, turning the words over and over in my mind.

"You were the greatest daughter a woman could have ever hoped for, my love. You worked so hard after you found out about her illness, sacrificed your planned future for cleaning creepy men's mansions just to pay for her care."

"Not all of them were creepy," I said, not much louder than before. "Just you."

Ethan chuckled, and I allowed a tiny smile to form.

"You rest, love. I can stay or, if you'd like some time alone, I can let you be and come back later."

"I'm not tired," I said, still quiet.

"Hungry then?" Ethan asked.

"I don't know," I answered, fresh tears welling up in my eyes. "Would it be okay if you sent for food and stayed with me?"

Ethan smiled with compassion and ran his palm down my cheek. I leaned into it, not realizing until then just how much I missed his touch.

"I'll have to make you something and bring it up, darling. Sophie was supposed to work today, but her sister's cat ran away and they're putting up flyers as we speak. It's just you and me here today. The normal house staff have been put on vacation until you're feeling better."

"Why?" I asked. None of it seemed right.

"Because your pain should be felt in the privacy of your home, where you won't be trod upon," he answered, as though it was the most natural thing in the world.

# DELILAH ST. RIVERS

"Do you ever get tired of it?" I asked, looking at him.

"Tired of what?" He looked at me, tilting his head slightly and furrowing his brow.

"Being the strong one. Staying patient while I'm at my worst. All of it."

"Pet, if I can't handle you at your worst, I don't deserve you at your best," he explained, his face relaxing into one of reassurance. "These days are only temporary; you'll find good times again. In fact, I do believe this is one of the longest conversations since the news of your mother that you and I have shared. It's getting a little better already." Ethan smiled again, his eyes bright with optimism.

"I've been so self-absorbed that I didn't even think about how you've been feeling," I began, feeling dreadful about it. "I've slept and ate and moped in here the whole time, and you're still so well-put together even though you've been all alone with no one to talk to..."

"Well, I wouldn't say I've been all alone, darling. Aside from occupying myself with you, work, and your mother's situation, the housekeepers were good conversationalists. They told me of their lives and it helped distract me for a moment from what you were going through. It was mostly Sophie who kept up with it, always coming in with a new tale or a joke she'd heard. She's thoughtful, that one."

I shrugged my shoulders. She and I weren't exactly best friends, but she was tolerable.

"How have you been holding up?" I asked him softly. "I know you were getting close to Mom, too. Do you feel at least a little angry for what she did?"

"Are you asking me this because you want to know the answer, or so you can validate your own anger by having someone who feels the same way by your side?" Ethan asked back.

I thought for a minute before answering. "Okay," I conceded. "I can't reconcile the two. I miss her so much, but I'm also so angry at her. At the same time, I understand that there's only so much people can take and I know she was only human and such a proud woman, too..."

"I was, at first, angry at her for abandoning you," Ethan confessed. "But like you, I see she was faced with an impossibly difficult future, and I had a sneaking suspicion that she would have wanted some control over how she passed, just as it seemed she had quite the control over how she lived. This whole ordeal with your mother's condition was terribly unfortunate. And I'm sorry for you, Pet. I'm so sorry for you."

"I'm sorry, too," I said, sniffling.

"For what?"

I sat up and adjusted myself until I leaned upon his chest, pulling his arms around me.

"For another afternoon wasted while I did nothing but bawl like a baby. I thought I was done with this part," I said.

"Stop." Ethan's voice grew a fraction harsher. "If you invalidate your mourning I shall treat you like my school teachers did me and make you write lines until you've finally learned that no one speaks disrespectfully about my darling, not even you."

"Write lines?" I smiled against his chest. "And what would those lines say?"

"*I am allowed to mourn as I see fit*, or something to that effect. Fifty times. And don't test me on this, darling, you won't win." His fingers dragged across the back of my neck slowly.

I shivered at his touch and snuggled tighter against him.

"It's weird not calling Rico every day anymore to check in on her. It's so different now."

"I know. When he and I last spoke, he was settled in San Antonio with his family and had found a job where he could work with children. He was a very good nurse to your mother and bid me to send his best wishes to you when I got the chance."

I thought about sending him a card or a memento of my mom at some point as I sighed deeply.

"Thank you for being here for me; for being everything I've ever needed and then some. For being you," I mumbled. The tendrils of deep, exhaustion-fueled sleep were finding me and dragging me down as I spoke.

"Only for you, my sweet girl. Only for you." I faintly felt his kiss on my head as the darkness took over, and I was soon aware of nothing else.

IT WAS DARK WHEN MY EYES OPENED. Ethan was snoring lightly beside me and the rest of the house was quiet. I rose from Ethan's outstretched arm and sat on the edge of the bed, both feet resting againt the floor. I leaned until my elbows were on my knees and my face went into my hands. My stomach gurgled in protest of another missed dinner and I groaned.

I couldn't even remember the last time I'd felt hunger or anything besides my own turmoil, and it lightened my mood considerably. I looked around for my crutches, supposing that while I was awake I might as well use the restroom before heading downstairs for something to eat. They were against the wall by the bedroom door, and I groaned inwardly, looking

# DELILAH ST. RIVERS

back at Ethan's sleeping form. He'd really done so much for me; I didn't have the heart to wake him.

I stood slowly, not putting any weight on my broken leg as I leaned heavily on the bed.

*So far, so good.*

I set my foot flat on the carpet and gradually rested there, feeling for any sort of discomfort and bracing myself for shooting pain.

Nothing. I felt nothing but the carpet between my toes.

I leaned to one side to take a step forward and was rewarded with a shaky, unsteady knee, atrophied from disuse. Stubbornly, I took another step, then another, until I got to the end of the bed. With a deep breath, I let go, praying I wouldn't land on my face.

When I reached my crutches, I was sweating and shaking, but smiling, for the first time in almost two whole months.

By the time I was done in the bathroom, I forgot about food as I set the crutches back against the wall by the door. I was too excited that I had no pain. I wasn't filled with adrenaline or anything that would numb or cover up the pain, if there was any to be had. My heart raced and I couldn't stop smiling as I climbed into bed next to Ethan. If I was truly healed, it meant no more cast. No more being cumbersome, or burdened by a useless leg. I looked up at Ethan's peacefully sleeping face.

*We could dance.*

My heart skipped a beat at the thought of being whisked around the house once again, staring into his eyes as he'd hold me in his arms.

I nestled into his chest and ran my hand across it, feeling the muscles beneath his shirt and thinking of all the other benefits that could come from being able-bodied once more. How I could better serve him and submit to him when we played. How I could run and jump into his arms when he'd come home after a business trip.

We could go to Paris...

Dance in a huge ballroom together like he promised in South Carolina...

I felt my face grow warm when I thought of the other activity he promised would happen in the same ballroom. I imagined how his lips would trail along my skin, how we'd be breathing hard and sweating as our bodies clashed together in the passionate fury I'd come to expect. I could almost hear his name echo off the walls as he would bring me to orgasm time and time again with his lips, his hands, his...

I sat up and searched his wrist for the watchface and lit the backlight. 4:07 a.m. That was a bit too early for even my dom. I lay back against him and did my best to go back to sleep.

# CHAINS OF SATIN

It didn't work.

Like a starving man with an open buffet table standing before him, I couldn't stop my need for him from growing. Within minutes my hands began to wander and I soon found out that he'd fallen asleep fully dressed, as though he didn't want to leave my side to change. I felt my heart melt at the thought of his dedication, and I kissed his forehead softly while I reached down, unbuttoning his pants and gingerly retrieving the sleeping flesh that I sought. I slid my body down the side of his until my nose brushed against the silken skin.

I grew damp with anticipation as I took him into my mouth and rolled my tongue around his hardening cock, awakening it and, moments later, him.

"Darling?" He sat up on his elbows to look at me before throwing his head back. "Ohh, sweet girl...bloody he—that's...oh, Pet?" He lifted his knees to bring my gaze up at him.

"Do you want me to stop?" I asked, trying to keep the dejection out of my voice.

"With all my heart, no, for God's sake. But wait, darling, wait," he chuckled as he pulled away from my mouth once more, forcing me to return my gaze to him. "Are you alright?"

"I'm alright," I said, stroking him with my hand, making the last-minute decision not to tell him what I discovered about my leg. "And if you don't mind, I'd really like to keep sucking your dick."

In the dark, Ethan let out a deep breath.

"How could anyone refuse such an act from such a beauty?" he asked, placing a hand on my head as I took his partial erection wholly into my mouth. I hummed in contentment as he threw himself backwards onto the pillows with a groan.

"Christ, your mouth will be the death of me," he whispered as I slowly began a rhythm of movements, twisting my hand up and around as my mouth slid up and down his shaft. I shifted my weight and brought my other hand up to tease and tug at his testicles, never breaking the pace.

Ethan hissed as he reached into my hair with both hands.

"Slower, love," he panted out. "It's been too long. I fear if you keep going like this, I'll be no use to you soon. Slower, *ahh*...Right there... There's my good, good girl."

Ethan's words, coupled with his sighs, were driving my own desire, intensifying it until I felt my own walls spasm. The grip I had on his cock tightened, causing him to inhale sharply.

"*Shit*," he cursed in a hoarse whisper. He sat back up and grabbed me by the shoulders, pulling me off him to kiss me deeply. "I want to taste you, precious girl. I need to."

He sat me up, and we carefully peeled off the rest of our clothes before my thighs touched his ears as he pulled me down onto his waiting mouth. A world of blissful sensations exploded within me as his lips met my dripping entrance and my clit met his nose.

"Ethan," I whined, feeling prickles of electricity form between my hips, my lower belly tightening. I reached down and grabbed a handful of his sleep-tousled hair to further steady myself as I rode his magnificent face. The coil within me snapped and I cried out his name. He moaned as I gasped, practically weeping at my body's brutal, unforgiving assault of pleasure. Ethan listened for my cries to soften before slowing his pace until he stopped altogether.

"I was almost ended by your cries alone, my sweet Pet." Ethan groaned, moving to caress my collarbone with his lips. "The things you do to me...the things you make me feel..." His teeth bit into the curve of my neck and I gasped at the contact.

"You say that now. Wait till I'm toothless and saggy," I joked with a giggle as he pulled away from me and stood. I blinked the blinding dazzle out of my eyes when he turned on the light. It took a few moments until I could focus on his breathtaking naked form standing before me.

"Up," he ordered, his face like stone.

I did as he asked, leaning all my weight on him to avoid giving away my secret. He held me tight against him, his erection pressed hard against my hip.

"Do you honestly believe age will take away your beauty in my eyes? Or that it would make me want you—want this—less?"

"Ethan," I began, rolling my eyes and smiling in jest.

"*Sir*." His eyes were blazing as he stared me down, cutting my smile off. I swallowed hard.

"Sir," I answered him timidly. "It was a joke."

"How I feel for you is a joke?" Before I could protest, he commanded, "Kneel, now."

It was instinct to obey his sudden command. I took the position I'd practiced for years, and my eyes were laid upon him by the guidance of his impatient fingers under my chin.

"You're a goddess in my eyes and should be seen as no less in your own. Say it. Say you're a goddess."

"I am a goddess." The monotone sentence fell clumsily from my lips as his cock danced distractedly in front of my eyes. I wanted to taste him and would have done anything to do so right then.

Ethan reached down and gripped a handful of my hair in his hand

# CHAINS OF SATIN

and raised my head to look at him.

"Say it like you mean it or I will leave you a quivering, unfinished puddle of need for days to come."

"I'm a goddess," I repeated in earnest.

"Whose goddess?"

"Yours," I insisted.

He released my hair and shifted his hip, prodding my lips with the head of his dick. I opened my mouth eagerly and took him in, my eyes never leaving his.

"Mine," he agreed, baring his teeth as he leaned inward to thrust and hold himself down my throat. Reflexive tears sprang in my eyes as I happily held him there. He pulled back and stepped away as I gasped for air. His arm swooped down, and I was pressed against his body once more. He kissed me, deeply and thoroughly, bending me back as his tongue dipped into my mouth to consume and conquer mine.

"How I want to see that languid look upon your face when you feel yourself being filled with my seed. Lie back on the bed, my Pet. Don't keep me waiting any longer than you already have."

I pulled away from him, sitting on the silken sheets before pulling myself up to lie against the pillows, keeping our eyes deadlocked. Lust consumed his eyes as my dom followed me on all fours. He knelt between my knees and his mouth latched on my stiffened nipple. With a hard, unguided thrust, he tore into me, finding me wet and inviting.

I shrieked as he filled me, stretching me around his girth as he slowly stroked in and out of me. It was a snug fit; those weeks without him inside me left me unaccustomed to his size.

"Why would I ever cease to want that which belongs to me, my Pet? How could I—" he shuddered mid-sentence as he brought me to another rippling orgasm. I clenched around him, soaking the sheets as my walls gripped his flesh tight. "How could I ever stop wanting you?" Ethan whispered, bringing his lips to gently press upon mine.

"Oh, Ethan," I breathed, his words stirring something deep within me.

He brought one of my knees up against him and drove into me, crashing into me like a madman until my eyes rolled back and I could feel the stirrings of yet another orgasm approaching.

"Not yet," Ethan grunted out. "Almost..."

I could feel him swell within me as I tightened around him.

"Now," he panted out as he let loose inside of me, spilling into me as he buried his teeth into my neck, sending me spiraling into my own screaming orgasm. My contracting muscles milked him for all he had as he shook above me, quaking from the strength of his climax while he stroked me slowly through mine.

I struggled for breath to call out his name. Ethan released his teeth from my neck and found my lips, coaxing me into a relaxed state once more. Ethan collapsed and rolled off of me as we both gasped for air.

"Are you in pain?" he asked after a few moments, pulling me close. I curled against his body, shaking my head in answer as my eyes began to flutter closed.

"I love you, Ethan," I whispered.

His body stiffened as though I'd taken him by surprise, then relaxed as he let out a soft chuckle.

"Shh, my darling." His hold tightened and he kissed my head twice, lulling me into a sleep I didn't want but couldn't fight against. "Sleep now."

FROM THE DESK OF ETHAN ALDRICH III

My treasured Pet,

Emergency meeting called me away from my preferred place in your arms. You were the embodiment of sin this morning in the very best way possible. I cannot wait for more. Wear your circlet for me when next we come to bed— You'll set the pace, darling. Moan for me and I'll be as tender as though it were your first time. Scream for me, and I'll ravish you until you know nothing else.

Your choice, darling.

Think on it.

xx

CHAPTER THIRTY-SIX

# Petunia

MY MOUTH RAN DRY AS I READ his letter. Even through the daze of sleepiness, my lower belly fluttered and I wished Ethan were there beside me right then.

A series of impatient knocks sounded from the door and I sat up, beckoning whoever was behind to come in.

Sophie's red head popped in the bedroom.

"About time," she muttered, before seeing the box on the bed. "What's that?"

"A gift from Ethan," I answered, opening the box to show her. She gasped and reached for it, pouting when I closed it and put it on the stand beside me.

"I almost made him late this morning," she giggled, setting the tray down onto the bed. "But he left smiling, and that's all that matters, right?" Sophie winked at me.

"What do you mean?" I asked, keeping my voice even to mask the jealousy churning in my stomach.

"Oh, you know how he is! He's so open and friendly all the time. I guess it helps that he's been so lonely and stuff ever since your mom died and you were doing your thing up here and…Anyways, he just needed a friend, I guess."

# CHAINS OF SATIN

She batted her eyes at me and I felt my own narrow almost imperceptibly.

"He had the cook make this and asked me to deliver it to you after I was done with the living room," Sophie pressed on. She lifted the lid to reveal a brunch consisting of eggs, toast, strawberries, and cubed cheese. "He said to remind you not to forget about physical therapy and to tell you to read the letter he set beside you." She spotted the letter by my side. "Have you read it yet? What's in it?"

Sophie moved quickly and tore it from its place before I could register what she was doing. In a flash, she hopped off the bed to the opposite wall and read it.

"That's private!" I shouted as I struggled with the sheets to retrieve my letter. Unfortunately, she was a quick reader and in seconds she was staring at me with her mouth hung open and her face flushed.

*She looks like a fish out of water,* I thought.

"He seems so proper and in control all the time. I never saw anything like this in him…" Sophie muttered as she handed the letter back to me. "Jesus, Pettie." Sophie sat on the bed beside me. "Is he one of those closeted guys that like to be spanked and crawl on the floor to worship your feet or something?"

*Spanking Ethan?* I laughed in her face.

"Not in your life," I said, feeling smug with the knowledge that no matter how "close" she thought she and Ethan were, I knew him so much better. "But I know he'd be upset if he knew you read my letter. He's particular about privacy, you know?"

"Shit, I can see why," Sophie said. "He'd want to keep all that shit behind closed doors. Whips and candle wax coming from the same guy who takes you to a fancy dinner and says 'I love you' is just weird."

"Yeah," I said softly, looking down at the letter in my hand.

"God, it's always the well-put together guys that like the kinky stuff, isn't it? He never gave me the impression…I mean sometimes he gets this look in his eye when we talk, but I never thought *that* was behind it all, jeez." Sophie giggled and tossed her red hair to the side. "Well, anyway, enjoy your food. I should get back to wor—oh! I almost forgot! Before he left, he said to mention dinner tonight and tell you to wear the green number in your closet. He also mentioned something about discussing a contract?" She shrugged and closed the door behind her.

*A contract? The contract? What about it?*

*"He draws up a six-month paper."*

Madeline's voice rang in my head, an unwanted intrusion. Our contract was written in such a way that it had no end date.

275

*Does he want to change it?*

*What the hell did Sophie mean when she said that thing about that look in his eye when they talked?* I shook my head and looked at the note in my hands. *I pushed him hard and away through my grieving process...was he looking at Sophie the same way he looked at me before we got together?*

I'd told him I loved him earlier that morning, I remembered clear as day. I also remembered the way he tensed up and didn't say it back.

Quickly I reread the letter in my hands.

*So what if he didn't say it last night? What if I just caught him off guard, and at dinner he may want to forget about the contract and we could just be in an actual relationship? He clearly has feelings for me.*

I remembered what he did to Daniel for crossing the line with me and what Daniel said after the fact: *"Any man in love has it in him."*

Ethan bought the nursing home for my mother, he helped sell my house for much more than it was worth, took me in while I was injured, encouraged me to keep up with the therapy even after Mom died so I wouldn't lose progress with my healing.

He loved me. Ethan loved me. The proof was in everything he did, the words he said to me, and everything he was.

I smiled and began to eat as much of my breakfast as I could and set the plate aside. I went to the closet and noted the newly purchased garment bag hanging there. Unable to resist a peek, I opened the bag to reveal a dress that was emerald green, shimmering as it cascaded down to the floor. Gold trimmed the daring neckline and studded the black belt at the waist. Daring to touch it, my fingers were met by a buttery-soft material, and I discovered a slit that would reach up beyond my mid-thigh. It was stunning and left me gobsmacked for a solid two minutes while I stared at it. Ethan always had such exquisite taste, and I couldn't wait to put it on for him.

Shaking off the surprise, I grabbed clothes and privately took a quick bath without my crutches. I was exhilarated by each movement I made unassisted as I bathed and dressed. Walking down the stairs with the crutches to ensure no one could spill my secret before I was ready to tell Ethan, I met with the driver and was taken to the physical therapy clinic.

THE BUZZ OF THE SAW DIDN'T EVEN bother me as it cut through the plaster. During physical therapy, I shared my progress, but was met with a gentle reprimand and reminder that I shouldn't be putting weight on the leg until it was healed. Worried about further damage that may have been done to my leg, X-rays were ordered and much to my delight,

# CHAINS OF SATIN

the scans showed that my leg was finally healed. There was no permanent damage, no twisting or shifting of the bone as it mended, and I was finally able to get the cast off.

The spreader revealed a pale, hairy leg in need of a good washing, which Sue was kind enough to do for me. She helped me apply a good lotion to the dried skin, advising me not to shave it for a few days, until the dried cracks in my skin healed.

"The last thing you need is an infection," she laughed. I was still wobbly when I tried standing, and Sue gave me a cane to walk with while I built up muscle again.

"It'll take a few weeks," she said. "Start gradually, but make sure you're walking each day."

"It feels so strange," I remarked. "It feels like I've been in that cast forever."

"Oh, I bet!" Sue nodded. "Here are some pamphlets of dos and don'ts to read on your own time. Be sure to keep up with physical therapy for this stage of healing. Elevate your leg at the end of each day before bed and make sure you use an air cast at night while you sleep, in case you or your partner are restless sleepers. Other than that, you're pretty much ready to go, Ms. Barlowe."

"No crutches, ma'am?" Mark asked as I loaded into the back of the car, the surprise easily seen on his face.

"Nope, and hopefully never again," I said, smiling. "But I want to surprise Mr. Aldrich when I return home, so don't spill the beans."

"You got it," he said, shutting my door and getting into the driver's seat. "Home, then?"

"I think I'll go to Joyce's first."

The high-end boutique knew me by name at this point, and I knew they would make sure the delivery of my surprise would be remembered by Ethan until the day he died.

I explained everything to the ladies at Joyce's, and they showed me an array of sexy outfits that may be to my liking. I browsed through racks and shelves of different outfits until I hit upon a black, sleek, halter-topped romper. With a simple bow behind my neck, the garment held just a touch of spice. It was perfect.

The salesladies were more than happy to help find a comfortable pair of flats to match, finishing off the outfit with a golden Coach clutch. I decided to dress then and there, putting my other clothes in the shoe bag.

*Ding!*

# DELILAH ST. RIVERS

> I'm home from my meetings and am missing you terribly. I have a surprise for you.

> I'll be home soon. I'm not sure how long this will take, but I also have a surprise for you.

> I shall count the minutes until you are here, beloved.

---

AN HOUR AND A HALF AFTER ENTERING Joyce's in yoga pants and a sweater, I emerged wearing my new outfit. My hair was done up in a French twist and they'd been kind enough to help me accessorize with gold hoop earrings and a matching 24-karat gold necklace that said *Ethan* in elegant script.

It was well past six when I got back into the car.

"Ma'am, at the risk of sounding too forward, you could stop traffic."

"Thank you, Mark." I blushed at his compliment. "Mr. Aldrich is home; can you drop me off around back so he doesn't see us?"

"Of course, ma'am." Mark grinned in the mirror at me. "He's going to be one happy man."

He would be pissed that I didn't tell him, for all of thirty seconds, before he registered the outfit and the necklace. He would see the jewelry as his brand on my skin, a tag with his name on it. My gift for him to unwrap. I shivered as we pulled into the driveway and slowly parked behind the large home.

*This is stupid*, I thought to myself. I was never into grand gestures. *Chances are I'll get to the last step, trip into the door and break my nose before he even sees me.*

"Ma'am?" Mark prompted as he stood by my opened car door.

I took a deep breath. *Whatever happens, he's going to love this*, I reassured myself. *I've never done anything to cause him disappointment, not when I wasn't trying to at least.*

I took another deep breath as I stepped onto the smooth driveway, relying on my cane as I climbed the steps up to the back door.

"Good luck, ma'am," Mark said as he went back into the car and

# CHAINS OF SATIN

parked it in the garage.

I straightened my shoulders and waited for Amelia, who Mark messaged ahead of time, to have her ready and waiting to open the door.

"The office, ma'am," Amelia told me with a smile before retreating to her duties.

I turned and went down the hallway, careful not to hit my cane too hard against the hardwood floor as I approached his office.

"I honestly like you better on both knees." Sophie's voice floated from the barely-opened door.

My blood froze in my veins as I peeked in, holding my breath. *Why is she here after cleaning hours?*

"Like this?"

Ethan's voice was deep and almost seductive in its whisper. He was down on both knees, his back to the door. He appeared to hold something in his hands.

"Just like that," Sophie said, moving in front of him and leaning on his desk. A piece of jewelry on her head caught the light from the windows behind her. It only took me a moment to realize she was wearing...

*My circlet.*

My head spun. That *bitch* was wearing my circlet and he wasn't telling her to take it off. He was kneeling in front of her—

"It's so big; are you sure it's not too big?" Flirtation oozed out of her mouth like slime. My stomach lurched.

"The only way to find out is to go through with this, don't you agree?"

I must have moved or made a small sound because Sophie's eyes lifted just a touch and found me in the doorway. Ethan, unaware of my presence, took her hand and tugged, bringing her attention back to him.

"Should we do this again?" he asked.

*Again?*

With another glance at me, Sophie reached down to caress his cheek before lowering her face to Ethan's.

*I'm going to tear her to pieces*, I thought as I tensed and reached for the door. I watched her bend low and kiss Ethan and I stopped. The hand that reached for the door flew to my mouth, and I stumbled backward a step. I staggered out of the hall, my stomach churning, my eyes burning, and my mind racing with every step. I couldn't hear anything beyond the shattering of my heart. I opened the door to our room and sat on the bed in shock.

*He's done with me. He's done.*

"*...be his plaything then sends you on your way...You actually think he cares for you...You took a poor girl and made her believe you loved her...*" Madeline

279

was right. I was so blind, so stupid, so...gullible. *"Shame on you for being so gullible."* That's what she had said, and there was no denying it any longer.

My fingers traced the letters of his name on my necklace as my tears fell. I loved him and he was downstairs betraying me, kissing Sophie with the same lips that kissed me just this morning.

*I drove him to this.*

Being so absent in the wake of my mother's passing had pushed him right into her arms. It was why he couldn't say it last night, wouldn't say it back...

I removed the necklace with my shaking hands and walked over to the little desk beside the window. I found a pen and notepad, thinking about what to say while I arranged it on top of the desk.

I calmly called an Uber and wrote Ethan my goodbye. When I was done, I kissed the letter as though it was him touching my lips, then set the necklace on the notepad. I looked to my wrist, my bracelet sparkling as brightly as its companion resting upon Sophie's treacherous head, and fresh tears began to fall. A sub removing a collar was as heartbreaking as a nasty divorce, and my pain doubled as I unclasped the silver hoop and set it beside his name.

The Uber came and took me away quietly. I risked a look back. There was no dramatic scene of him chasing after me, begging me to stay. I turned my phone off after letting Shay know I was on my way to her, so he couldn't call me. He didn't know where she lived, either. This was his last chance and he didn't even know it.

Tears streamed down my face as the car drove me away from his home, towards my future without Ethan.

My Dearest Ethan,

I don't have the words to express the array of emotions coursing through me after seeing you in the office with Sophie. I'm hurt, angry, deeply sad, and utterly betrayed by the loss of you and your affection. Even with this knowledge, I still love you.

I understand now why you couldn't tell me you loved me back. I get it. To say those words and not feel them would have been unfair to me and I appreciate the gentleman in you to protect me from further pain.

Even now as you sit on your knees downstairs, in front of Sophie, kissing her as she wears my circlet, I'm trying to bear you no hard feelings. I understand that this is your nature, but I can't help but blame you for the way things have ended. And I can't sit by and watch you place my jewelry on another, so I'm leaving quietly. Consider it my parting gift that I didn't show you just how big of a brat I can truly be.

As it stands, I have to say thank you, and that I don't know how I would have gotten through these last six months of my life without your support.

I guess all that's left is to tell you is goodbye. I loved you freely and will probably do so until my dying breath. It's difficult to know it was one-sided, but that's okay. Loving you made me more confident and will make me more capable of facing my future without you in it.

Petunia

PRESENT DAY
OFFICE OF DR. JOSEPH HALL

JOSEPH HELD THE TEAR-STAINED LETTER IN HIS hands after he read it.

"Sophie found me in the office," I began, unprompted. "She asked me where the circlet belonged, claiming Petunia left it on the nightstand by the bed. She said she was worried someone would steal it. I told her she was thoughtful as always, and she could leave it on my desk." I took a breath, recalling the final moments that led me to Joseph's office. "Sophie noticed the little box on my desk after her hands left the circlet. She asked about it and seemed genuinely happy for us once I told her I'd planned to ask Petunia to marry me. She asked how I would propose and I recited something along the lines of what I planned to say. At this point, Sophie and I were almost acquaintances, and I knew she and Petunia were somewhat close. I was so nervous, I thought her insight would help.

"She suggested she wear the circlet and pretend to be Petunia. She thought it could help alleviate my nerves if I practiced the proposal and though I felt a twinge of uneasiness when she'd put it on her head, I allowed it for the sake of perfecting my proposal."

"Nothing happened between the two of you in the office that day?"

I shook my head.

"She tried to kiss me at one point, but I politely rebuffed her

# CHAINS OF SATIN

There was a difference between rehearsal and cheating, and I was not about to cross that line and ruin the friendship I developed with her and my relationship with Petunia. I felt no attraction to her whatsoever. That's not to say she wasn't attractive, but my everything belonged to Petunia. *Everything.*

"After that, Sophie insisted I get the wording right and we worked on it a few times when she kissed me again. I felt guilty, thinking I'd led the girl on, but she was persistent. I finally had to tell her flat out that I had no romantic interest in her. She raged and complained, throwing the circlet to the floor.

"It was getting dark and she told me with a smile that she had to go. She said it was time for me to find my girlfriend, though she spit the word as though it left a bitter taste on her tongue." I sighed and closed my eyes, leaning my head back against the chair. "I realized the time, realized it was odd that Petunia hadn't come home yet. I tried calling, but there was no answer. Sometimes after her physical therapy she would be tired, so I considered she may have gone up to bed to rest. I took the stairs in three bounds only to find my bedroom dark and empty. The only light came from the desk lamp shining on the note, the necklace, and her bracelet."

"Ethan," Joseph leaned back in his own leather chair. "My friend, what are you going to do?"

"If I knew that, my friend, your pockets would be a bit lighter."

"Well, throughout your entire story you have done everything for her benefit. So, what do you think would be best for her?"

"To be with me, dammit!" I pounded a fist on my armchair in frustration. "To be safe and loved for all time, to see that she needs to be with me, to see that I am what's best for her!"

"Or…" Joseph prompted.

I paused for a moment.

"Or?" I looked at the man across from me.

"Or…what if she needs this time for herself? The poor girl has dealt with being drugged, the death of *both* of her parents, an injury, an abusive past, and she's worked herself to the bone. While you may feel better with her near, she may never get over these events in a *healthy* way if she isn't forced to face them without you as a buffer."

"I've been too long without her—it's tearing me open."

"Perhaps time apart will help you see her less as an idol of perfection and more as an actual person, flawed and incomplete as the rest of us mortals. Caring for someone is the greatest act of kindness in and of itself, as long as you aren't selfish about it."

"Is there any hope at all?" I asked my long-time friend.

283

# DELILAH ST. RIVERS

"I think, if you play it right, and you give her plenty of time to discover who she really is without everything she's had to deal with, perhaps eventually you'll find your way back to each other."

"I'd tried calling, tried explaining —"

"I'm sure you did," Joseph interrupted.

"Even her friend wouldn't listen, and she had quite the vocabulary to express her anger at me," I chuckled dryly. "I want to do so much. I want to find her, kidnap her, tie her down —"

"The worst case scenario, I seem to remember," Joseph said, smiling softly.

"Alright, my friend. I trust you," I sighed and sat back once more.

Joseph looked up at me, and I was certain he could see the earnestness and pain in my eyes.

"Given the chance, what would you do?" I asked.

"If you have the patience," Joseph started, "I have a plan."

*Mina Rakastan Sinua*

Darling reader—

Interested in my side of the story? Check out Delilah St. Rivers' website for exclusive bonus materials, including never-before-seen chapters from my point of view.

I promise you won't be disappointed.

    xx
    Ethan Richard Aldrich the Third

Ethan and Petunia's story continues in *Chains of Pearls*, coming soon from Delilah St. Rivers.

# Acknowledgements

THIS BOOK IS NOW FOUR YEARS IN THE MAKING, and there are so many people to thank for bringing this little Covid project to life for me.

First, YOU, the reader. Thank you for jumping into this with me, exploring the world inside my little head, and continuing to turn page after page until you got here. Without you, this wouldn't exist on the scale that it does. Ethan wouldn't exist. Petunia would still be a two-dimensional character in my mind.

To Teddi, who sought me out on TikTok because I never put down an email to be considered for publication (squirrel-brain). You believed in my work so much you scoured the videos until you found mine, scooped me up, and held me to the bosom of your budding publication company, something I am eternally grateful to the universe for.

To Taylor. Oh, goodness, where do I start?! How many editors did I go through before you decided enough was enough and took on the job yourself, even though you were so busy? You taught me so much about my own story, molding it and shaping it to be the beautiful masterpiece it is today. I'll forever hold onto the lessons (and so much laughter) learned through our tandem edits and apply them to all my future endeavors.

To Sarah Rosenberg, who went through so much to help me get all the pretty graphics and logos, taught me all about Canva and Squarespace, gave me TikTok ideas, and made my gorgeous cover even more so, then made a "clean" one so it will sell in stores a little easier. So many Hiddles-pics for you, girl. So many.

To everyone on our discord for your support, advice, drama, and questions. We are a little family unto ourselves, aren't we?

To my beta and ARC readers, thank you all so much for jumping in and supporting this story from the beginning to the end of its evolution.

To my mom and my grandmother, without you, I would have never discovered the joy of reading, which evolved into the joy of writing. I, indeed, come from a long line of incredible women.

To Jessica and Jerrica, your unwavering support my entire life, listening to all my stories as we grew up and even creating some together for entertainment (back in the dark ages before the internet and subsequent technology…and kids).

To Natalia. You know why, and I love you each and every day for the rest of my life for it.

To Janelle, who taught me how good a physical book written by me feels in my hands and made that dream not so far out of my reach.

To Tom Hiddleston. Your reading of Einstein's Theory of Relativity way back in the early 2000s, along with E.E. Cummings' poem, "May I Feel," has persistently lived rent-free in my head and inspired my Ethan.

To all of my kids. You are my drive to do the best I can with what I have, the reasons my heart beats and my fingers fly over the keyboard day and night. (Special thanks to Rachel for introducing me to the Celsius drink, my version of coffee.)

To Anna, I know you're reading this even though I told you that you weren't allowed until you were in your 40s.

And once more to you, dear reader. You are the alpha and the omega in this industry. Thank you for making my dream of being a writer come true.

# About the Author

Delilah St. Rivers began writing stories at the age of three and has not stopped since. Escapism has always been an inspiration behind the stories that she chooses to write and tell. Anne Rice is one of Delilah's most-loved authors. She loves the bravery that Rice showed in her writing and the way her stories have lasted the test of time.

In addition to being a fantastic writer, Delilah has a beautiful family that she loves to spend time with. Her husband is her greatest supporter and he loves to tell everyone that one day, she's going to be a bestselling author.

Follow Delilah's journey on all her social media platforms and through her newsletter!

www.delilahstrivers.com
@authordelilahst.rivers on TikTok
@author_delilah on Instagram

*More from*
*Spellbound Publishing House, LLC*

*The Best of Choice* by Edward Lee Wolverton is a collection of poetry that explores themes of love, life, beauty, pain, belief, and acceptance.

Written over a lifetime, this collection of poetry explores humanity, delving into the good, the bad, and everything that makes us human.

Owen is a boy who realizes he is special—he can control fire. Then he finds a camp where everyone is like him. When the Master of the Elements is killed, Owen is sure that he is going to be next in line. All he has to do is help his friends find the Rings of Power. With his new friends by his side, he knows they will succeed. But when one of his allies turns out to be a traitor, he no longer knows what to believe. And though he thinks he knows what he wants, by the end of his journey, he's not so sure.

Argent, a young Merran with budding abilities, becomes a fugitive from the government that created him when he witnesses a kidnapping. He does everything he can to stay under the radar, but there are only so many places to hide in an underwater society. With the help of a friend and the resources of a mysterious family, Argent unravels the shady past of his race, and the part that the government played in starting a war that he's not sure he wants them to win. Espionage, secrets, lies, and love all come to a head as Argent confronts his future and his fate. Is he ready to fight for the ideals that have been ingrained in him, or will he make different choices when it comes down to it?

# Trigger Warnings

- PTSD
- Off-Page Car Accident
- Death of loved ones
- Nightmares
- Betrayal
- Grooming
- Hospitalization
- Injury
- Alcohol use
- Cancer
- Usage of Rohypnol
- Scarring
- Anxiety
- Grieving
- Broken Bones
- Intimidation
- Praise
- Dementia in a loved one
- Suicide and suicidal ideation
- Sex slavery
- Threesomes (MMF)
- Violence
- Degradation
- Non-con sexual activity
- Explicit sexcapades including:
  - bondage
  - usage of various sex toys
- Sex as coercion, punishment, and reward
- Dub-con
- Past abuses including:
  - flashbacks of gore
  - forced abortion
  - physical abuse
  - verbal abuse
  - sexual abuse

Printed in the USA
CPSIA information can be obtained
at www.ICGtesting.com
LVHW090747170424
777535LV00001B/72